Pricked

Scott Mooney

This book is a work of fiction. Names, characters, places and incidents are the product of the author's imagination or are used fictitiously. Any resemblance to actual persons, living or dead, business establishments, events or locales is entirely coincidental.

No part of this publication may be reproduced, distributed, or transmitted in any form or by any means, including photocopying, recording, or other electronic or mechanical methods, without the prior written permission of the publisher, except in the case of brief quotations embodied in critical reviews and certain other noncommercial uses permitted by copyright law. For permission requests, write to the publisher, addressed "Attention: Permissions Coordinator," at the address below.

Bleeding Ink Publishing
253 Bee Caves Cove
Cibolo, TX 78108
www.bleedinginkpublishing.com
info@bleedinginkpublishing.com

Quantity sales: Special discounts are available on quantity purchases by corporations, associations, and others. For details, contact the publisher at the address above.

Printed in the United States of America
PRICKED
Copyright ©2018 Scott Mooney
All rights reserved.
Paperback ISBN: 978-1-948583-05-3
E-book ISBN: 978-1-948583-20-6
Cover design by Strong Image Editing
Book design by Inkstain Design Studio

PRICKED

Scott [signature]
Ann Arbor Native

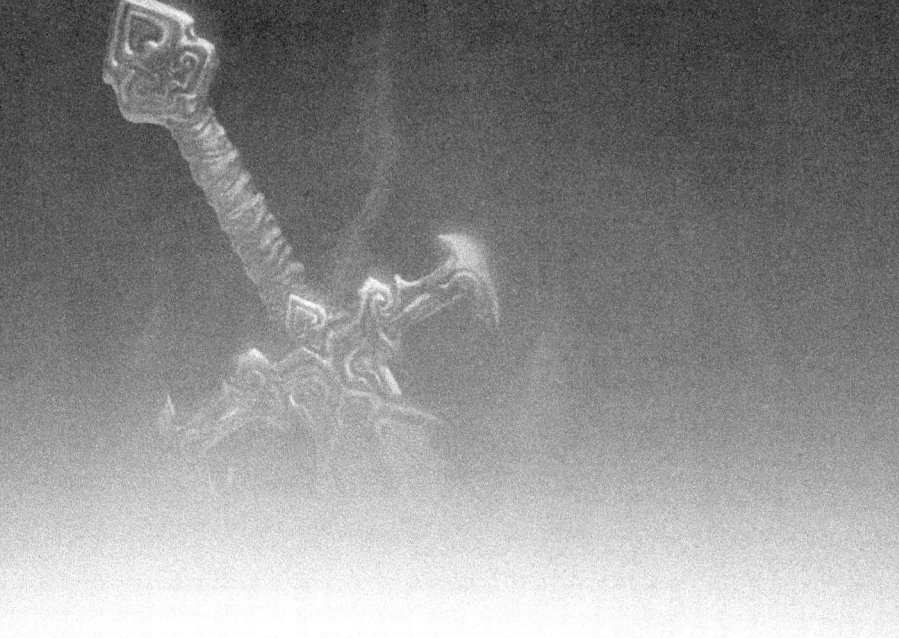

Once upon a Thursday, I was sitting on a damp bench in Central Park in the shade of a birch tree. I'd spent the last ten minutes trying to think of an eight-letter word for "a tiny monkey." The second-to-last letter was E, so I'd had to erase "capuchin." I pulled my leg up on the bench to get a better view of last Friday's *Times* crossword in front of me. Nothing came to mind.

It was the first sunny day in about a week, and puddles still dotted the city. But, puddles or no puddles, the sunshine had called most New Yorkers outdoors to bask. Central Park was ripe with the tangy scent of relaxation. I had finished my deliveries for the day and decided to spend the rest of the afternoon outside. It was the perfect weather for people-watching, and every once in a while, I actually figured out a crossword clue.

I picked a rose from my satchel on the bench beside me and rolled the stem absentmindedly through my fingers. Its blossom changed from red, to pink, to tangerine orange, the colors flowing into each other like dye in water. The petals turned a muted blue paisley for a moment, and then shifted to the reddish-green of unripe strawberries. None of it helped me think of tiny monkeys.

Frustrated, I flipped through the rest of the *Times* and scanned the headlines. Businesses failing. Politicians with wayward libidos. Jennifer Anniston heartbroken. The usual stories. There was a nice write-up on a string of arsons in Roosevelt Island. No suspects, totally unconnected victims, police baffled, that sort of thing. Now, there was a story. Just not, as I suspected, the whole story.

A sudden blast of wind nearly blew the newspaper off my leg, but I grabbed it just in time. A short, pale teen stumbled forward from a spot that had been empty a few seconds before. He took a handful of faltering steps towards me and stopped before he ran into the bench. The boy righted himself for a second, then doubled over, his hand on the bench's armrest. My heart started to slow down once I recognized him.

"Sonofabitch," the kid panted.

"Are you okay, T?" I said. I moved my roses to the ground to give him room to sit. He looked like he needed it.

Thomas "'Lil T" Daumen stood up and scowled at me from under his worn Mets cap. "I'm fine, Briar," he spat. "Friggin' puddles are everywhere, and the tread of my left boot is on its last legs." He paused. "So to speak."

T put his mud-crusted leather boot up on the bench and toyed with the loose sole. He muttered something foul under his breath, but I couldn't make it out.

"Where do you go to get a ten-block boot cobbled?" I asked, curious.

"I dunno," T said sarcastically. "I'll go ask the ogre I stole it from. Maybe he knows a good place." His voice cracked a little on the last word. He put his boot down, flopped on the bench, and continued to glare at me. His feet dangled over the grass, unable to touch the ground. I tried to picture him with a grin across his face and realized I'd never seen him really smile.

"Rose?" I said sweetly. I offered him the one in my hand as it turned sunburst yellow.

T flinched a little. "Hell, no."

I shrugged and put the rose back into my bag, where it returned to a dull red color. Some people you just can't help.

We stayed silent for a moment while T continued to breathe heavily. I straightened out the folds in my newspaper. He scratched his crotch unrepentantly. It seemed like the kind of shameless gesture you'd see from a zoo animal.

"Marmoset!" I burst before I could stop my mouth.

"What?" T scoffed, his face filled with genuine disgust. I scribbled the eight letters down on the crossword.

"Nothing. Don't worry about it." My cheeks burnt with embarrassment, but with a dark complexion like mine, I doubt T noticed. Besides, the giddy, little-kid feeling in my stomach was worth T's stares. Maybe I'd get this friggin' crossword after all.

"Shouldn't you be out delivering, flower girl?" he asked.

I shook my head. "Done for the day. I wanted to relax a bit before I head back."

"Must be nice, this easy life of yours," T snapped.

I ignored his tone. "You don't happen to know a thirteen-letter word for 'Jung's coincidences,' do you?"

T narrowed his eyes. "No. Those of us who actually work for a living don't have time for that crossword shit." He made a gruff noise and ran a hand over the stubble on the back of his neck.

I caught myself before I said anything rude and plastered on a smile. "To what do I owe the pleasure, T?"

He reached into the sports sack hung over his shoulder and pulled out a beige cylinder of parchment, handing it over without a word. My face scrunched up when I saw a brownish-black stain along one side.

The boy's face held the hint of a sheepish grin. "Chocolate churro. My bad."

I turned the letter over, where it was sealed the old-fashioned way. The blood-red wax still seemed warm to the touch. Looking closer, I saw the figure of a wolf pressed into the seal, reared up on its hind legs with its front paws in the air. To me, any heraldry involving a wolf rampant just looks like a badly drawn Scooby Doo. Still, the seal's significance was not lost on me.

Whatever the letter contained, it would not be good news. My hands started to shake a little as they held it.

I chewed on my lip and looked up at T. "Do you know what this is? Or which family it's from?" I tried to remember who T was working for these days.

T shook his head and hopped off the bench. "Sorry, Bri. You know the deal. Just the messenger. The Royals don't pay me to ask questions." He adjusted his foot in his left boot, frowning again.

"Later." He gave a little wave and took a step forward. The air seemed to rush and bubble around him, propelling him far into the distance. Luckily, I grabbed my paper before it got sucked into the vacuum of air T left behind. I caught a quick glimpse of him at the other end of the park, but in another step he was gone. One of the nearby sunbathers looked up for a moment, as if she, too, saw him vanish. She cocked her head to the side, shrugged, and went back to her *Cosmo*.

I popped the wax away from the paper with my finger and unfurled the scroll. Two short sentences had been written hastily in a deep red ink:

MEET ME TODAY AT SIX IN THE GRIMMOUR CHAPEL. LET YOURSELF IN.

Royals have a habit of assuming they can treat the rest of us like toys. Which is, sadly, pretty accurate. If I ignored this letter, the next one would come with a couple of knights who wouldn't give me a chance to run. It's good to be king. Or duke, or count, or whatever. I don't really keep track of that stuff.

I sighed, put the crossword into a side pocket of my bag, and promised myself I'd finish it sometime later that night, even though me completing a Friday puzzle was about as likely as me completing a marathon. Whatever. All I had to do was meet up with whomever sent the letter, and I was home free. With a little luck, they'd have a job for me. A job meant money, and I had debts to pay.

I walked deeper into the park where the cool of the shade was almost as soothing as the sunlight itself. A crowd of tourists had gathered around a street performer standing on a rock. The man was pulling a brightly colored rope of handkerchiefs from his suit pocket while mugging horrendously to the audience. It wasn't worth stopping. After twenty-two years growing up in the city, I had a pretty distinguished taste for street performers.

Sometimes it was hard to believe the things that passed for magic in this town.

The skyline peered down at me over the trees as I rounded Turtle

Pond. It would have been a nice day just to wander Manhattan and curl up in a coffee shop until the streetlights came on…but not with my luck. Instead, I had to call on a demanding Noble who could legally have me imprisoned for life. I would have much preferred the coffee shop.

I walked up the sandy brown path to Belvedere Castle. The grey stone structure towered over the rest of Central Park, clashing whimsically with the skyscrapers behind it. Its stone battlements and wooden pavilions were empty this late in the day, and I doubt anyone saw me as I walked briskly up to the door of its tower.

The iron handle stuck a little as I tried to open it. The meteorological station inside the castle was closed to the public this time of day, but after a second I heard the click of an unseen deadbolt and the door swung open. One of the perks of being a regular.

The inside of the castle was dark, lit only by the sunlight that drifted in through the half-round windows. But I knew my way by heart and went quickly down the curved staircase to the lowest part of the tower, a claustrophobic stone landing in the basement. To most visitors, this was a dead end. But when I squinted my eyes a little, I could make out a rounded wooden door in the staircase wall, popping out of the stone like one of those trick 3D pictures. Strange, looping designs covered the wood. The magic they contained kept the portal hidden from people not meant to find it. Sometimes the door appears to perfectly normal old ladies who have been living in the city for eighty years. Sometimes children who have used the door their whole lives lose the ability to see it when they lose their last baby tooth. It's impossible to predict. Magic isn't an exact science.

I opened the door and cringed at the ear-splitting creak of the hinges. No matter how much magic is in a door, there are some things only a can of WD40 can fix.

    I stepped up into the archway and drew my cloak around me as I was hit with a blast of cool, subterranean air. The climate always gets funky, traveling from Here to There. I was in a vaulted stone corridor lit by torches set along the walls in extravagant bronze sconces. The columns on either side of the hallway were topped with the grotesque faces of gargoyles. The stonework was impeccable, like a subway tunnel designed by Brunelleschi. Really, all the glitz was just a ploy to impress the handful of tourists who found their way here, but it was better than most of the other Doorways.

    After a few minutes of walking down the corridor, a faint, coppery glow was visible at the other end of the tunnel. The clean lines of the walls were also changing. Leaves, sprouts, and ferns poked their way through the mortar on either side of the hallway. The clacking of my boots faded as the cobblestones beneath my feet became overrun with a fuzzy green moss. The torches grew less and less frequent, and sunlight began digging through cracks in the ceiling.

    The farther I went, the more the wildness took hold of the corridor. Whole sections of wall crumbled away to reveal a thick hedge of thorny growth. When I reached the end of the path, the ruined brickwork fell away completely, and I was standing in a grove at the edge of a thick forest. Scattered bricks and stones kept the idea of a path that continued twenty feet further. Ahead of me stood an ancient stone arch, overgrown with ivy and a few choice bits of graffiti. I passed under the archway and nodded to the figure slumped against the other side, reading a 1968 issue of *The New Yorker*.

    "Evenin', Miss Briar," the middle-aged man said. He tipped his hat politely but didn't look up from his magazine.

    "Evening, Horace."

"You're back early. Done with your deliveries?"

"For now, I guess," I answered, smiling. "Do you keep tabs on everyone who comes through your Door, or do you just have a crush on me?"

As Horace looked up and smiled, a glint of sun flashed off of his gold tooth. "Being Doorman does have its advantages. Pretty much everyone goes through Belvedere at some point in the day. I keep track of the interesting ones." Horace, in addition to being one of the few authority figures I liked, was also a notorious gossip.

"You hear about those fires on Roosevelt Island?" I said. "There was another one yesterday. It's phigeons, right?"

"Must be. Seems like a new clutch of them is born every year. Whichever Doorman let that first phoenix escape through his Door should be hanged. It must've mated with every pigeon in Manhattan by now." He sniffed a very superior sniff.

I pulled out my incomplete crossword and showed it to him. "Ten down, thirteen-letter word for 'Jung's coincidences.' Any ideas?"

Horace scrunched up his weathered face for a second, and then shook his head. "Nope. Not a clue. I'm a strict Freudian, myself."

I took back the paper and grinned. "Sorry to hear that."

"You and my mother both," Horace replied. "Have a good one, Miss Briar."

Past the archway, I came to the crest of a small knoll. The sun was just dipping below the horizon, backlighting the vista before me. Directly in front of me was a ramshackle suburb of cottages and shanties, forming a ring of wood and plaster hemmed in by the dark Afterwoods on all sides. Some of the nicer houses looked like they'd been hand-plucked from the French countryside. Others looked like fifteenth-century subsidized housing—just cubes of cheap wood with small windows. The entire ghetto sported a forest of chimneys and towers that stuck up like pins in a pincushion against the sunset. The labyrinth of streets and alleys led all the way to the base of a steep hill in the center of town.

Atop this hill was Castle Fortnight, a veritable city of stone towers, turrets, and bulwarks, reaching impossibly high into the sky. The many spires were joined by open-air bridges, from which brightly colored banners and ribbons dangled in the wind. The lustrous white stone was flawless, giving the entire structure a corona that hurt the eyes. Castle Fortnight, the First Skyscraper, with its luxurious gardens, grand ballrooms, secret passageways, and aeries full of sleeping princesses. The center of the universe.

Places like this always have many names. The Lost Borough, Fairyland, Pucktown, The City that Always Dreams. Lately, it's been going by the Poisoned Apple.

Me? I just call it home.

I started down the hill into Commontown, making a mental checklist of what I had to do. If I had to "let myself in" to Castle Fortnight, I'd need to stop by my house and gather supplies first. It wasn't too far out of the way, and I thought it would be a good idea to check in with my housemates before going to the castle. At best, they might have heard something about why I had been summoned. At worst, they would know where to search for my body.

I entered the outskirts of SoLArca (Southern Little Arcadia—just because we live in Fairyland doesn't mean we're not New Yorkers) and made my way through the busy streets. Hawkers advertised a fire sale at the Alchemists'

Factory Store, while flyers for Goblin comedy shows were shoved in any available face. As I walked past, I saw a pair of Japanese tourists wearing "I WAND NY" shirts get sucked in by a vendor selling knock-off dragonhide gloves. It must have been their first time in the Apple.

I passed the Ballgown District and Lovers' Lane, finally winding my way through the Gingerbread Tenements towards Havmercy Park, on the outskirts of town. Our house was on the edge of the deep, dark woods, which sounded romantic until you had to scoop werewolf poo out of your front yard after every full moon. It was a modest, somewhat cramped little cottage that always seemed to be in a state of chaos, like if the Seven Dwarves had been frat boys instead of miners. The curtains were all different shades of blue (we'd lost half of them after our "Flaming Shots" party), and crushed beer cans constantly lined the walk. From the front, at least, it looked like any other low-rent house in the area. Its one notable feature was the circular tower on the west side. It wasn't particularly impressive in a town full of keeps and castles, but when you got inside, the bay windows on each floor of the tower gave you a stunning view of the rest of the neighborhood.

I opened the door and walked through the foyer to see the living room in its usual state of disarray. Various discarded pieces of clothing littered our second-hand couches, and concert posters covered most of the green and yellow wallpaper. I had added a few potted plants and shrubs to try to spruce things up, but the tube sock wrapped around my ficus somehow lessened the effect.

"Don't we look frazzled. What's up, Bri?"

Princess Jacquinetta D'Lucien Ardor sat on the floor of the kitchenette, nibbling a piece of tuna off a plate while looking through a copy of *The*

New Yorker that lay open in front of her. Her tail swished excitedly as I walked in, while the bottom of my stomach knotted up and my heart sank. I had been hoping to avoid her.

After six months of being a cat, she still refused to lick herself. Her glossy silver and white coat was matted and covered with flecks of dirt. I couldn't always tell what was grime and what were the distinctive black tiger stripes that ran down her back. I would probably have to give her another bath soon. The only thing that hadn't changed instantly with the rest of Jacqui's shape was her eyes, sparkling and blue. Hope and guilt kept me from fully acknowledging that, little by little, her eyes were becoming more catlike. Day by day her white corneas shrank, becoming a speckled robin's-egg blue.

I groaned my displeasure over the day's events. "I'm fine," I lied. "I just received a stupid summons to the castle."

She looked up from her paper and trotted over to me. "Oooh, called to the principal's office, huh? What did you do?"

"Nothing I can remember. It's not official business, either, because I'm supposed to sneak in."

Jacqui leapt up on one of the kitchen stools to be closer to my height. "Then it's probably another secret delivery. Just make sure they pay up front. I should know as well as anyone how cheap Nobles can be with their money."

"Speaking of which, have you heard anything from your parents lately?" I asked. I pulled a tea bag out of a tin on the counter and went to the cabinets to grab my favorite mug.

"Nope," Jacqui answered. Her shoulders sunk a little. "They still don't want to hear from me, whether I'm a human or a cat. They always were dog people." She tried to smile up at me, but pain marred her heart-shaped face. I could still see the emotions of my best friend easily, whatever her form.

I felt my eyes start to burn and turned away. I leaned down to my mug and whispered, "Bread and butter, bread and butter, bread and butter." As soon as I finished, hot water filled the mug from the bottom up. I found what was probably the only clean spoon in the house and stirred my tea around.

Jacqui scratched her ear with her back leg. It was one of the few feline mannerisms she'd picked up. "Alice is working late tonight. The Black Duchess had a soirée last night and needed extra maids to do overtime. But if you see her on your way into the castle, remind her we're out of milk."

The change of subject and the tea relieved me of some of my tension. "Well, if I'm not rotting to death in a dungeon, I can stop by Troll Foods on my way home. I have to grab some ammo out back, and then it's off to meet my mysterious Royal pen pal."

"Just remember, if he's cute, I have blanket dibs on all Royals," she retorted.

I rolled my eyes. "I somehow doubt it's from my secret admirer, Jacqui. I don't even know if it's a guy. But if it is and he doesn't try to execute me, I'll slip him your number."

Jacqui stuck her tongue out at me and returned to the paper while I crossed through the living room to the patio door. I walked out into the last rays of sunshine as they filtered through the evergreens at the edge of our back yard. A damp breeze blew in from the Afterwoods, carrying the scent of wet earth and pine needles. I took a few moments to look proudly at my garden. Even this early in the season, the trellises, shrubs, and branches held hundreds of blooms. What the garden lacked in variety, it made up for in sheer numbers. Spread out between the short stone walls on either side were rose bushes, rose trees, rose shrubs, and rose vines, boasting roses of every conceivable size, shape, and color. I planted them more or less by hue, and the garden shifted as I followed the paths from blue to yellow to red. In the center, I arrived at a tree ten feet high, covered only in blooms of the purest white.

I wandered the stone tile paths, collecting an assortment of roses that called out to me. Some days I'd be on a Tea rose kick or would pick only the freshest blooms. I always tried for a variety of colors, just to be prepared. For the break-in, I went for mostly miniature varieties. Maybe I was inspired by T.

I filled my satchel and turned to go back into the house. If I was lucky, I'd be able to get out without seeing Jacqui again. I didn't need the guilt.

A rustling sound in the back of the yard made me spin around. A well-muscled, six-foot-four man in a dark red cloak came out of the woods, a wicked-looking hatchet strapped to his back. As he made his way towards me, I noticed that the edge of the blade peeking over his shoulder was tinged with something dark. It wasn't rust.

"Hey, Cade," I called out as he approached. "Is that blood?"

"It's ichor, I think. Whatever basilisks bleed," Cade responded in his deep baritone. "We found a whole nest of them out in the Western Paths."

"Rough day?"

He shrugged. "If there weren't any monsters in the Afterwoods, me and the rest of the Red Hoods would be out of a job." He looked down at my satchel, and a frown crossed his tanned face. "That's a lot of roses. What are you stocking up for?"

"I'm not exactly sure. Some Noble wants me to sneak into the castle."

Cade rubbed the back of his neck, causing his clipper-short blond hair to stand on end. He looked past me towards the rest of the garden. "Well, you know, be careful." He shifted his weight uncomfortably and started to move towards the house.

"Cade Arden," I chastised, trying to keep my tone light, "when have I ever been anything but careful?"

Before I knew what was happening, Cade reached out with both hands to grab me firmly by the shoulders. "I'm serious, Briar," he grumbled. "After everything that's happened, you can't go barging into things like this. You think getting yourself killed will help Jacqui?"

I stood speechless for a moment. That many words in a row was unusual for him, and more importantly, Cade and I had an unstated "no-touching" rule, given our history. I rallied and twisted away from his grip. Mostly to make sure I didn't enjoy it.

"What else am I supposed to do, Cade? Getting Jacqui cured won't come cheap. You think I can just sit around and work a minimum wage job trying to pay for her treatment?" I had more to say, but the tightness in my chest made me pause.

Cade's hazel eyes narrowed, and the disgust I saw in them was like a slap to the face. "All of this happened because you started making *deliveries*." He spat the final word as if it were poison. "And if you keep it up, whoever did this to Jacqui will get you, too."

The pressure between my lungs had grown, and I could barely bring myself to catch short, helpless breaths. The rose buds around me blurred as my eyes began to tear.

Grimmsdammit, he was not going to make me cry.

"This is what I have to do, Cade. I don't like it. I wish I could go back. If I was the reason for Jacqui…" I gulped some air and tried to gather myself together. "But making deliveries is the only way I can fix things between us, and I don't need you making me feel guilty about it." I hoped my words conveyed a finality I knew wasn't in my tone.

Cade bowed his head a little, and I had to lean forward to hear his next words. "I just can't watch you get yourself hurt."

It took a moment for me to decide whether I was going to comfort him or hit him. I knew which of his shoulders he'd wrenched in a high school jousting match. I could make it hurt.

Apparently, after all this time, he could still tie me in the same emotional knots. I guess we both knew each other's weak spots. I hefted my satchel onto my shoulder and tried to clear my head of half-remembered feelings.

"I'll be fine. Don't worry about me," I promised with fake conviction. Even I didn't believe me. Sad, right?

Cade wouldn't meet my eyes. "Yeah, well." He gave a weak smile. "Don't come running to me to break you out of the White Tower when you piss off your mystery Noble." He took one last glance at me and turned to go into the house.

"Cade, wait." This wasn't how I wanted to leave things. "Can we talk later? On my way back, I could pick up some Chinese, and we could have dinner together." My intestines gave a kick, and I realized I didn't have the courage to eat with him alone. "All four of us. It would give us a chance to catch up."

He turned, his red cloak shifting slowly with the motion. He stared at me for a moment, and then his face broke into a grin. It was his real smile, the off-center one that showed his teeth. A smile I hadn't seen very often these past six months. "Sounds good. I could use a roomie dinner. See you then, Briar." I smiled back, and he went inside, leaving me alone with my roses.

All I could think of was a bright winter morning two months before, when a young fawn had hopped the fence into our garden and gotten trapped. Cade had bundled up in his cloak and tried to guide the poor thing to the back gate. He didn't know I was watching from the back window as he approached the deer slowly, arms open wide, talking in a gentle voice. In its panic, the fawn dashed all around the yard, sometimes drawn in by Cade's soothing tones, and sometimes bolting from his open arms. It got out, but it never actually let him help.

I could sympathize.

Jacqui's voice interrupted my thoughts as I heard her greet Cade in the kitchen. I put my hand over my eyes and rubbed my temples, not sure what just happened. Cade hadn't shown that much genuine emotion to me in the four years since high school. The way the concern looked in his eyes replayed itself in my mind, with a short intermission of how his hands felt as they held me. Everything that happened bounced around inside my head until it buzzed. With a sigh, I let my hand drop and felt a little better.

I saw movement out of the corner of my eye and turned. The roses nearest my hand flashed red, white, and orange in a Technicolor static. I pulled my hand back in surprise, and the roses shifted to their usual pink color. Only the bloom closest to me remained orange for a few seconds, until it flickered twice and changed back.

I stared for a moment, but nothing else happened. My power never had any effect on roses I wasn't touching. And I wasn't even trying to use it. I was just thinking about Cade…

Great. On top of everything else, now my magic was on the fritz.

The sunlight was gone, and my meeting at Grimmour Tower was fast approaching. I mentally shook myself for the task at hand. I needed to focus on breaking and entering, not childish fancies. Kiddie stories never helped me in the past, and Cade was no knight in shining armor. Whatever just happened between us could wait. Romantic aspirations were all well and good, but I had crimes to commit.

I made it out of the house without running into Cade or Jacqui, and apparently Alice still wasn't home. Avoiding my roommates made me uncomfortable, but at the moment I just couldn't deal with them. Besides, I would have to hurry to get to Castle Fortnight before six.

As I left Havmercy and got closer to the castle, the streets cleaned up noticeably. Bandits and panhandlers gave way to business people and lesser Nobility. Or, as I thought of them, bandits and panhandlers in nicer clothes. I turned onto Looking Glass Lane, the Poisoned Apple's answer to Fifth Ave. The buildings on either side of me got taller, and the dirt road beneath my feet changed to shining crystal cobblestones. To my left, a man in a three-piece suit yelled obscenities into a handheld crystal ball. To my right, the shop windows displayed flashy couture on a group of living statues. They looked bored.

I jerked my head to the side as a puff of silver flame flitted past my ear. I felt its warmth as it flew past and heard a tinny voice giggle. The glowing cloud raced up to a lamppost and lit it with some of its own grey fire before flying off in the direction of the next streetlight.

"Stupid wisps," I muttered. They worked cheap, but they were damned annoying.

A mix of colors and smells greeted me as I entered the marketplace in Liars' Square (which, true to its name, was a pentagon). The Square was packing up for the evening. A pay-as-you-go magic mirror salesman wheeled his gaudy cart past me as two kabob salesmen argued over the day's take. Liars' Square catered to a mixed clientele. It was a great place to go for knock-off designer wear, counterfeit spells, and "decorative" drug paraphernalia (as I recall, it was where Jacqui got her infamous glass slipper bong). Discarded newspaper and flyers lay caked into the crystalline cobblestones, lending the emptying Square a desolate feel.

At the center of the market was a large pedestal with a bronze statue of Molly Whuppie, one of the few worthwhile classic fairytale heroines, and a personal role model of mine. The sculpture showed her holding up the ring she stole from a giant, after tricking him into beating his wife and killing his children. So she wasn't the nicest fairy tale figure. At least she had spunk. Better than those boring, lay-on-my-back-until-I-get-rescued Sleeping Beauty types.

At the far end of the pentagon, the stones rose to become a curved bridge over the River Yester. Lamp posts on either side shed soft light on the workers straggling back from the castle. I reached the end of the bridge, where a large stone wall blocked the way. Riversgate was one of the largest entrances to the castle, and always heavily guarded. Battlements and arrow slits lined the top of the two-story structure, while a heavy, dwarf-iron gate manned by knights controlled who got in and out.

About thirty feet away from Riversgate, I paused and drew a rose from my satchel. It was a Yellow Tea Rose with petals so light, they were almost white around the edges. I held it gingerly in front of my face and closed my eyes.

I pushed aside my stress and concern and called up memories of clear water on bare feet, children playing and running, freshly-cut grass, merry-go-rounds, and a hint of the silvery laughter of the will-o-wisp. The afterimage of sunlight shining through clouds left a purple glow on the inside of my eyes. I focused and let all those images and feelings drift like apple blossoms down through my hand and into the rose.

I blinked a few times and looked down at the flower. The center was now a much deeper yellow, which flowed out into a shocking pink. I gave it a sniff. It wasn't very potent, but it should work for maybe ten minutes. I didn't have a lot of happiness to throw around.

I pulled my hood over my face and started towards the gate. That late in the day, there was only one guard on duty. He was covered from head-to-toe in gleaming iron armor, well-polished and covered in spikes. His open visor revealed a pair of small, piggy eyes, which narrowed into a scowl as I approached. I tried to make my gait as shy and demure as I could. At just over six feet, that wasn't always possible. It would probably be okay as long as he didn't see my dagger.

"Name and business," the guard barked.

"I'm Lily, sir," I answered, dropping into what I thought was a convincing curtsy. "I've been selling flowers all day, but I was wondering if you might have one, sir, for all your hard work." I offered him the yellow-pink rose with as much girlish charm as I could muster.

His eyes looked confused, but he still reached out a hand for the rose. Most people's hands worked quicker than their heads.

"I don't need—" the man started. The instant his fingers brushed the rose, his entire demeanor changed. His eyes widened, and laugh lines crinkled the skin nearby. He slackened his stiff military posture and dropped his halberd to the ground with a clatter. His entire attention was now fixated on the flower in his hand.

"Oh, wow! That's so pretty," he chirped, his voice full of pure joy. "Thank you so much! I love it!" He actually giggled a bit and bounced up and down on the balls of his feet.

I smiled widely at him. "You're welcome! Now, if you don't mind, I'm going to head inside and look for some more roses. I'll give you another one when I come out, okay?"

"Okay! Thanks, Lily! Bye!" the guard called as I moved past.

I couldn't help but smile. It felt nice to make people happy, even if it was a trick. The guard had taken the rose straight to the head. I didn't expect all the emotion I'd stored in it to hit him all at once. He would probably be back to normal in five minutes, and by that time I would be long gone.

The grounds of Castle Fortnight were all but deserted. A few servants hurried along the stone paths, but they paid me no attention. I walked alone through the vacant courtyards and empty, elegant gardens.

The castle itself was a hodge-podge of architectural styles. Ever since the end of the Crown Wars and the beginning of the Multiarchy in the 1940s, all of the Noble factions had built their own buildings around the original castle in the center. Elegant Baroque buttresses supported some towers, while others were decorated only with arrow slits and murder holes. Spires, domes, and minarets reached into the sky above me, each holding a different Court, House, or Dukedom.

Once upon a time, the titles meant something. You could still find old books detailing the genealogy of each House, with their dukes dotted and their marquesas marked. But with the Multiarchy in place, all the titles were up for grabs, except king and queen. The Apple was done with kings.

Royals nowadays used titles from every part of the world to stroke their egos. Czars had tea with earls and bishops, while sultans and daimyos played racquetball. It was all very cosmopolitan. Following tradition, most young Royals were princes and princesses until their twenty-first birthday. I assumed there was a system in place, but hell if I knew the proper way to address a viscountess.

An Art Nouveau clock tower to my right said it was twenty past five. If I hurried, I would be able to stop in and see Alice and still make it to the Grimmour chapel on time. If I were lucky, the Black Duchess wouldn't mind me borrowing one of her maids for five minutes. I went down a curved stone stairway leading to the flatlands on the eastern side of the grounds. Affectionately referred to as "The Desert" by those who didn't live there, this part of Castle Fortnight was designed with a distinctly French sensibility, all dusty gravel paths and swirling green topiary.

The Black Duchy was a wide, round pavilion with tall windows of tinted black glass set into a wall of hedges. The outside was still half-decorated with hanging fabrics and burnt-out torches. Sprinkled here and there were bits of shattered glass, spilled shrimp cocktail, and trampled corsages. I stepped around a broken syringe filled with what looked like confetti mixed with mercury. The Royals partied hard.

A couple of maids outside were able to direct me to the main ballroom, where I found Alice and the other servants trying to get mysterious stains out of the stone floor. I waved to her from the entryway, and she came out to meet me.

"Hey B, what's up?" Alice squeaked, almost skipping towards me. Her chopped black bangs flapped with the movement. Even in her bland, boring maid's uniform, she looked chipper and alive.

"Look what I found," she whispered. She turned her head and pushed back her hair, revealing a beautiful green stone necklace. "It was on the floor in one of the storage closets. Some Royal must have dropped it while banging a busboy or something."

I chuckled despite myself. Even on a stressful day, Alice could make me smile. "Very classy. It looks nice with your uniform."

She raised her eyebrows. "And that's saying something." She looked down at the black frock that was standard issue for Castle Fortnight maids. I knew she had made her own alterations to the dress, making it fit her more like a gown and less like a canvas sack, but it still didn't flatter her. Royals always kept their cleaning staff as unattractive as possible. It cut down on Cinderella stories.

"So what brings you to the castle?" she queried.

"I have to go meet with a Royal, one of the Grimmours. I think to get some sort of job, but I'm not sure yet. But I wanted to stop by and check in. I remember you saying something about a story you'd heard—something about a Marchioness?"

Alice's eyes glittered. "You mean the tale of the bear and the cursed tambourine?"

"Sure, something like that. Do you mind telling it to me?"

She looked around and drew close, as if she were about to divulge state secrets. "Once upon a time," she started, her voice taking up the richness of a storyteller, "there was a young Marchioness, whose father kept her hidden from the world on account of her breathtaking beauty. He kept her inside his tower and never let her see the face of a man. He planned to give her in marriage to a powerful lord in order to cement the alliance between their two houses. The Marchioness grew more and more beautiful with each passing year, but her heart grew sad and empty. She yearned for more."

"Okay," I drawled, "pretty standard." The story was nothing to write home about, but the music in Alice's voice made me want to keep listening.

She ignored the interruption. "One day, from outside her window, she heard the sound of music. Curious, she looked out and saw a fascinating sight. A giant black bear stood in the castle courtyard, jumping and capering while playing on a fiddle. Next to him, a young man played along on the tambourine. Now, the Marchioness had never seen a bear or a man before, but when she saw the pair dancing about, she was determined to join in. Filled with courage, she leapt from her tower window and landed softly in a nearby apple tree." Alice flung her arms out as she spoke, as if she herself were jumping into the air.

"She made her way down and jumped down right before the bear. The bear gave her a curious glance but kept playing. The young boy stopped playing, his cheeks flushed and ruddy from dancing. He kissed her hand and told her he was a traveling performer, sent to entertain her as a gift from her betrothed. The girl was flattered and asked if she might hear them play more. She spent the entire afternoon dancing and playing with the young man and his bear, until night fell and she snuck back into the castle. Before she left, she gave the young man one of her gold earrings to thank him for his company and for his music. The next day—"

"Sorry, Alice, I'm in a little bit of a rush. Let me guess. Three repetitions of her meeting the young boy, but on the third day, uh oh, she doesn't have an earring to give him."

Alice scowled at me. "You just don't appreciate the art of storytelling. But, yeah, that's pretty much it." She resumed her storytelling voice. "On the third day, the girl wanted to thank the tambourine player, but she was out of trinkets to give him. She was growing quite fond of the boy with his ruddy cheeks. She told him she would give him anything he desired. So the young man asked for her hand in marriage. The Marchioness paused, soaking in the feeling of her world changing around her. She said yes.

"As soon as she did, the black bear roared and charged at them, and in an instant he gobbled the young man up. The Marchioness screamed but was helpless to stop him. As soon as he'd finished, the bear transformed into a handsome but cruel man. He told the Marchioness that he was the powerful lord who was to be her husband and that he had brought the young man with him to test her fidelity. She failed. She was heartbroken. She clutched the young man's tambourine to her chest, but the lord had put a curse on it, and she fell into a deep, dreamless sleep. She was cursed to remain forever asleep until a prince of a prince entered her chamber. Her father laid her to rest in her bedroom, waiting for the moment when she would wake up, and he could comfort his daughter in the throes of her grief."

Alice fell silent. Her story hung in the air for a second, and I realized I had lost all track of the world around me. She was good.

"Well, that's kind of a downer," I scoffed, breaking the spell. "But is it true?"

"I think so," Alice answered cheerfully. "Actually, it was a sousaphone, not a tambourine, but sousaphones have no place in a fairy tale."

"Good to know. So the Marchioness was never rescued by a prince of a prince?"

"Not yet." Alice shrugged. "And it's been a century or two. She was shipped over here in the seventies when her family moved to the Apple."

"And which room is she in?"

Alice scrunched her face up as she remembered. "It's on the west side, right above the patch of daffodils. Can't miss it."

"Thanks, you're a lifesaver. Shouldn't you get back to work?"

Alice turned back to the maids glaring at her in the ballroom. "Oh, yeah, probably. But I'll see you back at the house?"

"If I'm not kidnapped by Royalty. I was thinking of getting some Chinese for dinner. Sound good?" Alice nodded. "And can you pick up some milk for Jacqui on your way home?"

"Yeah, definitely." At the sound of Jacqui's name, the first signs of a frown passed over Alice's lips. It was tough on us all.

I pulled my satchel up on my shoulder. "Oh, one more thing," I added. "You don't happen to know anything about Jungian psychoanalytic theory, do you?"

Alice shrugged. "Back in North Dakota, my parents sent me to a shrink to try to get me to stop dating my history teacher. Does that help?"

I laughed out loud, then tried to figure out if she was joking. Her eyes were bright and unreadable. I could never tell when Alice was being serious. "Probably not. Alright, thanks again for the story, Alice." I said my goodbyes and left her cleaning up champagne stains.

A curving stone path led me from the Black Duchy to the north end of the castle grounds. Grimmour Tower stood a little removed, the highest of all the buildings around it. The walls were made of a dark, slate-grey stone, and every inch of it was covered with imposing statues, carvings, and gargoyles. Not my particular taste in décor.

I circled behind the main entrance to the tower. Around the back, I came to one of the spots where the wall protruded an extra couple of feet. A thorny hedge stood surrounding the tower at about shoulder height. Underneath the dark umbrella of briars was a small patch of daffodils.

As I stepped into the bushes, the thorns twisted and curled away from my cloak. I waded through the thick hedge without a scratch. My dad's work clothes were still recognized by the Castle gardens, even after he retired from gardening years ago.

I reached the base of the protrusion, which opened a few feet off the ground into a tunnel that led up into the castle. It was just big enough for me to squeeze inside when I bent down. The inside was dim, but I could make out a faint point of light about twenty feet above me.

It didn't smell that bad for a latrine chute. I prayed silently that I had found the right one.

I braced my arms against either side of the chute and hefted myself up. The stone was dry, which was a good sign. I pressed myself close to the sides of the tunnel and inched my way slowly up the passage. The climb wasn't hard, just tedious. Good thing I was tall. Finally, my fingers reached smooth stone at the top of the tunnel. I extended my legs fully and climbed out of the latrine. I was in a small bathroom that, luckily, was empty. That could have been awkward. Most of the Apple had moved on to magic-based plumbing, but a lot of the older buildings still had the classic latrine style.

I made my way into the adjoining bedroom with as little noise as possible. A thin rail of a woman snored peacefully on the four-poster bed, and in the dim light from an overhead lamp, I saw cobwebs stuck to her sides.

Her nightgown looked expensive, if old-fashioned. I was in the right place.

The Marchioness was not the type I would have expected to jump out of towers or romance commoners. Maybe she had more fire when she was conscious.

I listened at the heavy oak door for a few moments before easing it open. Outside, the narrow stone hallway was empty. An expensive spell on the torches along the walls made the hallway look as if it were lit by fresh sunlight. It gave an odd contrast to the severe stonework and the dark carpets on the floor.

My steps were silent as I went down the hall and prayed my memory of the castle layout was trustworthy. A few weeks back, a minor Grimmour Noble had hired me and given me a brief tour of the castle. Apparently, he thought I'd be impressed by the historic vase collection or something. I don't pretend to understand rich people.

The Marchioness's room wasn't far from where I was going, and there were only a few deserted hallways to sneak through before I was at the stairs to the chapel. I took the wide stone steps two at a time. Thanks to the stupid sunlight spell, I was horribly visible if anyone should come along.

I came to a pair of wide, arch-shaped doors, each with a circular stained-glass window. My pocket watch said it was only five minutes to six. Just in time. I listened at the door to see if there was anyone inside.

Suddenly, the sound of clanking chain mail echoed up from the bottom of the stairs, followed by the muffled sound of human voices. Instantly, I felt my stomach curl into itself in fear. It felt like my digestive organs were trying to make a fist. I looked frantically around the stairwell to see if there was any means of escape. Nothing. My entire body shaking, I looked down the stairs and reached in my satchel for a single white rose.

Two castle guards rounded the corner, walking slowly as they made their rounds. Their blue-trimmed suits of armor were identical, except for a few necessary adjustments on the woman's outfit. My eyes fixed involuntarily on the large wooden crossbow hanging from the man's back.

Not giving them a chance to turn towards me, I sprang down the stairs three steps at a time. The guards had barely turned to face me by the time I reached the bottom.

I took a deep breath in and pictured the tense lump in my stomach leaping up into my lungs. There, it mingled with the terror that constricted my throat and the sticky, dry taste of fear on my tongue. I raised the rose to my lips and exhaled forcefully.

The petals turned a sharp, electric blue where my breath hit them and flew off the stem towards the surprised guards. The woman had her sword halfway out of its sheath when the whirl of blue petals hit her. She took a step back, as if struck. Her eyes widened with the panic I'd breathed into the petals, and her trembling fingers dropped her sword. The man turned swiftly, but before he could register what had happened to his partner, the cloud of blue banked off its first victim and flew at him. The swarm of petals rushed to him as if propelled by an unlikely wind. He let out a short gulp of terror and started to hyperventilate.

I watched this through blurred eyes as my head pounded. Using that much emotion at once always leaves me drained, and I fought to clear my head. All of my energy and adrenaline had gone into the rose. *Run*, a small, rational voice said to my legs. *Go. Now. Really, guys.* But my legs remained indifferent.

I finally managed to stumble forward in a half-jog, although my speed was hard to judge with the room spinning so much. The guards made no move to stop me, still spell-shocked. I staggered back down the hallway I'd come from. I tried to remember the way back to the Marchioness's latrine, but I found my sense of left and right deteriorating rapidly.

A polite clearing of a throat stopped me dead in my tracks. "Fairly impressive, Miss Pryce," a smooth voice said. "Drunken lurching aside, reports of your talents are only slightly exaggerated."

I spun clumsily to what I strongly suspected was my right. A tall, silver-haired man in a blue tunic and pinstriped pants observed me, an expression of detached amusement on his face. He stood in an archway that I didn't remember seeing on my way in. His gaze moved to the two frozen guards with disinterest.

"That will do. Follow me, please," he advised. He turned neatly and went through the arch.

The pain in my head started to clear, and I felt my heart rate going back to an almost normal level. After using up all of my panic in the rose, I was barely surprised to see a man appear out of nowhere. He had to be the one who called me here. His outfit practically shimmered with wealth.

I'd watched enough old detective movies to learn at least one thing: you should always follow the money. As soon as I shuffled my way close to him, the man began to speak without looking at me. "When will those guards be functional again, if you don't mind my asking?"

I cleared my throat of the bile that had risen during my escape attempt. "I'd give them another ten minutes of whimpering, and they'll be mobile, at least. Probably a bit jumpy for the rest of the night, but nothing permanent." I paused, not sure if I should push my luck. "You set them on me, didn't you? Some sort of test?"

He paused in the hallway and turned to give me a condescending look.

"Well, of course. I had to make sure you were resourceful."

"And if I wasn't?"

His lips twitched slightly, and he turned back around. "Breaking into Castle Fortnight is a serious offense. And no amount of resourcefulness could get you out of the maximum security floors of the White Tower. Besides, I'd much prefer your name didn't appear on any official Castle records this evening."

Alternating flashes of anger and fear passed through my mind. Whoever he was, he was a man of power. And he was hoping he could use me. A slimy little part of me was impressed I was even on his radar.

The man stopped suddenly and turned to face a doorway that had been sealed off with stone. He laid a hand on the wall for a few seconds and closed his eyes. The stonework slid away smoothly, the bricks melting into the walls on either side like some impossible Jenga set. In a few moments, the doorway was completely clear, without any sign of the vanished rock.

He seemed pleased with the surprise on my face. "Enchanted lodestone. It only responds to the touch of a Grimmour."

Inside the doorway was a lavish study. Bookshelves lined the curved walls, holding everything from rune-covered thirteenth-century manuscripts to first-edition Wordsworths. The man crossed and sat behind a large mahogany desk lined with papers and looked me over with a disapproving gaze. I waited for a moment, but he didn't ask me to sit.

I sat anyways.

"My name is Count Allistair Grimmour. I called you here because I need your assistance, and, unless I'm mistaken, you need mine." The Count's tone was brisk and businesslike, as if he were discussing forecasted stock dividends. "You wouldn't be here if I had any other option."

I sat forward in my seat. My heart had stopped pounding, and, despite how unnerving the Count was, I wanted to hear what he had to say.

"Two days ago, Rick Pearson, a student at Columbia, disappeared. He left for class in the morning and never arrived. His friends haven't seen him, his cell phone is disconnected, and no one knows where he is. And you," he said blandly, "are going to find him for me."

He pushed a picture across the desk. It was a shot of a kid a few years younger than me, with black spiky hair and a big smile on a wide but handsome face. He was at a party, laughing and pointing at something to his right. The picture had been cropped to show only him. Part of me strongly suspected the Count had gotten it off Facebook.

I looked up from the picture. "Okay," I said. "Why do you care?"

"Mr. Pearson," the Count sneered, "is dating my daughter. His disappearance has left her very upset." Disapproval dripped from every consonant.

"Your daughter? So he's a Royal as well?"

"No," he scorned, his tone clipped. "Pearson is from a small town in Indiana."

"Wait, he's a Know-Not? Your daughter is dating a Know-Not?" He nodded. "And he hasn't caught on that his girlfriend is Poisoned Apple Royalty?"

"Informing him of the Apple's existence would be a clear violation of the Compact. My daughter might not have the best taste in suitors, but she's not foolish enough to break the law."

Underneath his words rang the familiar tune of parental disapproval. I decided to play along. "Of course. But a girl of her station should be dating another Royal, no?"

He sat back in his chair and smiled ruefully. "Why don't you try telling Miranda that? My children are stubborn, Miss Pryce. They got it from their late mother. Miranda has been rebellious since I married my second wife, Braselyn. But I would do anything for them." He gestured to the wall behind me.

Twisting in my chair, I saw a giant oil painting hanging above a fireplace. I recognized the Count standing with his arm around a redhead half his age, who was posed somewhat provocatively for a family portrait. That must be the new wife. She was too young to be the mother of the two college-aged kids seated in the front of the portrait.

Miranda Grimmour was a stunningly fragile blonde, with flowing, winding hair that reached her waist. Her fine features were reflected on the young man next to her. His blond hair was cut short, but his face was just as pale and delicate. Both wore dark indigo outfits that made their blue eyes shine strikingly.

I turned back to the Count. "I understand. But why me? Any wizard with a crystal ball could find out where this Rick kid is."

He gave me a withering look. "Clearly, that was my first thought. But all the best wizards at the Academy of the Iron Wand have tried scrying him, and so far, all they've been able to tell me is that he is still alive. Something is clouding him from Academy magic. Which is why I need your talents."

A thought fell into place in my head, and I tried to keep the suspicion from showing on my face. "But sir, how am I supposed to give him a rose if I don't know where he is?"

"We both know that shouldn't be a problem." He opened a desk drawer and withdrew a thin black folder. Embossed on the cover was an old-fashioned crest centered in a pentagram. "While my friends at the Academy weren't able to help find Rick, they were able to point me towards someone who could." He opened the folder and read from one of the parchments inside. "In addition to imparting emotions to those around her, Pryce has demonstrated the ability to hone in on the emotions of others and track them over long distances."

It took me a second to comprehend what I was hearing. I'd only figured out the other side to my powers a year ago. Maybe ten people in all of the Apple had seen me track someone, yet here was a Royal reading about it from a folder. Suddenly, I felt very exposed and paranoid.

The Count must have seen my panic. "The Academy is always monitoring Free Spells like yourself. Sizing up the competition, as it were. Seeing if any of your non-Academy-sanctioned magic could be of use to them." He gestured to the black folder. "But don't worry, these records aren't accessible to the general public."

I shook my head. I hadn't even known there was a term for what I was. I would have to look up 'Free Spells' when I got home. "So the Academy can stalk the entire magic-using population of the Apple, but they can't find a single, disappeared Know-Not?"

He shrugged. "The wizards say they've never seen anything like it. Someone or something has completely hidden the boy from their sights. They said it is some sort of cloud that their spells can't pierce."

I blanched a little. The Academy was full of the biggest eggheads in the Apple, and if they couldn't identify something, it was probably trouble. It'd be like Stephen Hawking describing an object hurtling towards Earth as "kind of a space-related thingy."

"Do you have any idea who might have done this? Or why they would take him?"

"I've tried all the traditional routes of investigation and checked all the usual enemies of the Grimmours. So far, nothing. Only a few of Miranda's close friends in the Apple even knew she was seeing someone at Columbia."

Each new fact the Count gave me rushed out of my grasp. It was too much. "Do you think Rick disappeared on his own? Maybe he wanted to give Miranda the slip."

He shook his head. "As far as we can tell, he had no connections to the Apple beyond her. How could he find such a powerful spell to conceal himself? No, I'm afraid this is a kidnapping. Although," the Count leaned forward, "if he has decided to run away from my daughter, I'm sure you could *convince* him to return."

That was the final straw. I put my hands on the desk, ready to get up. "I'm sorry, sir, but this is just too much for me to handle. If these kidnappers can snatch a Know-Not in broad daylight and block the Academy's best and brightest, they are way out of my league. I'm just a delivery girl, not a private eye."

"I wouldn't send you alone. I've hired one of the Apple's most capable Knights to escort you during your search."

The idea of babysitting a duel-happy sword jockey didn't make the idea seem any more palatable. "I'm sorry, Your Grace, but this is more than I can handle. I—"

"I heard what happened to your friend Jacquinetta. How she was hit by a spell meant for you. Such a pity. But if you can find Rick Pearson and return him, Miss Pryce, I'm willing to pay in full for her to be treated at the Academy's Curse Reversal and Removal Department." I froze. The Count pressed on, and I could hear in his voice that he knew this was his ace-in-the-hole. "With my connections, I can get Jacquinetta the best care possible. She could be human again by the end of the month."

Human by the end of the month. I tried to picture it. I saw Jacqui back in her own body, not stuck in the house for days on end. I saw Cade smiling again, the worry lines gone from his eyes. I saw myself, no longer hard and guilt-ridden, giving up the work I detested. I could get back to the life I was living before.

But taking this job could get me killed. I would be going up against someone who had already pulled a fast one on the most powerful magicians in the Apple. I could act strong and talk tough with the best of them, but this was real. I could die. And worse, I could get others killed if I made a mistake.

Human by the end of month.

Dead by the end of the week.

Well, damn.

"Why don't you take a bit of time and think this over? Let me know later tonight." The Count's voice was cold and even. Whatever my reaction, he wanted to make sure I knew he wasn't going to beg.

I stood up slowly. I was relieved I didn't have to make the decision right away, but it was still going to be rough. For a Royal, the Count didn't seem like such a bad guy. He was just trying to look out for his daughter.

"Okay. Thanks. I'll let you know."

"Here is my card. Contact me as soon as you've reached a decision." He handed me a business card printed on expensive parchment, which I tucked into my bag. Even if I didn't take the job, maybe I'd hear something about the Rick kid that could help him. I turned to leave.

"Oh, and Miss Pryce?"

I looked back around, expectantly.

"If you'd like, you can go out through the front door this time."

I looked away a little sheepishly. "Sorry about the guards, Your Grace. Oh, and by the way, the Marchioness in the west turret needs dusting."

"It seems like this is our best bet to get Jacqui cured," Alice said wistfully, gesturing with her chopsticks. "Count Grimmour could get her treated by the best wizards in the city. Even if we had the money, we could never get that." She dipped a piece of Harpy Lo Mein in soy sauce and popped it in her mouth.

The four of us were on the couches in the living room, gathered around a huge spread of Chinese food on the coffee table. I had told them the entire story, hoping they would have some sort of insight. It felt good to talk to them again. It felt like this was the first meal all four of us had shared together in months.

"That's true," Jacqui conceded from her perch on the armrest. "Even my family doesn't have the kind of pull with the Academy that the Grimmours have. Not that my parents would help anyways. Still…" Her voice trailed off.

"What?" I asked.

"It's too dangerous. Whoever grabbed this kid is dangerous." She shook her head in a very uncatlike expression. "It's not worth risking your life on the off-chance you could find this kid and get me cured."

My stomach turned sour. "Jacqui, of course it's worth the risk. It's my fault that you—"

"We don't know that," she interrupted. "We don't know that the curse was meant for you. It could have been meant for any one of us, and I just happened to get home first that day."

"So you think it was a coincidence that someone sent a heavy-duty curse to our house right after I started making deliveries?"

"Maybe," Jacqui mumbled. "Maybe not. We might never know. But I do know that you won't be able to help me if whoever grabbed that Rick kid blows you to pieces."

She was right. This was too risky. I could get hurt, and there was no guarantee that it would do Jacqui any good.

"But the Count said he would protect you," Alice chimed in. "You'd have a Knight bodyguard to look after you."

"Right," Jacqui mocked, rolling her eyes. "Because some meathead in armor is going to be a lot of help against a world-class magician."

"I think she should do it," Cade spoke up. His deep voice cut through the room, even when speaking quietly. He turned to me on the couch and leaned in across the distance we'd kept from each other. "I think you can do this. You were the only one who was able to find that little girl in the woods last year. We had all the best Red Hood trackers out there, but only you could find her."

"But that was different," I argued. "That girl reeked of fear, and she was all alone in a snowy patch of woods without anyone else's emotions nearby. Rick Pearson was last seen in the middle of Manhattan, and the trail is already days old. I don't think I could follow it."

"So you won't try?" Cade's frown made me want to cry.

"I don't—maybe." I massaged my temples. "Listen, guys, I appreciate the input, but I'm going to have to think about this. I don't have to tell the Count for another hour or so." I met the eyes of my four roommates.

Alice's were filled with sympathy, Jacqui's with guilt. I couldn't tell exactly what was in Cade's. His were getting harder and harder for me to read.

Alice changed the subject and started sharing gossip from Castle Fortnight. Apparently, there were plans for a new bridge across the Yester that the Royals were trying to push through. I let the discussion flow around me, chiming in briefly here and there. My mind was still a blank canvas when it came to making a decision.

As usual, Cade began defending the Royals and any decision they made for the Apple. Part of the way into Jacqui's usual critique of the social contract, I heard a knock at the door. Glad to have an excuse to leave the conversation, I left my roommates to their argument and went to the door.

I had barely opened it when the figure on the other side panted, "Can I please come in?" He was covered head-to-toe in a hooded, royal-blue cloak filled with swirling, thorny patterns of a darker navy. The face beneath the hood was mostly hidden by an expensive-looking pair of brown aviators. He looked like he was about to spring across the entryway at any second.

It was late, and the fairy stories don't lie. Be careful whom you invite into your home. Especially if they wear sunglasses at night.

"Who are you?" I challenged, my right hand ready to reach for the bottom of the front hall coat tree where we kept our mace. The spiky kind, not the spray kind.

The visitor took off his aviators and looked at me out of familiar blue eyes. "Tarris Grimmour. Please, let me in. I can't be seen."

"Fine, come in." I stepped aside and let the kid in. He looked much more worn than he had in the family portrait in his father's office. Dark circles sat under his eyes, and his fair skin was ashen. Even so, the Royal was striking. Sharp cheekbones, full lips, thick eyelashes. His was a face that would always be more beautiful than handsome, but it was still perfect. I muffled a sigh. Royals got the best genes. Even with all the inbreeding.

"I'm sorry to barge in like this, Miss Pryce, but I have to talk with you," he pleaded.

"Just 'Briar' is fine, and don't worry about it," I waved it off. I found myself curious as to why he was here. "Follow me." I led him down the hall to the kitchen and sat him on a stool. "Do you want anything to drink?"

He shook his head. "You went to see my father today. He said you might help find Rick."

"I—" All of my indecision came flooding back to me and settled in my stomach next to the half-digested egg roll. "Yeah, I don't know. I don't know if I can."

Tarris's bright eyes stared evenly at me. "You don't know if you're able?"

I shook my head. "Look, I barely know how my magic works. It's not—"

"But the wizards say you can do it," he interrupted. "You can hone in on Rick's emotions to track him down."

Great. Apparently, the entire Grimmour family had read my file. "Maybe. But even then, how am I supposed to get him back? I just deliver flowers."

"If you could just find out where he is, that would be something." He leaned forward across the kitchen counter. "We have no other way of finding him. Can't you just try?"

I frowned, unsure of what to say.

"Please," Tarris continued, his voice getting louder. "If you don't help, you might as well be signing Rick's death warrant. And—" He paused, giving himself a moment to calm down. "My sister isn't taking it well. Rick means the world to her."

"Is that why you're here? For your sister?" Good Grimms, talk about pulling on the old heartstrings.

Tarris shook his head. "She doesn't know I'm here. But I can tell what she's going through. It's a twin thing." He gave a ghost of a smile, but I could smell the pain behind it. "Please, you have to help us. Rick needs you. You can't just stand idly by while—" Again, he reined himself in, before his true emotions came out.

The Count would probably flog the kid if he knew his son was out here begging a Commoner for help. Tarris had taken a huge risk sneaking out of the Tower to come try to convince me to find his sister's lost love. And he was right. If I could get the Grimmours some information, they might be able to save Rick Pearson.

Tarris looked up, his calm, polite mask in place. "Please."

The pressure became too great, and I felt my confusion fading away. For once, I could use this magic to make people genuinely happy. No tricks. I wouldn't have to feel guilty or manipulative. I could help.

"Okay," I huffed. "Okay, I'll do it." The addendum *Even if it kills me* seemed to hang unspoken in the air.

Tarris's face broke into a surprised smile. "Are you sure?" He didn't wait for me to reply. "Thank you. Thank you so much." He came around the counter and gave me a teeth-jangling handshake. "Just tell my father you can start tomorrow!"

I returned the smile, but the enormity of what I'd just agreed to started to hit me. This kid might have just guilt-tripped me into an early death. "Great. Should I send him a letter or try him by mirror?"

"He gave you his card, didn't he?"

"Right, but it didn't have any sort of contact details on it."

Tarris rolled his eyes. "Well, yeah. Because the card is Parchedment. Here, let me see it."

I pulled the card out of my pocket and handed it over. Tarris took it to the sink and let two big drops of water fall on it. "The wizards just came up with this spell. My family is the only one with access to it. Parchedment messages will get there faster than a carrier pigeon would, and it's more reliable than mirrors. You just need a little water." He handed the damp card over to me. "Now talk."

"What?"

"Talk into the card. It'll get to my father."

I wondered if the kid was pulling my leg, but he had the smug look that all adolescent males got when showing off a new gadget, so I decided to trust him.

I held the piece of parchment close to my mouth and tried not to think of how ridiculous I looked. "Count Grimmour, this is Briar Pryce. I've considered your offer, and I'd like to help. I can start looking for Rick tomorrow."

Suddenly, the card in my hand got very cold. The red ink that spelled out the Count's name and title began to swirl, each quill-stroke being pulled in a separate direction. The wolf on the Grimmour Crest also dissolved, until the entire surface of the card was being crisscrossed by what looked like shooting stars of red. Every so often the patterns looked a bit like words, and I could barely make out "offer," "Grimmour," and "Pryce" before the ink churned and they were lost.

Thirty seconds later, the ink stopped zipping around the page and resolved itself into a short message:

EXCELLENT. YOUR ESCORT WILL PICK YOU UP AT YOUR RESIDENCE AT EIGHT TOMORROW MORNING.

I stifled a groan. Not only was I risking my life to save a boy I didn't know, but now I had to get up early?

Tarris left after shaking my hand a half-dozen more times, and I went into the living room to break the news to my roommates. Alice was pleased, Jacqui seemed worried, and Cade looked vaguely proud. Whether or not they believed I was confident about my decision, I don't know. But I said goodnight anyway and went upstairs.

An hour later, I was lying sleepless in my bed, trying to make sense of my day. Deliveries had made my life unpredictable as of late, but this was a whole new story. I was plunging into something way over my head. Royals, kidnappings, and politics weren't my thing.

Sleep wasn't coming, and the cuckoo clock in the corner of my room told me there was no way I'd be getting enough sleep tonight. So I got up, wrapped a robe around myself, and padded to the window, stepping over the many piles of clothes on the floor. My room was situated at the top of our house's tower, and the one luxury it had to offer was an ornate bay window that looked out at the city. Even when the rest of my round room was a mess, I made sure to keep the pillows at the bay window seat clear. I even cut some yellow roses from the garden for a little vase along the sill. Let it never be said my failure as a homemaker was complete.

The Poisoned Apple looked tired. Puffs of fog rolled in for the night, giving the city lights a hazy, unfocused sheen. Just visible on the other side of Commontown were the trees of the Afterwoods, hemming in the urban sprawl like a warden. Rick Pearson could be anywhere. He could be locked in a grimy basement in Manhattan, or wandering the storied streets of the Apple confused and alone. No one should have to deal with the strange wonder of this place unprepared. The rules that governed this town were just as fractured and convoluted as those of the Old Stories.

Wisps of mist floated through the turrets of Castle Fortnight as its towers watched over the rest of the Apple. Miranda Grimmour was probably getting about as much sleep as I was. If Cade had disappeared into thin air when things were better with us, I know I would have been wrecked. The only thread Miranda had left to pull that could lead her to Rick was me. Without me, the two of them would float through the fog alone, separated. Lost.

I ruffled my hair and yawned. Star-crossed lovers. And me playing heroine. Putting my neck on the line for something I wasn't even sure I believed in. It was stupid. But maybe Cade was right. Maybe I could use my weird talents to make something go right for once. Even if love was just another passing feeling that I could dole out with a rose whenever I wanted.

Without thinking, I reached my hand out to the roses. When my fingertips got just a few inches away from the blooms, the petals shuddered and turned sea foam green. Then, in an instant, they blinked back to yellow and were still.

The tranquility was gone. I went back to bed and tried to count the seconds before sunrise.

Many seconds later, I was sitting in the kitchen nursing a cup of foul, instant coffee. Alice, the only legitimate morning person I have ever met, was perched on the counter scooping Lucky Charms into her mouth while humming. Today she had outfitted her maid's uniform with grey and black paisley tights and a small leather choker.

So far, the coffee only managed to raise my consciousness from coma to stupor. My limbs had that exhausted feeling like I'd been punched all over by someone with very small fists. I didn't do mornings. Nothing worthwhile ever happened before noon.

The grandfather clock in the hall read one minute until eight, when three sharp knocks broke through my early morning haze. The sounds were clipped, precise, and evenly spaced out. I decided I already loathed whomever was on the other side of the door.

I dragged myself to the door and opened it. The man on the other side lowered his hand, as if he were just about to start knocking again. He gave me a polite smile that I didn't bother returning.

"Miss Pryce, I presume?"

I grunted something affirmative.

"Antoine DuCarr, Knight Bachelor. It's a pleasure to meet you." He tried to take my hand and kiss it, but I turned the gesture into a firm handshake. Firm in the sense that I think I saw his eyes water a little. That would teach him to be sexist. Begrudgingly, I invited him in.

The word that came to mind when looking at Antoine was "groomed." Every inch of him had been expertly combed, ironed, shaved, pressed, starched, or polished. His curly chestnut hair was cut to frame his oval face, while his sideburns kept his round cheeks in place. An expensive watch chain hung from his emerald vest, which was worn a bit too formally to be fashionable. Each feature was adjusted to keep another in check, to make sure nothing was in excess. I found myself tilting my head to the side to make sure he actually had three dimensions. Some little girl somewhere was playing with a paper doll of a White Knight who looked exactly like this.

"Are you ready to depart?" he inquired.

"Just a second," I grumbled. While I looked for my keys, Alice swung herself off the counter and introduced herself. The knight took a large bag from his back and set it heavily against the wall. It was long and thin, like the kind architects used to carry blueprints.

"Would you like anything to drink? Water? Tea? Beer?" Alice queried while she led him into the kitchen. To his credit, he only hesitated a little before sitting on the dirty old stool she offered him.

"No, thank you, Miss. Is there anything I can do to help, Miss Pryce?" he offered to my back.

I pulled myself upright from digging under a couch cushion and bared my teeth at him. "It's Briar. And no. *Thanks.*"

Alice rolled her eyes. "You'll have to excuse her, Mr. DuCarr. She's not a morning person."

"Not a problem," he responded diplomatically. "You should see me before my morning Chai. But I'm sure I'll get to know Briar better over the course of the next few weeks."

Morning Chai? I winced as I pulled my keychain out from the pot of morning glories by the patio door. Dudley Do-Right and I would be spending a lot of time together these next few weeks. Whoopee. More reason to find Rick Pearson as fast as possible.

"You girls have a lovely home," Antoine offered. His gaze moved from a pile of old fencing magazines to the shopping bag full of beer cans sitting by the pantry door.

He's cute, Alice mouthed to me behind his back.

He's a liar, I mouthed back. "Found my keys. Let's go." The roses I'd picked the night before were lying in my satchel by the door, and I pulled it over my shoulder in one fluid movement as I rushed Antoine out the door. "Later, Alice."

"It was a pleasure to meet you, Miss," Antoine declared, his mouth flashing Prince Charming teeth.

"You too, Mr. DuCarr," Alice affirmed demurely. "You kids have fun!"

I slammed the door.

The morning air felt surprisingly good against my skin. The moisture still hanging in the air felt like the shower I hadn't had time for that morning. I took in a few breaths before I noticed Antoine waiting expectantly next to me.

"So where do we begin, Briar? I'm afraid the Count wasn't very specific about how these talents of yours work."

The knight's voice broke apart my early morning reverie. I waved a hand at him. "I wish I knew, myself, but in the past, I was only able to track people down once I'd had some sort of a…taste of their emotions. I needed some object or place that held a remnant of their feelings."

Confusion crossed Antoine's face. "And how does that help?"

"Once I get Rick's scent, so to speak, I can find places where other significant things happened. If we're lucky, whatever happened to him was emotional enough that I can track the kid down." It wouldn't be that easy, but I figured it was no use giving Antoine the minute details.

He dug in his pocket and produced a weathered-looking Columbia ID card. "What about Rick's dorm room? Would that be a good place to start? I've already looked through it, but maybe it will give you what you need."

"It might, actually," I acknowledged. I wasn't expecting Antoine to actually be helpful. "Will that get us in?"

He nodded. "It's got a spell worked into it that opens any door on campus. We'll still have to look out for security, of course."

"Sounds good. Should we head into the city?" He nodded, and we started walking. He set his pace to match mine. I sped up.

"So can you smell all emotions, then?" he prodded, jogging a little to keep up with me. We were about the same height, but I've got long legs.

"Not usually, no." Apparently, he thought the Count's payment covered pleasant conversation, but I was in no mood to explain the complexities of my powers. And to be honest, I had very little idea how they worked, myself.

"But once you've gotten a sense for a person, you can smell the— the leftovers of their emotions?" The wheels were spinning in Antoine's head, and I really wasn't feeling up for Twenty Questions about my magic.

"Something like that."

"Isn't that a little invasive?"

I gave him a look. "Do you want to find the kid or not?"

That shut him up for a minute. I led us down Drury Lane and towards Belvedere Door. It would be crowded at this hour of the morning, but this route would get us closest to Morningside Heights. I wove sporadically through the mess of hobos and Elvish newspaper salesmen, but somehow Antoine kept up.

"Is finding people what you normally do for the Royals?" Antoine ventured. "I think I've heard your name mentioned around the castle before."

"Not exactly." He was about to ask more, so I decided to change the subject. "What about you? Are you always assigned to missing persons?"

Antoine shrugged, apparently unaware of how I'd evaded his question. "Sometimes. All the jobs start to blur together after a while. You've got all the standard elements. Innocent in danger, distraught princess, heroic knight, magical helper figure…" He made a vague gesture in my direction.

My eyes got so narrow, I could barely see. "Excuse me— magical helper figure?"

"Yeah," he mused lightly, "you know, like a talking bird that leads the hero to his bride, or a magic trumpet that—"

"Magic *trumpet?*" I fumed, putting as much ice into the words as I could. We had stopped walking at some point.

His eyebrows went up in an expression of surprise, and maybe a little panic. "I'm sorry, I didn't mean anything by it. But you know the story; the boy has a magic trumpet that plays whenever he gets near the goblin king's treasure."

I pressed my forehead into my palm and tried to rein myself in. "Right. Of course. Magic trumpet."

"You're angry. I'm, it's just—"

"Save it," I quipped. His face froze. "I don't care whatever stories you make up about your life. Just kindly leave me out of them." I gave a sketch of a polite smile and started walking again.

"Sure," he assented, following behind. "I apologize. I didn't mean to offend you."

The walk to the Door was pleasantly quiet after that. We followed the crush of commuters into the Central Park sunshine and made our way to the street.

"We can get a cab," Antoine offered. He seemed happy to have something to jabber about. "The Count gave me money for travel expenses."

I shook my head. "I'm fine with the subway if you are."

"It wouldn't be that much just to get to Morningside Heights."

"I know, but—" I looked away from him. "I don't really like cabs."

"Oh, okay," he agreed. Apparently in less than an hour of knowing him, I'd already trained him not to ask questions. I'm such a sharer.

"It's not like I've had a traumatic cab experience or anything," I scoffed, rolling my eyes. "I just don't like the feeling of someone else taking me somewhere. With public transport, it's more like you… you earn it. You deserve to get where you're going."

I looked up into Antoine's dark eyes and noticed the little crow's feet of his smile. "The subway it is, then." I took him west a little ways into the city to the 79th Street station.

We stepped down into the gloom of the subway. Antoine offered to buy my ticket, but I waved him off. He fumbled with the ticket machine for a while before finally getting a MetroCard for himself. Not one to ride the subway much, I supposed.

"We just slide it through, right?" he asked as we neared the gate. I nodded. We slid our cards through and made our way towards the uptown platform.

His eyes narrowed in confusion. "Wait, how come your card is so much shinier than mine? How—" Revelation dawned on him. "That's a LeproCard, isn't it?"

I looked away. "I don't know what you mean," I sniffed. "Those are illegal."

His hand grabbed my shoulder gently, and his voice came out tight. "Briar, those things are dangerous. Do you know what the MTA did to the leprechauns who made those? Good Grimms, if they found out—"

"They're not going to find out, Antoine," I stated calmly. "I've been using this for, like, two years. Don't worry so much."

He frowned. "It's not just that. It's the principle of the thing. You're not paying."

"You're right, I'm not. But unless you're going to turn me in, let's keep moving."

That shut Antoine up, but I could almost see the moral indignation rising off him.

The platform was decently crowded, but I was able to push through to the first train that came. Being tall was nice sometimes. There were no seats, but Columbia was only a few stops away.

The subway car was filled with the usual cast of Manhattanites: overworked laborers, tittering schoolchildren, loud finance guys on Bluetooths, people plotting the murder of said finance guys. At the other end of the car was a girl with red hair so shiny, it almost looked lacquered. She wore a short green dress decorated with swirls of embroidered twigs and tattered purple leggings. Her head moved rhythmically to whatever song was coming out of her oversized headphones, and she was tapping a beat against her thigh with a small black wand.

There's an art to detecting the citizens of the Poisoned Apple when we're Topside. Us fey seem just a little more colorful, a little sharper around the edges; like we're Pixar characters in a Steamboat Willy world. Bigger, more vibrant, and oddly more believable than the Know-Nots. I'm pretty good at picking out characters like that girl from other New Yorkers, but then again, the wand was a big clue. Jacqui was always telling me I had to work on my feydar.

We got to Columbia's campus around nine, just as the students were hitting their snooze alarms for the first time. I was more than a little jealous.

Antoine stopped on one of the main paths and squinted up towards the buildings. "We should try to find a map or see if someone can give us directions to Wallach Hall."

"I think we'll be fine," I observed. "The buildings all have huge signs on them."

"It won't take long, just a couple—"

"Are you always going to be the woman and ask for directions?" I goaded, eyebrows raised. I took advantage of the shocked expression on his face and stalked off deeper into the campus. Just seeing the sea of Starbucks cups clutched in the students' hands was almost physically painful. It took a lot of willpower not to snatch one from a passing coed.

On the far edge of the quad was a row of more residential-looking buildings, with one clearly marked "Wallach Hall." I tried to be gracious in my success, but Antoine still seemed a little ruffled. We circled around back, where a small loading dock peeked out from between the dorms.

To my surprise, Antoine looked nonchalant as he walked up to the doors clearly marked "Private." They were heavy and didn't have handles. My first inclination would have been to push, just in case we were really lucky and someone had left them open. You never know.

I took a quick glance over my shoulder, but no one seemed to notice us. Hell, Columbia probably had employees who dressed a lot more casually than us. At least neither of us was wearing Birkenstocks.

Antoine took the ID card from his pocket and slid it into the space between the two doors. He ran it down like it was a credit card machine and whispered something Latin-sounding. The card left a glowing blue streak for a moment, and then the door creaked open.

Antoine smiled politely at me and gestured with his hand. "After you."

The clench in my stomach as we walked swiftly down the industrial-looking hallway felt almost familiar. It was my second break-in during the last eighteen hours. What happened to my life? It was like my high school counselor had been right about me all along.

The hall ended in a pair of metal doors. The seconds stretched out as we waited, but I couldn't hear anyone on the other side. All I needed was to get picked up by campus security for trespassing. That would make this the perfect day.

Antoine held up three fingers. I nodded and got ready to walk nonchalantly through. He put a finger down. Something was in my throat, but I knew swallowing it would make noise. One finger. Antoine gave me a significant look and opened the metal door smoothly. I followed him out into a long hallway of numbered doors, all of them closed. Antoine let the hall door close quietly behind him. From this side, it had a very clear "Staff Only" sign written in bright red letters.

"Rick is in room 1038. Tenth floor. We need to find an elevator," Antoine whispered. He led us down to where the hall turned. I heard a door open behind us just as we turned the corner.

"There," I declared, pointing ahead of us and to the left. A dull grey elevator sat idly with its doors open. We must have made our way to the center of the building. I jogged a little and stopped the doors from closing.

Once we were in and the doors shut, I let out the breath I'd been holding since we first walked in. I slumped against the elevator wall and waited.

"You okay?" Antoine questioned.

"I'm fine."

"Don't worry about it. You're young enough, you could probably pass for a student," he offered, giving me a tentative smile.

I narrowed my eyes at him but felt my lips tugging into a grin. "Oh, and you're so much older? I could totally see you walking around Columbia's campus with a backpack." He couldn't have been more than twenty-six.

The doors slid open as Antoine gave a little snort of a laugh. It wasn't the sort of laugh I would expect from a knight. "A grad student, maybe," he confessed.

The hallway we were now in was identical to the one we'd left, with the sole exception of the carpet color. Room 1038 was just a few doors away from the elevator.

"It's a single, so we shouldn't have to worry about a roommate bothering us," Antoine whispered as he pulled out the ID card.

"Unless Rick is back from wherever he went and he's studying in his room," I suggested. "Would I still get paid?"

"Cross your fingers," Antoine retorted as he pushed the door open. I crossed them tight, but there was no Rick on the other side.

Rick's room was small, but well-organized. The lofted twin bed was neatly made, and the desk underneath it had a series of wire baskets that held pens, pencils, highlighters, and other supplies. It looked more like those model rooms you saw set up at furniture stores than the actual living space of a boy my age. Posters of famous churches and cathedrals decorated the walls, each taped exactly perpendicularly to each other. This kid was Type A, with a capital A.

"So, are you getting anything? Are his emotions smelly enough here?" Antoine voiced. I gave him a look, but he seemed to be earnest.

"Maybe. I'll check. First, I'd like to take a look around." The bookshelves were lined with textbooks with names like *French Rococo Painting* and *Exploring Etruscan Bronzes*. A worn sci-fi paperback sat on his desk with a bookmark stuck halfway through. There was a small collage of famous Greek statues displaying their muscles and very little clothing next to the window. Notes from some sort of psych class were neatly stacked and color-coded on the side of his desk.

"So I think we can safely rule out a struggle," I offered wryly. "Unless the attacker was really fond of putting everything at right angles."

Antoine leafed through a book on Cubism which had been heavily Post-It flagged. "And it seems like he wouldn't have left town without all this stuff. I checked. His passport, MP3 player, asthma medication. It's all still here."

I frowned. I supposed it was a little naïve to expect a big, obvious clue to stick out to me when Antoine had already combed the room. "Alright, then," I volunteered, cracking my knuckles. "It's magic time."

My fingers floated over the selection of roses in my satchel, pausing here and there as something in my subconscious made its decision. It was funny how my magic worked like that sometimes, like I wasn't even making the decisions. Like I was just along for the ride. My hand finally settled on a large Blue Girl rose. It was a nearly perfect bloom. Purplish-blue petals unfolded from its center like a well-crafted piece of origami. Blue Girls were particularly odorless, by rose standards. Perfect for what I was trying to do. I assumed my magic knew what it was doing.

I stepped to the center of the room with the rose clutched to my chest.

My breathing slowed as I closed my eyes and focused. I exhaled strongly, trying to clear my nostrils of any unnecessary scents. All the frustration, fear, and stress that made up my morning started to pour out of me. I pictured my insides becoming hospital-porcelain clean. Sterile and white.

If I was lucky, I would still remember how to do this tracking magic thing.

I held the rose out, pointing it towards the architecture-covered walls and the color-coded pens, slowly rotating in place so I covered the entire space. I imagined all the Rick Pearson essence in the room being absorbed into the rose, filling it with all the feelings he had ever released into the small dwelling. After three rotations, I paused, opened my eyes, and looked down at the rose. The color hadn't changed, but the petals were trembling a bit. I brought it to my nose and took a deep breath in.

The emotions hit me like a shot of cheap vodka, so strong I could taste them deep in my throat. I gagged a little. There was the usual collection of extremely intense college emotions: the midterm anxiety, the post-frat-party giddiness, the post-dining-hall nausea. Pretty standard, as far as I could tell.

I continued to sort through the flavors, sifting out the weaker scents and picking up on the emotions that really defined Rick. Despite his OCD decorating style, Rick's room contained a good deal of contentment and happiness that broke through the more stressful emotions. I got the sense that he was friendly, hard-working, and maybe just a little bit anxious. There was a sense of doubt and uncertainty mixed in there too, as if he wasn't completely sure about the life he was living. But the freshest emotion I could smell was a heady cloud of joy, mixed with a little bit of lust. It seemed to be hanging most heavily over the bed.

It smelled like Rick was in love. Or at least he had been the last time he was in his room.

I was almost done with my categorizing when I noticed a sour note coming from the outermost petals of the rose. It stung my eyes, which I'd shut again while reflecting on the smells. It was an emotion I couldn't completely put into words, but if I had to try, it'd be the feeling of hiding. It smelled dank and almost sweaty, as if he had put a lot of energy into trying to conceal something.

Rick had a secret, and it was something he was willing to go to great lengths to keep hidden. Also, it smelled like used gym socks.

I opened my eyes and blinked hard. Antoine was looking questioningly at me, but spots kept flowing in and out of my vision. *Oh, right.* While I was sniffing through Rick's subconscious, I'd forgotten to breathe.

I tried to step forward towards the desk chair, but my arm bumped it and pushed it away. My knees had already started bending, and without the chair to support me, I overcompensated and started to pitch backwards.

The next thing I knew, Antoine was holding me upright and taking me slowly to the floor. I must have only blacked out for a second, but the sensation was terrifying. I gulped breath down so hard, it made my throat burn. The emotions I absorbed were swirling around my head so fast, it felt like it might explode. I pressed my palm to my forehead, as if that might keep my skull intact.

"Easy, Briar," Antoine urged softly. "Take it easy. You're alright." It was the tone of voice you used on a panicking horse. It helped. My muscles relaxed a little, and I allowed Antoine to take a little bit more of my weight. He was kneeling, holding me against himself with my legs splayed in front of me. The waves crashing in my head calmed a little, and my brain kick-started again.

Oh, great. I had just swooned into the arms of a handsome knight. Who the hell *did* that? And why did his cologne smell so good?

Clearly, that thought had to be shelved for a later time. I wasn't the "rescue me" type. Between this and my blushing schoolgirl episode with Cade the night before, I really needed to get my act together.

"I'm fine," I coughed out. "I'm fine. It was just—" I hacked out a few breaths. "Just a little too much."

"Here, lie down," Antoine entreated, guiding me towards the floor. "I'll get you some—"

"No, I'm fine." A little stronger now. I pulled myself out of Antoine's grip and got unsteadily to my feet. The tough girl act was a bit hard to pull off with my legs shaking so much. "I'll be back in a second." I scooped up my satchel and turned as quickly as I could.

I shoved the door open and found a women's bathroom down the hall. Someone was in there, but I ignored her and grabbed the nearest stall. As soon as the door was closed, my knees hit the linoleum. My stomach churned, as if I could vomit up the clouds of emotions rolling through me. *I will not throw up. I will not throw up*, I repeated to myself.

I fumbled around for a rose and clutched it tightly in my hand. Seizing the opportunity, the cacophony of feeling in my head traveled into the empty space in the bloom. The petals changed fitfully between, green, orange, and zebra-stripes, finally settling on a frantic rainbow paisley.

As usual, draining my emotions into the rose left my brain feeling numb and a little tingly. There was just a vacuum where the riot of Rick and my emotions had been. I looked dispassionately at the multicolored rose and let it drop into the toilet bowl.

I stood up and wiped off the front of my pants. Why was I so worried about puking anyway? Either I was going to, or I wouldn't. C'est la vie. I took some toilet paper and dabbed the perspiration off my face.

A scratchy ringtone version of Katy Perry rang out from the other half of the bathroom. "Hey bitch, what's up?" a nasal voice answered. "Yeah, just getting ready for lunch with Jeremy. No big."

I opened the stall door and went to the row of sinks. An angular-looking blonde in a tight black skirt stood applying copious amounts of eye shadow. She was chattering loudly into the phone held in the crook of her neck.

"Yeah, Tiff, he's real cute. He plays lacrosse, I think. Yeah, I know. He's like state school hot, but Ivy rich. His dad does something with oil shipping. Yeah, totally loaded."

Normally this sort of thing would probably have resulted in me actually projectile vomiting, but I felt supernaturally calm. I walked forward, gave the girl a slight smile, and splashed some water on my face.

"He's taking me to some sushi place. And paying, if he wants to get anywhere." She paused for a second. "I mean, yeah, why not? He's hot and rich. Were you listening, Tiff? I'll text you later and tell you how it goes. Later, bitch." The girl hung up the phone.

As I patted my face dry, I thought about how far, far away I was from the girl standing barely three feet from me. She reminded me a little of Antoine: uncomplicated, single-minded, sure of herself. Even after dumping most of my emotions into a rose, I would never be that…simple.

I stopped myself. Was the word I was looking for 'simple,' or 'happy?'

I reached down in my bag and grabbed the first rose I laid my eyes on. Keeping my body between the rose and the girl, I let the doubt and insecurity that I had kept leftover from Rick's room course down through my arm and settle in the rose. Its petals lightened from a bold red to a tentative pink.

"Big date?" I asked, turning to her and smiling. The girl nodded and gave me a judgmental look. Usually, I wasn't one for bathroom chitchat either. "Here," I urged, offering the rose. "This would look great in your hair."

"Uh, thanks?" the girl consented. The frown lines on her tan face deepened as her fingers touched the stem. She put the flower behind her ear and turned to the mirror almost reverently. She adjusted her dress, still frowning, but it looked like her eyes were dissatisfied with something more than her cleavage. The expression didn't fit her face.

I dried my hands and left the bathroom. I looked around for a second, momentarily disoriented by the identical hallways stretching in either direction. As I turned back the way I came, I caught a whiff of a strong, soapy smell. It was masculine and fresh, somewhere between dishwashing detergent and Antoine's over-priced cologne. I followed the scent back to the door of 1038 and knocked. Antoine opened the door, a concerned look on his face.

"I got it," I announced triumphantly. "I've got his scent. Let's go." I felt proud of myself, as much as my magically induced calm would allow.

Antoine opened his mouth to respond when a voice rang out from behind us.

"Excuse me, what are you two doing here?"

I tensed a little and turned. A hairy block of a kid stood wrapped in a towel, frowning at us. "You're not supposed to be here without a student. I'm going to call security." He backed away from us towards a phone on the far wall, keeping us in his sights.

Apparently, we couldn't pass for students.

I stole a glance at Antoine, whose eyes were wide. We couldn't afford to be detained by campus security. Not when Rick was getting farther and farther away every second. I grabbed a yellow rose.

I knew I should be worried, scared, or anxious, but I'd flushed most of those emotions in the bathroom. All I had to give was what I could still feel from Rick's room. My empty heart made it easy to focus on whichever of those emotions were closest to the surface. I inhaled, and then blew a stream of flower petals into the boy's face. They turned a bright tiger-lily orange as soon as they left the blossom.

I waited for a second, trying to see which of Rick's emotions I'd used. The boy shook his wet, shoulder length hair out of his face and looked straight at me. And then down. And then back up. A starry-eyed look of appreciation crossed his face. He adjusted his towel slightly.

Oh, Grimmsdammit. Just my luck. Love *would* be the first emotion to come to mind.

"Who are you?" the boy asked.

"Housing office," I declared. I usually feel something while blatantly lying— nerves, guilt, excitement. Something. "We're checking for asbestos." I nudged Antoine.

"Don't worry," he confirmed, clearly not on the same page. "We found it."

The boy didn't seem to notice Antoine at all. "When will I see you again?"

I jerked my head at Antoine and started towards the elevator. "Oh, probably soon. The asbestos is, uh, growing. Don't worry."

As soon as I reached the elevator, I jammed the button for the ground floor. Behind us, the boy shouted, "My name is Henry Ross! Add me on Facebook!" The doors closed, and whatever else he was yelling was lost.

I leaned against the wall, a headache burning its way through my temples. I had thrown a lot of emotion around in the past ten minutes, and it was starting to hit me. Six months ago, charging up more than one rose a day would have taken me out for hours. I guess I was getting in better shape, magic-wise. Three roses in ten minutes barely fazed me.

"What just happened?" Antoine asked. "What did that rose do to him?"

"Nothing," I protested. "It was just a little magic. He'll be fine in a few minutes."

"What did you do to him? It was like you—"

"It was a love spell, okay? We couldn't let him call security up here."

He looked at me in disbelief. "There's no such thing. Magic can sometimes daze people or play with their perceptions, but that's it. It can't change our feelings."

I looked away. "I can." It came out quieter than I intended.

His eyes widened. "But how?"

"It's what I do. Look, can we talk about this later? Are we going out the same door we came in or not?" Suddenly the elevator felt too small, and I was way too close to him.

The knight shook his head. "I don't think they'll bother checking us as we're leaving. Let's go out the front."

The security guard on the ground floor barely gave us a second glance when we passed him. I walked out the front door and onto the main quad. Antoine caught up to me just as I made it onto a patch of grass.

The sunlight seemed to make something in my head expand, and I stopped walking. No matter how much I squinted my eyes against the pain, it still felt like something was erupting out of my skull. When I opened my eyes, the grass seemed to pitch to the side like waves on the East River shoreline.

Strong hands steadied me and took almost all the weight off my wobbling knees. "Easy, Briar," Antoine's voice coaxed. "Easy."

My consciousness swam a little, and I focused solely on breathing. So much for being in good shape.

Antoine had to half-carry me to a questionable café across the street from Columbia's campus, where he plopped me in a booth by the window. My headache had mostly cleared up, but I still couldn't walk without support. It felt like I had oatmeal in my veins.

"I'm going to get you something to eat," Antoine asserted, pointing a finger at me. "You stay here."

My scathing retort died in my throat. Most days I'd rather starve than let a knight wait on me, but I reminded myself this wasn't some lovey-dovey date. It was more like a semi-conscious business lunch. And Antoine, being a gentleman, was acting stupid and chivalrous.

To keep myself occupied while he ordered, I looked around the room. Despite the grimy appearance, the restaurant was overwhelmed with students on their lunch break. Laughter and chattering filled the air, and I thought back to the two students I'd charmed in the dorm. The love spell should have worn off by now, but the girl in the bathroom…I poured a lot of doubt into that rose. I couldn't even remember why I did it. It was like the rose was in my hands before I even realized I had enchanted it.

Antoine returned with a mug of black coffee and two breakfast sandwiches. I begrudgingly let him have one.

"So, does your power always leave you immobile?" he inquired as he pushed the coffee in front of me.

I drank deeply from the mug of coffee, enjoying the burn as it drained down my throat. "Not usually, but I was still pretty woozy from inhaling all of Rick's emotions. I'm new at tracking."

"Speaking of which, are you picking up any sign of him?"

That took me by surprise. Between escaping the dorm and nearly passing out in the middle of Columbia's campus, I had forgotten all about tracking Rick's scent. For a second, I was afraid I lost it in the diner's stench of grease and stale coffee, but when I thought back to Rick's room, I could still detect a hint of the minty smell I had come to associate with him.

"He's definitely been here," I related, focusing on the subtle aromatics of the smell. "But it was a while ago, and nothing too emotional happened."

We fell silent for a moment. I took a bite of my sandwich and relished the fact that I didn't know what was in it. It was greasy and crunchy and cheesy and had some sort of meat. My arteries flinched a little.

"So, you can make people fall in love with you," Antoine began. I reached up to wipe some cheese off my mouth. Apparently, this was how he started conversations.

"Well, not just love. I can put any emotion into my roses," I informed him. "Usually, I don't do love."

His knife and fork moved smoothly as they dissected his breakfast sandwich. "Usually? You do this a lot?" Each word was precise, like the movements of his knife.

I might as well just say it. "That's what I do for the Royals. They pay me to deliver emotions." My spine straightened against the cracked green vinyl of the seat. Suddenly, this felt like an interrogation.

"Do the people know what you're doing to them?"

"No," I allowed. "Something in the spell makes it so they can't tell that the rose was responsible."

He looked up from his plate, and something flashed in his dark eyes. "And you're comfortable manipulating people like that for money?"

There it was. I'd had this talk more times than I could count, and there was always this moment. The disgust and judgment always came to the surface.

I met his gaze. "What, like I'm the only person who manipulates people? All I do is provide the service. It's no different from buying someone a drink at the bar or sending your friend a card to cheer them up."

"I think there's a pretty distinct difference between you and Hallmark. You get paid to turn people into puppets." He still sounded professional and uninvolved, but around his eyes I could see tension.

"That's not what I do," I defended. "My first client wanted me to give his depressed daughter a bouquet every week that would make her smile. That's all. He just wanted her to be happy one day out of seven. Are you going to judge me for that?"

He sat back a little, as if he were easing the attack. "But it's a trick. You give people emotions that aren't theirs. It's not real."

"Real?" I scoffed. Now I was starting to raise my voice. "Wake up. People get happy because their sports teams win and sad because they listen to too much Joni Mitchell. The emotions I give people *are* real, even if they're just borrowed."

"But the people don't know—"

"Of course you think what I do is wrong. You're a valiant knight, you fight evil, and you know exactly what is white and what is black. But for some of us, it isn't that easy."

That stopped him for a second. I'd struck a nerve. He opened his mouth to say something, but I raised my hands to stop him.

"Look, Antoine. I'm sorry. That was out of line." The headache was back. "I'm not saying what I do is right. But if we're going to work together, you're just going to have to look past it. It wasn't my first choice of careers." I wondered if the Count mentioned Jacqui to him or why I'd started making deliveries in the first place.

He dabbed his face with a napkin and gave me a forced smile. "Of course. I'm sorry I made you uncomfortable."

"Don't worry about it."

"Although, if you don't mind me asking, will that boy be in love with you forever?"

I gave him a little grin. "No magic can make a teenage boy that consistent. My roses usually last about an hour, depending on how much feeling I put into them. It's hard to tell. My power didn't come with a user's manual."

"Does it run in the family?"

"Maybe." I shrugged. "I was left on my adoptive father's doorstep when I was one. I don't know who my birth parents are." Years of practice made the sentence sound almost casual. Foundlings and orphans were pretty common in the Poisoned Apple. "My dad raised me himself, and he never found out who left me. I had one parent who took care of me, so why bother looking for the ones who didn't want me?"

"And nothing happened to you to give you this power?" Antoine challenged. "You didn't prick yourself on a magic rose while playing in a witch's garden or something?"

People like Antoine always thought that was how the world worked. And what sucks was, in the Apple, they were usually right. "No. The only witch in my neighborhood lived in a sixth story walk-up."

"So how did you figure out what you could do?"

I took a swig of coffee to give myself time to think. His questions were starting to irritate me, but I figured I owed him at least a little exposition for dragging my ass around Morningside Heights.

"I didn't find out I had magic until my last year of high school. It was the Spring Ball, and I didn't have a boyfriend, so I went with a few of my friends. We got all dressed up, rented a carriage, the whole nine yards. Before we left for the dance, I gave my date a boutonnière I'd picked from my dad's garden." I paused, almost feeling the smooth lapel of Cade's tuxedo beneath my fingertips as I pinned the rose in place. "I'd had a crush on him for about two years at that point, but I'd never said anything. I nearly puked just working up the courage to ask him to the Ball as friends.

"Long story short, I unknowingly enchanted him to love me for the next week. But unlike most people, the instant the rose wore off, he knew. He knew I'd done…something to him."

Antoine let the silence hang between us for a second. He'd adopted the perfect, 'I'm listening if you still want to talk' face. And it was working. Damn him.

"My friend tried not to let it show, but it got to him. He couldn't tell what emotions were his and what came from me. He said he forgave me, that it wasn't my fault, but…" I had a piece of ham caught in my throat and couldn't keep going. At least it was probably ham.

"What happened next?" he asked quietly.

I swallowed and glared at him. "Nothing. Nothing happened. Do not pass denouement, do not collect happily ever after. That's life. We moved on."

"That can't be the end of it."

"Trust me. It's the end."

The vinyl covering on Antoine's booth made a squeaky sound as he sat back. I stared out the window and let him stew for a minute.

"So how does the tracking part come in to all this?" he questioned, grasping at the conversation topic like a life jacket.

I popped the last bit of breakfast sandwich into my mouth and chewed. He could wait a little longer. "It's the same idea, really," I stated finally. "But instead of taking the emotions inside me and putting them in the rose, I use the ones other people have left floating around. Once I get them in the rose, it's just a matter of finding the scent."

The bell above the door rang as a couple walked in, sickeningly close to one another. The blast of wind that accompanied them had a clean, pleasant smell. I breathed deeply.

"Speaking of which," I added, grabbing my bag and downing the last dregs of my coffee, "I think I've got a trail. C'mon, DuCarr."

The smell led us to an intersection a few blocks away amongst a row of short, residential buildings. It was a strange sensation, smelling the city around me but being able to sense Rick's emotions like a disinfectant overlay on top of the smells of kebab and trash. It took me a minute to realize that the trail was leading to a point on the curb, just before the crosswalk.

Cloud cover had rolled in since the morning, but even through the increasingly muggy heat, the people of Manhattan jaywalked on. Antoine was silent for most of the walk over, watching me with interest. I realized I was walking nose-first, like a bloodhound on a trail.

"Is this it?" he asked as I stopped on the curb. I tried to focus despite the rush of students crowding the sidewalk.

I nodded. "Something happened here. Give me a second." I took out the Blue Girl that I had trapped Rick's emotions in and gave it a small whiff. Layers of feeling flowed into my nostrils, and I compared them to what I could smell on the street.

"Okay. We've got surprise, first. Then joy. Excitement. A little fear. But then it gets drowned out by the happier stuff." I crunched my face in concentration. "We're looking at maybe, six months ago? Maybe a little longer. The only reason I can still smell it is how strong it is."

"So what do all those mean?" Antoine asked. He guided me out of the way of a group of skateboarders while I stood in concentration. I distantly understood that I was being a terrible New Yorker by just standing in the middle of the narrow sidewalk.

I closed my eyes and could almost picture myself in Rick's body. My heart fluttered in frantic anticipation. My mouth opened a little in astonishment. I had to wipe my palms on my jeans to get the sweat off them. But the free-falling sensation in my gut felt familiar. It reminded me of the haze of affection hanging over Rick's bed, but fresher and more pointed.

"Infatuation," I deduced, opening my eyes and looking at Antoine. "Love at first sight. Whatever you want to call it. I'm guessing this was where he first saw Miranda and fell for her."

"On a dirty street corner next to a food truck?"

"Hey, Manhattanites have to take their fairy tales where they can find them," I chided, smirking. The beating of my heart slowed back to normal, but I still felt a warmth in my cheeks that I hadn't felt in a long time.

This kid really cared about her. That all-consuming, fixated feeling that I associated with high school and Cade. Who knew if it was true love, or if they'd last another six months. I'm not an expert in that area. But in that moment, I knew that what Rick felt for Miranda was a genuine, feel-it-in-your-blood kind of sensation that didn't come along every day.

"You said this patch of emotion was around six months old?" Antoine clarified.

"Give or take."

He frowned like he was considering not saying anything else. "But did Miranda fall in love with him then?"

"I can't say. I don't have her scent. But from what I could tell in Rick's room, he seemed to be happy and in love, so I'd assume she returned his feelings. Why?"

"It's just—" he started. "I've worked with the Grimmours for years, and Miranda has never shown much…consistency with her male companions."

I arched an eyebrow. "What does that mean for a Royal? She left her card with more than one gentleman caller during the same cotillion?"

Antoine gave a pleasing grin. "Something like that. But in all the time I've known the Grimmours, she hasn't kept the same suitor for more than a week or two. I was quite surprised when the Count briefed me and said she had a long-term boyfriend."

"Really? Flighty princess finds her one true love and settles down forever. I thought people like you ate that shit up."

"It's not that," he assented. "I was reviewing the Grimmour Tower security footage for the Count a few months back, and every day I was at the castle, there were couriers in and out. All bringing letters and gifts to Miranda from someone in the House of Liu."

"The House of Liu?" I queried.

"The Lius are an old Chinese family that immigrated to the Apple in the early nineteenth century. Pretty powerful, as far as immigrant Royals go."

"The Royals like to forget they were all immigrants at some point," I said. "But you think someone in the House of Liu was wooing Miranda while she was still with Rick?"

"It seems like it."

"Alright, we need to take a break," I quavered, my head spinning with motives and timelines. I led Antoine across the street to the edge of Morningside Park. There was an open bench overlooking the park, so I sat down and pulled a thin black notebook out of my bag. The night before, I had written down everything the Count told me about Rick's disappearance in the hopes I might be able to narrow down where to look for the kid.

"Do you think it's possible someone in the House of Liu wanted to get rid of Rick to get to Miranda? Or maybe she was seeing them both, and they just found out about each other?" I speculated, scribbling down a summary of what Antoine had told me.

"Possibly, but it seems like a lot of trouble to go through to get rid of one Know-Not."

"Is there anyone else who would want to target the Grimmours? Any longtime rivals or anything?"

Antoine looked across the sea of leaves in the park, thinking. "None come to mind. Count Grimmour is pretty well-respected in Royal circles. He's been Royal Liaison to the Academy of the Iron Wand for the past twenty years, so between his wealth and his wizard connections, nobody bothers him."

"Has anything changed recently?" I asked, writing Antoine's words in my own variant of shorthand. "Any shifts in power that might open the Grimmours up to an attack like this?"

"I hadn't thought of that," he mused. "Nothing recent. A few months back, Miranda's brother Tarris was appointed Royal Apprentice to the Exchequer, but that's not too important."

"Slow down," I interrupted. "Eggs-check-who-what?"

"Exchequer. Think of it as the Royal accountant. He handles all the tax money for the Poisoned Apple, checks the budget, handles financial matters, that sort of business."

"So if Tarris became his Apprentice, isn't that a coup for the Grimmours?"

"Not particularly. The position is more honorary than anything else. In the days of the Monarchy it was a powerful office, but nowadays the Royals don't get much from taxing serfs. Royal money mostly comes from their own Topside businesses. I couldn't see anyone resorting to kidnapping over it."

"Still, is there anyone else who might've wanted the job?" I pushed.

"Probably. The Exchequer's apprentice is selected from all the Royal princes who have turned twenty-one in the past year. I'm sure more than one family was hoping their son would get the appointment over Tarris. But just for the reputation more than anything else."

"You don't think the Royals would do this? Take his sister's boyfriend as a way to force him into giving up the post?"

Antoine looked mildly horrified. "You think a Royal family would stoop that low?"

I snorted. "Sure. I feel like they're always doing that sort of thing. Jockeying for position, screwing each other over."

"Kidnapping a mortal college student out of Manhattan is not only a flagrant violation of the Compact, but—" Antoine reined himself in. "I don't think that any Royals would dishonor themselves in that way."

"Okay," I allowed. "That's your opinion. But it seems to me that might be exactly the sort of motivation we're looking for. Is there some way we can check out which families have princes that age?"

"I'd have to check the Royal records, but it shouldn't be hard to find. In my opinion, I think it'd be more fruitful to see who would have a grudge against Miranda herself."

"We'll check that out, too. Besides, the Count made it sound like not many people outside of their family even knew she had a boyfriend, so there must be a personal connection in all of this." I closed my notebook, feeling a little better after putting all my thoughts down on paper. "Right now, I think we need more information."

I got up from the bench and started breathing deeply through my nose. There it was. Rick Pearson's toothpaste-green scent floating around Morningside Heights. An unconscious grin spread to my face. "C'mon. Let's see if we can find something useful." Without waiting to see if Antoine was following me, I followed Rick's feelings as they unfolded before me in a breadcrumb trail leading deeper and deeper into the city.

It took a couple of false starts before I found anything good. We passed a laundromat that bore the gritty, ground-in scent of tedium, while a few puffs of contentment drifted out of a run-down 24-hour sushi bar. I found a street lamp where he'd shared a particularly passionate kiss in the early morning. But the scents were all faded snapshots of a normal life. Nothing useful.

However, as we walked farther east from the campus, Rick's trail picked up an undertone of lemony excitement. It was the freshest trail I'd picked up of him yet. Probably not more than three or four days old. Right around the time he disappeared.

"I think I've got a trail," I crowed. Antoine had kept patiently at my heels the entire time I'd been roaming. "It's fresh."

"Great. Is it him being kidnapped?"

"I don't think so. It's him being really excited— but there's something wrong with it. It smells funny." I waggled my eyebrows at him. "Guess we have to follow it."

The scent led farther east to a small service drive nestled between a hair salon and a Korean grocer in a long string of storefronts. It was barely wide enough for a small car to scrape by, but the piles of trash bags on either side made it even narrower. Now that the sun was hidden, it was too dim to see very far, but it looked like the drive went back about thirty feet before turning to the right.

"What was Rick Pearson doing in a dark alley in Harlem?" Antoine pondered.

"I don't know. This looks like the sort of place tourists go to die. But whatever he was doing here, he was pretty damn excited about it. The whole place reeks of it."

"Well," he began, adjusting the strap on his shoulder bag, "I'll go in and check it out. Wait here."

The alley was creepy enough that I almost let him. But then I shook my head reluctantly. "Hell, no. I'm coming with you."

My eyes adjusted to the gloom after a few steps in. I watched my feet, but there were no syringes or shivs to step on. Alleys freaked me out a little. Give me a nice, torch-strewn dungeon or a haunted castle any day.

"Here, wait up a second," I cautioned. "Let me check to see what I can pick up from Rick." I stopped moving, closed my eyes, and took a deep breath through my nose.

Ugh. I have the worst ideas. My eyes immediately started watering from the putrid stench of the alley. Something egg-like was rotting in the trash pile to my left, while to my right, the sharp scent of nail polish drifted from the nail salon. To top it all off, someone in the apartments above us seemed to be cooking a tangy sewage broth.

The upside was, once I was able to set the horrible smells aside, Rick's wholesome scent of hygiene was easy to pick out. The excitement was still there, but it was joined by worry and trepidation— understandable, given his surroundings. But he still kept walking, according to the trail.

"He kept going in. He wasn't very happy about it, but whatever he was here for was so exciting, he didn't want to stop."

Antoine looked around the alley. "What do you think it was? Drugs?"

I frowned. That didn't seem to fit with the picture I'd assembled in my mind of Rick Pearson. "I don't know. There was a smell I found in his room—" I paused.

"What was it?"

"It's hard to put into words," I stumbled. "It was the feeling of hiding something. Of having a secret. I don't know what it is. Maybe he did drugs. Maybe he knew more about Miranda than he let on."

"We can't be sure of anything right now," Antoine contested. "Let's keep moving." He stayed in front of me as we walked around the trash, his hand on the strap of his shoulder bag.

Just before the bend in the alley, a pungent blast of fear hit me like a wall. Mixed in was the sugary scent of confusion, all intertwined with terror. Whatever happened here was sudden, scary, and quickly over. The excitement vanished instantly.

"Here," I stated. "I think it happened here. I just got a big burst of panic and then…nothing. The trail goes dead."

"Dead?" The knight's voice was choked with worry.

"That doesn't mean he was killed," I confirmed quickly. "The Count's wizards said he's still alive. It just means he stopped having emotions. He could have been knocked unconscious or been spell-dazed. What are you doing?"

Antoine was kicking the trash at our feet, moving what looked like a hobo nest to the side of the alley to expose the concrete. "Just a second. Something just occurred to me. Look at this."

He took out a shiny silk handkerchief and used it to grab a piece of newspaper, which he held out to me to see. It was much cleaner than anything found on the floor of a Harlem service drive should be. The paper was also stiffer than most, the type of parchment you only found in stationary stores and the Poisoned Apple. After a second, the headline sunk in too: "TROLL FOODS WORKERS IN UNION TALKS."

"Okay," I allowed. "So someone was reading a fey newspaper in the alley where Rick got abducted. I thought the presence of the cloaking spell made it pretty clear this had something to do with the Apple."

"Right," he contended, moving the final scraps of paper out of the way. "But they were arranged too perfectly. They were trying to cover this." He pointed downwards.

A ring of charred concrete filled the center of the alley, just visible in the gloom. Streaks of ash fanned outward, like someone had lit a firework the size and shape of a manhole cover. The ground in the middle looked slightly off, like the texture didn't match the rest of the alley. When I looked closer, it made my eyes sting a little.

"It's a Royal Door," he deduced. "I'd heard there was one in this area of Harlem, but I've never used it before."

"A Royal Door?"

"Sure," he admitted. "Only Royals and their people can use them."

"Royals have their own ways in and out of the Apple? How come I haven't heard of this?"

"They try to keep them secret," he explained. "In case of a peasant revolt, or the like."

How did I not know about this? "Are there Doormen to keep tabs on them, at least?"

"Of course not. Nobles come and go as they please."

I tried to let it slide, but not knowing things about the Apple bugged me. You never knew when those little pieces of information could save your life. "Okay, so where does this one go?"

"I'm not sure," Antoine answered, a little sheepishly. "But let's find out."

"Oh, right," I remembered. "I'm on an official job for once. Normally, the Royals like to keep me off the books."

He smiled. "And I've got a Royal Pennon, so we can—" His voice cut off sharply as the sound of movement echoed from around the corner. Multiple pairs of footsteps, muffled by the trash of the alleyway, were audible from right around the corner.

There was barely enough time for me to give Antoine a panicked look before three figures came into view. The first was a wiry old fey man; on the short side for a human, or on the tall side for a Little Person. He looked like an academic in a film noir, with a crumpled maroon sweater under a beige trench coat. A lit wooden pipe perched under his mustache, oozing black smoke.

Following behind him were two big men about my age, remarkably similar to one another. Their pitch-black dress shirts and slacks barely covered their jagged muscles and more than a few scars. From their piggish noses and slightly pointed ears, I could guess they had a little troll blood in them. One had a black ski cap pulled down almost to his eyes, while the other had a short crop of red hair. They both held paper fast-food bags soaked with grease. As soon as they saw us, their eyes narrowed, sizing us up. The grey-haired man held up a hand to them, as if telling them to stop.

"Good day," Antoine announced cheerfully. I couldn't tell if he was oblivious to the tension filling the alley or had just chosen to ignore it. "Are you here to use the Door?"

The old man took a drag from his pipe and nodded. At the same moment, a breeze shifted from behind the three men and brought their scents to me. The old guy smelled like decade-old tobacco and tweed, while his younger friends stunk of sweat and cheap cologne. But the smell that came from all three was the sticky, lingering scent of Rick Pearson's fear.

"After you, please," the smoking man said. "We're in no rush."

"No, no. After you," Antoine objected, gesturing towards the hole in the ground.

"You're quite kind," the other man commented. His manners were forced and brittle. "Which House are you with?"

I turned to Antoine, eyes wide, hoping he would read in my face that he should lie. But his eyes were still on the three men in front of us, and he smiled as he proclaimed, "The Grimmours."

The smoking man's smile instantly flattened, and his hand flicked towards us. At his signal, the two men at his side dropped their fast food and drew vicious knives from their sheathes.

As soon as the knives appeared, Antoine reached behind his back and unzipped his satchel. In one fluid movement, he drew out a gleaming rapier and dropped into a perfect, Cary Elwes-inspired on-guard position. He stepped forward to put himself between the half-trolls and me.

It took me that long to realize I should probably get my dagger out. I reached under my cloak and felt Prick's familiar weight as I grasped the handle. It felt perfectly balanced as I drew it; light enough to move quickly, but heavy enough to cut deep. The intricate silverwork in the handle resembled twisted vines that led up to the thorn-shaped blade. There was a subtle glow around the dagger's edges, just barely visible in the dim afternoon light.

Some girls got carriages, or ball gowns, or ponies for high school graduation. My dad, bless his heart, got me something a bit more practical.

The redhead reached us first, the narrowness of the alley forcing them to come at us one at a time. Antoine held his ground, his stance relaxed but ready. The point of his rapier hung still in the air, pointed directly at his attacker's eyes.

The first man lunged forward, sweeping his knife in a wide arc to knock Antoine's rapier out of the way. I flinched involuntarily, but the sound of metal on metal never came. Right before the blades met, Antoine swept his sword in the direction of the attack. The knife hit empty air, leaving the redheaded man unbalanced and unprotected. Antoine let his momentum carry him into a spin and jammed his left elbow into the guy's head. Before the half-troll had time to react, the knight slammed his boot down into the soft area behind the other man's knee, forcing him to the ground with a grinding sound. He hit the ground hard and stopped moving.

The man in the ski cap cringed a little after his friend went down but kept his eyes focused on Antoine. He rushed forward with an overhand swing of his knife. Just before the blade hit Antoine's shoulder, the knight shifted his weight so it missed him by inches. As the part-troll came forward, Antoine brought his knee up to the man's jaw. The thug took a few steps back, clutching at his mouth and howling in agony. Antoine stepped over the fallen redhead and put his entire weight behind a right hook. He used the hand guard of his rapier like brass knuckles, smashing the man's face with a clang. The man stumbled once and then dropped, unconscious.

It took Antoine less than thirty seconds to lay out two men much larger than him. Although he dressed like an anal-retentive Brooks Brothers clerk, in a fight he had the brutal efficiency of an MMA fighter. It was fascinating to watch. And a little terrifying. Living in the Apple, you got used to violence, but it was usually polite, ordered violence. Not jaw-breaking street fights.

As soon as the second thug hit the ground, Antoine swung his sword around to point at the old man's throat. "Don't move. Cooperate, and I won't hurt you."

The old man's eyebrows furrowed, but he remained still. Plumes of black smoke drifted from his pipe, filling his part of the alley with a haze. Antoine took a step closer.

Without warning, a form shot out from the cloud of pipe smoke and flew directly at Antoine's face. His rapier moved in a wide circle, attempting to block whatever it was, but the weapon passed right through the smoky shape. Antoine's movement took his face out of the way, so the projectile hit his right shoulder instead. He reeled back, but the thing had attached itself to him and began waving a plume-like tail as he tried to shake it off.

After a few seconds I realized it was a snake, formed out of the smoke and latched onto Antoine as if its life depended on it. It was about two feet long, with glowing cinders for eyes and a rattle made out of sparks. Antoine tried to grab the creature and pull it off, but as soon as his fingers touched it, he pulled back in pain.

I lurched forward to try to help, my mind racing. How did you fight smoke? I felt like I was moving in slow motion. I barely made it two steps before I noticed something else coming out of the roiling smoke above the old man's head. A large cloud the size of a watermelon burst open to reveal a pair of hazy wings. The rest of the cloud shimmered to form a sharp beak and talons. The smoke-hawk hung in the air for a moment before swooping down directly at my face.

Suddenly, I didn't feel like I was moving slowly. I leaned back limbo style, throwing my arm up to protect all those soft and important bits on my face. The bird's talons grazed my bare skin, but even their light touch brought screaming-hot welts to my skin. The pain overwhelmed me for a second, and I lost my balance. A trash pile topped with something sticky broke my fall, but my right shoulder blade hit painfully against the concrete. Served me right for trying to pull a Neo.

I took a quick moment to mentally check my body. I was mostly sure I hadn't stabbed myself. So far, so good.

I pushed the pain to the back of my mind and rolled to my feet. After eight months of training with Cade for his Order of the Red Hood combat exam, I knew the basics of how to handle myself in a fight.

Unfortunately for me, the basics did not include smoke monsters. I turned to face the hawk, which was circling around for another strike. The twin embers that formed its eyes glared menacingly at me. The three burn marks on my right forearm stung like a bitch, but for the moment, that just made me angry. I waited for the creature to come a bit closer.

The smoke bird whirled around in the tight confines of the alley and made another dive for me. When it was close enough, I whipped my cloak up and over my shoulder, slamming it down and causing a gust of air to blow towards it. The wind I'd generated hit the creature hard and blew it off course, but it didn't disperse it like I'd hoped. It wheeled dangerously close to the side of a fire escape but recovered and circled back to face me. It opened its beak and let out a shriek that sounded like water dousing the embers of a campfire.

Something about the uncanny nature of its cry shocked my brain into gear. *It's magic, dumbass*, I thought. *There's a spell in there somewhere.*

I took a wide stance with my weight evenly distributed, just like Cade taught me. I held my dagger at waist height and hoped I would be able to get a good swipe in without burning my hand. The bird recovered and was ready to dive at my face once more.

This time, I was ready for it. I waited until I could feel the heat from its talons and then spun, pivoting out of the way so the bird passed to my left. As I turned, I brought Prick around so it stabbed into the bird's side, right below where the wing attached to the body. As soon as the blade hit the smoke, orange and red sparks jumped out of the hawk like fireworks. As they fell, each spark reformed into a rune that hung in the air for a few seconds before winking out. I felt resistance in my arm, and I shifted my weight until I was able to put the blade entirely through the wing and out the other side. The two halves of the smoke bird separated with a crackle of light.

The wing and the bird kept moving forward towards the wall. The wing wavered for a second before becoming a puff of smoke once more, hanging in the air without heat or substance. The one-winged hawk hit the ground a few feet away, trailing sparks and symbols from the wound on its side. It somersaulted awkwardly and came to rest on the ground. Its beak opened to give one more steam-like shriek before the two eyes went dark, and only a bird-shaped cloud remained.

From across the alley, the old man gave a sharp grunt of effort. I turned to see Antoine trying to use a trash can lid to beat the smoke snake off his shoulder, but the metal passed right through it. The old man was motionless but still very tense, watching his creation intently.

I ran forward, jumping over the fallen thugs between Antoine and me. "Hold still!" I shouted as I grabbed his shoulder. He seemed surprised to see me but obeyed. I cut the serpent right behind its head, pulling down hard on the dagger until the creature was nothing more than smoke and sigils.

The smoking man let out a cry of pain. He didn't look so good anymore. His skin was grey and ashy, and sweat glinted on his forehead.

Antoine sagged a little after I removed the snake but still raised his sword to point at the man. In the alley above us, the cloud of smoke continued to grow. Here and there I caught flashes of claws, antlers, and gnashing teeth, waiting to be released.

Prick continued to glow as we advanced cautiously on the old man. He was starting to sag with effort, but the smoke above him failed to produce any more creatures.

When we'd gotten within five feet of him, he panicked. He grabbed the pipe out of his mouth and flicked the contents of the bowl at us. At the same moment, the cloud above his head rushed down and picked up the ash from the pipe and blew it towards us. As soon as it reached us, I had to shut my eyes fast against the acrid burning sensation. I couldn't open them if I wanted to. Having lost my sight, I instinctively tried to step forward and grab Antoine to steady myself.

Instead of finding him, I caught the side of my thigh on a trash can, which sent me forward onto my hands and knees. The concrete bit deeply into my palms. I managed to inhale enough of the smoke that I could do nothing besides hack and cough for a while. When I could finally bring myself to open my eyes, the old man and his minions were gone. The three men, our best chance of finding Rick Pearson, had disappeared into the thick, smoky air.

Wisps of smoke still hung in places, giving the alleyway the feeling of a late-night dive bar. Through the haze I made out Antoine leaning against the brick wall, examining the wound in his shoulder. The snake had burned right through his white dress shirt to the skin beneath. I wiped my skinned hands on my jeans to get some of the grime off them and got to my feet.

"Are you alright?" I asked. Immediately, I realized how stupid I sounded. It just seemed like the right thing to say, given the situation.

Antoine attempted a smile. "I'll be fine. The heat cauterized the wound."

I approached and looked closer. Right where he'd been bitten were two vicious-looking round burns, like he'd had a lit cigar pressed against his skin. The skin was a putrid mess of black and red boils, outlined by the singed remains of his shirtsleeves. My stomach gave a little kick of nausea. I was never good with seeing injuries up close.

"Those men smelled like Rick," I noted. "They smelled like his fear. If I could smell it on them, they must have been in close contact with him in the past hour or so."

"Is that why they fought us?" he said. "They only attacked when they found out we were working for Grimmour. Can you track them? They might lead us to him."

I took a deep breath through my nose. And then another. "Grimmsdammit," I swore. "I can't. I can't smell anything after that guy's smoke spell. My nose is completely clogged."

"Permanently?"

"I don't think so. It probably just needs to clear out. Speaking of smoke, what *was* that? I've never seen magic like that."

Antoine pulled himself up off the wall and put his rapier back in its satchel. "Neither have I. Either that was an enchanted pipe, or he was quite the Free Spell. Academy magic can't animate creatures the way he did."

I thought back to the symbols I saw when I cut into the smoke animals.

"But when I cut them, I swear they gave off Academy sigils. I'm no wizard, but it seemed like the creatures had some sort of Academy magic in them. Can someone be both a Free Spell and a wizard?"

"I have no clue. I can't imagine the Academy would allow something like that, though." Antoine looked over at me. "Wait, how were you able to cut them? My sword passed right through."

I grinned and held my dagger up for him to see. "I just had the right tool for the job. Prick here is made of forged dwarf iron, inlayed with some pretty serious disenchantment charms."

Antoine's mouth twitched a little. "Excuse me, Prick?"

"Well, when my dad got him for me, my friend Jacqui was on a big Tolkien kick, and she insisted that any enchanted weapon had to have a name," I admitted. "Prick fit with the whole rose motif."

"And the double entendre was just an added bonus?"

I gave him my best deadpan look. "What double entendre?"

He rolled his eyes. "Right. And does that work on all magic? Even yours?"

"That was kind of the point," I said. "Once I found out I had magic, it made sense to have something that could reverse it."

"By stabbing people."

"Not necessarily. All it takes is…well, a little prick."

"Charming. How did your father find something like that? I've heard of disenchanting weapons, but I've never actually seen one."

"I don't know," I related. "He wouldn't tell me. He just said he had the right connections."

"That's odd," Antoine said, then changed the topic. "If your nose is out of commission, we should probably make it back to the Count and tell him what we've found. Then once your nose clears, we can try to track the men who attacked us."

I shook my head. "That's not really an option. Emotion doesn't stick to people as well as it does to places and things. I could only smell Rick's emotion on them because they had been close to him very recently. By the time my nose clears, I doubt I'll be able to pick up their individual trails."

Antoine furrowed his brow. "Blast. Well, we should get back anyway to report to the Grimmours. I think this Door should get us pretty close to Castle Fortnight." He took out a black leather wallet from his back pocket and withdrew a small, credit card-sized triangle of felt. It was the same dark blue color of the flags that flew from Grimmour Tower. At the thickest end was the wolf rampant. It still looked like it should be drawn alongside Shaggy and Velma.

He walked over to the scorched circle of concrete and laid the Pennon in the center. He stepped back and said in a clear, official voice, "Antoine DuCarr and Briar Pryce, servants of the Grimmours."

At the last syllable, a faint shimmer of purple light emanated out from the Pennon to the sides of the circle. A gust of wind seemed to shoot up through the ground, propelling the Pennon up into the air. Antoine caught it as it drifted back towards the ground.

"Flashy," I scoffed, coming up behind him. "Now what?"

He put his foot into the Door, like he was testing the water of a lake. The tip of his loafer sunk into the concrete as if nothing were there. "Now we go down the rabbit hole," he retorted, smiling at his own joke.

I rolled my eyes. "You're going to be hearing from Lewis Carroll's estate for that. Do we just jump into the mysterious hole in the ground? Because if so, you are definitely going first."

He frowned, looking around the alley, until an idea seemed to occur to him. He reached up to the fire escape that hung above us. The final ladder was half-extended, leaving it just within reach. He jerked his left hand down, and the ladder opened with a clang. But it didn't stop at the ground. The fire escape continued to extend into the unseen depths of the Door. Metallic clanging noises echoed up from below as each section of the ladder slid into place.

Antoine arched his eyebrows a little smugly. "Ladies first."

"Are you sure this is safe?"

"Probably safer than standing around in a Harlem alleyway for this long."

He had a point. I shrugged and stepped forward to the ladder. When I tugged it, it seemed stable. It only wobbled a little as I grabbed hold of it and put my foot on the lowest rung above the concrete. So far, the fire escape seemed to be able to hold my weight.

I gave Antoine a mock salute. "I take but one small step for fey, and one giant leap—"

"Get on with it," he interrupted. I chuckled and moved my foot below the surface of the concrete.

My foot went a little numb and tingly as it passed below the ground and disappeared. The concrete felt cool on my skin as I pushed my foot underneath it. It wasn't unpleasant. It felt a bit like damp shade after a long day in the summer sun—cool and refreshing. I shivered a bit as each step took my body further and further into the chilly air beneath the street.

Finally, only my head was left above the surface, looking at the alley from a worm's-eye view. I took a deep breath, closed my eyes, and plunged completely under the concrete.

When I opened my eyes, I was clinging to the fire escape in a small vertical tunnel. It was about four feet in diameter, covered in old-fashioned flagstones. It reminded me of the summer when I was twelve that Cade and I explored the Brooklyn sewer system, looking for nixies. I couldn't see far enough down to tell what was below me, but a soft, sepia-toned light filtered up from somewhere. At the top of the tunnel was a perfect relief of the concrete I had come through, like I was really looking at the underside of the alley. I kept moving down a few more steps, when a strange rumbling sound came through the wall on my right. It sounded disconcertingly like a subway train passing right by my head. Apparently, I was neither Here nor There.

A few seconds later, Antoine's foot poked through the concrete above me. The top of the tunnel seemed to stick to his clothes for a second before slurping back into place. He made slow progress down the ladder towards me. With every rung, he had to switch hands to avoid putting weight on his injured arm.

"How far down does this go?" I asked when he got close enough.

"Not sure," he answered. "I assume we'll find out when we get there."

We kept climbing down in silence. The light from below got brighter, and I could see the flagstones more clearly. They weren't square at all, or else the design had changed in the short time we'd been climbing. Each stone was carved into the shape of a small leaf, arranged in an interlocking geometric pattern that covered the entire tunnel wall. At first it was just the outline of leaves, but then they began to pop out of the stone in relief.

As we went farther still, the leaves grew wild. All pattern was lost. It was like the sculptor had taken more and more of some illegal substance. The leaves poked out in clumps and patches and dangled from stone branches and vines. The wall's surface became smoother and shifted from dark brown to a dirty green. The stone leaves looked as real as the ones in my garden, carved with stems and veins, with little holes of caterpillar bites. A million tree house dreams from my childhood blew through my head.

Then the leaves began to move.

Slowly, at first. Just little twitches here and there, so small, I almost didn't trust my eyes. But pretty soon I was confident the leaves were swaying. Little gusts of wind seemed to run their way through the carvings, teasing them. Behind the leaves I heard the sound of summer breezes coursing through treetops. I noticed the steady tremolo of crickets in my ears but couldn't tell whether it had just started, or whether it had been there all along. Here and there, sunlight began to climb through holes in the leaves, creating a soft green glow around us.

Soon, the tunnel was nothing more than a clump of moving leaves with a fire escape bursting through it. The leaves ended abruptly, and at the bottom of the fire escape I saw a patch of grass much greener than any found in Manhattan. I hopped off the ladder and looked up. I had just emerged from the canopy of a giant oak tree in the middle of a field of tall yellow grass. The tree looked no different from the others surrounding the field, besides being much more up to fire code. A pair of cardinals sat on a branch right next to the ladder, chirping merrily. Something about the scene seemed a little off, but I couldn't put my finger on it. Probably a side effect of interexistential travel.

Antoine climbed down from the leaves and stepped off the ladder. As soon as he was off, there was a large metallic clang from above us and the ladder retracted into the branches. After a few seconds, there was no sign of it.

"I always thought it would be fun to live in a tree when I was a kid," I mused, looking up into the canopy. "I loved climbing through them. But I never did anything like that."

I walked around the trunk of the oak, tracing its rough bark with my hands. I had a goofy little-kid grin on my face, but I didn't care. Sometimes magic was just *so* cool.

A little to the side of where we'd climbed down was a heart carved into the tree, complete with initials and an arrow shot through it.

"Do you know an R.D. and a C.F., by any chance?" I asked Antoine.

He walked to me and looked over my shoulder "They're not people. It's a Royal Door marker. See how the C.F. is right by the arrow? That's the way to Castle Fortnight."

I followed the arrow to the tree line, where a path led into the Afterwoods. "That's convenient. Although I can't say it's a very tough code to crack."

"Well, even if a Commoner figured it out, they'd need a Pennon to make the Door work. Besides, even as it is, the code probably goes over a lot of Royals' heads."

I smiled at him, a little shocked. "Why, Mr. DuCarr, are you speaking out against our noble rulers?"

"Wouldn't dream of it," he murmured, his face blank.

"So what if a commoner stole a Pennon? Couldn't they get access to all the Royal Doors in the Apple?"

He shook his head. "It doesn't work that way. The spell in the Pennons only functions if it has been bestowed upon a Royal's vassal, and that vassal is using it at the Lord's behest."

"Wait," I challenged, my mind racing. "So if our chain-smoking friend and his goons used the Door to ambush Rick, then they were acting under Royal orders?"

"That's right," Antoine revealed, the gears visibly turning in his head. "The magic wouldn't work otherwise. They must have used the Door to move Rick after they knocked him unconscious."

"So we're looking for a Royal accomplice who gave them a Pennon to do his dirty work." I paused. "Or *her* dirty work."

"We need to get to the castle and tell the Count this right away. Maybe he can find out more." Antoine started for the path, and as he walked away, the zipper on his bag glinted in the light of the setting sun.

Shit.

"Antoine, why is the sun setting?"

"What?" He gave me a look like I'd just snorted pixie dust. But when he looked to the sky, his mouth started to form a foul word. "It was just after noon when we left the alley."

The wheels in my head were still grinding out of gear. We'd been in the leaf tunnel for all of ten minutes, if that. Did the Door take us to another time zone?

Antoine reached a conclusion faster than I could. "A Van Winkle! We must've hit a Van Winkle. Distortions like that are more common in these smaller Passways than in the bigger ones."

"And we lost, like, seven hours? Just like that?" I blurted out. I was beginning to feel nauseous. "You said it was safe."

Guilt blossomed behind Antoine's eyes like ink in water. "I thought it would be. Usually—"

"We could have found Rick by now," I admonished. I knew it was wrong to take out my frustration on Antoine, but I couldn't stop. "Who knows what could have happened to him in seven hours?"

Antoine started to say something but then stopped as a look of panic crossed his face. "That's not important right now. We need to move," he instructed. "Fast."

I was about to question why he suddenly decided to channel a B-movie slasher flick when the true significance of the sunset hit me. I hefted my satchel up on my shoulder and began to follow Antoine swiftly towards the path.

We were about to break the number one rule that all the folk tales and bedtime stories were created to teach: Never walk in the woods after dark.

Talking while the woods around me filled up with the things that go bump was probably a bad idea. But if I didn't talk, it would leave me free to think about glittering teeth, robber's knives, sharp claws… If I kept my voice to a whisper, that'd be fine. Right?

"How far do we have to go?" I hissed at Antoine.

"I'm not sure," he whispered from in front of me. He bent a tree branch back so it didn't hit me. "It should be close. The Royals wouldn't want a Door that was too far from the castle."

"So we'll be fine, right? The Red Hoods always patrol the woods close to town, and the sun is only just setting, and if we hurry—"

He stopped and put a hand on my shoulder. "Briar, take it easy. We need to focus. Everything's going to be alright. I can—" He paused and gave me a hint of a smile. "We can handle anything that comes along."

I tried to say something to thank him, but my voice was caught in my throat. Instead, I gave him a shaky smile and started to walk away.

While I walked, I tried to go over the day's events to distract myself from the gathering shadows. Something about being displaced in time seven hours made it more important to figure out the order of things. I went through the day, piece by piece, telling it to myself like a story. Somewhere in the grains of narrative, there must be a clue. My distraction worked pretty well, until a breeze made the ferns around us rustle like hobgoblins about to pounce. Time to start talking again.

"Where did you learn to fight like that?" I whispered to Antoine. "I don't think I've ever seen a knight kick someone's kneecap out."

"No one place in particular," he replied casually. "I was classically trained in combat in the Apple, but my patrons have sent me all over to learn more unusual styles. Some Capoeira from Brazil. Tai-chi at a school in Shanghai. A few hand-to-hand moves from the Mossad in Israel. I learned to handle a knife while running with a Parisian street gang for a few months."

"Really? You with a street gang? Somehow I can't picture it."

He turned back long enough to show a flash of teeth in the darkness. "You'd be surprised. I'm not always this…formal."

Talking about Antoine's badass-ness was beginning to curb my fears. "And so you've taken all these different fighting styles and combined them into a great, multicultural stew of face-breaking?"

"Something like that. When it comes to the Apple, most fey follow the more traditional rules of combat. They expect you to say all your 'en gardes' and your 'tally-hos,' but they don't expect you to spin kick them in the teeth." Somehow he kept his voice smooth and melodic, despite the darkness closing in around us.

"So are all your manners and formalities and sweater vests just part of a ruse to make people think you'll fight fair?"

"They're not a ruse, and I do fight fair, just…unexpectedly. Take in the alleyway, for example. It was two on one. If I had tried to duel them properly, they would have wiped the floor with me."

"Still," I continued, "aren't knights all about honor and chivalry? You must be breaking some sort of Royal rule fighting like that." My tone made it clear what I thought about breaking the Royals' precious regulations.

An owl hooted off in the distance, low and dangerous. My heart nearly exploded in my chest, but Antoine seemed unaffected. "To me, honor isn't about the places you are allowed to hit people. It's about the way you treat people. Protecting the innocent. Doing what you know is right." His voice had the fervor and warmth I associated with civil rights leaders and religious zealots. "When I pick which Royals to work for, that is always first in my mind. Not every job would allow me to act with honor."

There wasn't much I could say to that. My mind went back to all the deliveries I'd made that I didn't feel good about. Most of the time, I just avoided asking questions and figured I had to do whatever I could to help Jacqui. But who knew how many people I manipulated and abused along the way?

"That's why I took this job," Antoine continued. "You don't get much more clear-cut than this. A missing mortal kidnapped by Apple Royalty, who would probably die without our intervention. I just hope we didn't lose too much time in that Van Winkle." As soon as he mentioned the Van Winkle, my brain gave a jump.

"Antoine," I called. My voice was the scary kind of calm you get when you say phrases like 'no survivors' and 'last call.' "How do we know how much time we lost?"

He peered at the sky. "Well, sunset is around seven or eight, and I don't remember exactly when we went through the Door, but—"

"Right. It's around sunset," I agreed. "But what day?"

His eyes widened so far, it seemed like his eyebrows were trying to retreat over his scalp. "No. It's not possible. A Van Winkle big enough to dislodge two people more than a few hours? Couldn't happen."

"It happened to Rip, didn't it?"

He didn't have a response to that.

"You're probably right. I'm sure it's still today. I hope," I whispered.

"But if it's not…" Antoine let the sentence dangle.

I put effort into making my smile brave. "That's just part of the fun of the Apple, right? We've got time travel; we've got sword fights; we've got deep, dark woods. It's never boring."

The smile Antoine returned was tepid at best. It was barely visible in the fading light. He shook his head. "You're right about that."

My mind spun, trying to find a new topic of conversation. This time it was to distract Antoine more than to make myself feel better. "Do you ever feel like you have a split personality?"

"What?" Antoine asked. The question took him off guard, which was exactly my intention.

"I mean, not really, but you have the side that pays homage at court, adjusts his tie, and follows etiquette, and then you have the side that breaks jaws and brawls in alleyways. You don't see a conflict there?"

The dark had pushed us closer and closer on the path until we were almost brushing shoulders as we walked side by side. In my peripheral vision I saw Antoine cock his head to the side as he considered what I'd said.

"I don't think of it like that. It's not a Jekyll and Hyde thing. I don't suddenly become a Neanderthal just because I'm fighting someone. I'm still me."

"But is one just an act?" I asked, genuinely interested. "Or is one closer to who you are, deep down?"

"I couldn't say." He looked perplexed. "It's not like either is a lie. Does it have to be one or the other? Am I not allowed to have layers?"

"Well, sure," I conceded. "It's just strange. With my powers, I get a good sense of the types of people in the Apple, and most are pretty straightforward. They're either a witch or a princess, a hero or a villain. Not many people have…depth."

"I thought you said you could only smell the emotions of people whom you've scented."

"That's usually the case," I allowed. Somehow it didn't feel wrong to open up to him a little more. "Most of the time, I can't smell what people are feeling in the moment. But sometimes if an emotion is particularly strong, or if it's one the person feels a lot, I can smell it. It's hard to explain."

Antoine was walking so close to me now, I could feel the pressure of his gaze on my face. "So what do I smell like to you?"

I tried to put a little distance between us as I shook my head. "I don't like to use it on people if I can help it. Sure, sometimes I need to get a read on a client, but not on—" What could I say? Were we partners? Friends? "—not on people I spend a lot of time around."

"I don't mind," he coaxed. His voice had a sort of syrupy quality that I was unfamiliar with. "I've got nothing to hide."

"You wouldn't enjoy it. Most people don't like to find out what emotions they've been leaking most of their lives. It's unnerving."

"Try me." There was that deeper tone in his voice again. It was equal parts amusement, cockiness, and…invitation?

"Fine," I agreed, more to shut him up than anything else. I stopped moving and glared at him. "If you want me to sniff you that badly, stay still."

He stood in front of me, hands at his sides. We really didn't have time for this, but I walked up close to him anyway. There was no way to do this that wasn't incredibly awkward. The closer I got to him, the better reading I would get.

I kept my eyes down as I pushed his personal bubble to the popping point. The heat from his body was palpable in the chilled evening air. I leaned in so my head was right above the crook of his neck, framed by the muscle of his neck and shoulder. I pushed all the air out of my lungs, closed my eyes, and inhaled.

The scent of his cologne hit me first, followed by aftershave, starch, and laundry detergent. But my nose was usually capable of getting past the physical smells when it wanted to, no matter how strong they were. Antoine smelled good. Not, like, tasty good, but good good. Paid his taxes on time, good. Helped little old ladies across the drawbridge, good. It wasn't the type of neurotic do-gooding people felt like they had to do, or the self-serving charity that made people feel better. It was a mix of the stone-like smell of a strong moral compass, combined with a tangier overtone of determination.

Everything else seemed to be pretty balanced. Sometimes he was sad, sometimes he was happy, and sometimes he was angry. But overlaying all those scents was the stale stench of restraint. I didn't need powers to tell me that Antoine worked hard to keep himself in check, but my nose told me it was more than that. He was always holding back, keeping his emotions in a vice so only a polite portion leaked out. The stronger the emotion, the more effort he put into suppressing it.

I knew then that my earlier comments about his split personality were off the mark. His psyche wasn't cut in two halves; it was one psyche, cut off from the world. Only a miniscule amount of what went on in the depths of Antoine DuCarr ever made it past the surface.

"You're a good man," I declared, taking a few steps back. I kept my eyes closed, knowing I wouldn't have the courage to say what I had to say while looking into his eyes. "You're one of the most morally grounded people I've ever sniffed. But it's like you've stunted yourself. All the feelings you have inside are cut off and restricted. You never reach any heightened state of emotion. You're always in balance, but you never let yourself go to an extreme." I swallowed and opened my eyes.

Even in the dark, I could tell Antoine was confused. I'd seen it before. Whenever I told people what they smelled like, they got this way. It was like hearing or seeing a recording of yourself. Challenging the image that people had of themselves in their heads by showing them reality was always painful.

"So what should I change?" he asked finally. He sounded a little fainter than he had a few minutes ago.

"I can't tell you that."

"But—" he started and paused. "If I always suppress any emotion strong enough to change me, how do I break the cycle?"

I shrugged. "I wish I could tell you." A skittering sound came out of the darkness somewhere to the left side of the path. I wasn't sure if I was terrified or relieved to have an excuse to end the conversation. "We need to go."

For a few minutes of walking, there was silence. From us, as well as from the creepy-crawlies that seemed to be coming out into the twilight.

"What if you gave me a rose?" Antoine's whisper broke the silence.

"What do you mean?"

"You say I'm holding all my emotions back. What if you made me feel uninhibited or…emotionally volatile in some way? Maybe that's what I need."

My stomach did a little soft-shoe just thinking about it. "You actually want me to use my power on you? To change you?"

He looked right at me. "I trust you. You can always poke me with your dagger and make it go away, right?"

"It wouldn't go away," I cautioned. "I mean, the emotion would, but you'd still have the memory. And I don't know what happens when the person knows they're getting a rose. Maybe it doesn't work if you're expecting it."

"So why don't we try?"

"No," I said. "I don't rose people I know. I did that with Cade and we've never been able to get things back to normal."

That seemed to occupy him for a moment. "So Cade was the one you gave your first rose to. He was your— well, is your…"

"Is my roommate. Was my…" I made some scathing air quotes. "First true love."

"I see," he ventured. "So you're single now?"

Somewhere in the process of whipping my head around to look at him while putting one foot in front of the other, I tripped. My boot snagged an unseen root along the ground, and I started to approach the ground at an alarming rate. There was a sharp tug, and I felt Antoine's grip around my upper arm supporting me. The path loomed about six inches from my nose. I pushed myself back upright awkwardly and stepped away from Antoine as quickly as possible. Maybe I'm a little impolite.

"Uh, thanks," I stammered. "I must've caught my foot on something." Not my most eloquent recovery.

"Are you alright?" he asked, back to following his chivalrous knight script. The "milady" part was unspoken but implied. I didn't like this cardboard cutout version of Antoine, but right now it seemed safer than the man who had just propositioned me for mood-altering magic roses.

"Fine." My ankle was actually a little bit twisted, but like hell was I going to say that to him right now. I sucked it up and started walking again. The slight limp probably didn't show in the dark anyway.

I noticed Antoine running his hands through his hair a couple of times, and I took a little sniff to see what he was feeling. What was he nervous about?

"What I was saying before, are you seeing—" Antoine started.

Just when I thought I was safe.

"Listen," I interrupted, cutting him off. This had gone on long enough. "I don't really want to get into my personal life, if you don't mind. We should really just focus on getting back to the Apple, figuring out what day it is, and finding Rick Pearson." I tried to keep it from sounding too harsh.

His shoulders sagged a little, and I could smell the disappointment as it leaked out of him like a deflating Macy's float. "Sure. I'm sorry, I didn't mean to pry."

"Don't worry about it," I said. My voice had gone quiet again to avoid attracting attention. The purplish haze of sunset was quickly draining away to become true night. Antoine overtook me and sped down the sloping path in front of us. I matched his pace but kept a few feet behind him.

What was up with him? First he was all nervous and excited to ask about my pathetic excuse for a personal life, and then he got mopey when I put the kibosh on the subject. Sniffing him was clearly a mistake. His feelings were changing quicker than a hormonal teenage girl in the midst of her first crush—

Wait. No. Not possible.

Was Antoine interested in me? In the sweaty-palms, batting-eyelashes sort of way? I winced. That would explain the rapid emotional changes and the heavy investment in my opinion of him. He had just been on the verge of truly expressing himself, for once, and I crushed him without even thinking about it. For someone so attuned to feelings, it seemed like I was always accidentally hurting them.

But was I interested in Antoine?

That was the million-dollar question. Suddenly, this whole arrangement became a lot more complicated. But there was no way I was going to figure any of it out while I was still lost in the woods and (possibly) in time. It would all have to be shelved until we made it back to civilization. If I was going to be devoured by flesh-eating wolves, my last thoughts were definitely not going to be, 'Does he like me, or does he *like me* like me?'

I refocused on my surroundings just in time to see another root in my path. Having Antoine catch me for the second time in three minutes would not help things, and he'd already sped up and widened the distance between us. I stopped and gave the root a dirty look as I stepped around it. The woods were getting a little thinner now, so hopefully we were close to Castle Fortnight. I kept my eyes on the ground, determined to keep a better eye on where I was going.

Which was how I saw the roots burst up out of the ground and wrap themselves around my legs. Constant vigilance, that's me.

If you ever find yourself encircled from the waist down in thick, prehensile tree roots, your first reaction will probably be to try to move your legs. That was mine. But take my advice: don't. It's really not a good idea.

As soon as I started moving, the roots tightened, and I threw myself off balance. I reeled forward, and this time Antoine wasn't there to catch me. I was able to get my arms in front of me to absorb some of the impact, but the force of the dry, cracked earth on my ribs was still enough to knock the wind out of me.

Antoine had kept walking while I stopped to glare at the root, and now he was far enough away that he hadn't heard me fall. I tried to draw in enough breath to shout to him, but the hot pressure in my lungs made it impossible. He just kept walking.

With a jerk, the roots began to drag me farther away from Antoine. Branches and stones scraped my belly as I was dragged down an incline beside the path. I flung out my arms to try to grab something to hold on to, but everything I touched was pulled along with me. All I could manage were a few sputtering coughs to try to stop my chest from collapsing. It felt like my ribs were giving my lungs a bear hug.

I rocked to my side long enough to get my hands around Prick. In my mute, breathless panic, I started hacking away at the thick plant matter around my lower body. By some stroke of luck I avoided stabbing myself, but the things were undeterred. I couldn't get a clear shot at them while they were behind my back. So I decided to change tactics.

I took Prick in both my hands, raised it over my head, and plunged it into the dirt. It sank into the soil up to the hilt, and there was a popping sound in my jaw as I gritted my teeth and held on. The roots started tugging more violently at me, but the dagger held firm.

I chanced a quick look behind me to see where the roots were taking me. I was halfway down the slope of a giant sinkhole of sandy dirt. While there was grass and ferns surrounding the lip, inside the hole, nothing was green. At the center was a huge, gnarled oak tree that looked like it had been standing there for centuries. Its trunk was a tapestry of holes, notches, and knots. The root system started about a foot above the soil, as if the ground level had lowered since the tree was planted. A few of the roots, including the ones around me, were splayed out onto the soil like tubery tentacles. Looking up, I noticed the oak's leaves were all wrong. While the rest of the forest was green and lush with spring rainfall, this tree's leaves were a thick, unnatural brown texture that reminded me of leathery human flesh.

"Briar?" I heard Antoine's voice from the distance. I still couldn't talk, but I was able to cough pretty loudly. Within seconds, I saw him come over the crest of the hill I was being dragged down. "Fitcher's Bird, are you alright?" He had drawn his rapier and was running towards me. Suddenly, I was very okay with him playing the stock character of the white knight. The roots had stretched me out completely, and my grip on Prick's handle was starting to weaken.

Antoine charged down the slope with his rapier held high over his head. Just as he brought it down in a powerful two-handed chop towards the roots that held me, one of the strands of wood came undone and rose to meet his blow. The sword sank halfway into the snakelike root but didn't sever it. Instead, the root jerked down and pulled the rapier from Antoine's hands. Before he could recover, it jerked in a violent motion that dislodged the sword and sent it whirling end-over-end towards Antoine's face.

Almost faster than my eye could see, he threw himself on his back to avoid the sword, crying out when his weight landed on his injured arm. The rapier hit the top of the slope above us with a tinny clatter.

The root Antoine had been fighting took that opportunity to twist itself around his waist, pinning his good arm to his side. I saw the tip of the root rise up behind his head, as if it were sniffing the air. Then it pressed itself against the burn on his shoulder. He hissed with pain and began twisting back and forth, trying to remove it.

Meanwhile, one of the roots curled its way up my body as I clung to my dagger. I gasped when it slithered against the bare skin of my arms. With an invasiveness that I'd never associated with plant matter, it curled around my neck to my face, dragging itself lecherously across my skin. I could see the dirty, purple-brown tip of the root come towards me, like a potato shoot growing in fast-forward. My urge to scream was immediately taken over by my urge to keep my mouth closed as tightly as possible.

A quick glance to my left showed Antoine rolled over onto his front. The root was behind him now, pushing him into the ground like a dirty cop. But he'd managed to claw his way a little ways up the sinkhole, and his free hand reached out futilely for his sword.

The frisky root by my face suddenly wrapped around my forehead and yanked my head back aggressively. My neck muscles strained against the pressure, but with my arms stretched out in front of me, I had no way to resist. I rolled my head to the side to try to avoid the root's grip.

Looking behind me, I saw that I only had a few feet left before I reached the bottom of the sinkhole and the base of the tree. As I watched, a jagged crack formed vertically in the bark of the tree. It widened until it formed a gaping, serrated mouth. Through the jagged bark teeth, I saw the heart of the oak was dark, rotting, and crawling with maggots and centipedes. As my last fingers were pried from Prick's handle, the mouth seemed to give a cheeky smile.

As I was dragged, my shoulder bounced painfully off a rock in the ground. The impact flipped me onto my back, the perfect position to watch the tree monster draw me into its maw. At the last second I was able to get my boots on either side of the jaws, bracing myself against the pull of the roots. The tree tried to readjust its grip on me, but for now we were at a standstill. The burn in my thighs, however, told me it was only a matter of seconds before I couldn't fight it anymore.

The sound of blood pounding in my ears overwhelmed me, but under that noise I heard the beginnings of another. It was footsteps, racing towards the sinkhole. Just as my muscles began to succumb to the inevitable, I focused everything on listening to the steps as they bounded down the slope and came to a stop just a few feet above my head.

In that moment of distraction, the tree's mouth opened a little wider, and a black, greasy tongue snaked out of the darkness and curled itself around my right ankle. The forked tip moved up into my pant leg, and the instant it touched the skin on my ankle, I gasped. The tongue was wet and oily, with a feverish warmth that felt unnatural against my skin. As soon as I felt it slither against my skin, my knee buckled and I began to slide belly-up into the darkness.

Just before the tree could close its teeth over my legs, a strong hand gripped my wrist and stopped me. Clearly I should have been grateful, but all I could think of was kicking. I had to get the slimy tongue off my skin, to stop it from touching me. Whoever was behind me pulled me back from the tree a foot or so, but the tongue remained wrapped around me, having stretched to its full extent. I heard a grunt of effort from behind me, and an axe flew in an arc over me into the tree's gaping mouth, cutting the tongue off at the stem. The tree started shrieking like a pig at the slaughterhouse, and a mossy green fluid spattered wildly from its wound. The roots still pulling at me shuddered with pain but didn't let go. The detached half of the tongue loosened its grip but continued its disgusting ascent up my leg. I was able to kick it off without bruising myself too badly in the process.

The hand on my wrist pulled me back into a familiar-feeling lap between a pair of familiar-looking legs.

"Briar?" Cade almost shouted. He leaned over me so he could finally see my face, but in his surprise, he almost pushed me away into the tree creature's mouth.

Before I had time to respond, a silver streak shot past my head so close, the wind teased my hair. I instinctively dropped low to the ground in the opposite direction, as the arrow sank into the tree's core and sprayed putrid chunks of wood everywhere. Two identical metal arrows followed in a lethal staccato. With each landed shot, the tree writhed in pain.

After the third shot, the oak squealed with rage and tugged the roots still wrapped around Antoine, taking his feet out from under him. He dropped quickly down the side of the hill towards the tree's trunk. I wasn't sure if the tree was still hungry or planning on using him to absorb any further arrows. Before I knew what I was doing, I grabbed Prick from the dirt above me and threw myself over the roots attached to Antoine's body. I hacked frantically at them but wasn't able to sever them. My attacks must have loosened their grip though, because Antoine was able to break free and roll to the side. As he hit the dirt, he swallowed a cry and clutched at this shoulder.

The unseen bowman above us let loose one final shot into the dead center of the tree. The arrow burst through the opposite side of the trunk in a shower of sawdust and bark. The roots twitched a few more times half-heartedly, and then went still.

"That was not...what I meant," I gasped to Antoine, "when I said...I wanted to live...in a tree."

His grimace took on a hint of a smile, and something passed between us as Cade came over. He ignored Antoine completely and rushed to my side.

"Good Grimms, Briar, are you alright? Are you hurt?" Seeing Cade hovering over me with concern in his eyes made it a little hard to breathe. But besides a few scrapes, I seemed okay. For a moment, I considered faking injuries in the hopes Cade would try to heal me with true love's kiss.

"I'm fine," I wheezed. "I just have a few cuts. And a burn. From a smoke hawk. It clawed me in the alley."

Another face appeared in my view, this one much closer than Cade's. "Uh, that doesn't sound so good, man. She might be in shock, or concussed." Martin 'Scuff' McCorryn peered down at me clinically. At three-foot-six, he didn't have far to peer. His voice got loud and pronounced, like I was a hearing-impaired mental patient. "It's Scuff, Bri. Just lie back and try to relax, okay? That's a good girl." He began pulling vials out of the bandolier he wore over his shoulder. It hung right below his red cloak and right above his offensive green Hawaiian shirt.

I narrowed my eyes at him. "Dammit, Scuff, I'm not in shock. We fought a guy with a pipe in Harlem, and then we climbed a fire escape through the ground— Wait," I halted, turning to Cade. "When was the last time you saw me?"

Now the two Red Hoods gave me seriously worried looks. "This morning," Cade enunciated slowly. "You need to rest or something, Briar. You're not making any sense."

He tried to coax me into lying down, but I pulled myself up into a sitting position. "I'm *fine*, guys. Really. It's just that we time-traveled and I wanted to make sure we didn't go too far into the future."

Okay. Maybe I *did* sound a little less than lucid.

Scuff took my head in his hands and peeled back an eyelid, checking for a concussion. Sitting up, I was about the same height as the Little Person. "Easy, McFly," he chided. "We just want to make sure you're up to speed." I grumbled a little but consented. While he might not look it, Scuff was one of the Order of the Red Hood's best field medics. Even if he did have a reputation for using some of his herbs for more…recreational purposes.

"She's telling the truth," Antoine confirmed from the ground. "We hit a Van Winkle on our way here." He was still crumpled in the spot where he landed, but he managed to keep the pain out of his voice. Holding back again.

"Cripes on a bike," Scuff swore, looking at Antoine's wound. "Let me take a look at that. Here, you take care of the Bri-ster, she's just got some scratches." He tossed a roll of bandages into Cade's hands.

"Who are you?" Cade challenged Antoine pointedly.

Antoine slowly pulled himself up and offered a hand. "Antoine DuCarr, Knight Bachelor. And you are?"

Cade ignored the hand and the question. "You're her bodyguard?

Where were you when Briar was attacked?"

"I was with her, but the tree ambushed us, so—"

"So you let a Blighted Oak take your charge, nearly devour her, and then depended on her to save you?" Cade's voice was coldly furious.

"Perhaps if the Red Hoods did a better job of keeping these areas clear of hostiles, we wouldn't have run into any trouble," Antoine said. Now his hackles were up, too. Scuff stopped applying cream to Antoine's wound and stiffened.

"If we didn't come, she would have died," Cade growled, his voice low and dangerous. "You are supposed to protect her, and you—"

"That's enough!" I shouted. Everyone turned to look at me, including a few nearby crickets. "I don't know what stupid little testosterone-fueled pissing contest I've wandered into, but it ends now. Stop marking your territory and get ready to move out. We still need to get back to the Apple, and it's only going to get darker."

After my outburst, it was quiet for a full minute or two. Cade pulled a torchstone necklace out of his shirt and shined its light on my forearm. His hands were steady as they uncorked a jar of poultice, but I could smell the anger still rising off him like musk. He gently applied the thick, greenish poultice to my burn. It smelled like aloe and blueberries, and the cool feel of it on my skin was nothing short of heavenly.

"Is that too tight?" he ventured as he covered it up with a bandage.

"No, that's good. Thanks, Cade." Was it my imagination, or did his hand linger a little bit on my arm?

As soon as I said Cade's name, a burst of frustration and jealousy floated from Antoine's direction. Grimmsdammit. Sometimes it would be nice to be ignorant of what people felt.

"So how did you guys find us?" I asked. If I couldn't stop the impending he-man battle, I could at least delay it.

"We got word there were two incompetent travelers stumbling around the woods after dark, and decided to check it out," a voice from above sneered in a British accent. I looked up to see a stocky brunette with a crossbow start down into the sinkhole. As she walked, she slid a tiny round mirror into a pouch on her belt. The movement exposed dangerous-looking veins in her arm. "I just got off the mirror with HQ." She pronounced the H snootily as 'heych.' "They said to patch up the civilians swiftly and escort them back to town. Afterwards, we're supposed to go up to Hag's Pass and look for that tribe of Eisenhans that have been running about. Apparently, they've found a Passway to Chelsea, and it's only a matter of time before someone realizes they're not just a band of abnormally dirty hippies."

"Anya," I sneered, my voice getting brittle, "were those your arrows that barely missed us?"

She stopped a few feet above us and tossed her long ponytail over one shoulder. Somehow she made the gesture martial, rather than girly. "They were. I would have had a much better shot if you weren't flailing around so much. Ran into a bit of trouble, did we?"

Anya Koronik was the final member of Cade's Red Hood cadre, and by far my least favorite. She was dressed simply in a grey flannel shirt and black jeans under her red cloak, but her movements showed a savage sort of power. Although she was only a few years older than me, her once-pleasant face was taut and lined with scowl marks. They deepened as she narrowed her brown eyes at me. The lighting from her torchstone necklace gave her entire expression a campfire-horror-story kind of glow.

"What Anya meant to say is that a little bird told us there were a couple of people who needed an escort," Cade offered, finishing up my bandage. I suspected Cade wasn't being euphemistic. Nowadays, there weren't many talking animals in the wild, but the Red Hoods had connections with those that were still out there.

Antoine's wound looked considerably better with a thick layer of gauze covering it. My own burn was starting to feel much less painful, and I hoped Antoine's was improving as well. Scuff put his tools back in his bandolier and wiped his hands clean on his cargo shorts.

Anya cleared her throat. "Well, boys, let's get a move on, shall we? Cade and I will take point. You two," she glared in the direction of Antoine and me, "stay in the middle and *do* try to be quiet. Scuff, why don't you position yourself in the rear?" Scuff and I caught each other's eyes and tried not to giggle. Position yourself in the rear. Did she even listen to herself?

With the Hoods' help, we were able to find our way back to the path. Their torchstones lit the way as the five of us marched, and suddenly the Afterwoods seemed a little less scary. It wasn't long before we got out of the old-growth pine forest and into the sparser woodland that surrounded the city. We could even see the stars poke out between the leaves above us.

Antoine walked silently beside me. This close, I could smell the slightly moldy stench of his shame. What Cade said about Antoine's failures as a bodyguard clearly had hit home. I tried to think of some way to tell him it was okay, that I didn't hold him responsible for the Blighted Oak attack, but nothing seemed right, so I gave up trying. Hello, awkward tension.

Anya and Cade walked ahead, talking to each other in low tones. Every so often, Anya would half-turn and give me a scathing look. She'd always had that 'brothers-in-arms' sort of bond with Cade, and I hated her for it. I swear, if my life were a nineties teen movie, Anya would be the bitchy cheerleader with no redeeming qualities. Except that I'd seen her use her crossbow to pin a man's hand to a tree at fifty feet. I was pretty sure there weren't any scenes like that in *She's All That*.

My thoughts were interrupted by a melody coming from behind me. Scuff was absentmindedly humming a pretty, lilting song under his breath. It took me a second to place the tune.

"Hey, isn't that from the *Lord of the Rings* soundtrack?"

He stopped humming and smiled at me. "Yup. Seems appropriate, what with the dangerous journey through the wilderness and all. Besides, Cade got tired of my one-man rendition of *Into the Woods*."

"What did you think of the Peter Jackson version?"

"I owe that man my life. I mean, sure, he should've cast a *real* Little Person as Frodo, but those movies were the best thing to ever happen to me. Do you know how easy it was to get laid after those came out? All I had to do was put on my British accent," he said as he shifted to a pretty terrible Cockney, "and ask if anyone had room in their bed for a poor hobbit from the Shire."

I snorted. "You're terrible." I gave Scuff a quick glance. He was pretty good with bizarre bits of trivia. "You don't happen to know anything about Carl Jung, do you?"

"Maybe," Scuff answered, his face scrunching with effort. "Is he that troll who tends bar down at the Woodsman's Log? Big scar on his face? I think he's Jewish?"

"Never mind," I sighed. I was going to finish that crossword if it killed me. Although I supposed the monsters and kidnappers would be more likely suspects.

We finally broke through the last of the trees and found ourselves in a parking lot. It looked like a blacksmith's shop, filled with broken down carts and carriage wheels.

A movement in the darkness made me jump. A single orange cigarette light floated in the darkness, jerking up into an unseen mouth, followed by a sound of satisfied inhalation.

"Took you long enough." Lil T's voice rang through the dark. "They got the ransom note hours ago."

"Good Grimms, T, are you trying to give me a heart attack?" I said, stalking towards him. Cade and Anya followed behind me, bringing the light of their torchstones. "And why the hell are you smoking? Aren't you, like, twelve?"

"Hey, I'm sevent—hey!" T yelled as I pulled the cig from his mouth and threw it behind me. He gaped in shock for a second.

Cade frowned. "Briar, careful with the fire in the wilderness, please."

"Bite me, Smokey."

T recovered and gave me his best prep school scowl. "As I was saying, I'm here with a message from the Grimmours. You and the knight are summoned to the Tower immediately. They need to fill you in on recent developments."

"What recent developments?" I asked.

"If I knew that, there wouldn't be much point in going to the Tower, would there? Now come on. I have to escort you." T turned and started towards the end of the parking lot.

"Well, as much as I'd love to stay and chat, we're already behind on our patrol schedule as is," Anya scoffed, her voice dripping condescension. "Ta!" She turned to the woods and gestured to Cade like he was a dog on her leash.

Cade ignored her. "I'll see you back at home, okay Briar?" For a moment he just stared at me, and then before I could say anything, he wrapped his arms around me in a hug. At first I was in shock, but it didn't take long for my arms to grab him back and my head to find the curve of his neck. He felt solid. Not many people succeeded in making me feel small, but Cade's arms always made me feel encompassed. Bundled up like a nice little package, safe against the world.

As quickly as he embraced me, Cade untangled himself and took a step back. This wasn't the first time I was grateful my dark skin didn't blush. "Take care of yourself," he called as he turned to follow Anya.

"Yeah," I stammered. "You too." Crap. It had been four years since I'd been that close to Cade, but apparently all it took was one hug to make me into a bashful high schooler again.

The Hoods walked silently back to the woods, and I watched their torchstones shine through the leaves like paper lanterns. T cleared his throat impatiently, and then led us through the parking lot and into the Cast-Iron District. The street lamps had just come on, and the roads were filled with fey unwinding after a long day.

T slid quickly through the revelers, panhandlers, dust dealers, tourists, and businessmonsters as we walked uphill towards Castle Fortnight. He must have turned off his ten-block boots for our benefit. Whatever the Grimmours wanted with us, it must have been important to saddle us with a babysitter.

"I'm sorry," Antoine said from my side as T took the lead.

"For what?" I asked innocently, but I could guess what was coming.

"For the woods. Cade was right, I could've gotten you killed," he acknowledged, pitiably morose. He sounded like Eeyore, and it was kind of pissing me off.

"Listen, Antoine," I started. "Don't beat yourself up about it. It could have happened to anyone."

"But—"

I held out a hand as we turned a corner. "Not another word. Don't let Cade get to you."

We walked a little further down one of the broad avenues that approached the Apple. I didn't usually come from this direction, so I wasn't totally sure where we were. Somewhere near Goblin Town.

"So that's Cade," Antoine said. Worst conversation starter ever. "Your roommate."

"One of my roommates," I corrected. I really didn't want to get into all this now.

"How many people do you live with?"

"There are four of us. Me, Cade, Alice, and Jacqui. Besides Alice, we were all friends in high school. Jacqui and I have been best friends from about kindergarten until—" I cut myself off before divulging anything, but Antoine caught on.

"Until?"

I sighed. Antoine deserved to know why I was involved in this whole quest in the first place. "We've just been having issues lately. About six months ago, she was turned into a cat."

Even in the Apple, that wasn't a sentence you heard every day. Transformations were heavy-duty magic. "A cat?" Antoine said.

"One day, about a month after I'd started making deliveries, a basket was delivered to our house full of baked goods, addressed to me. Jacqui was the only one home, so she signed for it and looked inside. She tried a slice of apple bread, and…" I pulled myself together and finished the story. "She was cursed. But the Count said if I can find Rick, he'll pay to have her fixed, and everything will be alright again."

Antoine gave me a look out of the corner of his eyes, and I could smell the warm, cinnamon scent of admiration rising off him. "That's a noble thing you're doing for your friend."

I rolled my eyes. "Yeah, right. I'm the reason she got hit with the curse in the first place."

"And you don't know who did it?"

"Nope," I answered. "There was a note, but it just had nonsense on it. As soon as Jacqui's fixed, though, finding out who did this to her is the next step."

I didn't realize it while we were talking, but we'd already made it to the outskirts of Castle Fortnight. The guards at Oncegate took one look at T and waved us through. The castle grounds were just as busy as the rest of the Apple. The night watch patrolled in circles with their lanterns held high, while maids and valets walked from tower to tower laden with scrolls, food, and laundry. Above us, the turrets were strewn with amber light, shining high above the rest of the city.

T took us through the front entrance to the castle. It was a strange experience for me. Usually I was stuck going through back doors, tunnels, grates, or the many secret entrances that peppered the grounds. Instead of cobwebs and dark hallways, we walked through opulent carpeted foyers lit by crystal chandeliers.

We made our way through the main section of the castle to Grimmour Tower. We took a sweeping spiral staircase up to the family's quarters at the top and stepped into a massive sitting room the entire width of the tower. The semi-circular room was split into two levels, with a wide staircase leading up to the second tier. The walls were lined with glass shelves that held a wide collection of expensive crap. I saw vintage Yankees paraphernalia shelved next to stuffed griffin claws and gleaming medieval armor.

We took the stairs up to the higher level, where several chairs were arranged around a wide stone fireplace. The floor here was covered by a richly textured red carpet that looked more comfortable than any bed I'd ever slept on. A gust of cool, refreshing air blew from the fireplace, where a pale blue fire whirled like cotton candy over the logs. Tarris and the Count sat to one side of the fireplace, while Miranda Grimmour sat curled up on a chaise lounge on the other side.

"You're here," the Count said, rising from the largest of the armchairs. "My wizards were unable to scry your location, and I thought you'd been killed." He didn't seem too emotional about it.

"Did you find out anything?" Miranda asked. Her eyes were red and leaking, but that did nothing to detract from her beauty. She was breathing unevenly, as if we had just caught her at the end of a long sob. Each little breath made her golden curls dance playfully across her shoulders. The rich blue dressing gown she'd wrapped herself in revealed a generous amount of thigh. She was a breathtaking mess.

"My daughter, Miranda," the Count informed us. I recognized her from the Grimmour family portrait, but apparently Royals still liked their introductions. "Miranda, this is Briar Pryce."

"A pleasure to meet you," I remarked, dipping my head just far enough so it wasn't an insult. I really wasn't in the mood for displays of etiquette. And, for all my talent with emotion, crying people made me incredibly uncomfortable. "Sorry we're late. We got hit by a Van Winkle." My legs ached from walking, but no one offered us a seat.

"Ah," the Count said. He didn't sound super concerned with our well-being. "That would explain the problems my wizards were having. Were you able to find any leads?"

"We did, your lordship," Antoine confirmed. "Three men whom Briar suspects are the kidnappers attacked us in Harlem, not far from Rick Pearson's dorm." He gave the short version of our fight in the alleyway, although he downplayed his own role in the fight considerably. "But once Briar cut the snake off me, the magician blinded us with smoke and disappeared."

"You let them escape?" Tarris asked. He drew his hands back through his hair, making short blond tufts stand up. He was wearing a vest and tie, each fashionably rumpled.

"He had some sort of weird, smoke teleportation spell," I said. "It reminded me a little of Academy magic, but different somehow."

"I'll check into it at the Academy," the Count offered. "They won't be happy to hear of a rogue wizard combining his powers with wild magic."

"So what is this about a ransom note?" I asked.

"It arrived a few hours ago," Tarris said, pulling a small scrap of parchment from the inside of his vest. "It claims to be from the kidnappers and says the only way that we will see Rick again is if I step down from my position as apprentice to the Royal Exchequer." Guilt pulled at the corner of his eyes and gave him the scent of mothballs. Why was he holding on to the letter in the first place?

"So we can assume that the ones responsible for Rick's kidnapping are Royals trying to blackmail Tarris into giving up his position," the Count said.

That seemed reasonable enough. "And the men who kidnapped Rick used a Royal Door, meaning they had to have been following orders from a Noble," I added.

"But it still doesn't make sense," Tarris protested. "Being apprentice to the Exchequer is barely important at all these days."

The Count fixed him with a glare. "The enemies of our family would do anything to harm our reputation. This is exactly the sort of tactic they would use to make us seem weak." Tarris didn't look convinced.

"Can I see the letter?" I asked. Tarris offered it to me without getting up, and I begrudgingly walked over to take it. Manners to the wind, I sat on a nearby loveseat and inspected the letter.

It was short and blunt. Tarris's summary pretty much covered all the bases. The language was formal, and the handwriting was precise. I gave it a whiff, just to make sure.

"Can you get anything?" Antoine questioned. He looked as if he would have loved to sit next to me and look over my shoulder, but decorum held him in place.

"Nothing," I answered. "But that doesn't mean it's fake. The only way I'd get something is if Rick had been in close contact with the letter while experiencing an intense emotion. Objects and people don't hold feelings as well as places do."

"The letter isn't a fake," the Count said sternly. "We've kept this incident to ourselves, and there is only one family with anything to gain from Tarris's abdication. The House of Liu is behind this."

"But Father—" Tarris started.

"Minister Liu has been quite open with his opinion that his son Sho should have gotten the position. Taking Rick Pearson gives them the leverage they need to remove you from power." The Count's eyes were sternly fixed on Tarris's, but the younger man refused to raise his head.

"But power? I didn't even want—" Tarris started.

His father cut him off again. "If we give in to their demands, the family reputation would be damaged irreparably. Just the fact that my only daughter has taken up with an Other Worlder is embarrassment enough." Miranda looked away sharply, but her long hair hid her expression from me.

"So what are you planning to do?" I asked.

"I will not take this sort of attack against my family lightly," the Count fumed, standing and moving over to the fireplace. The blue light from the fireplace cast him in silhouette as he lowered his head. "And so we will go to war."

"War?" I asked, dumbfounded. "With the House of Liu?"

"They need to be taught not to interfere with the Grimmours," the Count said. "Battle is our only option." He grabbed a poker from the rack next to the fireplace and started stabbing the logs with a controlled fury. From their silence, I gathered neither of his children agreed with what he was saying.

"But, Your Grace, are you sure?" Antoine questioned. "Maybe we could find more evidence before—"

"I don't need more evidence," the Count interrupted. For a man embarking on a war, his voice was measured and controlled. He turned around, the poker clenched in his hand trailing blue sparks. "The Lius have tried to make a mockery of us, and they will suffer for it. My people delivered a declaration of war to them an hour ago."

The shock on my face and the disapproval on Antoine's must have done something to calm the Royal. He put the poker back on the rack and wiped his hands together. "Now, if you'll excuse me, preparations must be made." He gave his son a pointed look. "Tarris, can I trust you to assist Mr. DuCarr and Miss Pryce? Finding Rick Pearson would still be to our advantage, war or not."

"Of course, Father."

After the Count walked out, Tarris began to pace. "I'm not convinced this was planned by the Lius. There is no love lost between our families, but I cannot imagine them resorting to kidnapping over nothing more than an honorary position."

"And if they did take Rick and reveal themselves as fey, they've broken the Compact. No Royal would take that kind of risk if there wasn't a large payoff at stake," Antoine said.

"Some Royal did," I pointed out, "or otherwise those goons wouldn't have been able to use a Royal Door."

"But it couldn't have been the official action of a whole family. My guess is one rogue Royal planned the whole thing—" Tarris ventured.

"Did you find out anything else?" Miranda asked.

I shook my head. "I wish I had better news, Miss Grimmour, but that's all we've gotten so far. Have you guys figured out anything else on this end?"

"Nothing," Miranda said desperately. "My father's wizards are trying to break through the spell blocking Rick's location, but so far all they've been able to tell us is that he's still alive." She shifted on the couch. "I just can't believe the Lius would do something like this."

"Whether it is the Lius or not," Tarris said, "we still have to find Rick.

Either we can exonerate the Lius and stop the war before it starts, or we can prevent him from being used as a hostage against us." He turned to face Antoine and me, and I could see a commanding quality in his eyes that reminded me of his father. "Now, what can I do to help you two?"

"Actually, if you don't mind," I began, "we need to ask your sister a few questions, if that's alright with you, Miss Grimmour."

She stole a quick glance at her brother, who nodded slightly. "Of course," she agreed, turning a somewhat dampened smile to me. "And call me Miranda, please." Despite her obvious grief, the princess's voice had an airy, conversational tone that instantly made me more comfortable.

I pulled out my notebook and flipped to the first empty page. "Alright. So Antoine tells me you were receiving a lot of letters from one of the Lius this summer. Who were they from?" I asked. Antoine gave me a pointed look. He clearly disapproved of my bluntness.

If it bothered Miranda, she didn't show it. "Sho Liu, Minister Liu's oldest son. The one who Tarris beat out as the Exchequer's apprentice. We were…involved briefly before I met Rick. The letters didn't start pouring in until after I'd broken up with him, though. He didn't take it well."

Out of the corner of my eye, I saw Tarris make a face. Apparently, Miranda was understating Sho's distress.

"Do you think Sho could have taken Rick to try to get back together with you?"

Miranda frowned, and her earlier tears threatened to spill over again. "I don't know… I can't imagine Sho doing something like that. He wouldn't— I mean, he said he'd do anything to get me back, but that's just what guys say, right? He's not a bad guy. A little obsessive, but not violent or anything." Her voice shook, but she still smelled like she was confident in her opinion of Sho.

"We can't tell anything for sure yet," I insisted. "Even if the Lius were behind this, it doesn't mean Sho was involved." But even as I said it, I circled his name on my list of suspects. With both political and personal reasons to take Rick, Sho might have been crazy enough to kidnap Rick and use him to blackmail Tarris.

"Do the Lius have any properties in Manhattan where they could possibly have Rick?" Antoine asked. "If Briar and I could check them out, we could prove Sho is not behind this." I gave the knight an appreciative glance. He was skillfully pumping Miranda for information without pointing the finger at her ex.

"I don't know of any," Miranda said. "It seems like mostly they spend their time in their palace within Castle Fortnight. I don't remember Sho having much to do with the Other World at all."

"I don't think they would risk keeping a kidnapped Know-Not in their quarters," I said. "But that might be our only option."

"What do you mean?" Antoine asked.

"If I can get onto Liu turf, maybe one of them will have the scent of Rick's emotion on them. Then we'd know for sure."

"Wait—you can smell his emotions on other people?" Tarris asked.

"If they've been in close contact in the past few hours," I admitted. "And the stronger the emotion, the better. The men we fought in Harlem had a huge dose of his fear on them."

"He was afraid?" Tarris asked.

"Rick is never afraid," Miranda said defiantly. Both Grimmours looked distraught, but Tarris recovered his composure first.

"If you just need to sniff the Lius, there might be another way," he suggested. "I know it's last minute, but you'd be able to get close enough to smell them at tonight's ball."

"A ball?" I gaped. "Two of the Apple's most powerful families are about to go to war and blow the Multiarchy to smithereens, and the Royals won't even cancel their ball?"

"Well, no," Tarris said. "The war is the reason we're having the ball. Both sides always meet on the eve of war. It's tradition."

I had to be misunderstanding something. "You're about to fight to the death, and the only way you can respond to it is to have a *dance?*"

"I mean, we could have a masque," Miranda offered, "but the Haus of Stieg just threw a really good one last week."

"And besides," Tarris added scornfully, a touch of bitterness in his voice, "it's not like any of us will actually see battle. That's all done through mercenaries these days." I couldn't put my finger on what he was upset about. Did he hate the war, or hate that he wouldn't be fighting in it?

"So the entire House of Liu will be at this ball tonight?" I asked. "And they can't stab us until after it's over?"

"That's pretty much the idea," Tarris said, smiling a little. "And you're in luck… I still don't have a date."

It was decided that I would go with Tarris, and Antoine would go with one of Miranda's ladies-in-waiting. Count Grimmour had already determined that Miranda would go dateless, to emphasize the deep wrongs that had been committed against the family.

That left me with an hour to get ready for my first (and, if I had anything to say about it, last) Royal ball. It wasn't enough time to get home, change, and come back, and I doubt that anything in my closet would be considered classy enough. So Tarris called for a guard to escort Miranda and me to the Grimmour's fairy godmother.

Miranda was assuring me that Crea was one of the Apple's best when our escort arrived. "Right this way, ladies," he entreated, gesturing to the door. Then our eyes met, and he let out a little whimper. It took me a moment to recognize him as one of the guards I'd bespelled the day before. Without checking to see if we were following, he turned and walked quickly out of the sitting room.

He kept a good ten feet ahead of us as he escorted us through a maze of hallways to a lower part of the tower. Something wasn't right. I threw those fear petals at him over twenty-four hours before. He shouldn't still be feeling the effects. Maybe my own fear at the time caused me to overdo it?

We came to an open door about halfway up the tower that opened into a bright, high-ceilinged round room. Apparently, the hoity-toity interior decorator that went to town on the rest of Grimmour Tower had not been allowed in here. Instead of dark wood and threadbare tapestries, the room was festooned with spell-powered Christmas lights, fashion posters, and fabric swatches. A few dressmakers' mannequins lounged casually against the far wall, puffing long cigarettes and ashing out the window. Three raised circular daises took up the center of the room, while against the walls were dozens of tables and shelves containing all sorts of sewing materials and tools. I saw spools of golden thread so fine, it had to be nixie hair, bolts of sky-blue fabric complete with moving clouds floating by, and half-completed dresses that hissed at Miranda and me as we walked in.

In the center of this explosion of color was a small, squat woman dressed incongruously in a yellow and black checkered shirt and overalls. Her wavy black hair was pulled back in a functional bun, revealing a weather-worn brown face. From her head to her bare feet, she was perhaps five feet. She scowled at us as we walked in, but I noticed a spark of humor in her eyes.

"Oh, wonderful. Not only is the brat back, but she's brought a friend." Her accent, like her ethnicity, was hard to pinpoint. Maybe somewhere in the Middle East, or possibly India?

"Hey Crea, nice to see you too," Miranda said good-naturedly. She walked up to the platform on the right and climbed onto it. "This is my friend Briar. She needs a gown for the battle ball tonight."

"Tonight?" Crea challenged. "You want it tonight? You think I can just wave my hands and come up with a ballgown for any hussy you take in off the street?"

I started to protest the word 'hussy,' but Miranda's laugh cut me off. "Uh, yeah, Crea. You're a fairy godmother. One of the best, in fact. You can do a lot by waving your hands." I was surprised how easily the older woman's griping made her smile. Miranda looked like a different person from the distraught girl who'd been crying in the study twenty minutes earlier.

The compliment brought a genuine grin to the dressmaker's face. "Well, then, aren't you lucky you came to me? Let's do one last fitting of your dress first, though." She pointed at a closet full of hanging dresses and made a come hither motion.

At her gesture, dozens of objects around the room floated up and started to rotate around us. One of the dresses, a somber, floor-length blue gown with black accents, glided off its hanger and floated towards

Miranda. Simultaneously, her robe unwrapped itself and flew to a peg on the wall, leaving her standing on the platform in her shift. A measuring tape nearly hit me in the head as it whizzed over to take Miranda's measurements. The gown floated patiently beside her as the tape ran up and down her limbs.

Crea clucked her tongue. "Well, well. Your boyfriend's kidnapping agrees with you. You're down a half-size."

Miranda frowned and looked away. "I work out when I'm stressed."

"Well, don't worry about it," Crea said, her voice tender. "We'll just take the waist in a little. Now, Briar, was it? Step on up, honey. Let's see what I can do for you."

I hung my cloak up on a hook by the door and climbed up easily onto the platform. One of the benefits of my height. Once I was up there, I wasn't really sure what to do with myself. I self-consciously crossed my arms, decided that was awkward, and then let them dangle at my sides for a while before stuffing them into my pockets. It was my high school senior portrait all over again.

Crea snapped twice, and a cloud of tools rushed to her side. She began to circle me, while the measuring tape, a spool of ribbon, a box of pins, and a color wheel floated attentively behind her. Her eyes looked me up and down as she moved, but they seemed oddly vacant, as if she were seeing something that wasn't there. At the edge of my hearing, I thought I heard her mumble, "That's odd." But she shook her head and went over to her fabric rack.

"Is this your first ball, Briar?" she asked rhetorically. Apparently, whatever she saw had already told her the answer. "And you'll be going with Tarris? I already fixed him up a nice coat for tonight. I'll make sure you match." A roll of dark navy fabric peeked out from a box across the room and flew over to the platform.

"I thought you guys had to sing happy-go-lucky nonsense songs when you did these magical makeovers?" I said as the cloth spun lazily above Crea's head.

"Oh, please," Crea scoffed. "That's all Disney's idea. If you ever catch me saying any Mary Poppins bullshit, just punch me in the face. Now, what shoes are you wearing?"

I looked down at my mud-covered boots. "Um, do you have any I could borrow?" I asked as sweetly as I could.

The godmother rolled her eyes. "You are helpless." She walked over to a wicker bin and opened it up. After a few seconds of pawing through it, she pulled out a pair of silver heels with blue filigree decorating them. "Here. These are the ones," she said. They took flight from her palm and landed softly on the dais in front of me.

I squeezed out of my boots and slipped a foot into the new shoes. "These are too big," I said.

"Those are just right," Crea announced. "Trust me."

Her abruptness startled me a little. "But see, my toe barely gets to the front of the shoe. I'll fall out of these."

Crea gave me a stare. "What part of 'trust me' don't you understand? Those shoes—"

"Easy, Crea," Miranda said. "Briar has probably never been to a fairy godmother before. Have you, Briar?"

I shook my head.

"What do you know about them?" Miranda asked me.

"They're humans, right? But they can use a type of magic that's different from the kinds that wizards or witches use. That's about all I know."

Crea made a huffing sound while she flipped through a book of color swatches. "That's all? I mean, we like to keep a low profile, but…" She found what she was looking for, and a spool of light blue lace leapt out of a cupboard and flew to her hand. "I'm one of the few left who works traditionally. I do the usual— makeovers, gowns, even carriages sometimes. My grandmother taught me."

"So is it passed down through generations?"

The older woman shook her head. "Nope. But it takes a special sort of person. Our magic affects, well, fate, for lack of a better term. We don't usually predict the future, like those smarmy frickin' oracles, but we can give boons or curses to change how it unfolds."

"And the dresses you make are actually spells?" I asked.

"Sort of," Crea said. "That's how my talent manifests. I mostly just work in the boons and blessings department, but different fairies specialize in different things."

"I like to think of Crea as the Q to our James Bond," Miranda said. "She gives us exactly what we need to wear for whatever we're doing."

"Well, let me guess: this shoe is supposed to fall off Cinderella-style and lead me to my one true love?"

"Hell if I know," Crea said. "But those are the shoes you're supposed to wear tonight. I'm pretty certain." Miranda's head snapped to face the old woman. She looked shocked at Crea's admission of uncertainty. "What?" Crea grumbled. "For some reason, my magic doesn't like her. Do you mind telling me what you do, Briar?"

The question always stumped me. I usually went with the simplest answer. "I deliver flowers," I replied. And changed hearts. And fought smoke monsters. And travelled through time. And solved kidnappings. Thank Puck I didn't pay taxes, or the IRS would have a field day with my "occupation."

Crea seemed to pick up on the fact that I wasn't telling her everything, but she didn't call me out on it. "Well, whatever you do, you're hard to place. You don't fit." I gave her a confused look. "What I mean is that you don't have a nice, clean archetype. You're pretty, but not beautiful. You're a fighter, but no warrior. You could almost make a good oracle yourself, but…"

"I'm a dumbass?" I retorted sarcastically.

"Oracles don't change things. Neither do fairy godmothers, really. We just influence. But you…you're a tricky one. I'm thinking floor-length, sleeveless, but I can't get a clear picture." She scowled at me once more and turned away, like it was my fault she couldn't make the perfect dress for me.

While we'd been talking, her pair of shears had cut a complicated pattern out of the dark blue fabric. I felt an uncomfortable lurch as my shirt and pants began to fly off my body of their own accord. If I was lucky, the underwear I put on in my early-morning haze would at least be clean. As my jeans reached my ankles, I had to do a couple of hops to keep from being tripped. My shirt seemed more polite.

The dark blue fabric soared towards me in two pieces and wrapped itself around my body. One wrapped tightly around my legs, while the other swooped between my armpits and my shoulders in a complex, toga-like arrangement. The fabric was cool and soft against my skin. I wasn't used to ballgowns comfortable enough to sleep in. Or ballgowns at all, for that matter.

In front of me, the box of pins opened up and a cloudburst of needles emerged. For one heart-stopping second, every pin hung in mid-air and rotated to point at me. Before I could move to protect myself, they darted forward and stabbed themselves into the fabric to hold it in place. I gasped, but none of them so much as grazed my skin.

"Nice trick," I conceded, my voice a little higher than usual. "So what kind of person makes a good fairy godmother?"

Crea circled behind me, and I could feel the fabric shifting a little as it adjusted itself under her gaze. "It depends on what they do. My grandmother and I are needlewomen, but some work in talismans, or magic food, or tarot cards. It manifests in a lot of different ways."

"And your magic will work on this dress to make me…what? Incredibly beautiful? Super strong? Able to leap tall towers in a single bound?"

I felt the fabric move scandalously down my sternum, exposing more cleavage. "This dress," came Crea's voice from behind me, "is exactly what you need. Nothing more. Nothing less."

I was still voting for super strength.

Forty-five minutes of fitting, pinning, lacing, and refitting later, I was standing in the Grimmour's foyer in an ostentatious gown with more blue ribbon in it than Michael Phelps's bedroom. The ribbon snaked its way through the dress before gathering in a giant bow on my backside that made my butt look like a couture Christmas present (although I didn't share that opinion with Crea). The dress was beautiful, however, and settled over my body like a fine mist. A pair of mauve opera gloves completed the picture, giving me a touch of refinement that I didn't know

I had. The only part I couldn't stand was the size of the shoes. They threatened to take me down with almost every step. Taking the stairs to the first floor of the Tower had nearly been the end of me.

Tarris stood next to me as we waited for Miranda to join us. He wore a trendy blue blazer that looked like the product of a torrid love affair between a military jacket and a high school bandleader's uniform. It made his eyes practically glow in his pale face. The cream-colored ruffled shirt he wore under it wasn't tucked into his pinstriped grey dress pants. He looked like he'd wandered off a high fashion runway and into a high fantasy novel.

Antoine swung by his quarters in the castle to pick up one of what I could only assume was many formal outfits. He wore a midnight-blue waistcoat and cravat over a white shirt and forest green slacks. The light in the foyer glinted off the matching silver of his cufflinks and watch chain. As I was beginning to expect from Antoine, his entire outfit was wrinkleless. He looked sober and austere standing next to Tarris's more edgy ensemble.

Tarris had already introduced me to Antoine's date, Aelexis. The handmaiden was clinging to Antoine's arm and laughing a grating, Julia-Roberts-on-nitrous-oxide whinny at something he'd said. She wore a gauzy, tight-fitting ballgown that shifted from blue to green as she moved. The Royals only choose the fairest of the lower classes to serve them, and she was no exception. She had a strikingly angular face with brown eyes and long wavy hair, although her teeth and ears were a little pointed. Not that I judged on things like that.

Just as Aelexis was pulling Antoine's arm down to whisper something insipid in his ear, Miranda rushed down the stairs. "Sorry I'm late!" she announced, throwing a wrap around her shoulders as she ran. Crea's black-and-blue mourning dress had come out wonderfully, making her every inch the grieving, wounded beauty.

"Don't worry about it," Tarris allowed. "Although, you don't want to forget that." He pointed up. During her flight, Miranda had left a shoe sitting on the stairs.

She turned to face me and rolled her eyes. "Ugh. Please excuse the cliché." She stomped up and snatched the shoe.

Antoine politely untangled himself from Aelexis and drew me aside. "Is your nose ready to try and pick up any Rick-related signs of guilt?"

I swallowed and looked away. "I'll try. Like I told you, I usually can't pick up lingering scents like that."

Antoine's face got a little closer, and he stared for a second. "Usually? When can you do it?"

"There's nothing—"

"Briar, what aren't you telling me?" He'd kept his voice even and unaccusing. I could lie, tell him he was wrong. Tell him there was nothing I could do.

Damn, he was good.

"There's something I can try, but it's— It's risky. It's unpredictable, and I don't know how the magic would work, surrounded by so many people."

"What gives us the best chance of finding the people who took Rick?" Antoine put his hand on my arm. "I trust your judgment."

I weighed my options for a second. I really didn't want to do what I was thinking, but if I was honest, it was the only way to get any information. There was no way I'd pick up any of Rick's emotions that had rubbed off on the kidnapper unless they came straight from slapping him around.

Once I made up my mind, it didn't seem so bad. "Okay, I'll do it. But

I need a kitchen."

Antoine gave me a skeptical look but nodded and led me back to the group. "We need to stop by the kitchen, Tarris," he reported. "If you don't mind."

Tarris seemed just as surprised at the knight's directness as I was. "Is Briar hungry? There will be food there. The caterer is a brownie—"

"No, I just—" I started. I didn't want to explain everything. "I need to go to your kitchen."

"But Briar, we're already late and—" Tarris said.

"You can go ahead," Antoine said smoothly. "I'll make sure Briar gets there. We'll come as soon as we can."

Tarris shrugged. "Okay, I guess. I'll take these two, then. See you soon." He offered his arms to Miranda and Aelexis. As she walked off, Aelexis gave me a smile that showed a little too much of her pointed teeth to be friendly. I had definitely pissed off Antoine's not-completely-human date.

I could worry about that later.

A butler appeared out of nowhere to lead us to the kitchen. I wasn't sure where he came from or how he knew where we were going. Royal magic was ridiculous.

The closest kitchen was a small, windowless room that looked like it belonged more in a Washington Heights efficiency than a Royal palace. I guess the Nobles didn't care where they stuck their servants.

"A little cramped," Antoine said as he stuck his head in the door. I turned to thank the butler, but he was already walking briskly away. I thought I saw his shadow disappear as he rounded the corner, but I couldn't be sure.

"Do you need anything for your...whatever it is you're doing in here?"

Antoine asked. I shook my head. "Then I'll just wait out here until you're done." He started out the door.

"It's okay," I ventured. "You can stay if you want. It's no big deal."

"Are you sure?"

"Yeah," I said. I *was* sure. "It's just a little magic. No animal sacrifice or anything."

Antoine gave me a warm smile. "Thanks."

I smiled back for a moment before catching myself and turning to the row of cupboards above the sink. "Can you help me find a kettle?" I started going through the cupboards but found little besides china and dinner service. The size of the kitchen made it hard to maneuver, and Antoine and I had to squeeze awkwardly past each other a few times. I didn't find myself minding.

After a few minutes, we unearthed everything I'd need. A kettle, a mug, and a spoon. Antoine looked confused but didn't press me with questions as I set the kettle on the stovetop to boil.

"I figured out how to do this right after my friend Jacqui was transformed," I said. I fiddled with the knob on the stove, even though I knew it was on. It was better than having to look at him. "It was awful. I felt horrible. Too bloated with guilt and regret that I couldn't do anything to help her. So I tried to use a rose on myself.

"It didn't work at first. I can't *give* myself a rose, and apparently that's part of the spell. But I figured out a way around it."

Antoine furrowed his brow. "So how would giving yourself a rose help you track down the person guilty of kidnapping Rick? How does changing your emotions help us?"

I smiled. "You can't think of any feeling that would help me find the kidnapper?"

"Concentration? Focus? I don't know. Are those even emotions?"

I shook my head. "Empathy. If I can give myself enough empathy, I can get reads on everyone's emotions, not just people I'm close to. But it's hard to control."

We both turned our heads sharply as the kettle began to whistle. It had been on the fire for maybe a minute, tops. As I turned the stove off, I noticed a band of runes around the base of the kettle. Apparently, it didn't need any magic words or anything. Nice. Being the Royal Liaison to the Academy of the Iron Wand must have its advantages.

I took a rose out of the silver clutch I'd borrowed from Miranda. Most purses weren't designed for transporting plants, but I found one long enough in a walk-in (and in and in and in) closet next to Crea's atelier, that was filled with Miranda's discarded formalwear. I was only able to fit three Miniature roses, but it was better than going completely unarmed.

The rose on top was a typical, Valentine's Day, light pink rose with a soft, sweet smell. Perfect for superficial attraction, in case I needed to distract or lure. But it would work pretty well for the delicate flavor of empathy as well.

I took the rose in my hand and held it out to Antoine. "Do you mind?" I asked. He looked puzzled but put out his hand to take it. I grabbed both his hands and the rose and held them tight together while I closed my eyes.

Antoine was nervous. I could smell it. His fear wasn't focused on my magic, or the thugs after us, but sprang from what he'd learned in the past day of his life. His ordered, structured view of both the Apple and himself was coming apart at the seams. A Royal had violated one of our most basic laws and snatched a mortal. Antoine's role was always to protect the

Nobility; now it seemed like he had to protect others from them.

I focused on all the anxiety emanating from him; let it swirl into my nostrils and deep into my lungs. My own fears and concerns intertwined with his, mixing into a more pungent whole. If Antoine and I couldn't save Rick, Jacqui would be stuck as a cat forever. If we didn't stop the Grimmours from going to war, they could destroy the Multiarchy and plunge the Apple into chaos. Suddenly, the combined force of both our emotions gushed out of my lungs, and I gasped as my eyes fluttered open.

"What is it?" Antoine asked, putting his hand on my shoulder but not breaking the connection with the rose.

"Nothing," I said. My mind recited a litany of *it's okay, it's okay, you're okay*, while in reality I felt aftershocks, just like I did when I first tried to use a rose on myself.

"What did you feel?" Antoine questioned, his tone guarded. It was funny how when people realized you could smell their innermost feelings, they still tried to stop their voice from showing any emotion.

"You're a little nervous," I pointed out. "And now I'm nervous. It worked." As I spoke, I sent that feeling of connection, of my-pain-is-your-pain, down into the rose. I removed my hand from his, and instantly the connection was lost. Antoine's panicky feelings left my mind.

"So if it worked, why the boiling water?" he queried.

I shook my head. "The empathy is still in the rose. It's not in me." I picked the petals from the rose one by one and put them in the mug. They swirled up as I poured the hot water in and swished it around. The water turned a pale, unnatural turquoise.

Antoine made a suspicious face as I blew on the water to cool it. "Rose tea?" he asked.

"It's not the most delicious thing in the world, but it gets the job done."

"You sound like a frat boy about to swill cheap beer."

"Shut up," I said, sticking my tongue out at him. It was a decidedly modern reference for Antoine to make, and I realized I didn't know as much about him as I thought. Did he grow up in the Apple his whole childhood, or did he spend time in the Other World?

I took a hesitant sip. The tea was still pretty hot but tasted decent. Empathy tasted cool and herby, like a health food shake.

"Bottoms up," I said and offered the glass up to Antoine in a mock toast. The tea took me four good gulps to finish, but it was still another minute until the buzz of the magic hit me.

It started in my stomach. In all my experiments with self-targeted roses, that was where it always hit me. The tingle spread upwards, and just as it hit my eyes, I saw what I'd been missing. It was like my eyes were opened for the first time. Antoine wasn't just scared for himself. He was scared for me, scared for Rick, scared for the future of the Poisoned Apple that he had sworn to protect. His worldview had changed so much in the past day, he worried he would no longer have the strength to fight all the wrongs around him. What I told him in the woods about his inability to have strong emotions still weighed on him. It was the feeling that there was something wrong with him, at his very core, that could never be fixed.

My eyes began to tear up at the sheer, overwhelming fact that I wouldn't be able to help the ones I loved. Danger would come to call and find me lacking.

"Briar?" Antoine asked. No one had said anything for a good minute or two, despite the riot of emotions I felt bouncing around the room. "Are you okay?"

This wasn't mine. These feelings were his, mostly. They could have been amplified by the magic, by my intense feelings of empathy. But knowing that didn't make the feedback I was getting from Antoine any less painful.

I focused hard and shut off most of the flood of emotion. "I'll be fine," I assured him. "Just needed a second to adjust. On the upside, though, it worked."

I took a step forward, and my knee gave out, sending me clumsily into the counter. Antoine moved to help me, but I held up a hand. All I needed was to empathize with his sympathy for me. My brain would probably explode.

"Let's just go, okay? The fresh air will probably help." I hurried out of the kitchen, Antoine closely at my heels. The butler appeared again, wordlessly leading us through a series of stairwells that emptied out into the front foyer.

It was a bit chilly on the grounds of Castle Fortnight, but my dress was the perfect weight for the evening. Probably Crea's doing. I noticed a few other people in formal dress heading in the same direction as us. Apparently, War Balls were big events.

"So, you can give yourself this rose tea anytime you want?" Antoine asked as we walked.

"I could," I said, "but I don't."

"Why not?" Antoine questioned, curiosity rolling off him like steam. "Who wouldn't want to have the perfect emotion for the situation? You could break yourself out of a bad mood just by sipping some tea."

"Normal tea puts me in a pretty good mood by itself. The problem with my magic tea is that I can't be sure what sort of dose I'm getting. It's all or nothing. Like right now, I'm supernaturally sympathetic. I can't just give myself a quick pick-me-up."

"If you practiced, maybe, or just drank half a glass—"

"I don't want to!" I exploded, louder than I intended. "You can't control everything. I don't want to decide my emotions every day for the rest of my life."

Antoine bristled. "So it's okay for you to meddle with everyone else's feelings but your own?"

"That's not it—" I covered my eyes and rubbed my temples. "I don't know how I feel about it. Sometimes I feel like I should just give up my power altogether. Sometimes I think I should be changing more. Pushing people in the right direction. But— I can't make that decision for myself. Not now."

The crow's feet next to Antoine's eyes softened. "I'm sorry. I shouldn't have brought it up. I didn't realize—"

"No, it's not your fault." I still couldn't look at him. "I clearly need to rethink my line of work. But for now, let's focus on getting Rick back."

We remained silent as Antoine took us to a round, squat building the size of a football field towards the center of the grounds. There were no windows, and the only element I could see that broke the grey stone façade was a single, oak-paneled door with a few guards posted outside. I could hear a faint murmur of conversation and soft music.

I yawned as the head guard took our invitation from Antoine and gave it a look. It seemed to take forever, and I felt a huge need to get going and do something else.

Stupid, I told myself. *Stupid, stupid, stupid.* That was the guard's boredom, not mine. On the walk over, I'd let my defenses slip, and I couldn't afford to do that in the ball itself. I would need to focus if I was going to get any useful information out of the evening. As we passed the guard, I pictured a giant sheet of metal forming itself over my brain, and the random feelings seeping in instantly cut out.

A harried-looking woman in the robes of the Academy muttered something as we neared the door and looked into a small hand-held crystal. A green rune came to life in its depths, and she waved us through. If only LaGuardia had a system so simple.

The inside of the building was not what I expected. It was empty. A panicked voice in my head immediately concluded it was a trap, but a quick look at Antoine showed me I had nothing to worry about. There was a perverse kind of pleasure in knowing that the nonsensical paranoia I felt was all mine.

We were in a large, round room the entire length of the building. It was totally bare, without any furniture or decoration. The only aesthetic element to the room was a weird zig-zagging pattern along the walls.

Pieces fell into place. I could still hear the music and polite laughter, but it was coming from above. And the patterns on the walls were actually thin, architecturally disguised stairs leading to trap doors in the ceiling.

"Nice trick," I said to Antoine as I started towards the nearest stairway.

"You figured it out?" he said. A little disappointment drifted through my defenses. "It usually takes people a few minutes to understand the Wedding Cake."

"The Wedding Cake?"

"Well, this building is traditionally called the Maid Maleen Memorial Marquee, but most Royals just call it the Wedding Cake."

"Why?"

"You'll see."

I started up the stairs, which were narrow and a little uneven. The damn shoes Crea made me wear threatened to spring off at every step.

"Why the big empty space here, if everything is up on the roof?" I asked.

"If the weather is nice, most events use the roof anyway. But the trick with the Wedding Cake is that when they close that door, no light can get in. There are no windows, no chinks in the wall, and all the entrances are sealed. The room is probably the biggest place in the Apple where true darkness can exist."

"So this is where the Royals throw really sweet blacklight raves?"

I heard Antoine chuckle behind me. "Well, there's that. But there are certain creatures that the Nobility deals with who can't or won't come out in the light. This is the only place where the Royals can host them comfortably."

I tried not to think about what kind of beings Antoine was talking about, or what dealings they had with the Royals. Maybe he meant really sun-sensitive albino people.

Yeah, right.

The trap door opened of its own accord as we got close to it, and the stairs continued up to the roof. I stepped out into the ballroom and gave a low whistle of admiration. Say what you will about them, but the Royals know how to throw a party.

The top of the Wedding Cake was strewn with miniature turrets of varying widths and heights, like the world's most complicated layer cake.

Some were big enough for a couple to privately dance, while one was wide enough to hold an entire buffet. The entire roof looked like an upside-down chandelier with beautiful people spread out at all heights, chatting, eating, or looking aristocratically at the rest of the guests. In the very center, a large circle had been cleared, and musicians were setting up on the edge.

My stomach growled noticeably, and I realized it had been a while since my last meal. Rose petal empathy tea was surprisingly unfilling. "First stop: buffet," I proposed.

Antoine frowned. "Shouldn't we find Tarris and the others first?"

I let my shield drop a little as I took his hand. My hunger got worse. "Oh, come off it. You're starving, too." I led him briskly through the crowd and up the steps to the buffet.

It was heaven. Bruschetta with goat gruff's cheese, vegetables with ambrosia dip, stuffed giant mushroom. They even had finger sandwiches. There must have been ogres in attendance.

All the food was in rich-person portions, so I took about four of everything to start. People stared at my overflowing plate, but I couldn't care less. A lot of the Royals could stand to eat more.

"Didn't my father give you a per diem for food?" Tarris's wry voice came from behind me. I turned guiltily to face him, Miranda, and Aelexis. He chuckled, but Aelexis looked at me like I was growing a unicorn horn out of my head.

"Hey, sorry we're late," I apologized through a mouthful of wish-fish pâté.

"You didn't miss much," Miranda said.

"I can take that one off your hands," Tarris suggested, pointing to me with one hand and offering his other arm. I scowled but walked towards him anyway. Aelexis all but pushed me out of the way to get next to Antoine. I felt a wisp of pleasure and tangy desperation. She wanted him bad.

Good for her. Who was I to get in the way?

"Father made me promise to present you when you showed up," Tarris said, gesturing towards a raised dais on the other side of the roof. I shrugged and placed my arm in the crook of his. The touch of his bicep was firm against mine, and for a second—

I felt confident and at ease in the crowd of Nobles, sure of myself and my position in the courtly game, as if I had been born into it (and I had, hadn't I?). But my poise hid a deeper depression and wrongness. No matter how comfortable I was here, it could all fall away in an instant. Things were already going to hell, and how could I feel safe when—

My left foot caught on the back of my damn shoe, causing me to stumble briefly and bringing me back to myself. I gasped for breath, realizing that I hadn't been breathing for the past few steps.

"Wait— can we, uh, wait a second?" I stuttered thickly.

Tarris removed his arm and turned to face me, concern written across his face. "Are you alright?" He held out a hand, and it was almost instantly filled with a flute of something blood red and bubbling. It wasn't magic. Just expensive catering.

I shook my head. "I'll be fine. Sorry."

"Don't worry about it," Tarris said dismissively. He looked around the room casually, totally unintimidated by the rich and beautiful people surrounding him.

I had felt that just a second ago. Not just sympathized with it or understood it, but *felt* it. Deeply. They weren't just free-floating feelings, but attitudes, beliefs, even memories. I had, for all emotional purposes, *been* Tarris Grimmour. If it wasn't for my shoes, I could have been lost completely.

What the hell did I do to myself?

I called up every scrap of strength I had and coiled them around myself. Clearly it wasn't my brain I needed to defend, but me. All of me. I would be myself, feel what *I* felt. I'd open myself up only the smallest bit to get what I needed.

"Are you okay to keep going?" Tarris asked, concerned.

"Sure thing." I gritted my teeth, smiled, and took his arm. I could do this.

Tarris led me up to the Grimmours' seat of power. The Count was perched on a twisted black oak chair that was half-throne, half-barstool. He wore what would have been a plain black tuxedo, except that the jacket had been extended to spread out around his knees like a long, flowing robe. To his right, seated primly on a chaise lounge, was his young wife, Braselyn. The redhead was dressed in a tight-fitting orange cocktail dress that was simply sizzling. As in, smoke floated up from it to tease playfully at her hair as I watched. The fire-dress didn't exactly fit the somber tone of the rest of the crowd. Her green eyes looked at me appraisingly, somewhere between a high school mean girl and a jungle cat.

"Briar, good to see you," the Count said. "This is my wife, Braselyn Tintino-Grimmour. Darling, this is Briar Pryce."

"Charmed," Braselyn said. Or sort of said.

Her voice was somewhat human, at the source. But it had layers of sound whistling above it, like a bad pop song. I heard whistles, flutes, maybe even a harp singing "charmed" as her mouth moved.

You didn't last long in the Apple if you couldn't hide your surprise, so I smiled as if nothing had happened. "Likewise. It's a lovely party." It was the best I could think of. Maybe I should have siphoned off more of the comfort that Tarris felt in party situations.

"Thank you," she chimed, keeping eye contact. Her voice was still a whole wind section. Combined with her aggressive staring, it was starting to get a little creepy.

"I appreciate you coming," the Count said, taking command of the dais with his voice. "I hope you have a successful evening. Please let me know if you need anything." He gave a magnanimous sweeping gesture to dismiss us. Interview over, I guess.

Tarris and I walked back down the stairs as the Count leaned over to say something quietly to Braselyn. When I looked back, she was still staring at me.

When I was sure we were out of earshot, I leaned into Tarris. "Uh, about your step-mother's voice…" I couldn't think of a polite way to phrase the question.

"You don't know her story?" he asked. I shook my head. "I'll tell you." I started to thank him, but he held up a hand. "*If* you tell me what you and Antoine were doing before you came here."

I pouted a little. You never got something for nothing when it came to Royals, but Tarris seemed like a good guy, and I could use less secrecy in my life.

"I had to do a little magic," I admitted, trying to keep it casual. Like I'd just had to powder my nose. "I gave myself supernatural empathy so I could sense people's emotions better."

He recoiled a little but stopped from withdrawing his arm completely from mine. "So you can feel what everyone is feeling?"

It would be nice to have a solid five minutes where I didn't feel like a freak.

"It's okay. Not yours," I said quickly. "I'm reining it in. Just point me at the suspects." I kept my voice light and easy. "Now, what's the deal with Braselyn's voice?"

"She was cursed," Tarris whispered. He relaxed a little but still eyed me nervously. "That's how she met my father. She went to the Academy of the Iron Wand to get it removed."

"Whoa, wait. Start at the once upon. How did she get cursed?"

He rolled his eyes. "I'm not usually one for stories, but fine. Once upon a time, a beautiful daughter of the Tintino family fell in love. Maybe. Or she just slept with some guy. I don't know. But she got pregnant. Big scandal. Her parents wanted to cover it up, so they took the baby and hired a witch to take their daughter's voice so she couldn't say anything."

"But the witch screwed up and gave her a trumpet voice instead?"

"No. The witch went through with it. Braselyn's voice is sitting in a perfume bottle on her father's mantle."

"But how—"

"Now who's rushing?" Tarris and I took the steps up to a small turret with a semicircular red velvet couch. We sat conspiratorially in the part of the couch farthest back. "After Braselyn was cursed, she was banished from the Tintino house. She couldn't think of anywhere to go, and couldn't even ask anyone for help, so she fled to the Academy.

"When my father first saw her, she was being dragged out by security. No one knew who she was, or what she was trying to say by flailing her arms around. He convinced the wizards to at least inspect her, and they found out that her voice had been taken."

Picturing the Count taking pity on an anonymous, voiceless girl didn't really mesh with my idea of him. "That was nice of him."

Tarris shrugged. "Well, she *is* gorgeous. Anyway, my father footed the bill for her recovery. The wizards couldn't restore her old voice, so they put in an iron one. Once she could talk, she told my father her story and he took her in. Not long after, they were married. And that was how I ended up with a step-mother barely older than I am."

"What happened to her child?"

He raised his eyebrows in mock interest. "No one knows. Her parents probably gave it to some commoners to raise."

I felt my muscles constrict in my stomach. "Wait, when did this all happen?"

"About five years ago." I let out the breath I didn't realize I'd been holding. Braselyn wasn't my mother. Being a foundling sucked sometimes.

"Does she know about Rick's disappearance?" I asked.

"Of course," Tarris answered breezily. "My father tells her everything." His voice conveyed a bitterness I didn't need magic to sense.

"And how do you… get along with her? Does she like you and Miranda?" What could I say? Step-mothers don't have a great reputation in these parts.

"She likes us well enough," he replied. "She treats us like her own children." He paused.

"But?"

"The Tintinos are hardcore religious. Like, Inquisition-throwback religious. Even though she's been on the receiving end of their crazy moral judgment, Braselyn still acts like her family's daughter." He stopped once more, but I stayed quiet until he started up again. He wanted to say this.

"The first time my sister missed her curfew when she was in secondary school, Braselyn cried for a week straight, saying Miranda was on her way to being a loose woman. She never punishes us; she just acts like we've let her down. That's how she emotionally blackmails my father into punishing us."

"What happened to Miranda?"

"She was confined to the tower for a week and lost her carriage privileges for a month. And for my sister, that was just as bad." Tarris gave an undignified snort. "She doesn't walk anywhere."

I got up from the couch and went to the edge of the turret. I scanned the crowd for Miranda and found her surrounded by a group of Little People in formalwear. She was smiling graciously, but she didn't seem overly enthused.

Tarris came up behind me. "It's been hard on her. Rick was… something else. We had classes together at Columbia. He kept her sane, even when she was wrapped up in all the craziness of the court and the Apple." I felt sorrow surge against my defenses, but I gritted my teeth. If I was going to feel sorry for Miranda, it would be my own feelings.

"Well then, let's get him back," I said. "Where are the Lius?"

Tarris looked around, swearing quietly under his breath. "They're still not here. I can't believe it. Showing up late is a huge insult to us."

While looking through the various groups of people, I saw one figure sticking out about ten feet away. He was dressed in a black tux, and I mean *black*. The dress shirt, cuff links, and bowtie were all a solid, shiny black that caught the eye. Even the watch on his wrist was a burnished black metal.

His jet black hair was slicked back from his long face. He had a prominent nose that made him look angular and hungry. I could see that his eyes were an eerie, icy blue.

Because they were staring right at me.

"Who is that?" I whispered to Tarris, angling my body so the man in black couldn't see me point.

Tarris looked over, so casually that I barely even noticed. "Oh, him? Isaak Krakelev. I'm surprised they let him in. Then again, he always had a knack for showing up where he wasn't wanted."

I risked a quick look back at Isaak and saw he was still staring at me. "How do you know him?"

"He dated Miranda a while back. Well, maybe 'dated' is too strong a word. They were involved. I got the sense he wanted something more serious, but that was during my sister's wild days."

"What's he doing here?"

"I don't know. Maybe he's trying to get her back."

"Isn't that a little tasteless, considering her boyfriend has been kidnapped?" I asked. Isaak was still staring, but now he was smiling coyly. Apparently, he'd noticed me noticing him.

"Hmm?" Tarris mused, turning back from watching his father reprimand a caterer. "Yeah, maybe that's it. He never took no for an answer. My sister was one of the few women who gave him trouble."

I peeked at the man again. He wasn't particularly handsome, at first glance, but he was undeniably male. Pure, sexual hunger all directed at me.

Why in the world was it directed at me?

"So he's a real ladykiller?" I inquired. My face felt a little hot.

"He has a reputation. The word is, the Krakelevs are descended from incubi, or Lidérc. Although I think they might be responsible for most of those rumors. But even in his own family, Isaak is considered a bit of a manwhore."

Out of the corner of my eye, I saw Isaak dip his gaze to my legs and slowly draw his gaze upwards. I suppressed a shiver. My legs felt suddenly colder. I tried to convince myself it was a breeze, and not the sexual powers of a horny Royal.

I frowned. I hadn't felt any breezes before. I looked down.

"Tarris," I said, trying to keep my voice to a quiet panic, "why does my dress have a slit all of a sudden?" I tried to shift my stance to minimize the opening, but it was useless.

Tarris looked down and gave a little chuckle. "Why, Miss Pryce, how scandalous," he noted drolly. I punched him in the arm. "Ow! Easy. Crea probably put some time-delayed stitches into the slit that just came apart."

"She can do that?"

He nodded. "Once, I made fun of one of her dresses, and she sabotaged my jeans to turn into jorts right when I was going into a big Gov lecture."

"So why did this slit appear now? And why does it feel like it goes all the way up to my armpits?"

Tarris failed to suppress a smile. "Well, maybe it was to help you catch Mr. Krakelev's attention."

"Why the hell would I want to do that when I'm supposed to be here to check out the Lius? Unless— Does that mean I'm supposed to check out Isaak's emotions, too?"

"Maybe."

"Did Crea's magic just tell us who the kidnapper is?" I asked.

"Not necessarily. Fairy godmothering doesn't work like that. Just because one of Crea's dresses gets you some guy's attention, doesn't mean he's the kidnapper. Or your true love. Usually, her magic just gets you a leg up on exploring your best option at the time."

"Meaning...?"

Tarris wiggled his eyebrows. Good Grimms, he was enjoying this. "Meaning you should go talk to him. I've never had any of Crea's clothes lead me astray."

I looked down at the bandleader jacket he was wearing. "So what's that doing for you?"

Tarris grinned, opened it up, and drew out a handful of golden-egg quiches. "Two words: Snack. Pockets."

I snorted and shook my head. "And how much do you pay Crea again?"

He popped a quiche in his mouth and grinned. "Not enough. Go do your magic on Isaak."

My fingers clenched into fists involuntarily, and I reworked the psychic armor I would need to go back into the crowd. Letting myself be hit on by a sleazy Royal lothario was not how I pictured my detective work going. But I gave Tarris my best tough-girl grimace and went down the steps in my oversized heels. Jacqui had better appreciate her opposable thumbs after all of this.

My feet had barely hit the bottom step when Isaak was at my side. I hadn't even seen him start to move from where he'd been watching me. Creepy. Maybe he wasn't completely human. Or maybe I wasn't paying attention.

"May I have this dance?" His voice was deep and rich, with a little bit of a crackle that resonated in my toes. He leaned in much closer than he needed to and put his hand possessively on my glove-clad elbow. There was a huge silver, ankh-shaped ring on his hand. Oh, the pretension.

I squeezed out a smile, but I'm pretty sure my eyes were narrowed. "I would, but there's no mus—"

Before I could finish, a swell of brass music sounded from behind me. Either Isaak had the world's best luck, or he had planned it to the second. Without waiting for me to respond, he took my arm and led me to the dance floor. I started to protest but bit it back. The only way I was going to get a read on his emotions was to be close to him. Surely, I could last one song.

The band was playing something brisk and upbeat (did they miss the memo about the imminent war?), and Isaak put his arm firmly against my back and grabbed my hand. I reluctantly followed him as he moved me around the floor. I took the opportunity to give him a quick sniff, but I didn't smell any of Rick's emotional residue on him.

"Does the beautiful lady have a name?"

Puke. "Why, I'm Lily d'Lis, sir," I answered. I'd given my alias enough in the past that it was second nature.

"Isaak Krakelev. The pleasure is all mine," he said, giving a suggestive weight to the word 'pleasure.'

"So, how do you know the Grimmours?" I asked. As I danced, I focused on letting my empathy open a little pinprick-sized hole in my defenses.

"Oh, Miranda's an old friend," he purred, flashing shiny white teeth. His bright eyes bored into mine, and I tried to figure out some way to avoid them. I ended up staring at the spot between his eyebrows. "How do you know them?"

"I just met Miranda myself," I responded coolly. "She seems great." I let myself sympathize with him a little.

As I expected, I felt a sudden pull towards Miranda. It wasn't just physical. It was a draw to possess her, own her, make her mine. But there was also hurt there. She'd rejected him when so few women had. It cut him deeply every time he saw her.

I closed my eyes for a second and carefully discarded all the emotions I'd picked up from Isaak. This case was awkward enough without me catching a girl-crush on Miranda from her ex-boyfriend.

"Miranda's alright," Isaak said, twirling me around. I could taste his bitterness in the back of my throat. "But I must say, she isn't half the dancer you are." His hands slid a little bit further down my back.

I swallowed and forced a flirtatious laugh. It was the only thing to do to stop my knee from connecting with his crotch.

James Bond used his sexuality to get information out of women all the time. Why couldn't I? Just because I was a girl? Letting this creep grope me was like a feminist act. Right?

"Is that why you're not with her?" I asked cheerily. "I heard you two used to be an item."

He gave a throaty laugh. "No, it wasn't the dancing. We just didn't click."

"So you're not here to get her back?"

Before he answered, I felt a flow of emotion, half-determination, half-desperation. That was his plan. But it seemed that wasn't his only plan. "How could I think about Miranda when I have such a vision of loveliness in front of me?" His hand traced gingerly up mine, until I felt his fingertips reach over the top of my opera glove and touch bare skin.

The music changed to something fast-paced, and our bodies moved closer and closer to the new rhythm. I tightened my grip on the taut muscles of his back and grinned at him.

"You're not that bad a dancer yourself, Mr. Krakelev."

"Call me Isaak, milady." His face was close enough to mine that I could feel the heat of his breath tickle my collarbone. My fingertips curled into the fabric of his shirt.

He dipped me, and his leg grazed mine as he stepped forward to hold me. I heard only the rhythm of the music in time to our breathing.

This was getting fun.

Before I knew it, Isaak pulled me up and we were doing some complicated side-by-side step with our hands clasped straight out in front of us. All I needed was a rose between my teeth. I remembered the steps from somewhere. It had worked for me before.

He twirled me back to face him, and his stomach rubbed tantalizingly against mine. I looked up to meet his eyes and felt a heat that matched my own.

"Perhaps we could go somewhere, Isaak?" I suggested throatily into his ear. He grinned, nodded, and put his arm around me possessively as we exited the dance floor.

On the edge of the dance floor, I saw Miranda's shocked face, but I barely gave her a second look. She was getting what she deserved. If she wanted this, she'd had her opportunity. I was young and beautiful— what was I doing wrong?

Isaak let his hand drop from my shoulder to my hip, drawing me closer to his warm body. There was a faint sense of wrongness about that, some odd feeling of discomfort, but I dismissed it because otherwise it felt good. I let out a laugh and wormed my way closer. My hand played with the silver ankh ring, pushing it up and down his finger.

Suddenly there was a tension at my waist, and before I could react, I had the breath taken out of me by my own forward momentum. The ribbon tied along my back was caught on something. I heard a yelp from behind me. I stumbled backwards, nearly falling out of my own precarious heels.

I felt someone collide solidly with my back, and then the sound of falling silverware brought me back. All the lust and callousness that I'd been feeling was still there, but I could tell it wasn't mine, it was Isaak's.

Perrault's panties, I'd been about to…

I pushed every last feeling out of me, mine, Isaak's, I didn't care. I mumbled some sort of apology to the waiter I'd knocked over and just ran.

"Lily? Wait!" I heard Isaak shout behind me.

The heels slowed me down a little, but I was good at slipping through crowds. I ran in the same direction we'd been walking before, and came to a pair of large turrets that held the restrooms. This was probably where Isaak was planning on taking me if Crea's dress hadn't had other plans.

I wanted to get it off me as soon as I could. Whatever magic was in it had saved me, but it was what drew Isaak to me in the first place.

I pushed through the door with my shoulder as soon as the tears started. Inside was a posh bathroom complete with soft lighting, floor length mirrors, tasteful ferns, and even a sofa.

A short, matronly woman coming out of one of the stalls started as I came in. She took in the tears brimming in my eyes. "Oh, honey, what's wrong?" she coaxed. Her voice held all the warmth of sisterly bathroom chitchat.

"I'm. *Fine*," I said. I might have bared my teeth a little.

She left without washing her hands.

I slumped against the counter and splashed water on my face. That was too close. I'd become a walking emotional clone of Isaak Krakelev for a few minutes. Hell, I'd even absorbed his dance moves. The other times I used my magic empathy, it'd been like adding other people's emotions to my own, but this was different. None of my feelings got through. I had stopped being me.

I blotted my face with a paper towel. It was excessively soft. I would have loved to dump some of these emotions in a rose and forget about them, but I didn't trust my magic at the moment.

"Briar? Can I come in?" Antoine's voice called from outside the door. For a second, I heard Isaak's voice in my head.

I considered not answering.

"Briar?"

"Fine. Come in."

Antoine shuffled in, looking ashamed. I braced myself, but I couldn't feel his emotions. My mental armor was all I had.

"Are you okay? I saw you run in here—"

I held up my hand. "I'm fine. I just sampled a little too much of a suspect's feelings. No big."

Antoine met my eyes and held them for a beat. He didn't buy it. "Did you get anything useful?"

The question took me aback. I had been so focused on what Isaak's feelings had almost made me do, that I hadn't even thought about what they meant. The strongest feelings were all centered around Miranda. I could see him doing something drastic to get her back.

"Maybe. I think Isaak Krakelev could have been involved in Rick's kidnapping. He's a Royal with a motive. That's the best we have so far."

Antoine moved closer to me. "Well, Sho Liu and his father just arrived. Are you up to checking him out?"

My stomach gave a little kick. I wasn't ready to open myself up to more outside emotions. "Yeah, I'll be okay."

"Bullshit," Antoine said. I think my jaw dropped to my belly button.

He sounded surprisingly natural when swearing. He stepped all the way inside the bathroom and ran a towel under cold water. I held up a hand before he got too close.

"Wait," I said. "I'm not sure I can handle anyone in my bubble right now."

"What happened?"

I squelched the shudder that almost ran up my back. It didn't even make it past my armpits. "I got a little too far into Isaak Krakelev's head. I couldn't control it."

"What emotions did you pick up?"

"Horniness, mostly. But it wasn't just emotions. I mean, it was, but—I had these flashes of what the emotions were tied to, the way he felt about dancing, the fantasies that let him sleep at night. It wasn't pleasant."

Antoine frowned. "I would think not. From what I've heard of Isaak, he's not the sort of person you would want to delve into. Is that why you were…" I stared at him, daring him to say 'crying.' He fumbled for a second. "…in such a rush to go to the bathroom?"

I laughed, but with my nose still running, it sounded a little bit more like a sob. "I was in a rush to go to the bathroom *with* Isaak. It was only Crea's dress that snapped me out of it. But it was too close."

He tossed me the towel underhand, and I draped it over my entire face. Between the darkness and the wetness, it did feel good. "But you're okay now. I'll keep a better eye on you for the rest of the night."

"How will you know I'm me and that I won't take on the personality of another sex-crazed Noble?" My voice was a little hollower than I'm used to.

"What, you don't think I've learned to recognize your charming self by now?" he quipped through a grin. "If you ever stop being interesting, I'll shake you until the Royal emotions fall out."

For some reason, it was really important to me that Antoine found me interesting.

I took the towel off my face and forced a determined grin. "I'll hold you to that, DuCarr. Let's go find the Lius."

Antoine turned and left, so I took a quick moment to check myself out in the mirror. Even I am a little vain sometimes. Whatever mascara Miranda had slapped on me hadn't smeared, and my dress managed to escape tear-free. That cheered me up a bit.

Back outside, the dance floor was in full swing. We circled around the outskirts and stood near the band. I couldn't see Isaak anywhere, which was probably for the best. I couldn't be sure what my reaction to him would be. Two redheaded Little People wailed into saxophones almost as big as they were, and a hairy Eisenhans, half-naked and covered in tribal tattoos, flipped his hair around in a circle while laying a bass line. The stage lights glinted off his bare, metallic chest. The violin, unamused by such theatrics, played itself while hovering five feet off the ground.

"There's Sho Liu and his father," Antoine said, pointing at a pair of people ten feet away. Surrounded by attendants, it was still easy to tell who was in charge of the Liu clan. Minister Liu wore a long crimson robe with a matching pointed hat that must've added another foot to his height. A curtain of beads hung down to cover his face.

At his side, Sho Liu looked fashionably uninterested in everything around him. He was taller than his father and dressed in a brocade jacket with a red sash tied around his waist. Even at a distance, I could see the model-sized cheekbones that jutted out of his angular face.

"What's the plan?" I asked Antoine. "I'll need to get pretty close to pick up anything useful, and I'd rather not have to dance with another Royal."

"That's how a girl gets a reputation," Antoine said sagely. Before he could continue, the Minister leaned in to whisper something to Sho, and the two left for a private turret at the edge of the Wedding Cake.

I frowned. "Well, let's see what I can get." Without thinking, I took Antoine's hand and started towards the Lius. His hand was limp for a few seconds but then slipped to encase mine.

That Aelexis girl was going to bite my face off if she saw this.

I took us to the turret and leaned casually against the wall. Antoine followed suit, drawing close as if we were two lovers chatting conspiratorially. I crossed my fingers, hoping he was acting.

"At least give me a chance to explain myself," a voice whispered harshly from upstairs.

"Can you even see what you have done?" another voice answered. It was more raspy and accented, leading me to assume that it was the Minister. "We are on the verge of war, and you—"

"If you would just listen to what I have to say—"

"You have shamed me, Sho. I don't want to know any more about this scandal than I need to."

My heart pounded as I strained to hear everything I could. This sounded promising. I closed my eyes.

My focus floated up over the wall, and I tried to feel whatever emotions were up there. Judging from the voices, Sho was at the farther end of the turret, and all I could feel from that direction was the odd stab of anger.

But Minster Liu was broadcasting loud and clear. I opened myself up to his feelings.

The anger hit me first, the sheer frustration that, after everything I worked for, Sho could be so disrespectful. He was throwing away all the family had built, and for what? I was overwhelmed with a deep suspicion of Sho. I didn't know everything, but I knew enough to know that he was going down a bad path. *What has he done to us?*

There was a pressure on my arm, and my mind snapped back to myself. I shook my head and noticed Antoine's hand around my shoulder. He drew me closer as I heard footsteps going down the turret stairs. As Sho and his father turned the corner towards us, Antoine pulled me into his arms to block me from view.

"Are you okay?" Anotine asked. He still had his arm around me stiffly. "Your face got…odd."

"Odd?"

"You were scowling, but it wasn't your usual scowl," Antoine said.

I pushed him lightly and stepped back. "I'm glad you're so familiar with my scowl," I chuckled faintly.

"Let's find—" Antoine started, but he was interrupted by a large, thrumming bell. The party went silent as it rang twelve times.

"It's midnight already?" I asked.

He nodded. "Party's over."

"Really? I would've expected the Royals to go much later."

"Not at their official balls. A lot of magic only lasts until midnight, and the Royals don't like to be seen without their glamours."

"Really? My magic is still going strong." Just to test, I let down my defenses a bit, and Antoine's good-natured concern for me rushed forward.

"It's mostly a fairy godmother thing. I'm not sure if it's part of their magic, or if they just do it out of tradition."

I looked down at my gown. It didn't appear any different. "So this is just another expensive, individually-tailored piece of fabric now?"

"I'm afraid so," Antoine replied. "It still looks great on you, though."

I felt my ears get hot, and I turned away from him. The sound of raised voices broke the silence.

"You are leaving without even addressing me, Liu?" Count Grimmour thundered from the center of the party. A circle of party guests was gathering around him, and I looked at Antoine. He nodded, and we went to join the crowd.

"I have nothing to say to a power-hungry warmonger who would risk the stability of the Multiarchy over a lie," Minister Liu retorted calmly. He was no longer whispering, and his voice contained a quiet strength that matched the Count's imperiousness.

"A lie? You've endangered the Apple by knowingly breaking the Compact, kidnapping a non-fey—" Tarris joined in from beside his father. He had none of his father's regal poise; instead, he shouted at the top of his lungs, and I could feel the rage rolling off him through the crowd. His father cut him off with one hand.

"We are getting close to finding the non-fey in question," the Count said coldly. "And when we do, we will bring the full weight of the Multiarchy against you. Until then, we will be satisfied by meeting you on the field of battle." He turned his back on the Lius. Tarris, Miranda, Braselyn, and all their hangers-on followed suit.

"Well, that was diplomatic," I muttered to Antoine.

"I must say, most balls don't end in a screaming match," he said. "This is new."

"I guess it *is* a war ball," I said. "Let's catch up with them."

It didn't take us long to find Miranda as she walked a little bit behind the mass of Grimmour courtiers. She waved to us faintly.

"Ugh," she grumped. "I've forgotten how tiring these things are. I had to stop three old geezers from falling asleep in my cleavage. Did you have fun at your first ball, Bri?"

"It was an interesting experience," I answered carefully.

She raised an eyebrow. "Did Isaak Krakelev contribute to the night's interest?"

There was no way for me to stop the face of disgust that his name called up. "Definitely not. I just danced with the slimeball to check him out as a suspect, and he seemed to take that as an open invitation. Don't worry," I said hastily as Miranda's eyebrows went further up. "I fought him off."

"Good call," she said wryly. "You weren't missing much." I think I heard her mutter, "What was I thinking?" under her breath.

The crowd we were trailing went as a mass through the castle grounds. Our general destination was Grimmour Tower, but individual groups and couples split off here and there. As soon as we left the more formal atmosphere of the Wedding Cake, I began to notice how informal the people around me really were. A square-shaped man in a top hat was whispering something vile into the ear of a giggling blonde half his age. Two old women with butterfly wings were gossiping loudly, between very unladylike belches. I started to grin. It wasn't my responsibility. I was off the clock, and everything was right with the world.

"Briar?" Antoine prompted from my side. "You're making strange faces again."

His observation sobered me. I had been subconsciously soaking up all the cheerfulness and irresponsibility of the drunks around me. I shook my head. It was a weird feeling. All of the affective parts of being drunk, without the more physiological side effects.

I would have to give it a try at our next house party. Seemed like a good buzz.

The group took a different way to the tower than Antoine and I had taken earlier. It led us along a crenellated marble battlement high up in the castle. We walked between the spires of Castle Fortnight in the lantern-lit night. At that height I could see into some of the windows, catching glimpses of fantastic boudoirs, ballrooms, and conservatories. The styles ranged from wood-paneled medieval elegance to stark, metal post-modernism, but they all shared an extravagance of wealth.

Between the towers I could see the skyline of the rest of the Apple, for what it was worth. Rarely did a building make it over four stories, and those that did leaned precariously. Even in Commontown the lights were still blazing, but instead of daylight spells and wisp light, they were mostly dim, flickering torches. Not a great idea in the districts of town where everything was made of wood.

"So, has your father made any decisions about the upcoming war?" Antoine asked Miranda. Small talk in the Apple.

She shrugged. "They haven't ironed out the specifics. He's still rounding up mercenaries and getting curses on order from the Academy."

"Have the Lius decided on a theatre?" Antoine queried.

I frowned. "Theatre? What theatre? Is there also a pre-war musical revue or something?"

"A theatre of battle," Antoine answered, smiling. "Since the Grimmours are the challengers, the Lius get to decide where they'll fight."

"I hadn't thought about that," I admitted. "Isn't there an arena in the castle or something?"

Antoine shook his head. "The rules of the Multiarchy state that no battle can take place within Castle Fortnight. Everywhere else is fair game. The last Royal war wasn't even close to the castle." He got into lecture mode. "The Crummond-Lockstone House War in '73 took place entirely in East Hempstead."

"*East* Hempstead?" I scoffed. "Where's that? I've only heard of West Hempstead. It's that residential neighborhood right next to that big empty field, right?"

Miranda and Antoine both looked at me silently for a second.

"Oh," I murmured quietly.

"The Lockstones apparently had a weapons cache in East Hempstead, and the Crummonds tried to smoke them out. The spellfire they used got out of control. After it burned down the entire district, they called the whole thing a wash."

I couldn't believe Antoine could be so calm about calculated class warfare. "And the people of East Hempstead?"

"Oh, don't worry. I think they got most of them out in time."

"So they could do what? Go back and live in the rubble?" A few people in the crowd turned around as I shouted, but I didn't give a dwarf's ass.

"If you go into the field, the Crummonds built a beautiful memorial statue—" Antoine's eyes were wide with fear.

"You knew? You knew that was how Nobles fought their wars?" The hot rage making my eyes water felt great. At least I knew it was my own emotion.

"This is the way it is," Miranda said quietly from my side. I'd forgotten she was there. "It's not that different from the Other World. The Royals make the wars, but they rarely participate in any of the fighting."

"Miranda," I started, reining myself in a little, "what they did to Rick is awful, but this sounds like it could get a lot worse. And we don't even know if the Lius did it. I got a bunch of weird emotions coming from Isaak Krakelev, and—"

"I know," Miranda interrupted. Her jaw shifted, and she no longer looked like the wounded princess. Her voice was quiet but iron strong. "I know this is selfish, but if we can pressure the Lius into giving Rick back, there won't even have to be a war. We must do this."

"But we have no proof!" I argued. "You might be destroying the Apple on nothing more than a hunch."

"It's not a hunch," Miranda said. "I wasn't sure until I saw him tonight, but Sho…he still loves me. Even when he knew I was dating Rick, he still sent me letter after letter, begging me to take him back. When they stopped, I thought he'd moved on. But tonight— tonight I saw that ignoring him only made it worse."

I shook my head. "I'm sorry. I can't do this. I can't be involved in the genocide of innocent commoners. Tell your father to find someone else."

"Briar," Antoine cut in. "I'm sorry I didn't tell you how Royal wars worked earlier, but think this through. Without you, the Grimmours have no chance of finding Rick and calling off the war."

"You mean the war they might have started with the wrong people?" I yelled. I stopped moving and ignored the dirty glances from the people who had to move around me on the battlement. "This whole Rick-thing is just an excuse for your father to go after his number-one enemy. But from what we know, any number of the Royal families could have been involved in the kidnapping."

"I'll prove it to you," Miranda insisted. She stopped too and stood up right near my face. Her arms were at her side and stretched tight from her shoulders to her clenched fists. "I *know* he did it. And I know a way you can get into Liu Palace."

I took a step back before she did. Normally I wasn't one to back down, but I didn't want to antagonize Miranda if she had information that useful. "Really? Why didn't you say so before?"

She broke eye contact and glanced down at her shoes. "I don't know. I guess… I guess I was hoping that you'd find something to exonerate the Lius. I was close to Sho once, and I didn't think he would do this. But after tonight, I'm almost certain he did it."

Poor girl. It was tough to think your ex would risk destroying an entire city just to get back at you.

"Listen," I said, patting her on the shoulder, "we don't know anything for sure yet. We'll look into the Lius, and then check out that Krakelev guy. I'm going to find Rick before your dad and Minister Liu get the chance to burn everything to hell."

"I'll hold you to that," Miranda said. She cracked a bit of a smile. "Meet me tomorrow morning at eight at the first-floor entrance to our tower. I'll get you into Liu Palace. I'll go find Tarris and fill him in on my suspicions." She waved goodnight to the two of us and hurried ahead to the rest of the Grimmours.

I groaned. "Are you kidding? I have to get up early again? I thought detectives worked mostly at night."

Antoine chuckled. "I think that's only in noir." We started walking together along the battlement. He ran his hand through his chestnut hair a few times. The night air had gotten chilly, and I noticed myself moving a little closer to Antoine's body. Just for the warmth.

"Long day," I huffed out. I could see my breath.

"Not that long," Antoine said. "We lost seven hours in that Van Winkle."

"Oh, right," I remembered. "How could I forget? I'm still tired, though."

"Me too. Do you want me to pick you up at your house again tomorrow morning?"

I smiled at him. "Thanks, but I think I can get to the Castle on my own. Now that I'm here on official business, I won't even have to ensorcell any guards."

"I really don't mind—"

"Please, Antoine, you'll already be on the grounds—"

"I can deliver the clothes you left at the tower," he insisted. His voice went deeper. "I'd like to, if it's okay with you."

I looked at him as we walked. His dark eyes were earnest.

"I don't—" Something caught in my throat. "I don't mind. I'll see you then."

"Great." His grin caught the light and gleamed for a split second. We kept walking, closer now. I noticed our steps were in rhythm, and our hands were close enough to almost touch.

We rounded the corner of a tower, and a shape emerged out of the darkness. My hand scrabbled wildly for my nonexistent dagger before I realized who it was.

"There you are!" gushed Aelexis. "I couldn't find you after the ball let out, so I thought I'd wait here while the rest of the Grimmours came by. Hello, Briar." The last two words had the same vitriol evident in any death threat.

"I'm so sorry, Aelexis," Antoine apologized graciously. "I completely lost you in the crowd."

Aelexis clasped her hands behind her and pulled her shoulders back. Suddenly, her teeth weren't the pointiest things on her. "Oh, don't worry about it. I was just hoping you could escort me home."

"Oh," he said. He looked quickly at me and then back at her. "Well, I can walk you home, and then—"

"Great!" Aelexis chirped. She turned her cobra smile on me. "Goodnight, Briar! I think I saw Tarris up ahead." She slipped her arm through Antoine's and all but pulled him away.

"I'll see you tomorrow, Briar!" Antoine called from over his shoulder.

My face felt hot for some reason. I didn't feel like going back to Grimmour Tower just to be on the periphery. And besides, I was exhausted. Van Winkle lag or not, I needed to rest.

The night air was cool, and it was time to go home.

I got home a little after one o'clock, and my roommates were all still up and in the living room. It was Thursday, after all. Alice was plopped on the couch, sipping a beer, with Jacqui curled up on her toes. Cade sat on the floor holding the long, gold-framed mirror that usually hung above our mantel. Alice wore a flirty purple cocktail dress and slippers, while Cade had gotten into sweatpants and a Witchdale High Athletics T-shirt.

Alice gave a low whistle as I entered. "Hey, sexy. Nice dress."

"Thanks," I sighed, finally kicking off the oversized heels. "I had a

Royal ball to attend."

"A ball? Was it any good?" Jacqui asked, raising her head to look at my dress. Balls were the only part of Royal life that Jacqui truly missed.

"Not so much."

"Did you find that kid?" Cade asked. "I filled these two in on your adventures in the woods."

Seeing Cade in the Afterwoods seemed like forever ago. "Nope, still working on it. And trying to prevent a cataclysmic war from engulfing the Apple. But enough about me, what are you guys up to?"

If Alice caught my snarky tone, she chose to ignore it. "I just got back from ladies' night at Charming's, which Cade was too boring to come to," Alice said teasingly. Cade rolled his eyes and fiddled with something on the back of the mirror.

"Is the mirror acting up again?" I asked, flopping down on the armchair next to Alice.

"Yeah, I think these runes are just getting old. I'm going to try it again." He reached around and pressed a knob worked into the ornate design of the mirror frame. At once the mirror leapt to life, showing us a wavering picture of a rerun of *The Office*. A faint harp melody played over some of the dialogue.

"How is it?" Cade asked from behind the mirror.

Alice and I looked at each other. "There's a bit of magic static. And the picture quality is good, but…" I started.

"Nobody has skin. Unless this is some Halloween special I missed, Michael Scott is not a skeleton," Alice deadpanned.

Cade frowned and grabbed a screwdriver, and then began scratching at the back of the mirror. The older a piece of magic got, the more it became distorted, and every so often the runes needed to be put back into shape.

"Do we need to call a spell check to come fix this?" I asked. Cade was silent but shot me a look of wounded male pride.

"I don't know how any magic works," Alice admitted, running her hands over the magic lamp on the end table. It didn't offer any wishes, just light. "All I know is where to push it to make it turn on. At least with electricity, I knew the basics. Electrons, and all that."

"Well, if the wizards made it easy, there'd be no need for the Academy, would there?" Jacqui said thickly. She looked like she was about to fall asleep. As far as I could tell, her cat shape didn't come with a nocturnal sleep pattern.

Jim Halpert gave a bony grin to the camera as Cade continued to scratch at the back of the mirror. "I took rune shop in high school," he grumbled. "I should be able to do a simple tune up." He must have hit the right rune, because the channel suddenly switched to Animal Planet. The humming was gone, so he must have done something right; although the animals on the Serengeti were all being represented by people in eighteenth century period dress, so maybe I was being overly optimistic.

I stood up and stretched my arms to try to get some of the tension out of my shoulders. "Well, I'm going to change out of this dress."

"Okay, but you have to come back and tell us more stories. I want to hear how the ball was," Alice pleaded. She watched appreciatively as a woman in a hoop skirt bit the petticoat off of a smaller woman by the watering hole. I could actually get on board with this. In my opinion, period dramas could use a few more maulings.

The stairs up to my room never seemed longer. The dress slid off easily, and I hesitated before hanging it on a plastic hanger with the rest of my dress clothes (two collared shirts, a plain black funeral dress, and a pantsuit that Jacqui's mother handed down to me when I was fourteen). It probably needed something special like a garment bag or a cedar hanger or something, but at this hour of the night I couldn't care less. I pulled on a pair of gym shorts and my worn *Goblinpalooza Tour '03* shirt, topping it off with a maroon hoodie for extra comfort.

As I dragged myself back down the stairs, I heard a shout, followed by a string of Cade's favorite curse words. He ran down the hall, clutching his hand, and pushed open the door to the bathroom with his shoulder.

I ran forward and looked in. He was bent over the sink, running water over his hand where a giant glyph had been burned into his palm. The zigzagging symbol made his skin a naked, raw red.

"Are you okay?" I asked instinctively. Without thinking about it, I reached forward and touched his arm.

The pain hit first. It felt like someone had pressed a hot poker into my palm, and I'd tried to hold on to it. I gave a little yelp and held my crumpled hand against my chest.

"Briar?" Cade turned to me, concern evident in his face, but I didn't even need to look. I was still hooked into his heart.

The wall hit my shoulder blades as I leaned backwards and shut my eyes tight, sliding down the wall as my legs weakened. It was too much. Feeling Cade show concern for me as I showed concern for him, and concern at his concern for my concern... The emotional feedback loop made my teeth vibrate. And something about Cade's emotions seemed slippery and odd, but I couldn't put my finger on it. When was this tea going to wear off?

"Briar?" Cade's hands moved my body back up the wall until I straightened. I opened my eyes and looked down. Staring at my palm and reminding myself that this pain belonged to Cade made the burning feeling fade. Mostly. For better or worse, I was starting to get pretty good at distinguishing my own emotions from all the other people's that had been flowing in and out of my head all night.

"Briar, what happened to you?" Cade peered down, and as he got closer, the interference drowning out my thoughts got worse.

"I'm fine, I'm fine," I said, squirming out of his hands and sliding out of the bathroom. "I just saw your hand, and I'm a little worn out, is all."

He didn't buy it. With the emotions still rising off him, I could tell. But he just stared at me silently and let me squirm on the hook.

Living with people who knew you well sucked sometimes.

"Okay. That's not all," I admitted. I looked down. There was no way I could meet his eyes while saying this. "I did some magic. On myself."

"What did you do?"

I balled my hands up in my hoodie pockets and curled up against the wall. "Well, I had to try to find the kidnapper at this ball, and I needed to get better at sensing emotions, so I…" My voice dropped to an almost-whisper. "I made myself feel empathy. A lot of it."

"You can do that?" Cade gaped. I hadn't been particularly forthcoming with him when I started experimenting with self-inflicted roses. Whenever my power came up, he usually went silent or left the room.

I nodded. "I just figured it out recently." More or less. Six months ago was recent. In some perspectives.

"So you can change your *own* emotions now?" Cade asked. He was hurt. The conversation was wearing at an old emotional scar. Somehow, the pain and bitterness it brought to the surface felt different than what I'd gotten from him previously. This was more…solid. I could trust this pain.

What the hell was wrong with Cade's emotions?

"I don't do it often," I said defensively. "I just—it was after Jacqui got hurt. I needed to get out of my rut and start working to fix her. It was Alice's idea."

A quick twinge of something hard and callous passed through Cade's face. I probably wouldn't have caught it if I didn't feel it simultaneously in myself. "You need to stop this. Changing the feelings of random Royals is one thing, but you're messing with your own heart now."

He might as well have socked me in the gut. It would have been less painful. "Is that what you think this is? That I'm some sort of magic junkie now? I do what I have to do just to get by. Jacqui was hurt because of me, everything was going to shit, and it's not like I had you to support me!" I turned and stormed out of the room. I wished the emotional link I had with him went both ways, so he'd feel some of the shittiness he made me feel.

I mean, I guess I *could* make him feel that.

Instantly I pushed that thought to the far, far recesses of my mind. No way I was going down that road.

I walked into the living room, where Alice and Jacqui were laughing uproariously at an interview with Bill O'Reilly where he and all his conservative friends had been dubbed over with the sound of donkeys braying. Apparently, our magic mirror was becoming a political commentator.

I debated getting close to one of them and skimming off just a little of the gaiety they were feeling to get me through the night. They wouldn't even know, and it'd be nice to decompress with my friends after the day I'd had.

I stopped a couple of steps from the couch. "Hey, guys, sorry. I think

I'm just going to go to bed. I'll tell you about the ball tomorrow."

Alice pouted and mimed throwing a pillow at me. "Booo, lame. Come on, stay up a little longer. Cade already told us you got Van Winkled, so you don't have any excuse."

"Sorry," I repeated. "Have a good night, though." I looked down the hall, where the bathroom door was shut. "Make sure Cade doesn't fry himself again with the mirror."

"No promises," Alice chuckled. "Goodnight!"

Jacqui gave me a sideways glance but said goodbye just the same. I trudged up the stairs and thankfully avoided Cade until I got to my room. I shut the door behind me and let out a huge breath. I wouldn't be able to avoid him forever, but with the way this week had been going, I would probably be arrested or cut to pieces before that became a problem.

I set the alarm on my old, worn-out cuckoo clock and tossed my hoodie on the floor. I gave a cursory glance at my armoire but decided I would figure out what to wear in the morning. What does one wear to break into a palace?

I collapsed onto the bed and spent a few minutes just curling up and letting my muscles unwind. It felt damn good. The soft light from my bedside lamp was warm on my face. Most of the time I didn't spring for expensive things, but the lamp was an exception. It was spelled to look and feel like afternoon sunlight filtering through autumn leaves, and every so often it gave the calm, rustling sound of wind in trees. And unlike most of the things in our house, the spell in it was holding up pretty well. I thought I'd heard an owl devouring a mouse once, but even that was sort of soothing in a *National Geographic* kind of way.

Just as my eyes were closing, I heard a scratch at the door. I kept my groan silent but dragged myself to the door and opened it.

"Hey, sorry. You got a second?" Jacqui asked from my feet. She always felt so guilty whenever we had to open doors for her. I could smell it.

"Yeah, come in. What's up?" I walked over to the bed and sat cross-legged on the floor at the foot of it. Jacqui jumped nonchalantly onto the bed. That was usually the easiest way to be face-to-face with her.

"I just wanted to see—" She took in the three burn marks on my forearm. "What the hell is that?"

Crap. I'd forgotten about them. Whatever Red Hood salve Scuff put on it had numbed it out completely, and between my hoodie and Crea's opera gloves, my arms were covered for the rest of the night.

"It's nothing. Just a little scratch from some magic," I said nonchalantly.

"What magic?"

"Um, a smoke hawk."

"Whose smoke hawk, Briar? Was it a friendly smoke hawk?" Cripes, Jacqui was going to make a great domineering mother some day. I felt a twinge of sympathy for her future teenage daughter.

"We got in a little bit of a scuffle, okay? It was nothing serious. I had Antoine with me the whole time."

"You were attacked?" she exploded. Her eyes narrowed into vertical slits. Angry cats could be pretty scary.

"It wasn't a big deal." I tried to brush it off. "This is the Apple. Even getting groceries, you can wind up in a duel or a dwarf rebellion or something. Remember that time we were at Macey's and that griffin escaped from the petting zoo? It was knocking over carriages and—"

"You're changing the subject." Busted. "Briar, if this is dangerous, you can't keep doing it. You have to walk away. We'll find a means to fix me another way."

"Jacqui," I started, "I'm being safe. Honest. I have one of the Royals' top knights on me like stink on trolls. If he's good enough to protect them, he's good enough to protect me, right?"

She stared at me for a long second before giving me a firm head-butt on the leg. "He'd better be. If anything happens to you, the Royals better watch out."

I smirked at her as I flopped back into bed. "Noted. Now let me get some sleep."

The mattress decompressed as she leapt off the bed and stalked to the doorway. "Alright. But Briar?" She turned and gave me a final look of concern. "Be careful out there."

"When am I not careful?" I mused as she left. I threw a nearby shoe at the door to close it.

Was I being careful? Was I leaping in front of swords as some sort of punishment for what I did to Jacqui? Would actually getting a limb chopped off help anything?

I turned over and pressed a pillow over my head. Those were clearly questions for a less-tired, future Briar.

A single word called me from the depths of near-comatose sleep. A single word, repeated rapidly and loudly, in a high-pitched voice from outside my window. A word so foul that even I am too much of a lady to write it.

I know. Me…too much of a lady. That foul.

I stumbled *Night of the Living Dead*-style to the bay window and threw it open. The morning was still a dim, delicious grey color. It was that cool, damp time of day that I always secretly loved but was rarely awake to experience.

That still didn't make me any less angry to be woken.

Hovering just above the tree outside my window was a pas de trois of aerial struggle and vulgarity. The word at fault was coming from the mouth of a small, plump chipmunk wearing a smart blue vest and a monocle. He was being held upside down by his pinstriped dress pants. They were almost all the way off him, held on only by tiny, rubber band-sized suspenders.

The two creatures pantsing the chipmunk looked up at me with large, feral eyes and shiny, white grins as I opened the window. Pixies might look like adorable little children with dragonfly wings, but don't let the looks fool you. They're almost as bad as actual kids.

The pixies began shaking the little chipmunk violently to get the suspenders to break. The one on my right, a Shirley Temple-esque blonde in a checkered blue frock, gave his paw a vicious bite. The chipmunk's obscenities gave way to wounded squeaks.

I opened my hand up and found a rose conveniently in it. Although I had barely opened my eyes, I found it easy to ball up all of the cottony goodness of my deep sleep and let it tumble down into the rose. The petals turned a pale indigo and drifted up off the bloom.

The petals danced in a cloud for a second, forming the outline of a rose bloom, albeit one disconnected and floating in air. Then they shot forward like a comet and burst upon the heads of the pixies.

The effect was instantaneous. They stopped shaking the poor chipmunk, although they kept their hold on him. Their creepy, almostinsectoid eyes drooped, and when they looked down at their victim, they just seemed bored. It wasn't a sleep spell, like a witch would do. It was just the gooey, languid feeling you have for the split second when you come out of a solid nine hours of sleep.

The blonde pixie cricked her neck, shrugged, and let go of the chipmunk. Her redheaded friend followed, and they lazily flew away.

The chipmunk dropped a few feet into the tree, but had the claws and agility to grab the first solid branch he hit. He scurried up to the part of the tree nearest to me and squinted at me.

"What the hell was that?" he screeched.

I rubbed goo out of my eyes. "Community service," I mumbled.

The chipmunk straightened his vest and suspenders, shot me a suspicious look, and skittered down the tree. I thought I heard him mumble, "Freak," to himself.

"You're welcome," I said to the morning in general and shut the window.

I sat down on the bay window facing in and tried to massage the sleepiness out of my face. My clock promised I could have another half-hour of wonderful, chipmunk-free sleep until I had to get up, but I figured that was out of the question.

I got up and threw the petal-less rose stem into the trash. I'd have to cut another rose to put in the vase by the window.

Which reminded me. I walked over to the window. From where I stood, there was no way I could have grabbed that rose from the vase without stretching out and bending way over the window seat. But the rose had just appeared in my hand...

Like, well, magic.

Did I have rose-a-kinesis now, too? That was a new one. I frowned.

One of the troubling things about being like nobody else was that you had no way of telling what was or wasn't normal. Did these sorts of things happen to all other empathic, rose-enchanting, feeling magicians?

I'd have to ask at the next convention.

I held out an open hand to the vase and tried to picture the closest rose rising up and flying into my hand. I strained whatever parts of my brain I normally used for my magic, but to no avail. After thirty seconds, I dropped my hand and let out a defeated breath.

I swear, the rose twitched a little in sympathy. Or maybe the stress was finally getting to me.

I yawned and paced around the room, throwing discarded clothes into my hamper and trying to work the kinks out of my neck. I pushed some of the food wrappers off my desk and into the trash. There was a sock hanging from the mantle of my fireplace, and I unhooked it from a picture frame and threw it in with the rest of the dirty laundry.

Bad choice. Not only had the sock been covering a picture of Cade and me from prom (why did I never have the balls to take that down?), but it had been blocking my view of a slender parchment note folded over once. On the outside of the note, in extravagant script, was written, "Briar Pryce."

It stood on my mantle to remind me. To remind me of when I came home from a delivery to find the note, a gift basket, and a newly feline Jacqui lying on the kitchen floor. It was closed, but I knew the six words printed on the inside.

The heart is only the beginning.

What the hell was that supposed to mean? I sighed and went to my closet.

If I was up anyway, I might as well do something good for myself.

Something better than reflecting on old memories. I pulled out my old pair of Witchdale High track pants and slipped them on. They'd been balled up in the side of a drawer for a long time. I stepped into my only pair of tennis shoes, kept the Goblinpalooza shirt on, and pulled my hair back.

I'm no athlete, but on the rare occasion I gave myself time to go running, I loved it. I opened my desk drawer and pulled out a small mahogany box the size of a deck of cards. There was a tiny crank on the side that sprang into motion when I whispered, "Obla di, obla da." A pair of slender, charcoal black vines slid out of holes in the side of my box, growing up towards me like a time-lapse video. I put the box into the back pocket of my pants just as the earbuds planted themselves gently into my ears.

Aretha Franklin's voice jumped into the opening lyrics of "I Say a Little Prayer for You." An appropriate morning song, I supposed. My music box had a weird sense of humor, sometimes. The model I had was supposed to respond to the thoughts and feelings of the user, but more often than not, it just seemed like it was on permanent shuffle.

Or maybe it was my head that was constantly on shuffle.

The stretches I learned during my one semester on our high school track team unfolded in my muscles. Funny, the sort of stuff that remains in our bodies that has nothing to do with our minds. It was my own little ritual of bending and reaching, holding and loosening. It felt really good.

When I was nice and limber, I went down to the first floor. Alice was eating something brightly colored in a bowl in front of the mirror and gave me a wordless wave as I walked through. My box shifted into "Gives You Hell" by the All-American Rejects, and I was still a little unsure why.

I paused for a second and patted Alice's head from behind. Nothing happened. My super empathy had finally worn off.

I chugged a glass of one of Cade's weird muscle-hydration potions in the kitchen (it tasted like citrus) and did one final roll of my neck. I noticed myself grinning. Except for the chipmunk profanity, this was actually shaping up to be a good morning.

When I opened our front door, I saw Cade a few feet ahead. Walking beside him was Anya, wearing a Red Hood uniform that matched his. As I watched, she stopped, took off one boot, and steadied herself by placing her hand on Cade's shoulder.

I shut the door behind me with as much self-control as I could muster. They probably heard it slam in the Bronx.

Anya finished shaking out whatever was stuck in her boot and slipped it back on her foot before they both turned around. "Life goes on," I muttered, and the music faded out of my ears.

"Morning, Briar," Cade said.

"What are you doing awake at this hour?" Anya snipped with faux British civility. Her little boot stunt left her standing way too close to Cade for my liking.

It was too early to rise to her bait. "Just out for a Friday morning jog. Where are you two off to?"

"We're heading uptown to meet with Scuff," Cade answered. "We drew the short stick and got early morning patrol around the Castle perimeter. Anya just stopped by to walk over with me."

"Oh, how nice," I replied blandly. "Although, Anya, if you're still living in Tinker's Cross, isn't that a little bit out of your way?"

Even in the dim early morning light, I thought I saw a little color rise into her face. Good Grimms, how I wished I was close enough to smell her embarrassment. "Oh, it was no trouble. It's not too far."

"Really?" I said. "It's at least half an hour. In the opposite direction. With no trolley service—"

"We should get going," Cade cut in. As was his nature, he caught on to the subtext about a minute too late. "See you later, Briar."

"Ta ta." Anya scowled at me as they turned to leave. "Have a nice run."

I watched them leave. She was still too close to him.

"Obla di, obla da," I whispered. The All-American Rejects came back on in the bridge, wailing about bitter teen break-ups.

Stupid box. Although, as I kept listening and began to jog up the street in the opposite direction from Cade and Anya, I thought maybe it had a point. The song was all about moving on and, more importantly, getting pissed.

And I'm always better at running when I'm angry.

When Antoine knocked on the door, I was pulling a batch of cinnamon rolls from the oven. They were the kind that came in a cardboard tube, but still. This was an impressive and unusual demonstration of my domestic skills.

"I got it!" Alice yelled from the other room. I heard her open the door and usher Antoine into the kitchen. He was carrying a small canvas bag with the outfit I had changed out of before last night's ball.

"Good morning, DuCarr," I said while pouring icing on the rolls. "Cinnamon roll?"

I popped one onto a plate and held it out to him. I had put an apron over my blue-and-white-striped shirtdress and had even taken the time to straighten my hair after my shower. A thick maroon belt set the whole outfit off and clicked pleasingly with my caramel skin.

Antoine stood staring at me in the kitchen entrance. "Did you rose yourself again?" He looked almost dressed down today. He was wearing a white V-neck shirt with a forest green blazer over a pair of dark-washed jeans and loafers. Maybe I was loosening him up. Although the scabbard attached to his belt wasn't exactly business casual, it did match the small pouch he had on the other side of his waist.

I scoffed. "What? I can't make breakfast without you thinking I'm emotionally doping?"

"Do you *remember* yourself yesterday morning?" he scoffed. He took the plate from my hand, and I threw a fork at him from my apron.

"Point taken. But, and I expect you to take note of this because it doesn't happen often, I am actually having a good morning."

"These are delicious," Antoine said appreciatively through a mouthful of bun.

"Made them from scratch," I smiled. The grandfather clock in the living room chimed a quarter to eight. "Can you eat on the run?"

"Mmmmmhmm," Antoine answered. I grabbed a cinnamon bun for myself and shouldered the satchel of roses I'd already picked. It was full of pastel-colored roses that had called out to me earlier. It looked like what I'd puke up after eating too much Easter candy. Maybe I *was* in a good mood.

I yelled a goodbye to whomever else was still in the house and pushed the front door open with my shoulder. Antoine followed me, and we made a beeline for the castle. Foot traffic was pretty heavy on the streets as the commuters flitted from home to cafes to early-morning diners to their jobs. A big crush of workers was going the same way as us, to polish shoes and balance books for Royals too busy to notice.

"How was the rest of your night last night?" Antoine asked after he'd licked the cinnamon off all of his fingers. I was still only halfway through mine.

"Uneventful," I admitted. "I didn't go back to the Tower after the ball; I just went home and went to bed. What about you?"

"I walked Aelexis home."

I waited for the follow-up sentence where he went back to his place. It didn't come.

"Oh," I said. Another topic didn't come to mind, so I decided to munch on my cinnamon bun while I waited for the tips of my ears to stop feeling hot. I was being silly. Whatever Antoine did after hours had nothing to do with me.

By the time we reached Grimmour Tower, the sun had warmed the morning air a little, but there was still a pleasant chill. A butler met us at the door to usher us in wordlessly. I thought he was the same one who helped us find the kitchen the night before, but the more butlers we passed, the more I wasn't sure. They all had the same look.

About a minute into walking through the chandeliered foyers and Rubens-strewn hallways towards Miranda's room, I caught myself yawning. First, it clued me in that my chipmunk fiasco a few hours earlier had really cut into my sleep. Second…

Was I becoming comfortable in a Royal tower? Not even batting an eye at the ridiculous excess of the solid-gold doorknobs around me? Unacceptable. I couldn't be. I couldn't be another Royal lackey totally at ease with the way they threw their money in the air while the people below them barely scraped by.

Antoine hadn't said much since the Aelexis conversation, but he looked over just as I began to enter identity crisis mode. Sometimes it seemed like he had his own empathy powers.

"You okay?" Antoine asked casually.

"Do you realize how often you've asked me that in the past twenty-four hours?" I kept the smile off my face, but I thought he could still hear it in my voice.

"Try getting attacked by smoke monsters less."

"Tell it to the cast of *Lost*. Thank you!" I shouted to the butler as he left us in front of Miranda's room. I think I heard a muttered, "Welcome," as he turned the corner. Yup. We were getting to be good friends.

The double doors in front of us were a light blue with white piping and two giant, brass knockers shaped like wolves. I hesitated with my hand before them, just on the off-chance they came to life and tried to take a bite out of me. But nothing happened as I took one of the brass rings and gave three loud knocks.

"Just a second," Miranda called from inside. There was a muffled rustling. "Okay, come in."

As we opened the door, a cloud of subtle, yet tangy potpourri hit me, as well as a slight undertone of something familiar. As I looked over, Miranda was sheepishly putting out a mostly-unfinished cigarette onto an ashtray by the window. She flashed a smile as she put a box of cigarettes into the pockets of her dressing gown.

"Sorry," she said. "It's gross, I know. I've been trying to quit, but with the kidnapping...please, take a seat."

Apparently this was only the receiving chamber to Miranda's quarters. Huge picture windows with light blue drapes lined the opposite wall, looking out the back of the tower toward the Afterwoods. Dark navy couches, chairs, and settees formed a circle in the center of the tiled floor, broken up by end tables covered in lamps and small metal sculptures. Doors lined the plastered walls on either side. The ones that were open went to a bedroom, a spacious bath, and at least two closets.

"Actually, we should probably get going," Antoine informed her. "The best time to sneak into the Lius' palace is probably while all the servants are still arriving. No one will notice a few extra faces if we can get past the guards."

Miranda slipped the ashtray into a large potted plant by the window. "Don't worry, I'll get you in. We won't even have to leave the castle." She stepped into a pair of blue slippers and held up a finger towards us. "Just one second."

While she stepped into the bathroom, I paced around the room. It had a great view, and from that high up, you could see for miles into the Afterwoods. Much farther than anyone alive had actually traveled into the woods.

I meandered over to Miranda's vanity table and gaped at the neat arrangements of jewelry boxes, perfume bottles, and makeup vials. Even I was impressed, and I put on makeup maybe once every six months (last night's ball used up my quota for this calendar year).

There was that smell again. A feeling very similar to the one I smelled in Rick's room, but tinged with Miranda's emotional signature. The shameful, stinky scent of keeping secrets was hovering around the drawers of Miranda's vanity. But this one had a stronger scent of deceit. Of desperation.

"Ready to go?" Miranda chirped from behind me.

I turned quickly and whipped up a smile. "This is beautiful," I said, pointing to a random open jewelry box.

"That? Oh, thanks!" she chirped. She walked over and looked at the jeweled necklace I'd pointed at. "They're real selkie tears. My father got it for me when he was in Avalon, for business."

"What business?" I asked conversationally.

"He was visiting some college of druids outside of Dublin with a bunch of guys from the Academy of the Iron Wand. They had some kind of 'you live in a magical pocket dimension, we live in a magical pocket dimension, let's be friends' conference."

"Sounds fun," I said. "I've never been to any of the other World Slips."

Antoine cleared his throat. "Uh, ladies? We have a palace to infiltrate."

"Right," Miranda said cheerfully. "Let's go."

Just as we turned to the door to leave, it crashed open to reveal a panting servant in a disheveled butler's outfit. He took a few gasps, straightened his glasses, and words started pouring out. "I'm sorry, your Ladyship, for the intrusion, but your father needs you right away in the drawing room. All of you." If he had anything more to say, it was cut off by a fit of coughing.

Before I could quip about what exactly constituted a drawing-room emergency, Miranda started out the door. She made surprisingly good time in her slippers. Antoine and I barely kept up with her as she dashed through a series of short hallways and down a narrow servants' staircase. We reached a small (by Royal standards) room decorated extravagantly in cream and gold. A few tasseled armchairs were set out in a small circle, and Tarris, Braselyn, and the Count were already perched nervously on them, still in their luxurious silk pajamas.

A man I didn't recognize, in the flowery robes of the Academy of the Iron Wand, stood in front of a large oval mirror with a silver frame. After a second, I realized it was hanging in midair. The mirror showed nothing but billowing smoke, so thick and violent, it seemed as if the very surface of the glass was changing shape. A faint whispering came from the mirror (the voice of a past English teacher said "susurrus" in my mind), and after a moment I could pick out the name "Miranda Grimmour" hissed repeatedly, overlapping until it became just noise. Antoine and I came up behind the chairs to watch over the Royals' backs.

Tarris spoke first as his sister came up to sit beside him. "It started maybe ten minutes ago. I was just watching the news, and all of sudden this thing, this cloud—"

"It's an invasion," the Count charged fiercely. "The Lius have sent this spell into our very house. Stop this!" he snapped the last part at the wizard.

"I'm trying, Your Grace," the nebbishy man protested, flipping through a thick spellbook, "but this charm is like nothing I've ever—"

At that moment, the murmuring of the mirror hit a crescendo, roaring Miranda's name once more before the storm clouds retreated to the edge of the frame. The picture now showed a dingy brick wall with a figure standing in front of it. At first it was too dim to see any detail, but as the view brightened, I recognized him as the old man from the alley. His clothes looked much more fey than what he'd worn in Harlem, with a silver poet shirt, a black cummerbund, and a black cloak with a high collar.

The Count started to shout something commanding, but the old man in the mirror held up a hand. "If you want to see Rick Pearson alive again, I suggest you shut up and listen."

If concrete had been poured down the Count's spine, he could not have sat up straighter. Clearly being told to shut up was not his favorite activity, but he bit back whatever acidic response he had. I was impressed.

"You've received our demands," the man continued, "and still nothing has been done. Tarris Grimmour still holds the position of Royal Apprentice to the Exchequer."

I was hit by a whiff of pain and regret from Tarris's direction, and from behind I saw his hands tighten into fists.

"Just to prove that we're not bluffing, I thought a demonstration was in order." The old man walked to the edge of the frame, and the viewpoint of the mirror swiveled to follow him. We could see a little bit more of the room, but nothing too descriptive. It was larger than it seemed from the previous angle, with high ceilings and a cracked concrete floor. There were two windows letting in dim light, but they were covered with those separated plastic curtains that were so popular in butchers' shops and slasher flicks. Nothing was modern enough to tell us it was in the Other World, or archaic enough to tell us it was in the Apple.

In the center of the room was a cage almost as tall as the ceiling itself. Unlike the uniform, factory-made prisons you saw on TV, this cage had character. The bars were all slightly different lengths and had a variety of nicks, scorch marks, and stains that looked suspiciously like bodily fluids. The places where the bars met were carved and ornamented with devious-looking designs. The entire thing looked like a giant birdcage designed by someone who hated birds.

Pressed against the back wall of the cage was a tattered, feverish-looking Rick Pearson. The polo shirt and jeans he was wearing were stained and ripped, and he had an open cut on his face, but he was alive. He coughed a few times and looked in our direction, but it seemed like whatever spell the smoking man was using, Rick couldn't see us.

Standing to either side of the cage were two seemingly homeless people. One was a long-limbed, bird-like man wrapped in layer upon layer of fleeces and coats. The other was a stout, older woman with a long plume of greying dreadlocks that reached almost to her waist. Her flowered dress was faded and torn, presumably from years on the street. She was staring right at Rick and stroking the bars slowly, like a tiger playing with its prey. Her movements were strangely stilted and robotic.

The smoke magician continued. "It seems as though you've begun to doubt our commitment, Count Grimmour. You think we'll just wait around while you consider our demands. I'm here to show you how wrong you are." He gave a self-satisfied grin and walked closer to the cage.

I noticed out of the corner of my eye that the Grimmour's wizard had edged out of the frame of view of the mirror and was whispering something under his breath. He brought his hand up and trailed a line of orange sparks into a symbol. I'm no wizard, but I've seen enough magic to know it was the rune for place, or location.

"Now let me introduce—" the old man in the mirror started, but then he cocked his head to the side for a second, like he heard something. "Now, none of that," he chided casually and waved his hand. All of a sudden, the other wizard's glowing symbol popped into nothing more than a puff of smoke.

"Where's the fun if you track my spell?" he grinned at us from the mirror. "Let me introduce Mr. and Mrs. Nibbel, my associates. Smile for the camera, will you?"

The two vagrants turned and grinned at the camera, and I noticed what had seemed off about them before. They weren't even close to human. They moved awkwardly because they weren't wearing their own skin. The homeless people were just fleshjackets containing…something else. Maybe ogres, maybe something even more dangerous.

To drive their point home, the two creatures widened their grins. More and more teeth came into view until their mouths stretched the entirety of their faces. A black forked tongue whipped out of the man's mouth and wet his lips.

"The Nibbels have been taking care of Rick here for the past two nights. Feeding him, softening him, preparing him. If Tarris Grimmour still keeps his seat as the Exchequer's apprentice, they're going to spend one more night with him. And we all know what happens on the third night."

There was a brittle silence in the room as we waited for the smoke man to continue, but he just stared at us for a moment while his words sunk in. "You have until sunset to deliver your resignation, Tarris. Don't keep us waiting." With that, the picture on the mirror boiled into smoke again for a couple of seconds, and then went dark.

The silence broke into a burst of sound and sharp emotions. The Count got up to berate his wizard for failing to locate Rick, Braselyn at his side, while Miranda hid her head in her hands, and Tarris started yelling that he didn't even want the apprenticeship in the first place. I covered my mouth to try to block the smells of frustration, depression, anxiety, and concern that were pouring out of the Royal family.

"Of all the incompetent—" the Count started, advancing on the wizard.

"It's not my fault!" the wizard squeaked. "That man is— That's Elias Clewd! He was a Senior Runeist at the Academy before he— before he—" The little man's voice failed him, and he started to hyperventilate.

"Calm down, Eldon!" the Count snapped, further terrifying the other man. "You say you recognize him?"

Eldon nodded. "It was right when you started as Royal Liaison, Your

Grace. Elias Clewd was one of the top wizards at the Academy, a shoe-in for Head Magister, until he started his *experiments*." The wizard said it with such gusto, it seemed like he was waiting for an ominous thunderclap.

Tarris rolled his eyes and took the bait. "What experiments?"

Eldon's eyes gleamed with fervent sincerity. "*Terrible experiments*. It seems that Clewd had been hiding the fact that he was a Free Spell, and he began combining his own lesser magics with the great runes of the Academy to create something…" He gave a dramatic pause so long, Tarris finally jumped in.

"So what did the Academy do?" Tarris prompted.

"He was excommunicated, of course," Eldon said. "And he disappeared, taking a good chunk of the Academy library with him."

"Could he have been the one responsible for the cloaking spell that kept the Academy from scrying Rick?" I asked.

The wizard nodded. "He knew the Academy's magic as well as anyone. I wouldn't be surprised if he figured out some way to cloak himself from their magic while he was in hiding. Nobody has seen or heard of him in years."

Tarris turned to his father. "And all the while he's been nursing a secret hatred for the Academy, and anyone associated with it."

"What are you implying?" the Count asked.

"I'm saying if you were a little more aware of the wizards' affairs, we wouldn't have a scorned wizard with Academy-proof magic after our family. He's the perfect ally for whatever Royal is supporting him."

The Count's voice got low and dangerous. "Do not speak of things you don't understand, boy—"

"He's right, Father, if you would only—" Miranda started.

"Miranda!" Braselyn's iron voice rang out in warning. It was the first time she'd spoken all morning.

"Could you all stop for a second, please?" I gritted out in the polite tone I would use to talk down an angry Eisenhans. The Grimmours turned to me as one, mostly just shocked that I had the gall to interrupt all four of them at once.

I had all kinds of gall.

"I think the kidnappers gave us more than they meant to with that message," I said quickly, before their shock turned into threats of execution. I turned to the wizard. "Is there a way you can play some of that back? The part near the end?"

He swallowed, looked at the Count, and nodded at me. The Count inclined his head, and Eldon placed his hands on the mirror. "*Recitum*," he declared forcefully, and the image sprang to life. It was hazy for a few moments, but then it focused in on the part of the conversation when the smoking man was first introducing the Nibbels.

"There," I said, pointing to the edge of the screen. "Out the window."

"I can't see anything," Tarris muttered angrily. "The coverings are too thick to make out anything useful."

"Just watch that red patch of light," I said. After ten seconds of tense scrutiny, it disappeared, and another green patch appeared below it.

"It's a traffic light," Braselyn whispered in her reed-instrument voice.

Tarris swore softly under his breath. "A traffic light. They're in the Other World!" He threw an arm around me. "How the hell did you see that?"

I gave a small smile. "Just ADD, I guess. I saw it change while the smoking guy was rambling." To be honest, I hadn't been totally sure that I'd seen it. "And that narrows things down a little, but the Other World is a big place." There was a dangerous amount of hope in Tarris's eyes all of a sudden, and it made me anxious.

"Not that big," Tarris said. "Those monsters were using fleshjackets, which means they have to be close to the Apple for them to work. Unless they have really good spells in them, that means they're probably in Manhattan."

"Still," I argued, "even Manhattan is a wide area to cover."

"We were going to investigate the Lius," Antoine announced. "We'll keep an eye out for any properties they might have in the Other World."

The Count nodded. To dismiss us, I supposed. "I'll send more of my people on patrol, but we've already checked out all of the Liu territories we know about." Braselyn gave us an icy smile, and the two of them glided out of the room with the wizard at their heels. That woman really didn't like me for some reason.

Tarris pressed the heel of his hand into his forehead. "I don't understand why we can't just give in to their demands. I don't even want to be apprentice to the Exchequer."

Miranda put a hand on his shoulder. "We'll find Rick. It's not your fault," she said firmly.

Her brother gave her a small smile. "At this point, I can only hope. I'm going to go see if I can find any records of Liu properties that Father might have missed. Good luck."

As he left, Miranda turned to us. She looked a little harried, but still in control of herself. Maybe the reality of her boyfriend's impending consumption hadn't hit her yet.

"We should go," Miranda began. "If the Lius are behind this, it'd be better to figure that out now so we can refocus our efforts."

"Are you okay?" Antoine asked.

She squared her shoulders and looked at us. "I'm fine."

A familiar scent hit me, the one I smelled earlier in her quarters. Deception.

We followed her down a spiral staircase into the basement of the castle. I stared at the back of Miranda's head, wondering what her secrets were. The smell I picked up in her room could have had nothing to do with Rick. For all I knew, those drawers held her teenage love letters to Lance Bass or something (let's all agree the nineties were a confusing time for everyone). We all had secrets. Maybe she and Rick just had a stronger scent of hiding things than most people. They did have a whole star-crossed-lover thing going.

Or maybe they were caught up in something bigger.

As soon as we got below ground, the space opened up into a huge, vaulted series of chambers much larger than the tower above us. Apparently, that was only the tip of the iceberg.

"I'm not supposed to know about this," Miranda confided. "I don't know why our tower was built the way it was, but— this is how I used to visit Sho when we were dating. Just over here." She led us through a small portion of the hockey rink-sized collection of shelves that was the Grimmour family wine cellar. "The farthest part of our basement abuts the servant's room in the Lius' catacombs."

I tried to suppress a giggle. *Abut.* "Wait, did you say catacombs?"

Miranda nodded. "They're pretty big for a family that immigrated to the Apple this century. Some people say the Lius had them shipped over from their ancestral palace in the Forbidden City."

"How do you ship a tomb from half a world away?" Antoine asked.

"Big ships, I guess," Miranda said with a shrug. She took us to a small hallway in the back corner, which abruptly ended in a stone wall covered by a threadbare red tapestry.

"Seriously?" I scoffed. "The old secret-passageway-covered-by-a-tapestry trick?" I took the tapestry in both hands and yanked it off the hook it was hanging from.

A thick cloud of dust rose from the tapestry as it hit the floor, revealing a regular, completely solid wall.

"Uh, no," Miranda said. She eyed the fallen tapestry and frowned a little.

"Oh," I said. "Sorry."

Miranda stepped closer to the wall on the right and placed her hand on the stone. After a moment, the bricks creaked and rearranged themselves into an archway leading into darkness.

I gave a low whistle of appreciation. I forgot that all the Grimmours needed to do to remodel their tower was put a hand against the stone.

"Follow the main passageway through the tombs, go down the stairs, go straight, and then when it dead-ends, go right," Miranda instructed. "The ladder at the end of that hall will take you to a storage room behind the kitchens. From there, it shouldn't be hard to get out and poke around."

"You're not coming with us?" I asked.

"I would, but if the Lius captured me, they could force my father to surrender. That's really all a princess can do to contribute to a war. Avoid being kidnapped." She plastered on an ironic grin, but I could smell the bitterness behind it. "And you'll need these. It's pretty dark in there." She held out two torchstone pendants, which Antoine and I took and put around our necks.

"You thought of everything, didn't you?" I smiled at her.

"I always do," Miranda said. "On the off-chance you're questioned, just say you're from the Blacksmith's Guild. I know Sho was doing some sort of business with them the last time we talked. Good luck!" She put a hand on each of our shoulders and gave a little squeeze before turning to go out the way we came. As she walked away, I saw the confidence that powered through her every step. Whatever jokes she made about being a wilting princess, Miranda Grimmour was a strong young woman. Much stronger than the rest of her family gave her credit for.

"Miranda's hiding something," I told Antoine after she was definitely gone. "I smelled it in her room."

"Yeah? Do you think it's the same secret that was in Rick's room?"

"Maybe," I conceded. "Maybe not. Maybe it's nothing. But it has to be a pretty emotionally-laden secret for me to smell it without doing the whole rose ceremony I did in Rick's room."

"Rose ceremony? What is this, *The Bachelor*?"

I groaned. "I had to get saddled with the one Royal knight who watches reality television."

"Listen," Antoine began, his smile fading, "Miranda's a princess; I'm sure that comes with a whole host of secrets to keep. I bet you'd smell that in most bedrooms in Castle Fortnight."

"You're probably right. And besides, she's one of the few Royals I've met who I actually like," I confessed, making sure my torchstone was outside of my shirt so it cast the most light in front of me. The hole in front of us was still pretty dark.

"She's changed a lot in the past few months," Antoine said. "During my last job with the Grimmours, she was just a spoiled little girl. Maybe it takes tragedy to make someone grow."

"Remind me to put that in a fortune cookie," I muttered. Gazing ahead of us into the blackness, I was starting to feel a little uneasy. "Why are all the clues hidden in such creepy places? First an alleyway in Harlem, now a creepy Chinese tomb…"

"Want me to go first?" Antoine said mockingly.

"Bite your tongue, DuCarr," I snapped with false anger. Even pretending to be mad gave me the push to take the first step down into the tomb. Sometimes all it took was having something to prove.

After a few moments, my eyes adjusted to the low light being given off by our torchstones. The passageway leading us deeper into the tombs was claustrophobically tight, and Antoine and I had to go single file. As we left the dim light of the Grimmour wine cellar behind, I began to regret my big mouth.

The cracked sandstone walls on either side of us were riddled with rectangular holes about two feet across and two feet tall, just large enough for someone to lie down in. Not comfortably, of course. But then again, I supposed that wasn't the point. Every so often, a small pot or incense holder would be sitting on the lip of some lucky ancestor's tomb. I wondered if anyone would go through the effort to make my afterlife smell pretty.

The gritty sand piled on either side of the hallway made me think no one had been down in this part of the tombs in a long time, probably since Miranda took her last trip to see Sho. Cobwebs hung in wide arcs along the ceiling, making the hallway seem more round and tunnel-like.

"I would've expected a little more extravagance when it came to the ancestral tomb of the Lius," I said.

"This is only the servants' section," Antoine explained. We were both talking pretty quietly, although I couldn't imagine anyone could hear us.

"I guess if you work for them long enough, you get a free slot down here."

"That's decent of them. Most Royals would just as soon toss their servants in the river when they're done with them."

"What makes you say that?"

"You should've seen my dad's retirement package after working in the Castle gardens for fifty years," I grunted. "It makes the river look like—"

"*Wait*," Antoine hissed, reaching an arm out to grab my shoulder. I instinctively took a step back, which put me incredibly too close to him. "Did you see that?"

"Antoine," I whispered fiercely, "if you are trying to scare me, I swear to Bluebeard I will kill you and bury you right here." I still couldn't bring myself to step away from the protection of his arm.

"Stay still. I saw something move around the corner in front of us."

"What did you see?" I gulped.

"I don't know. Something. It slithered away before I got a chance to look at it."

"*Slithered?*" I whisper-shrieked, probably louder than I should have. Somewhere on the edge of my hearing (or maybe my imagination), I heard something rustling along the floor.

Antoine smoothly and silently took his rapier out from the scabbard. "We need to keep moving. We should be close to the stairs Miranda told us to take."

I took out Prick and held it in front of me. We went slowly, step by step down the hallway. After we passed the branch where Antoine saw whatever he'd seen, the hallway widened, and we were able to go side-by-side. I used my left hand to hold the torchstone necklace out in front of me, but so far, nothing. The floor in front of us was empty.

There was only a quick scrabbling noise above us before a long, many-clawed thing shot at us from the ceiling. I threw myself back just in time, and it landed heavily where I'd just been standing. Antoine took a swipe at it with his sword, but the snake-like creature wriggled around his attack and went back the way we had come. After a few seconds, the sound of claws on stone faded completely.

I rolled to my feet and went to Antoine. Instinctively, we stood back-to-back, our blades pointed at the darkness outside the range of our torchstones. I kept looking up nervously to check the ceiling. After a few minutes of panting, nothing else came at us.

"What the hell was that?" I whispered. My lungs still hurt from throwing myself to the ground.

"I don't know. It didn't stay still long enough for me to see," Antoine replied. "Thing came out of nowhere."

"Alright, we need to get out of here. Whatever it was could come back at any minute, and we're sitting ducks."

He straightened but kept his sword out. "No arguments here. I think I see the stairs up ahead."

They were. We stepped cautiously to the lip of the stairs and pointed our torchstones down. The steps led down into a small, narrow chamber about fifteen feet long with a high ceiling. In the center of the room was a simple, undecorated sarcophagus, nothing more than a rectangular slab of stone. Another passage split off from the room to the left, and the door Miranda told us to take was at the far end.

Of course, the main detail I noticed was that the walls were writhing.

About a dozen or so copies of the creature we had seen earlier covered the room, clinging to the walls in-between all the corpse holes.

Each was about six feet long and about as wide as a fire hose. Legs stuck out from their scaly green hides at random intervals. Their heads looked like a terrifying, tooth-filled cross between a piranha and a bulldog, with shocking orange hair for a mane. They started to move languidly, orienting themselves towards us. The sound of their bellies sliding across the stone made a hissing sound that made me think of some sort of terrible, terrible hive. Sharp little tusks gleamed all over the chamber as they grinned reptilian grins in unison.

"*Draconis Orientalis*," Antoine muttered from beside me.

"Latin?" I squeaked. "You're really speaking Latin right now?" One of the closer serpents twitched its head at the sound.

"Chinese dragons. Pretty young ones." Antoine murmured softly. "A whole clutch of them."

"What do we do?" The dragons were still inching towards us ever so slowly.

"I think I have an idea," he said, grabbing his torchstone pendant. "They hate bright light."

"So they'll be afraid of our torchstones?"

"No," he answered darkly. "They hate it, like they want to rip it apart." He gave a quick tug on the necklace and broke the string that hung around his neck. "Get ready to run."

In a blur, he threw the necklace into the corridor that split off to the left. As soon as it hit the wall, a bright flash of blue sparks lit up the tomb. The dragons all whipped their heads around and hissed as they surged forward towards the fizzling torchstone.

"Go!" Antoine shouted, but he didn't need to tell me. I was already taking the stairs down two at a time. We only had a few seconds before his torchstone died out completely, and the only other thing in the tomb that would attract the Chinese dragons was the pendant hanging around my neck.

I squeezed past the coffin on the side farthest from the dragons and made it to the far door with Antoine close behind me. I kept running, but about ten feet outside the room, the hallway split in two. I slowed a little and tried frantically to remember what Miranda had said when she gave us directions.

"Right!" Antoine barked from behind me. I stole a look backwards as I turned the corner. No ravaging horde of snake-dogs yet.

I took one step into the new hallway before I stopped short. Antoine bumped into me, but I grabbed the wall to make sure I didn't go forward any farther.

Stretched in front of us was another dragon, this one twice the size of the others. Its body was as thick as a dachshund's and covered in sickly green scales. It was impossible to tell how long it was, as it was coiled up and covered the entire hallway. It slowly lifted its head and turned to focus on my torchstone. Something told me we'd found the clutch's mommy.

At the end of the hallway, I could barely make out a small, round room with a ladder going into the ceiling, right where Miranda said it would be. Of course, she forgot to mention the three-hundred-pound, fanged boa constrictor.

Without warning, the monster sprang forward with its claws aimed directly at my neck. Antoine pulled me back around the corner, but not before one of the talons grazed my left shoulder. I bit the side of my cheek to keep from crying out. Those things were *sharp*.

The creature flowed around the corner to face us with shocking speed.

I guessed the thirty-or-so legs weren't just for show. It reared up on its hind legs so its mouth was level with my eyes.

Before it could attack again, Antoine stepped forward and slashed upward with his rapier, tracing a maroon line across the thing's pale underbelly. It twisted out of his range and fell back to the floor with a guttural grunting sound. It backed up a little, keeping its eyes trained on Antoine's blade.

The knight took advantage of its hesitation and leapt, hooking his boot into one of the tombs on the left side of the hallway. He pushed off it *parkour*-style and propelled himself over the dragon and into the intersection of the hallway as his sword flashed downward into the beast's side. It hissed and scuttled back into the left side of the hallway.

"Go!" Antoine shouted as he drove it further back and away from the room with the ladder. "Get to the end of the hall. I'm right behind you!"

I danced around to the right side of the hallway, almost tripping on the tail end of the dragon. Turning the corner, I started to run towards the ladder. The hall wasn't that long, and if there was some kind of door, maybe we could keep the dragons out long enough to get up the ladder.

A muffled grunt from behind me stopped me in my tracks. I turned my torchstone around to see that the dragon had found its way around Antoine's sword and head butted him in the jaw. The momentum drove him back onto his ass. The monster gave a satisfied growl and drew itself up, ready to go in for the kill.

I ran back towards them, my mind blank with fear. The dragon seemed to be just hanging there with its mouth open, delaying the moment when it would sink those knife-sharp teeth into Antoine's flesh.

My left hand found an urn in one of the tombs, and I flung it haphazardly towards the creature. To my surprise, the urn flew true and crashed right into the creature's mouth. It hissed and drew back a little as it tried to shake the pottery shards out of its teeth, but unfortunately, it was only stunned.

I used the force of my run to stab out wildly with Prick when I got close enough, but the dragon swerved and I ended up only getting the side of his head. My faint, obscure hope that it was somehow magical was dispersed when Prick's cut did nothing but make the thing bleed a little. Behind me, I heard Antoine leap to his feet.

The creature turned back to me slowly with blood dripping down the side of its face. It looked pissed.

"Run!" I shouted, turning on my heels and pushing Antoine ahead of me. I heard the monster's claws behind me, only about two feet back and gaining. We were halfway to the room at the end of the hallway, but there was no way we were going to make it. I felt the hot breath of the dragon as it panted behind me.

Before it could bite, I took a page out of Antoine's book and jumped up. I put one foot on a tomb and used it to spring forward to the other side of the wall. I ping-ponged back and forth for a few steps while still keeping momentum. The dragon snapped at my feet, but he was just the tiniest bit too short to get to me.

I ran like that for a few seconds before I saw Antoine reach the round room, glance back and then grind to a halt. Even in the swinging light of my torchstone, I could tell from his posture something was wrong. He turned and pointed to my right shoulder.

It was hard to twist and see what he was pointing at, but it didn't take a long look. While I'd been watching my feet, two of the baby dragons had crawled along the ceiling and were waiting hungrily on the wall where I was about to jump.

I tried to hold back my momentum, but my footing slipped and I began to fall. I saw the Momma dragon open her mouth below me.

In a last ditch effort, I kicked out as I fell, catching the big beast right in the snout. It wasn't anything more than a tap, but it forced the terrifying jaws shut for a split second. I'd take it.

I hit the ground hard, but the pain was a bland undertone to the adrenaline that screamed throughout all my senses. I sprung up from the ground like my track coach had taught me and thanked my lucky stars I'd stretched out my leg muscles while jogging that morning.

But I was still too far from the room. The dragon on the floor recovered and was reaching out a claw to hook me. I wouldn't make it.

I flung myself forward, sacrificing my balance for a few more seconds of not being mauled. The creature saw what I was doing and also pounced forward. I passed through the doorway in mid air, already rolling to try to kick the monster away when it landed on me.

There was a bright purple flash, and my vision went black.

I felt myself hit Antoine, taking him out at the knees as we both tumbled to the floor. A metallic rasping sound told me that Prick had flown out of my grasp and flung across the floor. At first I thought I'd broken my torchstone, but I would've felt the spell burn out onto my skin.

A second later the purple afterglow in my eyes faded, and I saw its source. Three giant Chinese characters floated in the empty doorway, their curves traced in neon purple light. The dragons on the other side of the doorway hissed and clawed the air, but the spell seemed to have stopped them.

Once I realized there was no giant lizard about to crush me, I became very aware of how entangled Antoine and I had become after my jump. His arm was pinned beneath me, and my leg was between both of his. It would have been sexy if it weren't so painful and awkward. Story of my life.

I cleared my throat and rolled carefully away from him, securing Prick at my waist. "Are you okay?"

"A few bumps here and there, but nothing too bad, thanks to you. That thing almost had me before you hit it with that pot. I owe you."

"Please," I scoffed. "I've stopped keeping track of who saved whose life after yesterday. Let's just call this whole quest a wash."

"That's probably for the best," he conceded. "I was planning on pushing you into danger just so I could even the score."

"Ha ha," I said evenly. "Now let's get the hell out of here, just in case that barrier spell has a time limit."

He looked back at the dragons. "The Lius must have put those things in sometime after Miranda's last trip. I assume she would've mentioned man-eating serpents in her directions if she'd known."

"They do seem to stand out in one's mind," I deadpanned.

"Wait here. I'm going to check if there's anyone above us." Antoine grabbed the ladder and tested how sturdy it was. At the top was a wooden trap door with a faint light coming from the cracks. Satisfied, he climbed to the top and pressed it up just enough to see through.

"Looks clear," he said quietly. "Come on up."

He pushed the trap door open silently and climbed gracefully up. I followed, pulling myself into a small storeroom filled with burlap sacks and boxes of ingredients. It smelled spicy and exotic. I probably couldn't name even a third of what was in the room. There was only one exit, which cut down on our chances of getting lost.

"I don't hear anything," Antoine said. He was already listening at the closed door. "I say we walk out as quickly as we can and try to blend in. Follow me when we're out there; I think I remember where the Lius' personal quarters are."

"Geez, have you been in every palace in the Castle?"

"A fair amount of them," he admitted. "I've worked for a lot of Royals."

"I have, too," I said, "but they don't usually invite me back to their pads. What did Miranda say our cover was? We're from the Blacksmith's Guild?"

"Yes," Antoine replied, giving me a sideways look. "Do you know anything about smithing?"

"Uh." I paused. "Not really. My knowledge of swords pretty much amounts to 'insert pointy end into bad guy.'"

He smiled, his hand on the door handle. "Let me do the talking, then, if we're caught."

The door opened into a short hallway. To one end were crashing sounds from what must've been the kitchens, but the other end seemed quiet enough. Antoine jerked his head in that direction, and we went up a wooden staircase until we came to a sliding, paper-screen door.

He slid it open, and we walked out as nonchalantly as we could. We were on a wide wooden walkway that wrapped around the inside of the palace. I saw a few servants here and there, but they all seemed too busy to give us a second glance. On one side was a grid of paper screens like the one we had just come through, and on the other was a wooden balustrade that overlooked a massive courtyard. In the garden's center was a cherry tree, maybe six stories high, that reached up and over the series of balconies that encircled it. Its branches twisted and swirled around each other, like calligraphy done in bonsai. Lit paper lanterns dangled from many of the branches, their light faint in the early morning sunshine. Cherry blossoms were everywhere, drifting slowly to the ground in a pink shower.

"Wow…" I gasped.

"I thought you'd like this. Pretty impressive, huh?"

"…those petals must be a *bitch* to clean up," I said. Antoine rolled his eyes. "What? I'm a gardener's daughter. Now, where to?"

"Up there," he said, pointing. Across the courtyard from us was a five-sided tower that loomed over the rest of the palace, its point as high as the top of the cherry tree. "Sho's quarters should be up there."

I gave a good sniff but smelled only cherry blossoms. "I don't smell Rick's scent. I guess it would be too convenient if Sho had stored him here and given us a trail to track."

"I can't imagine him stashing a kidnapped non-fey in his room and somehow managing to keep it hidden from his father."

"Yeah," I agreed. "Minister Liu didn't seem very happy about whatever Sho is doing. Do you think Sho kept him in the dark and kidnapped Rick all on his own?"

"Let's find out," Antoine answered. We circled the tree to the other side of the walkway, and he opened a screen, revealing a shoddily-built staircase. The wood of each riser wasn't completely flush with the white stucco walls as it spiraled up.

"Servants' staircase," Antoine whispered as he started climbing. The planks creaked suspiciously under his weight.

"I never would have guessed," I muttered. Falling down these was probably what had filled half of the tomb we had just walked through.

We went up three flights, and at each landing there was a paper screen. As we rounded the third landing, one screen opened and a young girl in blue robes rushed past us with a full tea set. It was the first person we'd seen on the stairs.

"Is it always this empty?" I asked after she passed us.

"It must be the war," Antoine deduced. "The servants are probably rushing all over the Apple, making preparations."

"Royals don't even do the prep work for their wars? Figures."

After the seventh flight, I could tell we were in the tower. The wall opposite the paper screens had small windows to let in a little natural light. It was still pretty dim in the stairwell, though, and I stumbled more than once on the uneven steps.

Finally, Antoine raised his hand in front of a screen. I thought he was about to open it, but then I heard the rustling of papers. Someone was right on the other side of the screen.

Antoine held up a hand for silence and inched the screen open just a crack. Through the opening I saw the back of Sho Liu, barely three feet away. He was sitting at a great mahogany desk, reading a scroll. The rest of the study, at least from what I could see, was empty.

We'll have to wait, Antoine mouthed at me. Our faces were close enough that I could feel the tiniest bit of breath he put behind each word. I shook my head.

I slipped a rose from my bag and held it up. It was a light, It's-A-Boy-And-We're-Reinforcing-Gender-Stereotypes blue. What emotion could I use to get Sho out his office and make sure he'd be gone for a while?

Even before my conscious mind made a decision, the rose petals started to swirl and become a fiery orange. My hand started shaking a little, as I felt all the adrenaline and excited energy from my morning jog flow down into the rose. The petals started to twitch hyperactively, and then shot all together through the crack to swirl around Sho's head.

Immediately he stood up, loosened his tie, and reached for a small, palm-sized magic mirror on his desk. He tapped on it impatiently until a face appeared.

"Rachel, hold my calls, will you? I'm going out," he instructed quickly as he pulled off his dress shoes. Rachel said something on the other end, but I couldn't make it out. "I *know* we're supposed to meet in half an hour. Just tell them I'll meet them at the warehouse at noon instead. I'm going for a jog." He slipped off his shoes and started working on his belt when I looked away.

He was jogging? That was specific.

After I heard his pants hit the floor, followed by more rustling, I looked back. Sho had changed into a pair of gym shorts and a tank top and was doing stretches. He started with a hamstring stretch that was one of my favorites. He had nice form, and his body was in very good shape.

After a few minutes of stretching, he seemed to get impatient and started for the door. Just as he was about to leave, he stopped, turned around, and went back to his desk. After a few seconds of looking around, he took a few of the scrolls he'd been looking at and put them in a black wooden box. He murmured something under his breath, and the box snapped shut, a shower of gold sparks flying out of the keyhole. Satisfied, he galloped through the door on the other side of the room. I heard him clomping down the stairs for a while until the sound faded away.

Once it was silent, Antoine and I went into the room and closed the screen behind us.

"What do you think that meeting at the warehouse is about?" Antoine whispered. He went to the black box and tried to open it. "Damn. No way we're going to guess the right magic word for this."

"Don't need it." I grinned at him and pulled out Prick. Antoine moved out of the way, and I jammed the point of the dagger into the keyhole. There was a little resistance, but after a couple seconds, a few sparks shot out and the spellock clicked open.

I took out the scrolls and spread them across the desk. Most of them were contracts that were more or less unintelligible to me, but I scanned them anyway.

"Here's something," Antoine said. "A rental agreement for a storage space on the Lower East Side, from some shady rental company. There's a non-disclosure clause in there, too."

"As in, 'don't disclose that I'm hiding a kidnapped Know-Not in there?' Is that included?"

"Doesn't say. But I was thinking the same thing."

The scroll he was pointing at just looked like a lot of numbers and legal jargon to me, but I nodded. "Do you see a date on there?"

Antoine's finger traced along the page. "There. He just signed it yesterday."

"Okay," I mused. "So Rick disappeared Tuesday, yesterday was Thursday. Where was he for those two days? Why move him now?"

"Maybe we were getting too close to him in Harlem," he suggested. "There's an address on here, but this says Sho already signed for the keys, and it doesn't say which unit he rented. There could be hundreds."

I pulled out my notebook, copied down the address, and checked my watch. "Dammit. Okay, Sho said he'd be there at noon, but maybe we can get there first. If we can't find it by ourselves, we can wait for him to come along and try to sneak in after him."

Antoine frowned. "I guess that'll have to do. We don't have any other options. Maybe you can ensorcell someone who works there and they can tell us what unit we're looking for."

"We'll see—" I started, when a pair of footsteps came up the servants' stairs and stopped in front of the screen. Antoine and I froze and looked at each other. At the same time, we sprinted quietly for the screen on the opposite side of the room. Just as we closed it behind us, I saw the servants' screen start to open.

The staircase we were on now could not have been more different from the one we'd come up on. It curved beautifully down, with a smooth railing of polished mahogany that featured carved dragons running along it. But we didn't have time to stop and admire it.

"Antoine," I called as we raced quietly down the stairs, "we left all of those papers out on Sho's desk. He'll know someone was there."

"I know. We just have to hurry," he whispered shrilly.

The staircase emptied out onto the top balcony surrounding the courtyard. This level was empty, except for a pair of Nobles in fancy robes. Antoine instantly shifted into his relaxed, professional knight persona, but I felt like I was about to throw up. We were coming out of the private quarters of the Lius and could not look more out of place.

The two Nobles gave us a scandalized look, and then hurried off.

"Shit," I cursed. "If they tell the guards, they'll lock down the entire palace. There's no way we'll get out through the front."

"Well, I'm not going back through the tombs," Antoine said. "That's suicide. We'll have to go up and out."

"What?" I stammered, but he was already moving to the balcony. He jumped up on the railing in one smooth motion and grabbed one of the cherry tree branches. I gasped, but the branch seemed more than strong enough to hold him. After that, he just needed to shimmy up a little until he was close enough to the roof of the palace to pull himself over.

"Come on," he called from above me. "You just have to get close enough so I can pull you up. Trust me."

Damn it. I did trust him.

The railing wasn't too high, but once I climbed on top of it, I had a good view of how far down the ground was from there. But my body was already in danger mode, and there was barely any hesitation as I hopped off onto the branch.

My ribs hit the bark hard, but besides emitting a very unattractive grunt, I didn't seem to be hurt. For a stomach-turning second the branch moved a little but then steadied. A shower of cherry petals fell down from the motion, and I got one in my mouth.

Antoine had been so graceful; I barely managed to caterpillar-crawl up the branch until I was close enough to his outstretched hand. He was perched on the clay tile roof and looked pretty steady. From below, I heard someone shout in surprise. So much for a stealthy exit.

For safety's sake, I got a little closer before reaching out my hand to his and pushing off the tree towards the roof. I was in the air for one terrifying moment but landed securely with Antoine's help.

The clay-tiled roof slanted pretty gradually, and I didn't have much trouble following Antoine as he climbed up and over the peak of the roof to the outside wall. At the base of the Lius' private tower was a series of statues of Chinese warriors looking out at the rest of the Apple.

"I hope these aren't terra cotta," Antoine mumbled quickly. He looked through the pouch on his belt for a second before pulling out a small locket of blonde hair tied with a blue ribbon.

"Is this really the time to reminisce over past girlfriends?" I spat.

He gave me a quick look of good-natured exasperation before he tied the locket around the stone sword of the statue closest to the edge of the roof and tested its strength.

"Let down your long hair," he murmured to the locket. A bright glow ran down the length of the locket, like the kind you saw in hair conditioner commercials. When the glow hit the end of the strand of hair, it began to grow.

It was fascinating to watch, but after a couple of seconds I started to see where Antoine was going with this. "Oh, hell no. You've got to be kidding."

"It's the only way out, unless you'd rather go with the guards or the dragons," he said. The hair had already started to pile onto the roof. Antoine gathered the hair into two strands and tied one to his belt. The other he threaded through the belt loops of my shirtdress. I hoped they were strong enough to support my weight, or I would be all kinds of naked as I plummeted to my death from my first failed rappelling attempt.

"I think it's long enough now," he advised. "It's just like walking backward. Down the side of a building."

"Oh, thanks," I scowled at him. He didn't seem to mind that I was taking my fear out on him.

"I'll help you get over the side of the roof."

We walked to the edge, and I resolutely kept myself from looking down. I'd learned my lesson. It was equally as hard to turn my back on the five-story drop and face the palace.

"I'm just going to lift you down, and then the hair rope will support you, okay?" Antoine said. He put his hands around my waist and looked into my face.

I shut my eyes and took a breath. "Yeah," I said, opening them and looking at him. "Let's do it."

Without any more fanfare, he lifted me up in a weird little ballet lift around the waist and lowered me over the side of the roof. For a second, my feet kicked out with nothing below them and I felt a kick of panic in my gut. Then the hair finally went taut and I felt it holding me somewhat painfully by my waist. At least the statues were sturdy enough to hold us.

Antoine let go of me and turned around, and then he casually stepped backwards off the roof and let the hair catch him. "The trick is to sit back into it." Our two harnesses of hair were just about even, and I saw Antoine brace his legs against the wall and start to walk backwards down it. I followed suit. The hair kept growing, keeping us even as we made our way slowly down the wall.

"This isn't too bad," I admitted. After a few feet, I got the hang of pushing away from the wall with one foot while moving the other down.

"Not everyone gets used to it so easily."

"I used to watch a lot of *Alias*. Jennifer Garner did stuff like this all the time. In heels."

"I have a confession to make," Antoine said, "just in case we fall hundreds of feet to our deaths in the next few minutes. Sometimes you make pop culture references that I completely do not get, and I just go along with it."

I narrowed my eyes at him. "Let's keep it that way. Trust me that they are both apt and hilarious."

After a few more minutes, we reached the ground. As soon as we were standing upright, Antoine undid our harnesses and whispered, "Gothel is here" to the hair. The strand glowed once more and began to retract into a small braid again.

We were standing about twenty feet from the edge of the Afterwoods and could still hear the sound of shouting and general hubbub coming from the Liu's palace. Once the hair shrank down again, Antoine gestured for me to follow him as he ran towards the woods.

"Didn't we learn this lesson yesterday?" I asked as we got into the woods proper.

"It's not night," he replied. "We'll be fine. But I think it makes sense to circle back through the woods to get to Grimmour Tower."

The Afterwoods were practically idyllic at this time of day. There was filtered sunlight through the leaves, birds chirping, a nice breeze, and not a single man-eating monster as far as the eye could see. We kept far enough into the woods that we wouldn't be seen, but not anywhere near the Deep Dark parts.

"So what do you think our next move should be?" I asked as Antoine helped me over a fallen tree.

"I say we check back with Miranda and tell her what we've learned. After that, we should have plenty of time to get to Sho's mystery warehouse before he does."

"Works for me," I agreed.

Once we were close enough to Grimmour Tower, we were able to surreptitiously slide into the flow of traffic along one of the main castle roads. Castle Fortnight was almost encircled by the Afterwoods, which the Royals assumed were as good as most walls at keeping peasants out. Between the nasties that lived there and the Red Hood patrols, using the woods to break in would not be a wise choice.

We didn't get very far into Grimmour Tower when a musical voice asked, "Can I help you?" Turning, I saw Braselyn, dressed in a killer power suit, coming out of a stairwell into the main entry hall. The professional attire didn't do anything to hide the otherworldly look in her eyes as she stared us down.

"We're here to see Miranda, milady," Antoine said graciously, bowing. After a second of him glaring at me from the corner of his eye, I gave her a perfunctory curtsy.

"My daughter is indisposed, I'm afraid," Braselyn whistle-sang as she approached us. Her iron voice made it hard to tell exactly what she was feeling. "I'll let her know you stopped by."

"It will only take a second," I said.

"May I be frank, Miss Pryce?" Braselyn added snidely, turning her glare onto me full-force. She didn't wait for an answer. "I don't know what magic you do, but giving my stepdaughter false hope that you can locate her little non-fey consort isn't helping our family. It's just cruel. All this nonsense is just going to break her."

It took me a second to parse the words out of the melody that was her voice. It took another second for me to get pissed.

"Your daughter is a lot stronger than you give her credit for, Countess Grimmour. She's been a huge help in our search for Rick. So if you'll tell her we have a lead, that would be *great*." Not waiting for a response, I turned on my heels and stormed out of the tower.

Outside, I stopped to take a few breaths. Antoine came rushing up to me. "What was that?" he snapped. His voice was harsh, but I couldn't smell any real anger behind the words.

"She was being a bitch," I answered hotly.

"That may be true, but you can't speak to a Royal like that."

I scuffed at the ground. "I know. That was dumb. But it's just— you don't think she's right, do you? Are we just leading the Grimmours on?"

He looked into my eyes. "Now's not the time to ask that question. We can't back out. Besides, Braselyn is terse with everyone. Maybe she's compensating for her voice."

I pulled out my pocket watch and checked the time. "Alright, we have plenty of time to get to the warehouse before Sho's meeting there." I paused, trying to plan the quickest route to the Lower East Side. "At this time of day, I think the East River Chute is probably our best bet. We can take a trolley there from the Riversgate stop, but then we might have to take a cab once we're Topside."

Antoine concentrated for a moment. "Yeah, sounds good to me. Although I know there's been some construction on the trolley tracks, so we might have to grab a broom service to fly us to the Chute."

If you think keeping track of the MTA was hard, try public transportation in the Apple. Getting where you're going is an art.

We got out of the castle with no problems. Besides the impending war, everything was pretty quiet at Castle Fortnight. The Lius weren't about to put out an alarm for us. Nobles are usually hesitant to admit they've had intruders on their grounds. It's very embarrassing.

After we crossed the bridge to Liars' Square, we waited along with a crowd of giggling goblin schoolgirls on a field trip. They were all dressed in blazers and pleated skirts. Very Upper East Side, if WASPs had craggly green skin, pointed ears, and inhumanly long fingers.

Liars' Square was bustling with traffic in and out of Castle Fortnight. Some people were taking early lunch breaks, some were grabbing a late-morning latte, and others seemed to be getting back from overnight shifts. It was a mix of off-duty servants and Royals slumming it with the common folk.

I took in the ebb and flow of shoppers in and out of the shops across from the trolley stop. Businessmen and minor Nobles flooded in and out of the Magic Beanstop with coffee in hand, while street vendors sold fake Gucci scabbards. But something was off. Everyone walked a little faster than normal and kept looking over their shoulders. Over the usual smells of the city was a gasoline-sweet scent of tension and fear.

The city was a powder keg, and if we didn't find Rick, the Royals were going to set it on fire.

One of the storefronts across from us was boarded up, which I found odd. Liars' Square was pretty pricey real estate, and I couldn't picture anyone letting a property go to waste. Just as I noticed it, I saw a man in a hooded black pea coat approach and knock a pattern on the shuttered-up window next to the door.

On his hand was a silver ankh.

My vision tunneled as I looked for a break in traffic. By the time one came, the door to the storefront had opened and let the man inside. I sprinted across the street, the taste of rage in the back of my throat.

"Briar? What—" Antoine started as I ran away. A cart honked from behind me, but I didn't have time to see if Antoine was following.

The door to the shop was locked tight when I tried to pull it open. I gave it a few yanks just to make sure. When that didn't work, I pulled out Prick and jammed it into the lock. Something gave a fizzing noise, and wisps of purple smoke flew out of the disabled spellock. If someone went through the trouble to magically secure this door, it was much more than an abandoned store.

I put a shoulder into the door, and it banged open. Inside was a dark room that at one time was a bar. The main level had been cleared away, tables pushed to the side, except for one big, round one in the center. Everything was in disrepair, and the oak-paneled walls were lined with broken chairs, empty crates, and a lining of cobwebs. The only light came from a single exposed bulb that hung above the table.

Standing around the table was a crowd of devious-looking guys in formalwear. Whether troll, dwarf, or human, they were all glaring at me. There was one other woman, a svelte dryad in a tight dress, and the twin sickles strapped to her back made her look just as dangerous as the men around her. Beneath the rank smell of intimidation, however, was a bit of peppery embarrassment. Heaped on the table were stacks and stacks of bills, arranged in neat and expensive piles.

"Krakelev," I said. I couldn't think of anything else. My hands were shaking, and in the gloom I could see the roses in my bag shifting wildly across the color spectrum. Were they glowing?

"Hey, you can't—" a big, dark-skinned ogre started, spittle dripping off his tusks. Isaak threw up a hand, cutting him off.

"Lily," he purred, his voice smooth, "what a pleasant surprise." He pulled off his hood and fixed me with a rakish smile. "But I'm afraid this isn't a great time for a reunion."

Something about his cocky charm pushed me over the edge. Without thinking, I grabbed the nearest rose from my satchel and started towards him. In my hand, the rose went from blue to a deep, blood red. It might have been the light, but I swore the flower swelled as it absorbed my rage. The petals looked pointy, somehow, and the thorns grew wickedly sharp as I neared him.

"Briar," Antoine's voice came from behind me. It was a warning.

I stopped about a foot away from Isaak. The rose in my hand showed up as a faint red glow in the buttons of his pea coat. One of the Green Knights standing behind him started to step towards me, but Isaak was completely unfazed. He didn't know what I held in my hand, or what the amount of anger crackling inside the rose could do to him. Stroke, heart attack, a berserk rage on anyone in sight. Usually I held back, so my roses didn't push people too far.

This time there was no holding back.

"Briar, don't." Antoine's words pulled me back from the edge. I'd never tinkered that much with someone's emotions, and Isaak's failed seduction wasn't a good enough reason to start. I let the rose drop to the floor, crushing it under the toe of my boot.

"Who is that?" Isaak asked, apparently more concerned with Antoine's presence than the glowing rose.

"A friend," I replied, forcing myself to smile at him. "Could we talk to you for a second? I promise it won't take long."

Isaak looked at the rest of the men gathered around the table, most of whom were staring at him and grumbling violently. "I don't think now is the best time—"

I grabbed a new rose and filled it without thinking. "Here," I offered, handing him the rose as it changed from yellow to a mint green.

"What—" Isaak started, but then the magic hit him, filling him with graciousness and the desire to help. It was an emotion I'd perfected after sniffing a host of genuinely helpful waiters, concerned parents, and the odd customer service worker who actually cared. It was one of my specialties for getting information out of someone.

"I'll just be a moment," he told the assembled group. When he took my arm in his, I had to fight the urge to backhand him. We went up to a small raised area with a bar covered in upturned stools. Antoine followed, but Isaak didn't seem to notice.

Once we were there, I jerked my arm away. "Alright, you need to tell us everything you know about Rick Pearson."

"Rick?" Isaak looked surprised. "You mean Miranda's little Know-Not? What about him?"

I got real close to him. "Do you know where he is?"

"Of course not," Isaak scoffed. I gave him a good whiff. Beyond the helpfulness that I'd given him, there was mostly just confusion; none of the anxiety or delight that people usually felt when they were lying. I couldn't be sure, but if I had to put money on it, I'd say he was telling the truth.

"Then what's with the rogues gallery over there?" I said, pointing towards the increasingly hostile group of criminals.

"We're just engaging in a little under-the-table…speculation on the outcome of the upcoming war," Isaak replied dismissively.

"You're betting?" I sputtered. "Betting on a war that could raze the entire Apple to the ground?"

He spread his hands and tried to give a charming smile. "You got me. It's times like these that are great for us entrepreneurs."

This was turning into an utter waste of time. "So you don't know anything about the kidnapping?"

"Of course not," Isaak said. "Sho covers his tracks pretty well. Most of the time."

"What does that mean?" Antoine prodded.

Isaak gave him a disgusted look. I could smell the helpfulness already draining from him. "Let's just say I was able to procure a little inside intelligence on the war preparations, and the Lius were especially sloppy about protecting their information as it pertains to their mercenaries, their supplies, and where they're keeping them."

"Isaak," I coaxed, leaning forward and smiling. "If you know anything, please, we need any information you have on the Lius."

Isaak put his face close to mine and smiled. The scent of his cologne cut into me like a very expensive knife. "What's in it for me, sweetheart?"

Damn it. The magic had worn off, and I didn't want to drain myself by making another rose. I'd have to play this a different way. "Listen," I offered, keeping close to him but keeping my voice professional, "if you've got a lot of money riding on this war, I can provide you with a play-by-play as this thing develops. You'll need someone on the inside of the Grimmour camp."

He made an exaggerated pouting face. "As beautiful as you are, I usually just speculate. Interfering in these matters isn't really my thing—I'll have to decline."

"I can put in a good word for you to Miranda," I said. "You still want her. I can smell— I can tell you still have feelings for her."

He let out a bitter chuckle. "It will take a lot more than a good word to get me another chance at her. She's turning the whole town upside down trying to get her little boy-toy back."

"Alright, fine. I didn't want to have to do this, but if you tell me everything you know about the upcoming war, I'll make sure get you a chance with Miranda."

"How do you mean?" he challenged. The rumble of his voice was reserved, but I could tell he was interested.

"Have you ever heard the story about the commoner who goes around delivering flowers for the Royals? Magic flowers that make people feel happy, sad, or any host of emotions?"

"Sure. It's a fairy tale. Magic can't change feelings."

I smiled and showed him the satchel of flowers at my side. "Really? You didn't feel a little burst of helpfulness in the past few minutes that you can't explain?"

He looked down at the bag and back to me and let out a little laugh. "No shit? *You're* the Rose? I was wondering why I even bothered talking to you after the stunt you pulled last night."

"So if you give me the info, I'll give you a shot at getting Miranda back."

"You'll make her love me?"

"No," I admitted. "I can't do love. Not true, lasting love." A lie, but I didn't want any of the Nobles thinking I could. "But I can do better. I can do forgiveness, understanding, nostalgia, or fill-in-the-blank. It would give you the opportunity to talk to her, at least, and maybe put her in the right mood to hear you out."

There was a second in which Isaak weighed his options, and I thought I'd read him wrong. "Deal," he agreed. "You give me the rose, and I'll tell you what I know."

"Doesn't work that way," I said. "I have to be the one to hand it to her."

"So how do I know I'll even see you again after I give you the info?" he asked shrewdly.

I offered my hand. "I'll make an oath."

He took my hand in his and looked me straight in the eye. "Do you pledge to deliver one rose for me if I provide you with information?"

"On my heart," I promised. There was a quick tingle of magic that raced like pinpricks up my hand. Oaths in the Apple were not a thing to be taken lightly.

"Bert!" Isaak shouted above the din of the crowd. A tall, gangly-looking Green Knight came over with a stack of papers. "Please give— ah, what was your true name, again?"

"Briar," I said.

"Please give Briar here everything we found about the stockpiles the Grimmours and the Lius have started preparing."

The Green Knight gave me a suspicious look, frown lines showing on his emerald skin. But after a short moment of hesitation, he put a manila envelope on top of the bar.

"Actually, just a moment," Isaak said. He stepped over to the table and put his fist lightly down on top of the envelope, knuckles first. I heard him whisper something at the edge of hearing, and black wax began to flow from a ring on his hand. When he removed it, there was a perfect seal on the folder with an ankh emblazoned in the center.

"A sign of my good faith," he said expansively as he handed the envelope to me.

"Nice doing business with you," I muttered, sliding it into my bag. "Just out of curiosity, which side are you betting on?"

Isaak looked away. It was the first time during our conversation that he didn't target me with his ice blue sex eyes. "The Grimmours. I'll always back Miranda."

It would've been cute if he hadn't tried to boink me in a bathroom last night. That kind of tarnished my image of him as a lovelorn romantic hero, pining for his lost princess.

We left the bar just in time to see a trolley pulling away. "Dammit," I grumbled.

"Briar, what was that?" Antoine said, his voice perfumed with frustration.

"What was what?"

"That. You charging across the street without saying anything. I looked over to see you gone, and I thought…"

It took me a second to remember the coursing rage that drove me to follow Isaak into the bar in the first place. I had poured most of my anger into that rose.

"I'm sorry," I admitted sheepishly. Seeing Isaak had made me forget that Antoine was right next to me. "I saw him over there, and I just lost it. What he almost did to me—"

"I understand, but you can't just charge off like that. We're partners." He cleared his throat. "Now come on, we need to hail a broom if we're going to make it to Sho's storage space in time."

Somehow, I felt like I was a child getting scolded. "Well, we got more info on Sho's activities, at least. Hopefully, what Isaak gave us will point to which storage unit we're looking for."

Around the corner was a broom service stand, one of the many that dotted the Apple. I didn't normally like to travel by broom, but we had to move fast. It was only a few minutes before a plump, flight-goggled witch swooped down on a big four-seater and hovered above the ground in front of us.

"Where to?" she asked as we climbed aboard. She was sitting sidesaddle, her traditional black-and-white striped stockings dangling just above the ground. The skin that showed over her black dress was tinged with light purple.

"The East River Chute, please," Antoine offered in his politest voice. I was sitting uneasily behind him. These things never seemed wide enough.

Without any warning, the broom shot up at a sixty-degree angle. I bit off my yelp of surprise, but my arms still flung forward to wrap around Antoine's waist. The rooftops of Liars' Square passed us at an alarming rate as we flew higher and higher into the sky.

"You okay?" he asked quietly. I almost didn't hear him over the rush of wind.

"Fine," I squeaked, trying to overcome my nausea with positive thinking. "I don't mind heights, I just don't like being so…unstable."

The witch steered us sharply to the right to avoid a flock of seagulls and I hugged Antoine tighter. Even through my fear I noticed Antoine's taut stomach. Yeesh, the knight did not skip his sit-ups.

"Sorry," I said when I could open my eyes again.

"Don't worry about it."

We leveled out a bit, and the witch pointed us towards the Ballgown District. Now that we'd reached cruising altitude, my blood pressure started to lower a little.

I made myself look down at the Apple splayed out below us. The view was the only redeeming thing about taking a broom.

The streets of Commontown spread out from Castle Fortnight like roundabout arteries. We were high above even the tallest buildings outside of the castle grounds. Here and there, other broomsticks flew, ferrying passengers through the air.

A huge silver mass caught my eye. Gathered around Blue Fairy Park was a group of fifty or so small figures in gleaming armor. As I watched, one of them hoisted a dark blue banner and the rest formed into rank behind it.

"Is the battle starting already?" I yelled to Antoine in shock.

"It shouldn't be," he called back. "The theatre hasn't been decided on, last I heard. But if mercenaries are already massing like that, it can't be far off."

"Shit," I swore to myself. I pictured battalions like that one spreading throughout the entire Apple like a virus.

I scanned the rest of the streets as we passed them but didn't see any other soldiers. If war was brewing, apparently the beans were still being ground.

After thinking of that metaphor, I decided I should've gotten some coffee.

Just as I got comfortable being balanced on the broom, the witch pulled into a dive. I wrapped myself around Antoine again, but, to be honest, it didn't seem like he minded. We pulled up to the broom service stop outside of the East River Chute. Once we were stopped a few feet above the ground, I disentangled myself from Antoine and stepped gratefully onto the ground. He tipped the witch generously, and we walked over to the station.

The East River Chute had expanded as the Apple continued to grow. There were now four separate chutes to accommodate more traffic. Each looked like those old Art Nouveau cage elevators, except made entirely out of rune-covered wood. An attendant directed us into the first available chute, which already had a woman and her daughter in it. There was just enough room inside the elevator for us all to stand, but not comfortably.

The attendant pulled the wooden latticework across the entrance, and there was a loud clunk as we sank into the ground. The girl gave a little squeal of excitement and buried her face into her mom's dress. After a few seconds, the sensation of falling went away, and, when I looked through the elevator's cage, there was only darkness.

It still felt like we were moving, but I couldn't tell in what direction. My stomach, already upset from our broom ride, didn't like it. But I guess that was the price you paid for traveling between Here and There.

There was another loud clunk, and the elevator skidded to a halt. I always felt like jumping during that moment, but I wasn't sure in which direction the momentum would carry me. After a few more seconds, the wooden latticework pulled back into a bark-shaped gap just wide enough for one person to fit through. We let the woman and her daughter go through first. Antoine gestured for me to go next, and for the first time, his chivalry didn't piss me off.

I squeezed through the door and found myself in East River Park. The elevator fed out into a big tree in one of the thickets that dotted the park. After Antoine came through, the opening in the bark folded back into itself, and there was no sign that it was secretly a Door to another world. A few other fey were nonchalantly getting out of a big birch tree across from us. A jogger looked over distractedly in our direction but didn't seem to care enough to stop and wonder why a crowd had gathered in this particular bunch of trees.

I checked my pocket watch. We had less than half an hour before Sho's noon meeting.

"Do you mind if we take a cab to the storage facility?" Antoine asked as we walked to the street.

I sighed. "Fine, fine. Although let the record show this is the first time I've taken anything but public transportation in months."

He laughed as he flagged down a passing cab. While he was giving the cabbie the address, I pulled out Isaak's folder and popped the wax seal. Inside was page after page of spreadsheets giving the location of various properties owned by the Lius and the Grimmours, along with notes on what could possibly be stored there. I leafed through until I found the most recent entries.

"Isaak's intelligence seems pretty up-to-date," I explained to Antoine as the cabbie sped us to the Lower East Side. "Here, see? There's an entry on the storage space he rented out yesterday. Unit number seventy-one."

"Does it say what he put in there?"

I waggled my eyebrows suggestively. "It says 'unknown.' But between that and the fact he took out the space in his own name and not his father's, I'd say it's a good place to check."

We pulled up across from a big warehouse building, and Antoine passed the cab driver some money. We got out and inspected the area. Sho couldn't have picked a better building to hide something. No one would expect a Royal to go within twenty feet of the "Quik-Save Storage Boutique," much less store something there. But as old and broken down as it was, the front door was chained and padlocked shut.

"Well, I'm not going to charm my way past that," I pointed out. "And somehow I doubt a place as gross as this would invest in a spellock."

"Should we wait?" Antoine asked. He gestured to a bus stop not far from the doors on the same side of the street.

"I guess. It's only about ten minutes until Sho gets here."

We sat in the bus shelter, and Antoine angled his body to get a good look at the entrance to the Storage Boutique. I looked up and down the street. There were definitely a few traffic lights that could be seen from the windows, if this was really where Rick was being kept.

"So, are you okay?" Antoine finally asked.

"From the broom sickness, or from the run in with Isaak?"

"Either. Both."

I chuckled a little. "I just get a little motion sick. And I overreacted about the Isaak thing. As much as he is a skeez, I'm glad you stopped me from giving him that rose."

"Yeah, what was that? I haven't seen any of your roses look so…evil."

I shuddered a little as I saw the pointy red rose glowing in my mind's eye. "I'm not sure. That was a little much. There was more emotion in that rose than I think I've ever put in anything. It was like my magic—" I stopped myself.

"What?" Antoine said.

"My magic has been getting a little unpredictable lately," I admitted. "It was like it took what I was feeling and…amped it up as it got to the rose. That rose had enough anger in it to give him an aneurysm."

"Your magic has been unpredictable, how?" Antoine said, worried. "Forgive me for nagging, but aren't we basing our search for Rick Pearson on your ability to sniff him out?"

"The sniffing isn't the problem," I explained. "It's just—sometimes it feels like the magic has a mind of its own. I still don't understand it all. Like today. I gave Sho the same energetic feeling that made me go jogging this morning, and then he did the same things I did. Same hamstring stretch I do and everything. Most of the time, I only give diffuse, general emotions. Not ones that lead to a specific behavior."

"Is that so bad?" he asked. "Maybe your power is getting stronger."

"If I knew what was happening and could control it, sure. But there was a guard at the Grimmours…I spelled him when I first went there, but he was still feeling it when I saw him yesterday. That should've worn off in a few hours, tops. What if my magic doesn't go away as quickly as I thought?"

"Well," Antoine pondered, "you're sort of working without a net here. No other magic in the recorded history of the Apple has been able to change a person's feelings. There's going to be some level of trial and error. Maybe it affects different people differently."

I leaned forward and rubbed my temples. "Right, but trial and error doesn't cut it when I'm messing with someone's heart."

Antoine gave me a reassuring smile. "Hey, they test medicine that way. Give yourself a break."

"It's just—what if I've totally changed people, and I don't even know it? You didn't feel what I was feeling when I was about to rose Isaak. It was like I wanted to—to totally change him. To rip him apart and rearrange his insides. Metaphorically," I added after Antoine gave me a disgusted look.

He was quiet for a moment after that, and I wondered if I had finally scared him off. But it wasn't long before he turned to me, concern in his eyes. "If I wasn't there, do you think you would have done it?"

"Maybe," I confessed. The reality of what happened finally sunk in. "I could have killed him."

"But you didn't."

"But I could have. Or twisted him so far that he would never bounce back."

"I'm not sure a change that drastic would be bad for Isaak. But," he said over my objection, "I see what you mean. You've never pushed your power as far as you have in the past couple of days. It's scary."

I nodded.

"You know, a beautiful woman once told me that I'd never grow unless I pushed myself emotionally," he said. "That if I let restraint rule me, I'd be stuck forever not knowing how far I could go."

My face felt a little hot. "Did she? Well, what *I* told you is that you're repressed. I think you might have hallucinated that other advice."

"Well, real or not, I think it's wise. How will you know what you're capable of, if you're too afraid to try? Maybe some people *should* be changed. You could…I don't know. Make smokers feel disgust at cigarettes. Or make depressed teens feel happy again."

I thought of the girl who I'd given doubt to in Rick's dorm. Was that a blessing or a curse? "I don't know. I feel like I'm not the one who should be writing people's stories for them."

"Even if it makes them happier in the end?"

"It doesn't matter. I'm not sure I could really change people for good. Permanently, I mean. But even if I could, is that what's best for them? And who gets to decide what emotions people should feel? Me?"

"Sho," Antoine said quietly.

"What?" I responded before I saw where he was pointing. Just a few minutes ahead of schedule, Sho Liu was walking towards us. He'd changed into a suit jacket over a powder blue dress shirt and jeans. It was only the slightest touch of feyness that separated him from the New Yorkers around him.

He rang a buzzer next to the door of the Quik-Save Storage Boutique, and after a minute or so, an old woman unchained the front door and ushered him inside. Sho said something to her, and she left the front door unlocked.

Antoine stood up from the bus shelter bench. "Should we try to slip in before the people Sho is actually meeting come?"

"I feel like this is our knee-jerk reaction," I joked. "Breaking and entering is just what we do now."

"In our defense, we haven't had a good break-in for an hour or so. It's about time."

I snorted. "After you."

The Storage Boutique looked more run-down as we got closer. The green paint on the door was cracked, and the bricks around the entrance were chipped and graffitied. Not a great place to store anything important, but then again, it looked shady enough that I could see Rick being kept here.

We walked in swiftly and closed the door behind us without a sound. The entrance led to a small tiled foyer, with a big corkboard covered in faded flyers and concert posters. After the door closed, the only light was from yellowy fluorescent bulbs strung along the ceiling. There was an office to the right, with a large window blocked by stained ivory blinds. From behind it, I heard Sho's voice and what must have been the old woman who worked here.

The foyer opened up into a surprisingly large warehouse filled with chain link cages holding all manner of refuse. Two of the units closest to the door were filled with purple seats that looked like they'd been torn from a movie theatre. Others were filled with racks of clothes, trash bags, or dirty old stuffed animals.

"Unit seventy-one, right?" I said to Antoine in the barest whisper. He nodded, and we crept into the maze of cages. The padlocks on each cage had numbers etched into them, but they were hard to discern in the dimness.

"This is eighteen," I offered as I squinted at one. At that moment, I heard a knock on the front door. Antoine pulled me into an aisle blocked from view just as the office door opened.

"Hurry," he whispered as we started scrambling from lock to lock. We'd turned down the right aisle, apparently, and the numbers were in the forties and going up. How we were going to open Rick's cage and get him out without everyone noticing would be the issue.

The sound of Sho and at least two more men talking was starting to come towards us into the storage area. Antoine and I turned a corner and followed the passageway formed between the concrete wall and a row of even larger cages.

"Sixty-eight, sixty-nine, seventy," I counted as the row stopped and the hallway dead-ended. "Grimmsdammit, where's seventy-one?" I looked about wildly.

"There," Antoine answered hollowly. He pointed to a metal door in the wall behind me. In addition to looking like it came out of a bank vault, it was marked with a small, white seventy-one. Two keyholes lined the right side of the door, and a third was built into a large handle.

The voices of Sho, his guests, and the old woman were getting closer, and there was nowhere to go.

Antoine pulled out his sword. "We'll have to take the keys if we're going to get through. How many of them can you take out with roses?"

"I— I don't know. Even hitting two people at once can be tricky—"

"Hey," Antoine said evenly, grabbing my shoulder and turning me to look him in the eye. "You can do this. I'd say it's a good time to test your limits, no?"

Seeing him grinning at me while we had our backs against the wall was all I needed. There was something about his open smile, the feel of his hands on my shoulder—but I'd deal with that later. Now, I had to focus.

I pulled two matching red roses from my bag and held them in either hand. Judging from the sound of Sho chatting about payment schedules, I only had a few seconds.

That was fine.

I didn't want fear. If they ran away, we'd be no closer to getting through the damn door. But if we could get them to stick around and not bother us while we let Rick out…

I let go of the reins, as it were, and felt the magic take them up. Whatever had been stirring in me the past few days, it was good at changing people. If I was going to ensorcell four people at once, I needed to let my power work unrestricted.

Something flowed down my arms like ice water and pooled into the roses. Like the rose I made in Isaak's bar, there was more feeling in these than I thought I could generate. But rather than question it, I let the energy swirl around until the roses positively crackled with it.

The old woman was the first one to come around the corner, and Sho almost ran into her when she stopped and stared at us. "Who the hell are you?" she barked. Behind the two of them, a pair of stout fey in cheap suits stopped and looked at us in confusion.

The magic running through my body raised my arms, and the two roses lifted gently from my hands. The stems hung in midair for a second, and the skeptic in me looked for strings. But they held perfectly still.

One of Sho's business partners stepped forward and started to say something, but as soon as he moved, the petals on the rose shot forward. All of the red in them faded into a sickly beige. The petals kept swarming forward, until the hallway was filled with them. There were more petals than two blossoms could possibly have produced, all writhing and diving at the four people like piranhas. Through the cloud, I saw the men swatting at the petals for a few seconds before they jerked in surprise, slowly putting their hands by their sides.

The dance of petals was beautiful, but it was more than that. I could feel each petal as it flew. Each was a little piece of me, thrown out into the world. The magic danced through the hallway, through me, through the petals, and through the people in front of me. My back arched involuntarily as I flowed out into the scene in front of me, the floral conductor of an unseen orchestra.

After thirty seconds, the petals dispersed in one big blast, during which the stems fell to the floor. The hallway looked like Times Square on the first of January; beige petals covered the floor like a shower of depressing confetti.

Sho, the old lady, and the two stocky men with them were completely still, their faces frozen in matching looks of loss. I'd hit them with all the powerlessness, all the thwarted agency I felt when my magic took over. Sho looked at us and weakly tried to say something but gave up.

Damn, that felt good. Good to let loose. Good to let go of that feeling of helplessness.

I took a deep breath and put a hand out to steady myself on the wall. There was still so much energy within me, roiling around in my head until it was hard to see straight.

"Are you alright?" Antoine asked. "That was amazing."

"I'm fine," I answered, straightening up. And I was, for once. I didn't feel as winded as I usually did after a huge burst of emotion. The exhausted Briar, the helpless Briar, seemed to have blown out into the petals.

I walked towards Sho and the rest of them, and their only reaction was to follow me with their eyes. The dusty smell of ennui filled the entire hallway. "They should be too overwhelmed to do much for at least half an hour," I said.

I circled the old woman and found a Gordian knot of keys hanging from her back belt loop. I unclipped it and thanked my wishing stars that the keys were labeled. Antoine patted Sho down and pulled a single key from his pocket that matched the ones I had. Sho tried to resist, but a meek hand-swatting was all he was able to muster.

After a minute of sorting, I pulled out keys Seventy-One A and Seventy-One B from the mass and made my way to the door. "You ready?" I asked Antoine.

He nodded and stepped to my side. I put 71A into the top keyhole and turned it until I heard a clang from the door. Same with 71B. I turned to Antoine, but he held out the final key to me.

"I think you should be the one to do this," he declared. I started to protest, but he pressed the key into my hand firmly.

"Alright," I conceded.

"Also, remember there could be traps on the other side of the door."

"Oh, great. That somehow makes your noble gesture seem a little less meaningful." I glowered at him.

The key fit smoothly into the hole, and I turned it until I heard a click. After that, I pressed down hard on the handle and swung the door out, keeping most of my body behind the door and only peeking my head in to look inside.

It was dark for a few seconds before a motion sensor kicked in and the light buzzed on. The room was about twenty feet by twenty feet, the same unadorned grey concrete. And it was filled with armor.

Suits of chain mail, with some plate mail and a few leather outfits, all lined the floor, arranged into piles by function. It reached halfway up the walls. If there had been weapons, there were probably enough suits of armor to equip an entire regiment of soldiers.

But there was no Rick. And nothing that smelled like him.

I found myself tearing up. "Damn," I burst out, to stop any other emotions from outpouring. "Damn, damn, damn."

Antoine stepped into the room, looking as crestfallen as I felt. "But this doesn't make sense. Why would Sho keep his own stock of equipment and go to such lengths to hide it from his father?" he asked no one in particular.

A piece of chain mail at the top of one of the piles caught my eye, and I pulled it out. "What is this stuff?" The suit was small, maybe only a foot and a half long. It had holes for a head, legs and arms, kind of like a—

"Is this a chain mail onesie?" I asked, stunned. "I know child soldiers are 'in' right now, but seriously?" It couldn't have fit a child over the age of one.

"Sho is up to something," Antoine said. "And I still think he might know something about Rick."

"Then let's ask," I suggested grimly, sliding Prick from his sheath. The lethargy zombies were, predictably, right where we left them. Sho's arm was completely slack as I raised it and pricked his finger the slightest bit.

The effect was instant. "Ow! Son of a—who are you?" he barked, snapping from listless to overloaded in a second. And bleeding.

"Sorry," I apologized brusquely, pulling a napkin from my bag and clamping it on to Sho's hand. The tiniest starburst of blood appeared on the white.

He pulled up into his best imperious Royal stance. "Is this a kidnapping? I'll have you know my father is—"

"Minister Liu. Got it. We know," I interrupted.

"We're very sorry for the inconvenience, Prince Liu. We just have to ask you a few questions," Antoine said sweetly. Apparently, he was playing the Good Cop to my Big Bad Cop.

"I'm not answering anything," he responded haughtily. "You stabbed me, and— what did you do to them?" He turned to the other three for the first time. They were still as statues.

Well, this would have to be done the hard way. "If you want us to fix them, you have to answer our questions. Where is Rick Pearson?"

"What? How should I know?" Sho fumed. "I didn't even know Miranda was seeing someone until he went missing and we were blamed."

I stepped towards him and gave a sniff. There was probably a more subtle way to smell him, but I didn't really care. He smelled of surprise, panic, fear, and some jealousy, but nothing that would suggest he was lying. Probably.

"So the Lius had nothing to do with his disappearance?" I pushed.

"Not that I know of," Sho said. "I'm not on the best terms with my father these days, but kidnapping isn't really his modus operandi."

This was all a dead end. "So what's the deal with your secret stash of armor in there?" I asked, jerking my thumb towards the storage room. "Why keep some of your troops' equipment hidden from your father?"

"How did you—who are you, anyways?"

I brandished Prick towards him and gave my best sneer. "Your fairy godmother. Answer the question."

"They're not for troops!" he blurted out. His eyes were fixed on the dagger in front of him. As if I would actually stab him. "They're for Commontown!"

"What?" Antoine and I said in unison.

"They're magic," he admitted. "They have spells in them for protection. I just knew—the Grimmours are going to come at us with all their Academy of the Iron Wand friends, and it's going to spill out and over onto the commoners like it always does. This will turn into another East Hempstead."

"So you were planning to sell these to desperate families in Commontown to make a quick buck?" I shouted. Suddenly stabbing him didn't seem like a bad plan.

"No!" he said quickly. "No. I just felt like this whole war was partly my fault, and if I could distribute these to some of the people in the battle zones…" He made a shrugging motion with his hands.

"Wait," I said, putting Prick back in my sheath. "You're saying this is some sort of aid package for the peasants? And what do you mean you're partially responsible?"

"I wanted to fix things, if I could. I— It wasn't right for Miranda and I to be together in the first place. Our families hate each other. I should've known things would come to a head if we dated, but…I loved her."

He wasn't lying this time. The soothing fabric softener scent of affection steamed off him. But it was faded and worn, like memories of an old love affair should be. It was love firmly in the past tense. In my head, I crossed Sho Liu off the suspect list.

"How are you going to get these to the people?" Antoine asked softly.

"Well," Sho responded shakily, "I'm trying to work with the Blacksmiths' Guild to help distribute the armor to people in the war's path, but it's hard to predict where the wizards' curses could hit. Both my family and the Grimmours have holdings and safehouses scattered across the Apple." He paused. "And you turned the men from the Blacksmiths' Guild into statues."

I scratched my neck sheepishly. "Oh. Sorry about that. I can fix them."

Antoine went quiet for a second and then pulled a pad of parchment out from his pocket. "Here," he offered, scribbling a name and address on the pad. "I have a friend who can help. His name's Halvern; he was a tactician during the Crown Wars. If anyone can get that armor to the people who need it, Halvern can."

"The Crown Wars? That was almost seventy years ago," I marveled.

"Gnomes age slow. He's still sharp as a snicker-snack, though. Give him my name, and he'll help." He handed the parchment over to a stunned Sho.

"But—thank you, I—why are you doing this?"

"Because," Antoine added with a gentlemanly smile, "if the Apple burns down, I'm out of a job."

"Here," I said gently. "I'll free your friends from the spell." I pricked each of the blacksmiths first, and then the old woman.

They were slower to come out of it than Sho was, maybe because they'd had the magic in their systems for longer. Or something. I'm not an expert. While they groggily looked around, I nodded to Antoine. "We should go."

"Who are you?" Sho demanded once more. "And why are you looking for Miranda's Know-Not boyfriend?"

"We're trying to save him and stop the war," I answered carefully. "That's all you need to know. Thanks for the information." I gave him one last smile, and then walked away.

My gut was roiling. "Where next?" Antoine asked as we left the building.

I kept walking so he wouldn't see my face. "I don't know. We spent half a day investigating the Lius, only to reach a dead end."

He sighed. "I know."

"While we've been wasting time, Rick is still trapped somewhere, the Apple is going apeshit, and things are only getting worse. Even if I did find Rick, curing Jacqui's curse doesn't mean much if our neighborhood is a war zone."

"Briar," Antoine said, walking evenly with me. "Let's wait a second and talk this through." He pulled me over to the bus bench we'd sat on earlier.

As soon as my legs stopped working, my mind went into stress overdrive. "What do we do? Our two top suspects are clean. I could smell the sincerity on both Isaak and Sho."

Antoine's face dimmed for a moment, only to be replaced by the optimism that usually filled it. "We'll crack this. We've eliminated some false trails, now we just need to get back on track. If nothing is panning out by investigating Miranda's beaus, maybe we should focus on Rick."

He sounded so Grimmsdamn sure. "I guess. But going around sniffing the city hoping to pick up on a recent trail is like trying to find a—" I paused mid-sentence.

I sniffed once to make sure.

"Shit. *Shit*. I've lost the scent," I exploded.

"What?"

"Rick's emotions. I can't—I don't remember what his feelings smell like."

Antoine frowned. "Why not?"

"I don't know," I said. "This hasn't happened before. I can't believe it." Maybe the mojo I pulled out in the hallway overwrote my memory of Rick's scent.

"Do we need to go back to his dorm? I still have the card key."

My head started to pound. I was royally screwing this up. Rick would die, Jacqui would remain a cat forever, the Apple would crumble, and all because I couldn't keep a stupid scent in my stupid head—

"Briar," Antoine said, taking my hands and holding them between us, "it's okay. We'll make a quick stop by Columbia and get back out there. It'll work out. I promise."

I bit my tongue before it could say an emphatic *bullshit*.

Once again, we walked through Columbia's quad towards Wallach Hall. The co-eds were out lazing in the spring sunshine, enjoying the Friday afternoon before a weekend that I could only assume would be full of binge drinking and casual sex.

And some people are pessimistic about our generation.

I paused to watch a Frisbee drift by dreamily over the grass. It would have been nice to grab a smoothie and lie in the sun for a while. Being a noble heroine had shitty hours. I could smell all the relaxation, the joie de vivre, all the fun these kids were having. And something else that smelled familiar, although I couldn't put my finger on it.

We'd almost made it to the back entrance when a head turned on the quad and my stomach sank. The big, hippie-looking kid I had enchanted the day before was sitting in a group of similarly granola students, and when he saw me, his face broke into a love struck smile. The mystery scent I'd been smelling was his rose-induced crush on me.

I tried to avert my eyes and start moving, but he'd already jumped to his feet and run towards us. "It's you!" he panted. "The girl from housing. With the asbestos." His blocky, honest-looking face was red, and his words were all overlapping. "It's me. I'm, uh, Henry. From yesterday."

There was no way my rose could have lasted this long. Even my strongest one was maybe twelve hours, tops. Except for the one that made Cade love me for a week, and that was a special case.

When this was all over, I really needed to sort out what was happening to my magic.

"Henry, uh, hi," I mumbled, grabbing Antoine's arm and trying to use him as a shield. "I remember you. We're back to check on—you know, the asbestos."

"Oh, great. I was just about to head back to my room, actually," he hinted, deception and love spewing out from his armpits. "Do you mind if I walk with you?"

I started to protest when Antoine cut in. "Actually, that'd be great. Lily here forgot her ID card, so it'd be quicker to just go in with you." Henry all but split his face open grinning, while I gave Antoine the dirtiest glare I could muster.

The assembled students said goodbye and we were walking towards Wallach Hall when another scent hit me. "Just a second, Henry. I have to fix my boot." I feigned adjusting my foot while I put a hand on Antoine's shoulder and leaned in to whisper to him.

"There's something up there," I said softly. "Something I recognize. My Briar senses are tingling. Just be on your guard."

I smiled and caught up with Henry. The security guard on the first floor gave us a cursory glance as Henry signed us in but didn't seem to care.

The scent got stronger as we rode the elevator up to Rick's floor. It wasn't Rick's smell; I was pretty sure of that. Whatever it was made me uneasy.

The door opened, and the sense of uncertainty was almost overwhelming. But I had something to take care of first.

"Henry, which one is your room?" I asked, trying to add a little sultriness to my voice. It came out sounding like I was just congested.

Henry and Antoine's heads whipped around in tandem, and I got a little surge of pleasure from the jealousy that puffed out of Antoine.

"It's, uh, this way," Henry offered, putting his hand out in an awkward approximation of chivalry.

We came to a room right near the elevator that had the names Henry and Sam on the door. Henry unlocked the room, and before he could step aside to let me in, I grabbed his hand.

"I am so sorry about all of this," I said. Prick was already in my hand,

and when I made the smallest cut on his finger, Henry twitched and pulled his hand back. There was only confusion in his eyes as he looked at me, and I smelled all the love evaporate from him.

I gave him a little bit of a shove into his room and closed the door. If we were lucky, his confusion would keep him from calling security. At least until we got out of there.

"Will he be okay?" Antoine asked.

"Probably," I sighed.

"Here, Rick's room is this way," he said, pointing.

I shook my head. "I'll meet you there. I have to take care of something first." Dealing with Henry made me remember what it was that set my senses off in the quad.

My nose led me to another section of the floor, to a single room with the name Kristi on the door. There were construction paper signs with the name of a sorority too, but I couldn't read them. Greek letters aren't too popular in the Apple; those myths usually live in Olympus, and that is a hell of a commute.

I knocked on the door, and the blonde I met in the bathroom yesterday opened the door. She looked different. Instead of a tight black skirt, she was dressed simply in a white tee shirt and grey yoga pants. Her heavy makeup was gone, and I saw the circles under her eyes from not getting enough sleep. The one thing I recognized was the pale pink rose I'd given her, tucked behind her ear. It still radiated doubt, the same feeling I was able to sense from so far away.

She was only supposed to question herself a little…

"It's you," Kristi said tentatively. "The girl from the bathroom."

"Uh, yeah. I was just checking, to see, um—I'm from housing," I stumbled. I should just stab her and get it over with. This was getting really awkward.

"What did you do to me?" she asked simply.

My jaw dropped a little. She shouldn't have had any idea that my rose did anything to her.

"After I saw you yesterday," she continued, "I just felt…unsure. About myself. About everything. And then I started thinking about it and realized it all changed the moment I saw you in the bathroom."

Damn. Apparently, I'd encouraged her to reflect so much, she'd figured it out on her own. What did I put in that rose?

"I'm sorry," I admitted. "I didn't mean to disrupt your life. I just thought you could use a little bit of perspective."

"I had it all figured out," she mused, the rims of her eyes getting wet. "I was going to go into marketing, marry someone rich and dumb, and get a condo in the Financial District."

"I can fix it," I said quickly. "I can make what I did to you go away."

She cocked her head to the side. "Make it go away?"

I nodded. "Here, let me come in for a second, and I'll—"

"No," Kristi declared quietly.

"No?"

"I don't want to go back," she proclaimed. "I look at who I was yesterday and…it was all so simple. Too simple. I'd rather take my chances."

My eyes started to water in sympathy. For better or worse, this girl wouldn't be going back to her sheltered world of cherry glitter lip gloss and boozy sorority mixers.

"Good luck," I offered quietly and turned away.

Antoine was leaning against the wall on the other side of the floor, looking as inconspicuous as an attractive guy wearing penny loafers and a scabbard could. "All set?" he asked as I walked over.

"Let's go," I said. "Once I get a quick sniff, we can get out of here."

We walked towards Rick's room, but all I could smell was the doubt from Kristi that had permeated the floor. Apparently, these inadvertently super-charged roses I'd been handing out were extra stanky.

"I was thinking – maybe we should do a little more investigation while we're here?" Antoine prompted as we approached the door to Rick's room. He pulled out his enchanted Columbia ID card. "Maybe there's another connection to the Apple that we're missing. Something that could turn up a lead."

It sounded like we were grasping at straws to me, but now wasn't the time to say that. "Yeah, sure," I agreed. "Once I remember his scent, we can—"

There was a thumping sound from behind the door, followed by a faint rattling noise. Without hesitating, Antoine drew his sword and pressed himself against the wood. I unsheathed Prick and took a position behind the opposite door jamb.

I gave Antoine a nod, and he swiped the card down the side of the door and jerked it open with his shoulder. As he entered, he scanned the room with his sword en guard, in some sort of medieval Black Ops spin move.

At the far end of the room, Elias Clewd, wearing the same clothes he'd been wearing in his mirror transmission, was pawing through Rick's desk drawer. As we rushed into the room, I kicked the door shut with my boot. As soon as it slammed, Elais turned to face us. In his hand was what looked like a small asthma inhaler.

"Drop it!" Antoine instructed, his rapier pointed directly at Elias's throat. I wasn't sure if he meant the inhaler, or the pipe that was clenched in the old man's teeth.

"Easy, knight," Elias purred softly. He put his hands up as if to surrender, but he kept holding on to the inhaler. "Let me go, and I won't have to harm you." For the first time, I saw him as a harmless academic, with the kind of soft-spoken voice that probably put whole lecture halls to sleep.

"Harm us?" I scoffed. "We kicked your ass back in Harlem, as I recall."

"Let me go," he repeated. "Mr. Pearson needs this. Let me go give it to him." He shook the inhaler so it gave a little clicking noise.

"And let our best chance of finding him get away?" I asked.

Elias shrugged. "Your funeral, I suppose." In a flash, he took his pipe and flicked it, pouring out a massive plume of smoke that billowed towards us.

I held Prick in front of me, trusting in its disenchantment charms to work as well as they did in the alley. I swiped at the cloud, and as soon as the blade hit, little blue sparks leapt out and seemed to take some of the smoke with them. But before I could make another attack, the cloud filled the rest of the room and started to burn my throat with the acrid fume of tobacco. The fluorescent light in the ceiling dimmed to nothing as more and more smoke rushed from the pipe.

Antoine and I both doubled over, hacking and coughing, trying to get the smoke out of our lungs. I made a few more swings with Prick as I went down to my knees, but it barely did anything. My eyes became bleary, and I thought of nothing besides getting the fumes out of my body.

"Here's a tip," Elias offered calmly from the other side of the room. I heard a click as he pocketed the inhaler. "When you're fighting a smoke magus, don't close the door. Enclosed spaces are our specialty."

My throat felt ripped and raw from exertion, and I still felt the smoke burning deeper and deeper. As I fell forward onto my hands, I felt the scratch of thorns as I brushed against my bag.

"I do apologize for this," Elias explained. "And I doubt my employer would approve, but really, it will be better for everyone when you're out of the picture. Rick Pearson cannot be found."

Each cough wracked my body further until I felt even my legs tensing. When I opened my eyes, I couldn't see anything—whether from smoke or oxygen loss, I wasn't sure.

I was going to die. After all we'd been through, I was going to be smothered to death in a Columbia dorm room. They probably wouldn't find us until we started to smell.

That wasn't the ending I was going for.

I reached out blindly in the dark, sensing the roses in my sack before I could touch them. In my mind's eye they stood out, little balls of light in the overwhelming dark.

My hands found one, and I clutched it like a life raft. A thorn pierced into the meat below my thumb, but I barely felt it. And something told me that blood could only help what I was doing.

For the second time that day, I let go. I let the magic course through me, taking all of me with it, into the flower. My personality rushed into each petal as they rose up off the stem, creating a shower of little Briars that spiraled for a moment before exploding across the room. Even with the smoke roiling around me, I sensed the rest of the room, my magic touching each and every object and bouncing back like echolocation. I felt Antoine as a swirl of tendons and emotions to my left. As his body struggled to stay alive, shame and regret surged through him that he'd failed. That he failed me.

Each petal swirled around and around before honing in on Elias Clewd and shooting forward. I felt the consciousness of my body dim, even as each piece of me invaded him.

Someone screamed.

I gulped air, gulped it until my lungs felt like they would burst. I opened my eyes, and as soon as my vision focused, I saw the smoke was gone. Elias was backed up against the far wall, covered in livid blue petals. I tasted the fear coursing through him like a battery on my tongue. He screamed once more, pointed at me, and turned to smoke. Even as a cloud, he moved nervously, finding the cracks in the window casement and seeping out into the Manhattan sky.

I lurched over to the plastic trash bin and spit up into it. Although not suffocating felt great, each breath seemed like I was trying to swallow a cheese grater. I still felt the smoke inside me, burning my throat and lungs.

Antoine was still curled up on the floor, coughing, and I stumbled over to him and put a hand on his back. "Are you okay?" I sputtered.

"Isn't that—" he started before another fit. "Isn't that my line?"

I grinned and started looking through Rick's bookshelf. True to form, Rick had sorted everything by size and color. "Found it," I boasted after a minute of searching.

"A clue?" Antoine asked, getting up and walking over.

"No. Air freshener. This place smells like the men's room at The Woodsman's Log." I sprayed the calming scent of ocean breeze over the length of the room, but it didn't do much to mask the deep, biting smell of tobacco.

"How do you know what the men's room smells—"

"Never mind that," I interrupted quickly. "Why was Elias even here?

Why get asthma medication for a boy who's going to be eaten in a few hours?"

Antoine shrugged. "I guess they want to keep him alive until then, just in case the Count gives in to their demand. Will you still be able to get a scent on Rick after the smoke?"

"Crap. I don't know," I admitted. Although I didn't want any more smoke in my nose, I took a deep breath to see if I could tease out Rick's scent from beneath the smog.

My eyes began to water from the smoky haze, but I pushed through it to the smell hidden beneath. Not unlike the air freshener, Rick's emotions were clean and crisp underneath everything else.

But there was something else, too.

I went to the window and opened it all the way. Late afternoon sun made the room golden, and a cool breeze danced across my face. After a quick exhalation to clear my nose, I drew air sharply into my lungs.

There it was.

"Antoine," I said, "we need to go north. Quickly."

"Why?" Antoine replied, straightening up immediately. "Did you get a trail on Rick?"

"No. Elias. I can still smell the rose I gave him. It's like a little piece of me is going along with him. And I think I can track it."

"So if he's running scared, you're hoping he'll lead us back to the place they're keeping Rick?"

I gave a Cheshire grin. "That's the plan."

Antoine gave me a look of determination. "Then I need to go to the bathroom."

It turned out, he just needed a sink for sending a Parchedment message to the Count telling him we were on our way. After that, Antoine was able to talk me into another cab ride up Broadway to Washington Heights.

The smell of the fear I'd put into Elias was still fresh, but it became harder to track the farther uptown we travelled. I would nose my way around a building, stop, and then pause to make sure I was going the right way. After about a dozen times of this, even Antoine was getting a little frustrated.

I walked around the corner of an underground parking garage, then doubled back. My nose was distracted by the smell of a hot dog cart down the street. It'd been a while since I'd eaten anything.

"You guys look like friggin' tourists," an obnoxious voice snipped from around the corner.

"'Lil T,' I groaned. "Please say you are here to deliver us food."

T meandered lazily towards us from the food cart. As he got close, he pushed the last bit of a hot dog into his mouth and grinned at me from under his baseball cap. "The Count thought you two might need backup."

"Great," I said. "Where is it?"

The kid glowered at me. "Very funny. You can take your sarcasm and shove it up your—"

"Wait, quiet," I said, cutting T off with a gesture. "I think I picked up the scent again."

I hadn't, but it did shut him up.

It took another hour of meandering through the square brick buildings of Washington Heights before I fixed on Elias's location. It was a big concrete warehouse with an art gallery's worth of graffiti ringing the first floor. From across the street, it looked like the only entrance was a pair of doors that were chained shut.

"Are you sure this is the one your nose has been telling us about, Scooby?" T said as we looked it over.

I flicked him off with one hand and used the other to point to the top floor. "Do you recognize those plastic window covers from the mirror message? Oh, that's right. You weren't important enough to see that. I almost forgot that you're clearly a supporting cast member on this quest."

"Supporting cast?" T sputtered. "I was the friggin' Call to Adventure! I—"

"Guys, come on," Antoine sighed feebly. "We need to figure out a way to get in there."

T narrowed his eyes poisonously at me. "I can get us in. *If* Briar asks me nicely."

One of the roses closest to my hand flickered dangerously. "How about if you get us in, I won't kick your ass?"

T gave me a saccharine-sweet smile. "Now, is that any way to talk to someone who is helping you?" Lang's bangs, he was loving this.

I gritted my teeth so hard, it felt like something in my jaw was about to rupture. "T," I began, forcing a smile, "would you help us get in there?"

T's eyebrows made an unpleasant arc. "What's the magic word?"

The first dozen words that came to mind were definitely not what he was looking for. "Please?" I squeaked out.

"Of course," T said. Before I could react, he'd grabbed Antoine and me around the arms and pulled us so we were touching him. "Hold on," he warned and jumped.

The ten-block boots pushed us a good fifty feet into the air before I even had time to start yelling. My surroundings dissolved into a rush of color and movement. Then for one awesome, terrible moment at the peak of our jump, it felt like we were weightless. Unwilling to think about what was about to happen, I caught a quick glimpse of streets laid out below me, the gritty storefronts glistening in the sun. Then I was screaming and falling, and the roof of the building was rushing up way too fast.

The three of us split as we hit the concrete, and I tumbled sideways with my hands over my face. The impact knocked the wind out of me, but given how high we'd been, I felt lucky. Something in the magic of the boots must have softened our fall.

There was a large part of me that felt like staying there. Just lying down on the roof and catching my breath. And a tan. But I pushed myself up anyway.

The first thing I did was slug T in the arm. Hard. "What the hell's the matter with you? You couldn't give us a warning that you were about to shoot us into the air?"

T grinned even as he rubbed his arm. "But that wouldn't have been nearly as fun. And look, roof entrance." He pointed over to a stairwell jutting out of the roof, the industrial grey door propped open with a cinder block.

"Alright," I admitted, "I won't kill you. *This* time. But what's our game plan? Rick is right below us."

"There's no way we can sneak in. There's a smoke magus and at least two other…things there guarding Rick's cage," Antoine said.

"Elias is still terrified of me. If we're lucky, he won't stick around for long. But I've tried giving roses to things in fleshjackets before. My magic can't get through their enchantments," I said.

T drew a matching pair of slender, curved daggers from his high tops. "Then I guess it's up to the men to cut 'em up."

It was so pathetically machismo, it almost made me laugh. I slid Prick from his sheath and held it by my side. "Yeah, right. I guess I'll let you guys play with your swords while I rescue the fair princess's boy toy. Are we doing this or not?"

"I'll take point," Antoine said, looking at T's matching daggers skeptically.

We went through the door and emerged into a grimy concrete stairwell with no windows. At the bottom of the first flight was a door with a crooked six painted on it. I could hear a strange whirring noise from within, but nothing else. Antoine tried the handle slowly but found it locked, so I peered down and looked at the keyhole. There was a slight shimmer of bluish light coming out. I slipped Prick's point in the hole, and the spellock fizzled. Antoine nodded his thanks, looked at both me and T, and then kicked the door in.

The room was much the same as when I had seen it that morning in the mirror. Various pieces of old furniture were pushed up against the walls to make room for the giant cage holding Rick Pearson. Mr. and Mrs. Nibbel were at the back of the room, using an old-fashioned sharpening wheel on two giant kitchen knives. As soon as they saw us, they readied their knives and hissed.

Elias was sitting at a desk with a hamburger halfway out of its greasy paper wrapper. He jumped out of the chair and spun around, but as soon as he saw me, his look of rage changed to fear. First he turned chalk white, then he turned into smoke. I noticed that even his hamburger became part of the cloud that quickly flew out the window.

At this point, a storyteller with a baser sense of humor would say he must like his meat *smoked*. But I won't go there.

The soapy, masculine scent of Rick Pearson was stronger than I'd ever smelled it before, and I could instantly tell what he was feeling. He'd given up. He'd heard he was going to die at sundown, and he was okay with it because it would end the terrors he'd experienced since Tuesday.

I felt a rush of wind as T used his boots to leap forward in an instant and slam into Mr. Nibbel, knocking the knife out of his hand. The man gave an inhuman growl and swiped at him, but T took a step back and was suddenly across the room, out of harm's way.

Meanwhile, Antoine engaged Mrs. Nibbel in a lightning-quick swordfight. The woman and her knife kept up with him blow for blow, her arms bending at unnatural angles under the fleshjacket. Worse still, she was grinning a creepy grin full of far too many teeth.

I ran forward to Rick's cage, and the scared little Know-Not immediately pushed himself to the end as far away from me as possible. Couldn't blame him, what with the nightmare creatures who'd been threatening to eat him for three days.

"Don't worry, Rick. We're here to help." I gave him a reassuring smile, but his dark eyes were wide with fear. It took a second of looking around, but I found the door to the cage and the rusty, fist-sized iron padlock that held it shut. I looked at it for a second and swore softly. It wasn't spellocked. That meant I'd either need the real key or a blowtorch. And my guess was that the key went up in smoke with Elias.

"Briar! I could use a little help here!" T shouted. He was circling Mr. Nibbel cautiously, and I could see why. The tall, gangly man had grown hands the size of carriage wheels. Each stubby, hoagie-thick finger had a long, yellow fingernail that had been filed (or more likely, chewed) to a vicious point.

Ew.

While he was looking at T, I ran forward to take a swipe at Mr. Nibbel's back. I was within a foot of him when he spun around with a predatory speed that twisted his entire human shell. Before I could stop or change directions, the monster caught me with a backhanded blow that lifted me off my feet and sent me flying.

It was like getting hit with a medicine ball shot out of a cannon. The breath left my body in a huff, and I flailed like a rag doll. A deep bellow let me know that I'd at least scored a hit with my dagger during my spasm.

That did little to improve my mood as I flew airborne towards the concrete wall.

My thighs hit the back of an old couch, and the momentum sent the upper part of my body spinning painfully into the threadbare couch cushions that, frankly, couldn't have been much more comforting than the concrete wall.

"Briar!" I heard Antoine yell, the sounds of metal on metal ceasing for a quick second.

Before I could right myself and get up, I saw Mr. Nibbel lurch into my field of vision and wrap a giant hand around my leg. I kicked at his hand and tried to squirm away, but nothing could loosen his grip. His awful toothy grin widened, and widened, and widened, until I was sure that he would gobble me all up.

I screamed.

Just as I felt myself being lifted towards his smile, I noticed movement near his wrist. That must have been where Prick grazed him. A small tear in the hobo flesh was flapping open, exposing grey, pustule-covered skin underneath. When his arm flexed to pick me up, something in his wrist gave a wet, snapping noise, and the skin started to rip at the seams. Strips of papery white flesh started to unwrap themselves from his skin like unhooked cables. A few oozing red runes splattered out onto the walls as the fleshjacket self-destructed. There was a small explosion of twisty, evil-looking sigils made out of something viscous that was too watery to be blood. I'm no wizard, but there was some bad ju-ju holding that fleshjacket together.

The creature called Mr. Nibbel began to assume his full size as the spell disintegrated, rising up towards the ceiling. Sinewy grey skin appeared from the haze of flesh and magic.

I pulled myself up and tumbled awkwardly over the back of the couch just as Mr. Nibbel brought an arm down onto it. The wooden frame split in two like it was kindling. The fleshjacket fell all the way to the floor, revealing the form underneath. Mr. Nibbel was a good fifteen feet tall, stooped awkwardly against the ceiling. He had the frame of a wrestler, but every grey muscle was covered in pockmarks and sores. A ratty green cloth tied around his waist was all that separated me from years of therapy. His bald, squat head was ninety percent mouth, and I saw hundreds of crooked yellow teeth as he opened his mouth to roar.

"Mountain giants!" I gasped. "T! They're mountain giants!"

I scrambled to get out of the giant's reach, but I knew it wouldn't do me any good. Mr. Nibbel leaned down, his mouth opening to take my head off in one bite. His black, sandpapery tongue reached out towards me, flinging spittle into my face. I wanted to close my eyes, but something about the sheer predatory perfection in front of me made it impossible.

I heard a blast of wind from the far side of the room and was able to look away. T stood perched on the remains of the couch. In his hand he held the plastic curtain that had covered the window, letting the light spill into the room.

Mr. Nibbel roared as the light hit him and pulled back for a moment. I heard a crackling sound, like oil on a hot skillet. A second later, Mr. Nibbel came back towards me, his hands outstretched to reduce me to a squishy, delicious pulp.

His fingernails were inches from my face when they turned brown, and Mr. Nibbel became nothing more than a sandstone statue. I sent a prayer of thanks to whatever deities were still listening to me, thanking them for the sunny day.

Across the room, Mrs. Nibbel and Antoine were still in a heated exchange of blades. Antoine was bleeding from a nasty cut to his shoulder, but it didn't slow him down. He was clearly the more skilled duelist, using his blade like a paintbrush, hemming in the monster on all sides, but she had preternatural speed on her side. Her flowered dress was cut to shreds where Antoine had scored hits, but she probably barely felt it beneath her fleshjacket.

Mrs. Nibbel spared one moment to look at her statuesque husband and gave a hiss of shock. Antoine took the opportunity to grab a lamp that sat on a stack of crates and smash her over the head with it.

The Blue Fairy bless him, he was being so unchivalrous.

Whether it was the lamp or the defeat of her husband, Mrs. Nibbel gave one final roar and ran for the other side of the room. Her hands swelled up to the size of hubcaps as she ran. She gave an impressive leap through the open window, and, through the swinging shades, I saw her hit the wall on the other side of the alley. Her claws sank into the brick, and she turned around to give one final hiss before scurrying, beetle-like, up the wall and out of sight.

"Antoine, are you okay?" I said, beating him to the question before he could ask me.

He grinned and shrugged. The bleeding from his shoulder seemed to have stopped. "Just a scratch. You?"

"Definitely going to be sore in the morning after that spin move he gave me."

"That's what she said," T muttered, as if by reflex. "Now, how's about we get Fido here out of his cage before the sun sets and our stone friend gets moving again?" He knocked on the side of Mr. Nibbel's leg for emphasis.

"Who— who *are* you people?" Rick Pearson asked tremulously from the far side of the cage. His voice was hoarse and timid.

Antoine turned to him and put on his least-threatening authority-figure smile. "I'm Antoine DuCarr, and this is Briar and T. We're here to save you." He somehow avoided making the last sentence sound corny.

"But why? Why me? I don't –" His voice caught in his throat, and it looked like he was going to cry. He buried his dirt-stained head in his hands, and all I could see was his matted black hair.

"Rick," I said, trying to keep my voice even, "I'll explain everything. Don't worry. But we need to get out of here, so you're going to have to work with us. You can trust us. Your girlfriend's father sent us."

Rick stopped shaking and pulled his head out of his hands, but his broad face was twisted in confusion. "What girlfriend?"

My mouth failed me for a moment. "Wait, what?" I finally stammered.

Antoine shot me a look of panicked concern. "Your girlfriend. Miranda Grimmour. Do you remember Miranda?"

"Miranda?" Rick asked. "Miranda's not my girlfriend."

A knot formed in my stomach that had nothing to do with recently being punched by an NBA-sized cannibal. Despite what a lot of the Old Stories said, magic couldn't make you forget things.

Although, magic wasn't supposed to be able to change your feelings, either.

I caught a waft of Rick's feelings, and I could tell he was being evasive. It was the same feeling of hiding that I'd sensed in his dorm room. And as much as I didn't want to shake his fragile mental state and see what fell out, we didn't have time to dance around the issue. "But you know Miranda?" I prompted.

"Well, yeah. I—uh, I'm dating her brother."

That took a second to process.

"Oh. You're dating Tarris?" Antoine asked. T took a step back from the cage and looked squeamish.

Rick nodded, a little embarrassed. He didn't smell comfortable, but at the same time, I sensed a glimmer of joy when he was able to say it out loud.

The love I'd smelled in his room wasn't for Miranda.

"Okay," I began. "Okay. But why would the Grimmours care that much to make up such an elaborate lie? I couldn't care less."

"The Royals aren't all as accepting," Antoine said. "Sure, it's much better nowadays than even five years ago, but having a gay son would definitely damage the Count's reputation in some circles in the Apple."

I smelled a puff of anger and confusion from Rick. "What apple? What are you talking about? Royals? Counts?"

Crap, this was going to be an awkward trip back to Grimmour Tower.

"Rick, I promise I'll explain everything. But first we need to get you out of this cage." The kidnappers had already blown the Compact to hell by revealing magic to Rick, so I might as well tell him what he needed to know to survive.

"You guys look around for the keys. I'll see what I can do with this lock," T said. He reached in his sports sack and pulled out a set of lock picks.

I rifled through the small camp the Nibbels had made in the back of the room while Antoine looked around Elias's desk. They'd set up a camper stove, and there was a cooler nearby that smelled distinctly of meat. No keys, but I found an impressive spice rack.

"Rick," I asked casually, "what have they been feeding you?"

The Know-Not's face paled a little. "Steak, mostly. A lot of meat."

"With spices?"

"Yeah, really strong ones. How'd you know?"

There wasn't a delicate way to put this. "They were fattening you up. The mountain giants were feeding you spices so you'd taste better. It's an old ogre trick. That's why they wait the traditional three days before eating someone." Welcome to the Poisoned Apple, kid.

"Oh. Okay. Gotcha," Rick answered robotically. The tart smell of shock was thick on him, and with a little luck, it would pull him through until we got him back to the Grimmours safe and sound.

"And just to cover our bases: No, this isn't an elaborate prank. Yes, magic is real. No, you're not dreaming."

Rick nodded distractedly, but I could tell his mind was racing.

I remembered our run-in with Elias in Rick's dorm. "Did they give you your asthma medicine?" I asked.

"Yeah," Rick replied. "I was having a lot of trouble breathing a couple hours ago, and that professor-looking guy left and came back with my inhaler."

I frowned. It still didn't make any sense. Why medicate a kid who was on the menu for the evening?

"Got it!" T called from the other side of the cage. The big, thick lock clicked open, and he was able to pull the door open with a scraping sound. Rick lurched forward out of the cage but stumbled on weak legs.

"Easy," I said, walking towards him with my hands outstretched. I considered giving him a little pick-me-up rose just so he'd calm down for the trip back but decided against it. The kid's head had been through enough in the past two days. Rick went over to the frozen statue of Mr. Nibbel and looked at it vacantly.

"Alright, Rick. We're going to take you back to Tarris, and you can finally put this behind you, okay? You're going to be fine." My brain could only come up with platitudes. I'm not the best in these situations.

"Uh, Briar?" Antoine said from over at Elias's desk. "We have a problem."

Before I could ask him what was wrong, he drew a small piece of felt from the desk and showed it to us. It was a Royal Pennon, with a wolf rampant represented in the dark blue colors of the Grimmours.

My mind went blank for a moment before a horrible feeling took root in my stomach.

"What the hell does that mean? Elias was working for the Grimmours?" I swore liberally.

Antoine's face was devoid of any emotion and his voice was hollow as he stated, "Royal Pennons don't work unless the vassal is following the direct orders of a Noble."

"So this was a set up? Count Grimmour planned the whole thing?" I asked the room in general.

T's face scrunched up with thought. "But why would he hire you to find Rick? I know the Count is a little Machiavellian, but he wouldn't plan to kill his son's boyfriend, would he?"

Antoine leaned against the desk. "This doesn't make any sense."

"I don't believe it," I said hollowly.

"Maybe the smoke magician did something to the Pennon's magic…" Antoine ventured weakly.

A thought struck me, and I reached in my satchel and pulled out the folder of addresses Isaak gave me. Thumbing through the entries for the Grimmours, I found the warehouse in Washington Heights where we were. "It's in here. It says this property has belonged to the Grimmours for decades."

Rick wrapped his arms around himself. "Would someone please tell me what's going on? What does that little flag thing mean?" he asked quietly. No one responded.

"I think we were never supposed to find Rick," I said. "The Count wanted to give the appearance of looking for Rick, but it was all just an excuse to start a war with the Lius."

"Why, though?" Antoine said, rubbing his forehead. "Why go through all of this? What could he possibly gain by provoking a war?"

"Power. Reputation. I don't know," I ranted. "Who understands the games these people play? At the very least, he would get his son's embarrassing boyfriend out of the way."

"I'm sure he had a good reason," T said. "A reason we're not going to figure out by standing around here. Let's take Rick back and ask him ourselves."

There was a tense silence for a moment. "You're kidding, right?" I scoffed. "He was going to have a Know-Not devoured by giants. We're not bringing Rick anywhere near him."

T gave me a look of surprise. "Briar, that's not our call. You're a vassal of the Grimmours now. He hired us to do a job. You're just the delivery girl. Right, Antoine?" he said, turning to face Antoine across the room from me.

As soon as T turned his back to me, I brained him with Prick's hilt. To my credit, he crumbled like a pack of cards.

"Briar!" Antoine sputtered. "What the hell?!"

I looked up from where T was lying on the floor and met Antoine's eyes. "He's just unconscious."

"Because you hit him!" Antoine said, somewhat hysterically.

My fingers found a rose and took it from my bag. "What are you going to do, DuCarr? Because there's no way in Sinbad's seas that I'm going to take that poor boy back to the man who did this to him." Antoine just stared at me, but I saw his hand poised near his sword hilt.

For a moment we just stared at each other, my rose in front of me. I wasn't even sure what emotion I would hit him with. Confusion, maybe? Rebellion? Compassion?

In my peripheral vision, I saw Rick looking back and forth between us, still confused as ever. Finally, the tension was too much for him, and he started crying.

Like we'd been lifted from a spell, Antoine and I both looked away. "Of course we're not taking him back," Antoine agreed. "I don't know what I was thinking. But did you have to knock T out?"

"There was no way he'd go along with it," I said. It was just sort of sinking in that I'd knocked someone unconscious. "And I don't know him well enough to be able to tell how a rose would affect him. Here, drag him into the cage."

Antoine looked shocked but lifted up the little guy and put him gingerly on the same bundle of rags that Rick had been sleeping on. I got the cooler from the back of the room and put it in there for him.

"I'll get Cade to send some plainclothes Red Hoods out here. They can let him out and take care of the Nibbels."

I took off his ten-block boots and placed them outside the cage. I didn't think they'd get to him through the cage bars, but who knew with magic? The cage door closed with a satisfying clang, and I kicked T's lockpicks out of reach.

"Who are you people?" Rick asked again from the wall he'd slumped onto.

I sighed and knelt down in front of him. "I'm Briar."

"Antoine DuCarr, Knight Bachelor," Antoine said. He frowned a little when the words didn't have his desired effect.

"I'm Rick," he stuttered. "Art history major."

"Rick, is there someplace we can take you where you'll be safe? The man who had you kidnapped could still find you."

"What about Tarris?" Rick asked. "Is he safe?"

"The man who did this to you is his father. I can't imagine that he'd…" Antoine trailed off.

"Tarris will be fine," I decided. "We need to get you somewhere where you won't be found."

"I need to get to Tarris," Rick said, his voice getting stronger.

"That's not wise," Antoine cautioned. "If the Count finds you, he could kill you. And getting you into the Apple while there's a war starting—"

"What apple?" Rick exploded. "You people keep talking and telling me what to do, but you won't explain anything! I was just chained up by monsters for three days, and all you can say is that I should go run and hide while my boyfriend is in danger? Well, screw you! I'll find him myself."

Wobbly and weak, Rick pushed himself off the wall and started for the door. He put a shoulder into Antoine as he passed.

I liked this kid.

"Rick, wait. I'm sorry," I said. "Really. I can't imagine what you've been through, and we're treating you like a child."

Rick stopped but didn't turn around.

"And you're right. Tarris could be in danger. But Antoine and I can go get him. If you can just think of a place you could stay, one where you wouldn't be found, we'll find Tarris and bring him to you—"

"I'm going with you," Rick snapped. "I don't care what sort of X-Files-Harry-Potter bullshit you people are wrapped up in, I'm making sure my boyfriend is safe."

"But Rick—"

"I love him," he said, turning around. "And unless you're planning on locking me back in that cage, you can't stop me from going to him."

I smelled him, and I knew it was true. In the past five minutes, Rick's feelings had coalesced; he was in love and didn't doubt it anymore.

It was a feeling I didn't smell very often.

I looked to Antoine, and, despite the reservations written clearly across his face, he nodded.

"Alright," I agreed. "We'll take you to Tarris. But first, there are some things I should explain."

The subway was surprisingly empty as we rode downtown towards Central Park. Rick and I took a bench in the back of the car, while Antoine stood protectively over us. We decided we didn't need to rush. Breaking into Grimmour Tower while they were on full red-alert would be suicidal enough, but waiting for the cover of darkness might give us the edge we needed.

"So, Tarris comes from a secret world of elite royalty who are currently planning on going to war over their fairy tale kingdom?" Rick asked. Back in the Nibbel's nest, we found him a purple track jacket to cover up his torn clothes. He looked a little less homeless that way.

"Yes, basically," I said.

"Hmph. He always told me he was from Westchester."

"Oh, I guess Castle Fortnight is a little like Westchester," I agreed. "Lots of disaffected rich people. Just with swords. And sorcery."

Rick mulled this over for a few moments. "But why does the Poisoned Apple exist? When did it start?"

That stopped me for a second. It wasn't something I really thought about. "I mean, why does Staten Island exist?" I quipped. "That's a much better question."

"The Apple isn't the only World Slip," Antoine said. "They've been found all over, throughout history. There's Shangri-La, Olympus, Mag Mell, Atlantis, Tripura, Alfheim, Mount Penglai…"

"I hear Cockaigne is nice in the spring," I offered.

"But those are just in stories," Rick said adamantly.

"Stories collect around groups of people," Antoine reasoned. "So do World Slips. That's just how it is."

"But do people tell stories about these places because they exist, or do they exist because people tell stories about them?"

A recording cheerily announced the 72nd Street stop. It was kinda sad the conductors didn't talk as much as they used to.

"Chicken. Egg," I muttered briskly. "C'mon, Rick. This is our stop."

This half of Central Park was already being shaded by the penthouses of the Upper West Side. The shadows made the damp, loamy smell of the woods that much more delicious. Central Park was packed. It seemed New York had decided to take a break from cubicles and cramped apartments to taste the spring air.

We passed a couple jogging on the path through the Rambles towards Belvedere Castle. "Remember, Rick," I warned. "I'll do the talking when we get into the Apple. I know the Doorman, but it's still a little difficult getting a Know-Not— a nonmagical person— into the Apple for the first time."

"They've really cracked down on immigration recently," Antoine contributed. "Everyone is afraid that brownies are going to come in and take human jobs."

Even in the dimness of the woods, I caught Rick's horrified expression. It took a second for me to replay the conversation in my head. "Actual brownies!" I added quickly. "As in, helpful household spirits."

"They'll work for practically nothing," Antoine said as we came out onto the deck of the castle. A huge group of blonde, statuesque tourists were taking pictures of each other and talking excitedly in Swedish. Across Turtle Pond, the open fields were dotted with picnickers and sunbathers escaping the approaching shadows.

I pulled out my pocket watch. We still had time to kill. "Let's wait here a few minutes," I suggested. "Is there anything else you want to ask, Rick?"

He took a moment as we walked over to the balustrade overlooking the pond. The poor kid still looked battered and bruised, but ever since he'd decided to help us find Tarris, he had taken on a much more energetic appearance. Under the dirt he was a good-looking kid, with a bright, wide smile that he'd shown a few times on the way over. He was a little on the short side, at least compared to me, but had the sort of taut, easy muscles that came from regular exercise.

Good for Tarris. If you were going to have a secret boyfriend kidnapped by mountain giants, at least he could be easy on the eyes.

While Rick was thinking, he put a fingernail into his mouth to chew absentmindedly. As soon as it touched his lips, he pulled it out and looked at it. "What the—um, why do I taste so good?"

"That must be the troll spices," I explained. "It'll be a couple days before you sweat them all out. Better than being eaten, I suppose."

"Sure," he agreed. The faint smell of shock still hung around him. He put his arms on the balustrade and started watching a pair of swans lazing in the pond. "So how come Tarris never told me all this? About the Apple. How come he lied to me?"

"I'm sure he wanted to tell you," I said, "but he couldn't. The first law of the Apple is the Compact: 'We never purposefully reveal the Apple to non-fey. It must reveal itself to those it deems worthy.' Even the Royals are bound by the Compact. It's enforced by powerful magic."

"But he made up a whole life while we were together," Rick said. "He told me all about how his dad was some corporate lawyer, how his stepmom was a big religious nut, the games he and his sister used to play on their property upstate—"

"Most of that was probably true. Or at least as true as he could make it. His mom is really religious, and being a Royal does involve lots of meetings and hostile takeovers," I said. "Everyone tells stories, even when they don't want to."

"I feel like I don't know him at all," he whispered softly, looking at the lake.

His words and a puff of desperation hung in the air for a moment. "Does that change anything? Because if you're going to back out of the rescue mission," I pointed out, "now is the time to do it. Your first trip to the Apple...it changes you."

Under his melancholy was still the metallic tang of certainty. "No," he said, resolute. "I love him. I don't have any other choice." There was a pause. "Ugh. In the future, stop me from getting that melodramatic."

I smirked and patted him on the shoulder. "Will do. If you don't mind me asking, how did this all start? What were you doing when you got nabbed?"

"I've been trying to piece that together. I remember being in my dorm that morning, and then..." He screwed up his face with effort. "I remember a note being slid under my door. Then things are hazy, and I was in an alley, and then I don't remember anything until I woke up in that cage."

"You got a note?" I asked.

"That's the last memory I have. I opened up the note, there was a flash, and then I was in the alley."

"Shit," I swore. "That sounds like a geas."

"You mean a goose?" Rick said.

"No, a geas. It's a spell. I've heard of them; they're powerful, illegal magic. Pretty rare. It's the closest thing to my magic the Academy has ever come up with." I had told Rick about the basics of my ability after I'd given a rose to a down-on-his-luck subway drummer to cheer her up.

"What do they do?"

"Well, in the stories I've heard, wizards put a geas on someone and they have to fulfill some sort of quest, or obligation. That must have been the source of all that fake excitement in that alleyway in Harlem. It's what lured you there, where no one could see you being abducted."

"So they brainwashed me?" Rick said.

"Basically. I'm shocked Elias and the person he's working for have access to that kind of magic."

"Magic," Rick said quietly. "Wow. I can't believe it's real."

"Rick," I started, peeling away from the overlook, "trust me. You ain't seen nothing yet." Something occurred to me. "Do you know anything about psychology?"

"I took Psych 101," he answered, "but that was two years ago. Why?"

I looked longingly out at Turtle Pond. "Forget it. Just a crossword clue. Does the phrase 'Jung's coincidences' mean anything to you?"

Rick stared at me. "Uh, no. Sorry. Should we get back to the part where we rescue my boyfriend and stop a war?"

I pulled myself away from the wall. If I was going to die, it would have been nice to at least get that damn crossword solved. "Yeah. Sorry. Let's go."

Antoine met us by the door into the castle. "Are you ready?" Rick nodded, and Antoine held the door open for us and followed us into the murky interior of Belvedere Castle.

I led the way towards the bottom of the stairwell while Antoine played tour guide from behind us. "Belvedere Door is the most frequented of the Doors into the Apple. It was enchanted in the 1870s, shortly after the castle was finished. It is known as one of the more stable Passways, at least for Commoners."

We made it to the bottom of the stairwell, where the Door itself glimmered slightly in the gloom. I turned to Rick. "Here we are. The Crossing of the First Threshold." Rick gave me a puzzled look. "Joseph Campbell? *The Hero with a Thousand Faces*? Nothing?" It was required reading at Witchdale High.

Rick shrugged. "I'm an art history major."

"It's a book about stories," Antoine explained. "You're at the part where your story changes. You go into the woods. You pull the sword from the stone. You open the box everyone tells you not to."

"You leave Tatooine with Han," I said.

Rick took a second to absorb this. "Okay. I'm ready."

"Can you see the door?" I asked.

"Door?" Rick asked. He squinted in the darkness. "Wait…yes. Has that always been here? The shape of the keystone in the arch is totally wrong for the period when this was built."

I smiled. This was a good sign. If he could see the door, it meant the magic of the Apple was close to accepting him.

"Open it," I said.

Rick made a swing and a miss, passing his hand through the air a couple inches above the handle. But on his second try he caught hold of it, turning to me for approval. I nodded.

I hoped he knew what he was getting himself into.

As soon as the handle clicked, coppery sparks started racing up and down the metal of the frame, outlining the entire door with light from the other side. Rick startled and pulled back, but his hand remained on the door handle. The looping designs etched in the door seemed to slither their way towards the handle, and soon both the carvings and sparks were spinning like a galaxy around Rick's hand. There was a moment of stillness as Rick looked at the magic in front of him with fear and wonder. Then the enchantment struck, flittering up Rick's arms and covering his body before winking out.

Rick's grip finally slipped from the handle, and he stumbled backwards, landing roughly on the opposite wall. He looked down at his hand in amazement. "What—what the…?" he gasped.

"You're one of us now," Antoine answered. "You've been marked."

Rick looked over his hands like he'd never seen them before. The magic of the Apple was clearly visible on him; there was the little oscillation around his edges that marked him as fey. He'd never be fully normal again.

None of us seemed to want to break the silence with small talk, so we went through the door into the hallway beyond like a group of penitent monks. Rick gaped at the carvings, the gargoyles, the columns—all the masterful stonework that filled the corridor. At a few points in the journey, we waited for him to examine a piece more closely. To an art history buff, this probably was as close as he could get to an honest-to-goodness fairy tale.

Finally, the stone crumbled away and the forest took over. There was still a little more sunshine left on this side of the Door—one of the weird peculiarities of the Apple. Most of the time, things like sunsets and phases of the moon matched up, but you never knew. Constancies in the Apple were like an honest wolf: rare.

We came out into the woods proper and towards the hill that held the Doorman's Arch. Horace was there, as usual, in a powder blue suit, sitting on a stool and playing a game of Chinese checkers against himself.

He glanced up at us, looked down, and then got up hastily as he noticed Rick's presence.

"Miss Briar! Mr. Antoine! Who is this?" he said, clearly surprised. People slipped through the cracks into the Apple all of the time, but they didn't usually go through the front Door. So to speak.

"Horace, meet Rick Pearson," I introduced. Horace didn't answer to the Royals, and I trusted him completely. The Count wouldn't know about us bringing Rick into the Apple.

"Hi, I'm Rick. Nice to meet you." Rick offered a hand, his full Midwestern politeness coming to the fore.

Horace shook his hand vigorously and adjusted his monocle. I didn't know if Horace had a background in magic, but it seemed like he was giving Rick some sort of aura reading or chi analysis or something.

"Miss Briar," Horace began quietly, "please tell me you haven't done something stupid and violated the Compact."

"Nope," I responded. "I mean, I've done some stupid things, but that wasn't one of them. That honor belongs to a smoke mage and his monster squad." I gave Horace the basic sketch of what happened to Rick over the past few days. As I spoke, the old man's round face melted from shock to concern.

Good old Horace. What a softie.

"So you've been snatched by monsters, held for three days, and you're now on a heroic quest to rescue your true love? Do I understand that correctly?" Horace said to Rick.

"Uh…" Rick looked to me, and I gave him a swift nod. "I guess. Yeah."

"Well. With that track record, you'll be a full Apple citizen by the end of the week. Permission to enter granted," Horace beamed, shaking Rick's hand.

We said our goodbyes to Horace and started towards the outskirts of Commontown. A handful of people were passing the other way, some carrying giant suitcases or steamer trunks, all with a distinct look of worry on their faces.

Preemptive refugees. Willing to leave everything they had to escape the coming battles. Muscles in my jaw clenched involuntarily.

The impending war didn't do much to squelch the gaiety of the rest of the Commoners getting off work. The streets were abuzz. Trolls lumbered here and there carrying briefcases in their trash can-sized fists, while a group of chattering nereids in cocktail dresses searched for a happy hour. A swarm of wisps, having already finished their race to light up the streetlamps, amused themselves by spelling out dirty words above a bodega.

"Where to?" Antoine asked as Rick spent a few more moments with his jaw on the ground.

"I say we stop by my place," I suggested. "Get Rick a clean set of clothes and a weapon. Then we hit Castle Fortnight, before Elias and the Count figure out Rick's gone."

"And how exactly do you plan on doing that?"

"If you can get us onto the castle grounds, I know a way into Grimmour Tower where we won't be seen."

"Sounds like a plan," Antoine said casually.

There was a pause. "No, not really," I pointed out. "But it's the closest thing we have to one."

Rick was silent as we walked the streets of the Apple towards Havmercy Park, taking in all the wonderful and terrible things the Apple had to offer.

I tried to place myself in his shoes, coming from a small town in Indiana all the way to this place between places.

A pair of ten-foot tall ice wights in pantsuits came out of a wine bar, their spindly legs ending in spectral Monolo Blahniks. A handsome cab driver was having a heated argument in Old French with a headless horseman who'd cut him off. It was like a carnival, a children's storybook, Paris, and a fever dream had all gotten off work at the same time and were sharing a flask of tequila on the commute home.

"So, how come there's no electricity here?" Rick said after he'd recovered his senses a little.

"Whatever causes World Slips makes the laws of physics a little wonky," I explained. "People have tried to get things like electricity and gunpowder to work, but technology just doesn't agree with the Apple. And we have magic, so it's not really worth it."

"Is my phone going to be okay?" Rick asked, pulling out a sleek little Samsung.

"Probably," I responded, "but it won't work while we're here."

Rick pressed a few buttons. "Huh. My background turned into a giant pentagram, and I have ten new texts from someone named 'The Erlking.'"

"Don't answer," I said quickly.

Rick jumped as a movement from the garbage outside of a twenty-four hour diner caught his eye. A wild, hairy man, probably a good seven feet tall, emerged from the pile of refuse and held out a coffee can. His skin had the burnished glean of rusted iron, and a variety of swirling tribal tattoos were etched into his metallic skin.

I slipped him a fiver, in the hopes that he'd invest in something to cover his teensy little loincloth. This wasn't a romance novel.

"What was that?" Rick muttered under his breath as we kept walking.

"An Eisenhans," I replied. "They're like barbarians, but, uh…made of iron." It was at times like this when I wished I could explain some of the stranger denizens of the Apple. But they simply are what they are.

We made it to my cottage, and Rick stopped short a few feet outside the door. "You *live* here?" he marveled. "It's like a Kinkade."

"Eh," I said, shrugging. "The rent is low." I opened the door and led them inside. "Hello? Guys?" I called out. There was no answer, but I heard the sound of the magic mirror from the living room.

We walked into the living room to find my roommates sitting rapt in front of the mirror. Cade had gotten it mostly fixed, so the only detail off about the newscaster on the screen was that he was constantly rolling his eyes.

"…with reports coming in on the first outbreak of warfare in the Furrier's Quarter between Liu and Grimmour forces. No casualties have been reported, but eyewitnesses claim there has been an exchange of curses on both sides—"

I dropped my bag and rushed to the couch. "When did this happen?" I exclaimed, forgetting any sort of pleasantries.

Alice tilted her face towards me, but her eyes were still looking at the mirror. "Just a few minutes ago," she said, her voice flat. My normally vivacious roommate looked drained, her pajamas clinging to her frame as she hugged her legs into herself.

I sat stunned for a few seconds, absorbing the information that was greeting most of the jovial commuters of the Apple as they got home. The boiling point had been reached, and we were facing violence. Not the personal, narrative-friendly duels we were used to, but war, brutal and dehumanizing.

Cade was still in his Red Hood outfit with his axe at his side. It looked as if he, too, had been drawn into the mirror's story just as he arrived home. "Who is that?" he asked, breaking eye contact with the screen just long enough to see Rick.

"Oh, sorry," I replied distractedly. "Rick, these are my roommates—Cade, Alice, and Jacqui. This is Rick Pearson."

Rick barely even flinched when Jacqui looked up and said, "Pleased to meet you." Apparently, talking cats weren't as terrifying as shape-shifting cannibals.

"*That's* Rick Pearson?" Cade asked. "The non-fey everyone is looking for?"

"Wait, what?" Rick asked. I'd explained the war situation to him on the trip over, but apparently he underestimated how his name was plastered all over the Apple.

"Are you going to stop this?" Alice asked, a note of pleading in her voice.

I couldn't even meet her eyes. "We're going to try," I answered grimly. "It's complicated. It looks like Count Grimmour set the whole thing up." I briefly told them about the Pennon we'd discovered along with Rick.

Alice shook her head. "Isn't there someone we can take the evidence to?"

Cade shook his head. "Getting enough Royals to agree to investigate the allegations would take weeks. Commoners don't have a lot of options when it comes to accusing Nobles of treason. Even if they violated the Compact."

"I think there's something we're missing," Jacqui said. "You guys are forgetting the usual culprit behind these sorts of things."

I gave her a confused look, but Alice beat me to the punch. "The wicked stepmother," she ventured.

"The Grimmour Pennon didn't necessarily come from the Count," Jacqui explained. "And I'm willing to bet that Braselyn, being so religious, wouldn't be happy about her stepson's boyfriend."

I swore harshly under my breath. "Do you think she could've done it?"

Antoine shook his head. "We can see if Tarris has any information. If Braselyn is responsible, we might have a better chance at stopping this war. But for right now, we need to get to Grimmour Tower."

He was right. Just when I thought we'd figured things out, more wrinkles started to appear.

"I'm coming with you," Cade declared, hefting his axe.

Antoine eyed the worn weapon with distaste. "This is a stealth mission. The fewer people we have, the better chance—"

"So you're bringing an untrained little Know-Not as backup?" Cade snarled, turning on him.

"Guys!" I yelled. At this rate, I was going to have to hose them down. Their macho rivalry cut the air like the smell of cat piss. "Give it a rest." I turned to Cade and tried to put a pleading look in my eyes. "Cade, if you break into Castle Fortnight with us, you can pretty much kiss your career in the Red Hoods goodbye."

"What about him?" Cade accused, pointing a little too vigorously at Antoine with his axe. "He's breaking all his knightly oaths to do this."

That gave me pause. Was Antoine throwing away his future by standing up to the Grimmours?

"This is the quest I was assigned to," Antoine said simply. "Find and protect Rick Pearson. And if we're right, and the Grimmours violated the Compact, I'll be fine. A Red Hood, however, has no right to interfere in Royal affairs—"

I raised my hand to cut him off and tried to speak in calm tones. "Cade, I can't let you do this. Besides, if things go south and the Apple erupts into war, you need to be here to protect Alice and Jacqui." All three of my roommates started to protest, but I beat them to the punch. "This is *my* story, guys, and I can't put you in harm's way to finish it."

Everyone was silent for a moment before Alice cleared her throat and sprang up from the couch, a little of her old energy back. "Alright, I'll make everyone snacks." She bustled off to the kitchen. If I knew her, and I did, her snacks would have enough sugar to bring us just shy of an insulin coma.

"Okay, Antoine, why don't you help Rick find a weapon? Our weapons closet is at the top of the stairs, on the left. Cade, can you grab Rick some clothes? I'm going to pick a few more roses, and then we need to get out of here A.S.A.P. before the violence spreads."

Everyone split up, and I walked out the door into the back garden. The sun had already set, giving us a little covering darkness for our stealth mission. Not as much as I would like, but it would have to do. Good thing I knew my garden, because the flowers were barely more than dark shapes in front of me, moving slightly in the twilight.

I walked swiftly towards the first rose bush and held out my hand. The roses seemed to turn themselves towards me, like sunflowers towards the sun.

This was getting strange, but now was *so* not the time.

As I picked the first one, a voice from behind me spoke suddenly, making me jump and jam my thumb into a thorn. "Briar? Oh, sorry," Jacqui apologized. She must've come out behind me without me noticing.

I stuck my pricked thumb in my mouth. "Ow. Grimmthdammit. Whadth up?"

She padded away from the door nervously and started rubbing herself against one of the stone planters near the door. "I'm scared, Bri."

I started pulling a few choice roses off the bush. "Me too."

"It's just this war…" she began quietly. "I don't know if it's going to stop. I feel like we might need to—leave."

"You mean, wait it out in Manhattan for a few nights?"

Jacqui jumped up on a wooden bench, and I went over to sit with her. "Leave the Apple. I've read the history books, Bri. These things don't blow over in a few weeks. The Crown Wars lasted five years. And now that it's actually come to bloodshed…"

"Don't even say that, Jacqui. We're staying in the Apple. This is our home. And we have to stay to get you fixed."

"We don't, though," Jacqui argued. "We could just leave. Go far, far away. The stories say if you get far enough away from the Apple and the other World Slips, curses just fade after a while. I've heard almost all magic dies once you reach Nebraska."

I paused for a moment. I'd heard those stories too but never thought anyone actually tried to follow their advice. The Apple was where we lived. It was magic. It was life. I couldn't picture leaving it for anything.

"Think about it," Jacqui pleaded fervently. "We could go right now. Get out before it all burns down around us. Please, Briar."

The thought sickened me. Not because the Midwest could possibly be that bad, but because I realized after all the pain Jacqui had gone through from her transformation, she'd become a coward. And I was responsible.

"Jacqui," I said softly, "please don't ask me to do that. You know I can't. That boy in there needs me. If there's a chance I can stop anyone from dying in this war, I have to try."

Jacqui looked out quietly for a moment towards the Afterwoods. It was dark enough by now that they were a heavy blue silhouette against the azure sky. Deep, deep within them, I saw something glowing with a milky white light. Probably a White Lady or a sprite out for a sunset stroll. Maybe even a unicorn, although they were rarely spotted this close to civilization these days.

Sure, the Afterwoods were full of monsters and robbers and Perrault knew what else, but I couldn't picture living a single day without their wild presence.

Jacqui looked up at me and gave me a Cheshire cat grin. "I guess I knew you wouldn't walk away from all this. Just promise me you'll be careful and you'll get out of there if it's too dangerous."

"I will," I promised. Even in my thoughts, I'd been so cavalier, but something about being with Jacqui made me realize how stupid that was. She was always there to remind me that there were consequences to every action.

"Good," Jacqui said. "Now, I'm going to go inside and help Alice with those snacks." Even before she was a cat, Jacqui's method of helping in the kitchen usually amounted to licking the bowls clean after a baking project. She pushed the door open with her paw and scuttled inside.

I made one last sweep of the garden, filling my satchel until it was almost overflowing with roses. Who knew what I might need to make it through the night?

Just as I made my way back to the door, it clicked open and Cade came out into the dusk. He'd changed out of his Red Hood outfit and was dressed simply in an off-white henley and a pair of dark jeans. His sandaled feet made no sound as he walked over and took a seat on the bench that Jacqui had just left. He didn't say anything, but his eyes were serious as they found mine and he gestured to the empty seat next to him.

Cripes, was there a sign somewhere that said, "For dramatic confrontation, sit here"?

I settled in beside him, and as usual, I felt the heat generated from his body against my skin, drawing instant goose bumps.

"I got Rick some clothes," Cade began. "He's changing now, and then you can head out."

Cade Arden, king of the oblique conversation starter.

"Are you sure you should be bringing Rick along?" he continued after I said nothing.

"I didn't want to," I admitted, "but there's not much I can do. It's his story as much as it is mine, at this point. He's got to rescue his prince."

"And you're sure that's what you want to do? Steal Tarris out from under the Grimmour's noses?"

"If Jacqui is right and this was Braselyn's plan all along, maybe we can stop the Count from continuing to fight the Lius." The roses in front of me bobbed a little in a cool breeze, just barely illuminated by the lights from our house. "I just don't know anymore."

"I don't have to tell you to be careful," Cade said. "If Count Grimmour catches you, there's no one to protect you."

"I know."

"If something happens to you…" he said softly, almost to himself.

The feeling of his hand close to mine was still throbbing through my arm, and it felt like the cool spring night was suddenly the inside of a pressure cooker. And, against my better judgment, I leaned in a little further and gave Cade a quiet sniff.

He was worried and flustered. The scents hit my nose in a jangle of anxiety and stress. Cade had been ungrounded. The Royals he was so quick to defend had finally done something he couldn't forgive. The people he trusted to run the Apple were threatening to burn it all down.

I knew I shouldn't, but I dug a little deeper through the emotions wafting off Cade. Most of it was nothing new. I'd known him for what felt like forever, so smelling that he was really angry about injustice, or that he felt most comfortable with his axe in his hand, wasn't new to me. But I'd never explored his emotions with my magic before.

There was something oddly pliant about his feelings that I'd sensed the night before when I was on empath-tea. Everything was normal, but it was like I was sensing it through Saran wrap or smelling it through a funnel. His emotions had a disjointed, unreal quality to them. I'd never run into anything like it before.

"You're still not over what happened at prom," I finally intuited, not looking at him. Ethics be damned; smelling his emotions was probably the only way I was ever going to figure out what was going on between us.

"Would you be?" he said, shifting uncomfortably on the bench. Away from me.

"I don't know, Cade. I don't know what you went through. We never talk."

"There's nothing you can do," he said, but it wasn't an accusation. I sensed a subtle shift in him, towards a deep-rooted resignation.

"At least tell me. After everything with Jacqui, with us…I just want to hear your side of the story."

He took a moment, and I could smell resolve gathering. He settled back into his seat, and we were still close enough to be almost touching. When he spoke, he kept his deep voice steady and fairly monotone, but I recognized the emotions swirling turgidly beneath.

"After you gave me the rose at prom and it wore off, I could still feel some of it affecting me. There was love there, and I—there was no way of telling if it came from you, or if I really felt that way. I'd never really had feelings that strong before, and it was like…I couldn't trust them. I didn't know what parts of me were really *me*. I guess I still don't."

The fairy light in the woods started to blur as my eyes filled up with tears. "I didn't know. I never meant to…"

"I know, and it's not fair of me to blame all of this on you, but— but that's what I'm going through."

I had no idea my magic had done so much to him. My eyes stung, and all I could do was hope Cade couldn't see me in the darkness. "I'm sorry."

He moved, and before I knew it, he put his arm around my shoulder and pulled me into his shoulder. I squeezed my eyes tight and tried to muffle the few sobs that came. All the things that had happened over the past three days, hell, the past six months, all came flashing through my mind, like a bad reality show montage. At the time, it had seemed so easy to keep it together.

After a few minutes, I wiped my eyes and tried to pull up, but Cade kept me gently pressed up against his body. His hand rubbed soothing circles on my arm, and I felt a lot of the tension ease from my body.

It was hard to feel small sometimes. Especially at my height. But Cade could make me remember how nice it was to have someone surrounding you.

I made a few disgusting snorting sounds and tilted my head so I could see Cade's face in profile. "I think I got boogers on your shirt."

He grinned, and I felt his genuine amusement and affection for me surrounding us like a cologne. "You can never just let us have a nice moment. You always have to have your jokes."

"I'm told it's one of my most endearing qualities."

He squeezed my arm, and it suddenly felt like old times again, hanging out together after school in Witchdale Park, sipping milkshakes and telling stories. "Well, I'm sure it wasn't me who told you that. You okay?"

I nodded and straightened. It felt good to be close to him again, but after everything…I knew I couldn't jump into things rashly.

"I think it's time I head out," I said, surreptitiously wiping my eyes on my shirtsleeves. I heard voices from inside, and Cade held the patio door open for me as we went into the living room.

Alice had a tray of double fudge-stuffed chocolate chocolate chip cookies cooling on the dining table. She smiled and offered me one as I walked in, but my stomach was still churning. Cade smiled and took two. He wouldn't be sleeping anytime soon.

Antoine and Rick walked down the stairs, Rick carrying a heavy iron mace awkwardly under his arm. He was dressed in some of Cade's old stuff— a clean pair of corduroys, a Hard Rock Café Poisoned Apple T-shirt, and a brown vest with a bunch of pockets.

"I got Rick a mace," Antoine said. "It seems to be a good fit."

"I play squash," Rick replied sheepishly.

"Nice," I said. "Are we ready?"

"Can I just walk through the streets with this?" Rick asked, looking at the mace in his hand.

"Uhm, duh," I scoffed. "Second Amendment. It also applies to maces."

Alice packed up a baggie full of cookies and promptly forced it into one of Rick's many pockets. She, Jacqui, and Cade stood there as we said our goodbyes, off to invade a castle, save a Prince, and stop a war. It weirdly reminded me of my dad seeing me off on my first day of kindergarten.

"Be careful," Cade called just as we headed for the door, his eyes catching mine.

Honestly, people needed to stop telling me that. It wasn't like it was doing any good.

The atmosphere in our neighborhood was a marked change from when we'd come into the house forty-five minutes before. The streets were practically empty, and those few people who were out were scared. A Roma woman all but carried her three young children in front of her, looking around frantically as they rushed down the streets. Even the will-o-wisps seemed to have gotten off the streets for the evening.

"Are we safe?" Rick asked quietly in the hush of an empty Looking Glass Lane.

I couldn't lie to the kid outright, so I answered simply, "We're going to be fine."

"But it's after dark," he said. "Aren't there monsters and things? Are we going to have to fight vampires?"

"Easy, Buffy. Most of the monsters seem to have gone home for the night," I replied. "And don't be silly. There's no such thing as vampires."

The streets began to be a little less empty the closer we got to the castle, but it still felt like we were walking through a ghost town rather than the usual bustle of the Apple. I couldn't be sure, but far off in the distance I thought I heard the sound of swords clashing, peppered by the occasional boom of a curse. But it could have been my imagination.

The walls of Castle Fortnight, on the other hand, were busier than I'd ever seen them. As we crossed through Liars' Square and took the bridge to Riversgate, a full battalion of knights had their weapons ready and aimed at us. It was a little concerning.

"Name and business," a knight demanded as we got to the gate, gripping her halberd tightly. The castle guards were tense, even though any warfare on castle grounds was forbidden.

"Antoine DuCarr, Briar Pryce, and Owen Bilson," Antoine responded smoothly. "Here on Grimmour family business."

If the guard was suspicious, seeing Antoine's Grimmour Pennon convinced her. She waved us through, and we started on the path towards Grimmour Tower.

"Owen Bilson?" I said quietly to Antoine.

"Hey, I'm new to this whole deception thing," he muttered.

The castle grounds bustled with the same sort of nervous energy the gate had. Patrols of armed knights were everywhere, but instead of making me feel safer, they reinforced the salty scent of fear on the wind.

All the lights in Grimmour Tower were blazing, and a constant stream of messengers, knights, and servants poured in and out of the front doors. The top of the tower was silhouetted against the newly risen moon, the macabre assortment of statues and gargoyles standing out in sharp relief.

Silently, we circled around to the back of the tower in the gathering darkness. I heard a constant stream of talking and movement coming from the arched windows. On the west side, however, was one window that was dimmer than the rest.

Underneath, I stepped into the hedge, being careful not to step on any of the daffodils. "This way," I instructed, and Rick and Antoine followed me as the thorns turned themselves away from my father's cloak. We walked inwards, towards the latrine chute that would take us into the tower.

"I'm not too familiar with medieval architecture," Rick said. "What is that opening for?"

Antoine and I had a moment of shared discomfort. "It's how they water the flowers," I answered. Not a lie, technically. Although there was also some fertilization that went into the process. "Can you guys fit in there?"

Antoine leaned down and looked up the tube. "Just barely. I'll go first," he said. He shifted his scabbard around to his back and pulled himself up into the chute.

"Can you do this?" I asked Rick.

He nodded and looked me in the eye. "I'll be fine." When I saw the look of determination on his face, I knew he could. Not just the climbing, but the whole quest in general. It wasn't that he wasn't scared, but he wasn't going to let fear stop him.

Tarris was a lucky kid.

Rick tucked his mace into a loop on his vest and got in the tunnel, dragging himself up in a series of starts and stops. As soon as he reached the latrine, I started up. The climb wasn't as hard as I remembered, or maybe I just had more adrenaline coursing through me this time.

When I reached the top and clambered out of the latrine, Antoine was already perched, listening at the bathroom door, and Rick had gotten his mace out and ready.

"I think we're clear," Antoine whispered. He pushed open the door to the Marchioness's room.

Predictably, not much had changed since the last time I was there. The girl was still on the bed, snoozing away while the castle was on red alert. There was just enough light coming from the slightly open door to illuminate her bed.

As soon as we entered the Marchioness's bedroom, frantic blue lights started tracing complicated patterns over the sleeping Royal's body. The electric blue lines formed a tangled knot that covered the skinny girl like a shield. Then, all at once, the lines broke and pieces of magic scattered into the air with a faint chiming noise.

The Marchioness shifted in her bed, yawned, and sat up.

My mind was sort of numb as I tried to comprehend what happened. Antoine and Rick also seemed momentarily stunned by the light show.

"Where am I?" the girl asked groggily. "Who are you people?"

While she was still in the fog of enchanted sleep, I drew a yellow rose from my satchel and quickly drew all of my stunned surprise into the bloom. The yellow became a deep marigold hue, with green tips on each petal. I pumped in enough magic to last a few hours.

Just as the girl started to get out of bed, I threw the rose onto her chest, still covered in blankets. Instantly, her face became even more bewildered and dumbfounded, and she sat back on the bed. She mouthed a few words and started looking aimlessly around the room.

"What the hell was that?" Rick whispered harshly.

"What did you give her?" Antoine asked.

"Just a little shock and awe," I replied. "She's been asleep for decades, she can wait a little longer. Just until we're done here." I silently hoped I hadn't put too much into the rose. All I needed was another broken psyche on my conscience.

"But why did she wake up?" Antoine said. "You said you used this entrance earlier this week and nothing happened."

I replayed the story Alice told me in my head. "'…and the Marchioness was cursed to remain asleep until a prince of a prince entered her chamber.'"

Antoine and I turned to Rick. "What?" he said.

"You're Tarris's 'prince.' A prince of a prince. Kind of," I offered.

"So I broke this girl's curse?"

"Looks like it. We like wordplay in the Apple," I explained. "Now, let's get going before I have to bespell Sleeping Beauty here again."

"Once we get into the hallway, we should be able to get up to the Royal quarters without incident. Everything is so crazy, no one's going to be alarmed by a few more people in the hallways," Antoine said. "If we get stopped, let me do the talking."

We slipped out of the Marchioness's room without anyone noticing, blending in with a crowd of servants who were delivering dinner up to the Grimmour's personal quarters. There were enough people in the hallways that no one gave us a second glance.

Once we were on the right floor, I tapped a butler on the shoulder. I was pretty sure it was one of the ones I'd talked to before.

"Excuse me, could you tell us where Prince Tarris is? We have a report to make to him."

"The Prince and the Princess are meeting with their father in the conference room, one floor up," the butler sniffed. He gave me a bit of a funny look, but the three of us were already heading to the nearest stairwell.

We walked up a winding, circular staircase hung with tapestries, and Antoine stopped us before we entered the next floor. There was a small window in the door that he peered through.

"It looks like there aren't any servants on this level," Antoine pointed out. Judging from the view out the stairway's slit windows, we were right by the top of the tower. "I don't know which room is—"

When Antoine cut himself off, I edged over to the window to try to see why.

Tarris and Miranda had just come through a pair of double doors, deep in discussion. I couldn't hear what they were talking about, but the conversation looked involved. Apparently, Royals dealt with war by getting fancy, as Tarris was in a blue vest and tie, while Miranda was in a chic green dress with lacy sleeves.

"You guys wait here," I whispered to Antoine. "If anyone sees you, take Rick and run. I'll grab Tarris."

He nodded, and I edged open the door and walked quickly into the hallway. Tarris and Miranda were talking quietly near a large stained glass window. Two identical stone carvings of nymphs were placed at either end of the window, making a sort of foyer to the room the twins had just left.

"Briar?" Tarris gasped as he saw me. "What are you doing here? Have you found anything out?"

"Did you find Rick?" Miranda asked, her worried girlfriend act firmly in place.

"I need to talk to you, Tarris," I began. "We have new information."

"To me? Why?" he said, feigning surprise. I still smelled a bit of fear of discovery.

"It's okay," I soothed quickly. "I know about you and Rick. And," I started, turning to Miranda, "I think it's great what you did to try to protect your brother, but we have bigger issues at stake here."

The Grimmour twins smelled of confusion. "Like what?" Tarris said. "Here, let me get my father, he's just in the other room—"

"No!" I barked. This was taking way too much time. "I think your father may have been involved in Rick's kidnapping. Or possibly your stepmother."

Tarris reeled back as if he'd been hit with a club. He took a faltering step away from me. "What? What are you talking about?"

"We found a Grimmour Pennon at the place where they were holding Rick. But please, we need to go. Now."

"So you found Rick?" Tarris asked. "Is he okay?"

"He's fine, but we need to get out of here before your father—"

"My father did all this?" Tarris interrupted. "He was going to—Rick was going to die because of him?"

I put my hand out to grab his shoulder. "We need to leave now," I said, "and then we can report your father to the Multiarchy and stop the war—"

Tarris broke free of my grip and whirled towards the double doors they'd just come through. "Tarris! No!" I said harshly.

Just as he was about to push through the doors, stone bricks slid from either side of the arched doorway and covered it completely. Tarris bounced off the wall harmlessly, and I looked over to see Miranda with her hand on a pillar.

"Miranda, what the hell?" Tarris spat angrily.

"Thanks," I said to the princess. "We can't let the Count know we caught on to his plan. Not until Tarris and Rick are safe."

Miranda caught my eye, her face etched with a resigned look of pain. "I'm sorry, Briar. But we can't let *anyone* know about this. I can't have the rest of the Royals tracing the kidnapping back to the Grimmours." With that, she called upon the magic within Grimmour Tower and blocked all the doorways in the hallway, trapping us.

"Miranda, what are you doing?" Tarris asked incredulously.

"I can't let you two leave," she answered quietly. "I'm sorry. If the rest of the Apple found out this was an inside job, the Multiarchy would only get stronger."

"What are you talking about?" I gaped, struggling to keep up. The hallway felt like it was contracting around me.

"Rick was never going to be hurt," she said. "Elias was going to stop the mountain giants from eating him. I just had to make it look authentic to convince Daddy."

"Make *what* look authentic? What are you saying?" Tarris protested.

"Tarris, I'm so sorry I had to put you through this, but in the end, it had to happen. Our family fighting the Lius will finally destroy the Multiarchy. And kidnapping Rick and blaming them was the best way to ensure our father would start a war. Don't you see? I had to do it."

"Miranda—" I started.

"See, when you were in the running for the position of the Exchequer's apprentice, I realized something," she began. "A princess doesn't have a future. It's all just waiting around for a man to finally deem you worthy. The Multiarchy, the Academy of the Iron Wand—they're all dominated by men. They refuse to share the Apple equally with women, or the poor, or non-humans." She looked pointedly at Tarris. "Or anyone outside of the establishment. What kind of future will you and Rick have if the Multiarchy is allowed to continue?"

"Pretty soon, I met a group that felt the same way I do. The Arsenic Queens want to free the Apple. They provided me with Elias and the mountain giants. They made the geas that lured Rick away from his dorm. They helped me form this plan to strike a final, fatal blow to the Multiarchy."

Everything in my head was spinning, and I tried to form a coherent argument. "You did all this," Tarris said, "to destroy the Multiarchy? Just because you were mad you couldn't be the Royal accountant's toady, you've become— become some sort of terrorist?"

"Terrorist? Extremist? Separatist? Traitor? Don't those words just depend on who's telling the story? When the Multiarchy falls, we'll be revolutionaries. Heroes who stood up to a corrupt dictatorship."

Miranda turned to me, and for a second, she seemed like the strong young woman I'd admired so much. "You have to agree with me, Briar. You've seen all the excess, the injustice, the pettiness that goes on in Castle Fortnight. Picture how the Apple would be without the Royals at the top, controlling it all."

"I know what you mean, Miranda," I said, my voice desperate. I could hear banging coming from the blocked door to the stairwell. "But this isn't the way to bring equality to the Apple. The war you started will kill people, Miranda. And without the Multiarchy, everything will be chaos. The Crown Wars nearly destroyed everything—"

"I'm not suggesting anarchy," Miranda scoffed, an edge of mania creeping in to her voice. "When the Multiarchy falls, the Arsenic Queens will be there to rebuild the Apple. We'll restore the Apple to what it was supposed to be."

There was a dull thumping from the conference room the twins had just left.

"Miranda," Tarris pleaded, his eyes starting to tear up, "don't do this."

"If you two can't realize what is at stake," Miranda said dangerously, "I won't force you to join us. But I can't let you spoil our plans by exposing what we've done. This war will cleanse the Apple of its enemies. For that reason, you two need to disappear until it's over."

She drew a small matchbook from a pocket in her dress and took out a single match. She lit it and mumbled, "Elias, I need you." I recognized the matchbook as the one she'd been using to "smoke" in her room. I couldn't believe I hadn't connected the dots sooner.

Tarris gave me a pointed look, and we both moved together. I sprang forward, taking Miranda out at the knees in the perfect football tackle that Cade had taught me in high school. We slid a few feet on the carpeted stone, with Miranda flailing beneath me, her frantic strength allowing her to push me to the side. As we both scrambled to our feet, I saw Tarris with his hand on the stone floor, concentrating. A second later, the stones covering all the doors in the hallway slid away with a grinding noise.

The conference room door burst open, and the Count stormed into the hallway. "Tarris! What is going on?"

"It's Miranda! She's the one who kidnapped Rick!" Tarris exploded, pointing at his sister.

Before the Count could react, Miranda rolled off the carpet and placed her hand on the stone. "I'm sorry, Daddy," she whispered. She made a little grunt of effort, and the nymph statue closest to the Count twisted suddenly and clocked him with a stone wreath.

Crap. The spell in the tower's stone was stronger than I thought.

"Father!" Tarris shouted. "Miranda! What did you do to him?"

The Count stumbled forward and collapsed at my feet. With him down, the nymph statue turned on me and aimed a punch at my head. It was fast but still made of heavy stone. I ducked beneath the nymph's fist, and its swing overbalanced it, sending it toppling into the nearby wall. With the statue out of commission, I wrapped my arms under the Count's armpits and dragged him away from Miranda. He was heavier than I expected.

I heard Antoine and Rick shouting as they ran towards us in the hallway, as well as the sound of many metal boots racing towards us. I looked down at the Count for a moment. He was bleeding from a pretty nasty cut on his forehead, but his chest was still moving with uneven breaths.

"Guards!" Miranda shouted. "They're trying to kidnap my father!"

Shit.

Tarris started to protest, but Miranda sent a column lurching towards him from the wall, and he yelled and rolled to the side. The guards skidded to a stop and drew their weapons.

There were seven of them, with the sound of more armored feet coming from the stairway. Antoine whipped his rapier around, forcing the guards to retreat towards the stairs.

I grabbed a rose from my satchel, hoping I might be able to stun at least some of the guards before they cut us to ribbons. The fear that made my heart race like a team of horses seemed like a good tool.

Before I could charge the rose, I felt a twisting sensation in my arm. Miranda had my arm twisted painfully behind my back, forcing me to drop the rose. The incoming guards had distracted me, and I didn't notice her lunge for me. I cried out in surprise, but before I could fight her off, she took the rose and ripped the satchel off my shoulder.

"Bitch!" I yelled.

Miranda grabbed a pedestal nearby and tapped into the Grimmour magic in the stones. A patch of bricks in the wall pushed themselves out and fell into the night. She looked me in the eyes for a moment, and then dropped the satchel and all the roses out of the tower.

"*Bitch!*" I repeated. Not my best mid-fight banter.

Well, if I didn't have my roses, I still had my dagger. I drew it, risking a quick glance back to see if everyone still had all their limbs.

Antoine was trying to fight four guards simultaneously, while it was all Rick could do to parry a few hits with his mace. Tarris managed to trap a pair of the guards behind a cage of pillars that he'd dragged up from the floor. As I watched, he sent a column crashing into another knight, trapping him against the wall. Not too bad for the good guys.

Miranda took one look at my dagger and turned to run. She dragged her hand along the wall, and with a creaking noise, part of the ceiling in front of her fell away. A large cabinet from the floor above us crashed into the floor, splintering into a pile of wood and broken dishes. A series of pillars sprang up in front of her like a fountain of stone, each from a different time or architectural style. Together, they formed a makeshift stairwell to the hole in the ceiling above. Miranda sprang up it without hesitation.

"Guys! She's getting away!" I called. Tarris stooped to check on his father, but the older man was still breathing, if unconscious.

Antoine had already knocked out one of the four guards he'd been dueling, and another was slumped against the wall, holding his hand to a deep gash between his chest plates. Rick succeeded in pushing the guard he'd been fighting back against the wall, but another group of guards was coming up the stairs, and I knew we wouldn't be able to stop them all.

"Stand down!" Tarris shouted, but if the guards heard him over the clang of battle, they didn't respond. I guess seeing your lord bleeding and unconscious on the floor trumped the usual chain of command. Antoine did a brutal spin kick and tripped up both the guards he was fighting, one of whom crashed into the knight Rick was whacking at with his mace.

"Come on!" I insisted before the guards could disentangle themselves from each other. Rick and Antoine started running towards us, and Tarris got up and looked at the impromptu stairway his sister had made.

As soon as Rick and Antoine were on our side of the hallway, Tarris sent up a wall, blocking the guards from getting to us. The sound of them pounding on the wall was all I could hear from the other side of the stone.

"Are you okay?" Tarris asked, giving Rick a firm embrace. "I'm so, so sorry—"

"It's okay," Rick said, his face buried in the taller guy's neck. "I didn't think I would ever see you again."

I hated to be a bitch, but we had to keep moving. "Guys, we need to stop Miranda. If she gets away, she'll do anything she can to keep this war going."

The two boys separated regretfully as Antoine started up the stairs.

"Careful," I warned. "I think she called in Elias."

We took the stairs up to what looked like a guest bedroom, sumptuously decorated, if you could ignore the gaping hole Miranda had punched in the floor.

"This is the top floor," Tarris explained. "She must be trying to get to the roof."

I stopped and listened, and I thought I could hear footsteps from above us. "Can you get us up there?"

Tarris nodded and put his hand against the wall. The bricks rippled like boiling water, and a stone ladder emerged, leading up to a small hole that formed in the ceiling.

Antoine barely waited for the ladder to finish before he started climbing, the rest of us on his heels. Halfway up, there was a crashing noise from below that sounded like a piece of the stone floor collapsing.

"Shit," Tarris swore. "The tower must be getting unstable from all the changes we've been making."

"Another reason we should stop your sister," Antoine growled as he reached the top of the ladder and climbed through to the roof.

The top of Grimmour Tower was lit only by a few torches and the moon. It was a large circle, about forty feet across with a small turret in the center that led to the floor below. A few pointed towers stretched up at random intervals, offshoots of the main building. All around the edges, gargoyles perched like an eager audience at a boxing match.

Miranda was standing in the center of the roof, surrounded by a group of five guards she must have recruited from the top floor. As soon as we climbed up the stairs, she screamed and pointed at us.

"There! That's the witch who enchanted my brother!" she sobbed. She'd gone into full hysterical princess mode. "You have to stop them from taking me!"

A pair of guards readied crossbows at us, and I barely had time to shout, "Down!" before they fired at us. I rolled to one side, while I saw Tarris drop to the ground. Within seconds, a pair of square stone pillars shot up from the ground and knocked the crossbows out of the guards' hands. They fell to the ground with the sound of crunching wood.

"Nice shot with those columns, Tarris!" I cheered as I got up into a fighting stance. The guards had all drawn their swords and were advancing on us cautiously. They'd spread out around Miranda in an arc.

"Technically, those were pilasters," Rick said. The three of us paused for a split second and gave him a look. "What?" he asked. "They were rectangular. Columns are rounded." He smelled a little like the ozone of someone in shock.

Before Rick could elaborate, a cloud of greasy smoke landed on the tower to my left. After a moment, it resolved itself into the murky form of Elias Clewd. His shirt and cummerbund were all askew, as if he'd put them on in a hurry to get here.

If he got to Miranda and teleported her out, we'd be screwed.

"Keep him away from Miranda!" I shouted.

I ran for Elias, waving my arms in an attempt to scare him off. Given the amount of fear I'd shot into him, I knew it would still be affecting him.

Elias drew himself up from where he was crouched and took his pipe from his mouth. When he saw me running towards him, his eyes widened.

Before I could react, he snapped his pipe towards me like a whip and a dart of smoke shot out. A burning sensation traced its path across my thigh, causing me to stumble. I kept myself upright by painfully slamming my palm against the rough, rain-hewn stone of the roof.

"I found a counter spell, you little minx," Elias spat as I regained my balance. "Courtesy of the Arsenic Queens."

I couldn't even process that. Besides the disenchantment charms in Prick, I had never found anything that could counteract my magic.

A cracking sound from the far side of the rooftop drew my attention. Miranda had animated the gargoyles and statues around her, and they were wrenching themselves away from their foundations and marching towards us.

"Elias!" she cried over the thump of stone feet. "Get us out of here!"

Before I could reach him, the smoke mage started running towards her. The statues formed a line between our side of the tower and Miranda.

A motley assortment of stone cherubs, wolves, gargoyles, and saints advanced on us, shoulder to shoulder with the tower guards. Rick gave a barbaric shout and smashed his mace into the statue of a portly friar. To all of our surprise, the rain-weakened stone of the friar's beatific face cracked to reveal an empty core.

"They're hollow?" Tarris shouted from beside me. "Grimmsdamn dwarven contractors!" He placed his hand on the ground and started animating the statues closest to him. Meanwhile, Elias rounded the side of the tower and was closing in on Miranda.

"Antoine!" I yelled. "Stop him!"

I ran after Elias, but an eight-foot statue of a knight in pointy ceremonial armor blocked my path. Miranda was getting better at the magic, and the knight moved with dangerous speed. I jumped back as it swept a stone broadsword in an arc at my chest.

Elias was inches away from Miranda, and I didn't have time to stop him. If they touched and he turned them both to smoke, we could kiss any chance of stopping them goodbye.

With a loud shout, Antoine threw his rapier like a throwing knife, and it sailed true into Elias's shoulder. The older man cried out in pain, and then evaporated into a cloud of smoke. Antoine's sword clattered to the ground, its tip dark with blood.

Weaponless, Antoine spun around just in time for a dwarfish guard with a cutlass to swing up at his face. Rick called a warning and stumbled forward just in time to block the sword with his weapon. The dwarf stumbled back, giving Rick the opportunity to use his mace like a golf club and lift the Little Person clean off his feet with a wild blow. But a nearby guardswoman knocked Rick's mace to the ground, and a group of guards and statues surrounded the two unarmed men.

Distracted, I moved too slowly as the stone knight aimed a kick at my midsection. His concrete boot knocked the wind out of me, and I fell backwards painfully onto my ass. My elbow hit the ground with a jolt, and Prick sprang out of my hand and out of reach. There were only six inches between my head and the edge of the tower, but I rolled to my left as the statue's sword slammed forcefully down on where I'd been, cracking the roof. Apparently, this one's sword was solid stone.

Something below us in the tower creaked, and with a large crunching sound, the roof tipped sideways. My stomach lurched as the entire tower tilted, and I slid even closer to the edge. The knight took a few awkward steps, as his stone boots failed to grip the crooked surface beneath him. He pitched forward, and just as I braced myself for him to fall on me, the tower shuddered again, sending him flying over the side of the roof.

I rolled awkwardly to my feet and looked over the edge, watching as the knight crashed onto the stone pavement hundreds of feet below me, scattering a crowd of spectators that had gathered to watch the bizarre spectacle taking place. A few floors below us, I caught sight of my satchel of roses. After Miranda threw it out the window, it had gotten caught in the antlers of a stone deer that adorned the pitched roof of one of the smaller side towers.

Which would have done me a lot of good if I were able to scale thirty feet of sheer vertical stone.

Turning back to the roof, my heart dropped. The guards, backed up by Miranda's animated statues, had their blades at Rick and Antoine's throats. Tarris had his hands up in a position of surrender, his face wrought with fear and anger.

Elias had turned back into his human form by Miranda's feet, but the gaping wound in his shoulder seemed to be stopping him from doing any magic right away. Miranda was holding a piece of cloth over the wound and trying to mop the sweat off his forehead with her sleeves. She looked from my captured friends to me.

"Surrender," she announced loudly over the rooftop. "Make an oath to support me, or I'll have you put in the White Tower for life."

Now who was the tyrant?

I looked around the tower, trying to think of a way to stall or prevent Miranda from putting the only people who knew about her plans away.

"Why not just kill us, Miranda? Make sure that once and for all your treachery doesn't come to light?" I shouted, inching backwards towards the edge of the roof.

The princess set Elias down gently and drew herself up to her full height. "No one has to die. I'm trying to make things right."

"What about the hundreds of commoners who have already been drafted into the war you started? They'll fight and die, but because you don't know them, because they don't have faces you recognize, that's okay?" I was sitting up now, with my arms inching backwards to the roof's edge.

The guards surrounding Antoine and Rick started to shift uncomfortably, but they still kept their weapons up.

"It had to happen this way," Miranda said fervently. "The people need the tragedy of war to see the Apple's true face. It's the story they need to hear. It's the only way to change people's hearts."

"Not exactly," I muttered.

I called on all the magic within me, all the emotion I'd ever felt coiled within my chest. The barriers I always had, the ones that separated me from the power I refused to let define me, fell away as my vision faded almost completely to nothing. There was just feeling, lighting the sky like fireworks in the summer night.

I felt the roses below, and with a beckoning gesture, I called two of them up to me. Somehow I was on my feet, although I didn't remember getting up. The roses shot up, covering thirty feet in seconds. The one that flew to my left hand was a pale cream color, with a wide, bouncy blossom. It felt of lazy afternoons and a baby's cooing. In my right hand was a slender red rose, its bloom just barely opening at the top. This was a rose with possibilities, its power red and dark beneath my fingertips.

The magic worked through my fingertips, sending each rose out in front of me in an explosion of petals. The light cream petals turned a soft, fabric-softener pink and danced over to the guards. The panicked, martial emotions that bounced around in the warriors dampened, and I eased them into a warm, loving stupor. Their weapons clattered to the ground, and I could feel a deep sense of belonging and comfort overtake them.

The red petals darkened and turned the black and shiny color of beetle carapaces. They darted swiftly over to Miranda like a swarm of hungry bats. She screamed, but I kept them hovering just inches away from her skin.

I walked slowly towards the princess, smelling the tangy scent of her fear as the petals pirouetted around her. "I could rend you," I intoned dangerously. My voice sounded strange and alien, even to my ears. The power I'd called up lent it a depth and a presence that wasn't entirely my own. "I could take your heart apart; make sure you never have another misguided, self-righteous feeling again in your little life."

A sob shook Miranda's frame, and I felt the terror that my presence inspired in her.

"I could dismantle you. Make you into the pretty, pretty princess you were supposed to be." My hand reached out and cupped her face, and I realized I wasn't the one in the driver's seat anymore. The magic was swirling through me too powerfully, coming from somewhere, someplace, maybe some*one* else. Part of me was terrified, but mostly I just felt…free. Unfettered.

Miranda's pale skin reflected a hundred colors of light as they surged around my body. Feelings flew freely like neon starlings from me, through me, all around the tower. They weren't mine. They'd been called up by whatever magic I'd tapped.

"Briar," a voice called from beside me. "Briar, stop."

I sensed concern and worry, and something that could have been love, but it seemed so petty. Just more emotions flitting around on the wind.

"Briar, this isn't you," the voice said. A hand grabbed my arm, and the pressure on my skin drew me back into myself a little. "You didn't want to be the one to write people's stories for them, remember?"

Antoine. Those were Antoine's feelings. I shook my head, and the light show that danced around me dimmed. I let go of Miranda and stepped back. The petals surrounding her dispersed, and she relaxed a little.

Maybe it was the excessive levels of magic leaving my body, or maybe I was just bad at these sorts of things, but no acceptably dramatic quip came to mind. I thought I said something like, "You're a prince-ass."

Then I socked her across the jaw.

As is the case with most princesses I've come across, Miranda's jaw was as glassy as Cinderella's slippers. She folded up onto the roof and lay there.

Antoine clicked his tongue. "Couldn't you have just bespelled her? Not that she didn't deserve it."

I shook my knuckles out. Between Miranda and T, I was getting pretty good at cold cocking people. "I didn't want to risk it, after I'd almost... thanks, by the way."

"Don't mention it—I knew that wasn't you. It wasn't what you wanted." Antoine put his hands on mine and gave me a tentative squeeze. His body moved close to mine, and there was a charge in the air between us.

I looked into Antoine's eyes, and through my fading magical senses, I could easily smell the scent of attraction and desire. But under it was the warm, coconut-oil scent of admiration. The beginnings of love.

How'd those emotions work out for Cade?

"Thanks again," I said, pulling gently away from him. Whatever Antoine had expected to happen in that moment, he was visibly disappointed. But, really. A rooftop embrace after winning a climactic battle? It was so not me.

Apparently, I was alone in that respect. As I turned away from Antoine, I noticed Rick and Tarris locked passionately in each other's arms. After a few moments of holding each other, they separated and Tarris looked into the Know-Not's eyes.

"You came for me? After I nearly got you killed?" he asked, his voice thick with emotion.

Rick's face broke into a wide grin, although I saw there were tears in his eyes. "I love you," he said simply.

The two boys kissed, tenderly and deeply. From across the tower, I felt the emotion released into the air, overpowering everything else. Almost erasing the magic of the stupor spell I'd put on the guards. It was true love.

The sprinkling of rose petals fell around the lovers, the black blossoms having lightened back to a lipstick red that glowed from residual feeling. Apparently, my power had a romantic sense of timing.

Voyeuristic as I was, I took a moment to drink in their emotions, standing above the unconscious body of the girl who'd almost taken this all away. Antoine stood by my side, stealing glances at me every few moments.

One happy ending later, Rick and Tarris separated, although there was a funny look on Tarris's face. "Rick, don't take this the wrong way," he began, "but why do you taste so delicious?"

Sitting in my living room in our worn-out easy chair, I did a complicated, butt-wiggling dance of victory. I'd spent the two weeks since Miranda's defeat lying low, slogging my way through *The Complete Works of Carl Jung*. But now, after days pouring through the obtuse psychoanalytic concepts, I found what I was looking for.

I took out the worn crossword puzzle I'd been working on in Central Park (that seemed like decades ago) and filled in the thirteen blank spaces of ten down.

Synchronicity.

I'd briefly skimmed through Jung's early work on the subject. Seeing meaning in causally unrelated events. Jung would've liked the Apple.

Yes, I could have Wikipedia-ed it. But that would be cheating.

Cade came in through the patio door, his tank top drenched from his morning jog. A steady rain fell outside, but that wasn't enough to keep Mr. Fitness indoors.

He kicked off his tennis shoes and grabbed a towel from a hook near the door. Running it vigorously through his hair, he turned his short blond hair into a puffer fish of spikes. He was still panting, his wide chest moving visibly. He noticed me watching, and, unexpectedly, grinned.

"You should have joined me out there, Bri. Hell of a nice day for a jog."

I smiled back and set my book and crossword to the side. "I was too busy mastering psychoanalysis. Try me. Tell me anything, and I'll tell you how it represents your deep desire to sleep with your mother."

Cade laughed, and I immediately felt warm. He'd been so…unreserved the past two weeks. It was like high school all over again. I didn't know if it was from our talk in the garden or Jacqui starting her treatments, but he moved and acted like he was the goofy, carefree teenager I'd fallen in love with years ago.

"I'm gonna make eggs. You want some?" he offered, hanging the towel back up and ambling into the kitchen.

"Chicken or cockatrice?" I asked.

"I think we're out of chicken," he called out, his head stuck in the icebox.

"Sure," I said. "Thanks."

"Scrambled, with cheese, onions, and garlic, right?"

He knew that was how I liked my eggs, just like I knew he'd joke about my breath after I ate them. "Yes, please."

I went over to the kitchen and poured him some of the energy potion he swore by. He took it with a nod of thanks and busied himself over the skillet. I made myself a cup of tea and sat on the counter while he cooked.

"Where are Alice and Jacqui?" Cade said. "Can you ask them if they want some?"

"They left early," I answered. "Alice took Jacqui to the Academy on her way to work. They have a full day of disenchantment scheduled for her."

Even though he was facing the eggs, I saw Cade's smile in profile. "She's looking better and better. Have you noticed her eyes?"

I nodded. In the week and a half that Jacqui had been going to the

Academy, she'd already started to change. Her eyes had gone completely human. They were the same eyes my best friend had always had. Before the curse.

Of course, the Academy wizards were cagey about the process, as most professionals were. They talked about the "strange and unprecedented nature of the curse" and warned of a "long and difficult road to being curse-free." But that didn't matter to me. They would fix her.

Of course, I couldn't stop her from thanking me unnecessarily, but hopefully she would get over that. It just reminded me that I was the one who got her cursed in the first place.

I was blowing on a spoonful of hot tea when I heard a knock on the front door. We hadn't received many visitors since the end of the war, and that was just the way I liked it. The only person in the past few days was a delivery boy with a bouquet of silver roses from Isaak Krakelev, and a double-entendre-soaked card reminding me of my debt to him. One rose delivery, of his choice. He implied that with Miranda's recent fall from grace, he didn't think he'd need my help getting her back, but he still wanted to keep me on retainer.

The bouquet went in the trash can, but I kept the card. You couldn't forget your promises in the Apple.

I hopped off the counter and went to the door. Opening it, I found Antoine there, smiling and holding a parchment. He had traded his rapier for a long, forest green umbrella, and wore a trench coat over a blue cable-knit sweater and khakis. "Hey, stranger," he greeted.

A usually dormant part of my psyche started freaking out that I was still wearing my pajama pants and a beer-stained T-shirt. And hadn't had my shower yet. And probably smelled like the onions Cade was frying in the kitchen.

"Antoine," I smiled, "come on in."

"Actually," he said, handing over the parchment, "I believe I'm supposed to escort you to the Count. If you'll come with me?" He offered me space under his umbrella.

I popped open the seal on the parchment, but it was merely a request for me to meet with the Count. Not too different from the first one that had started this whole mess.

"Can I have five minutes to change?" I asked.

"You look great," he offered, a little flirtatiously. And obliviously.

Okay, I was definitely changing.

Ten minutes later, I came down from my room to see Cade still cooking and Antoine sitting on the couch. Neither man was talking to the other, and the tension smelled like wet dog.

"Hey Cade, sorry. Rain check on the eggs?" I suggested.

"Yeah, sure," he muttered with a bitter glance at Antoine. But he gathered himself together and gave me a smile. "Means more for me."

"Just watch your breath," I said. He chuckled at our silly little inside joke.

I grabbed a hoodie from our coat rack to wear over my green camisole. I had put on jeans and a pair of black boots that added an extra inch to my height. I hadn't been back to the castle since the final fight, and I could use a little extra intimidation factor in case the Count was pissed at me for cold-cocking his daughter. I left my satchel of roses behind.

Antoine and I went out into the rain, and I walked awkwardly close to him under the umbrella. He was being all chivalrous and giving me the lion's share of the space, and I could see his left arm getting soaked.

"So, how come you're pulling escort duty? Isn't that a little below your pay grade?" I said.

"Well, the Grimmour's normal messenger refuses to see you, on account of you knocking him unconscious."

Oh, right. "T is still holding a grudge?

"You locked him in a cage."

"You helped."

"True," Antoine conceded, smiling. His pleasure at seeing me was thick in the air underneath the umbrella.

The streets were rife with late-morning commuters. The rain was just heavy enough for jackets, but it wasn't torrential. It was a warm, pleasant sort of rain, not too different from the shower I didn't get a chance to take that morning.

All the fear and paranoia from the war had been washed down the drains. Antoine had taken my place in all the resulting Noble councils and investigations over the past two weeks. He'd provided all the evidence we'd gathered and worked with the Grimmours in the peace process. According to the castle gossip Alice had overheard, the Lius were making the Grimmours pay heavily. In exchange, they agreed not to dig too deeply into what had really happened with Rick Pearson. The rumor mill guessed rightly that things were not as they seemed, but so far the tabloids hadn't guessed about Rick's connection to Tarris or who was really behind the kidnapping.

Antoine filled me in on what I'd missed as we walked. Inquisitions, exploratory commissions, the works. It sounded like the most boring two weeks ever. I owed him for taking on the burden of looking out for Tarris and Rick throughout the whole ordeal. The only good story he had to share was about a curse fire in the Gingerbread Tenements. A wayward Grimmour hex had ignited an entire building, but all the Commoners got out safely, thanks to the enchanted armor Sho Liu had distributed to the district.

You had to take your happy endings where you could find them, I guess.

All too soon, we reached the tower. It had been rebuilt since the battle, but sculptors were still working on the top floors to replace the statues that had been destroyed.

I smelled a funny scent of anxiety coming from Antoine as we climbed the stairs to the Count's office. It kept increasing until we were standing outside the door.

"Briar," he started before I could knock. "Listen. I've been thinking a lot lately."

Never a good thing to hear from a guy.

"After everything we went through, I realized there are a lot of problems with serving the Royals. I keep thinking of T and how he was going to send Rick right back to the person who we thought had kidnapped him."

"Okay," I offered, because he seemed desperate for me to say something.

"I'm going to start doing some pro bono work, when I can," he said. "Start helping regular people with their problems. See what I can do to help."

Relief washed over me as I figured out what he was talking about. "Sort of like a detective agency."

"Sure," he said. "Whether it's kidnappings, or investigations, or missing persons, people would come to us and we could —"

"Sorry," I interrupted. "We?"

Antoine grinned sheepishly. "I was wondering if you'd be interested in helping out, here and there. I could use someone with your talents."

I arched my eyebrows. "As a magical helper figure?"

He grinned and rolled his eyes at me. "As a partner. What do you say?"

I smiled at him. That sort of thing sounded right up my alley. With the bonus the Count had given me to keep away from the press, I could afford to do some charity.

"I'd love to," I said. And I meant it.

"Great. I'll let you know once I get things started up. Oh, and Briar?" he said as I went to the door.

"Yes?"

"Remember when you told me I should let my emotions out more?" he said, a glimmer of mischievousness in his voice.

"Yeah? What about that?"

Instead of answering, he closed the space between us and firmly grabbed the back of my head. Before I could react or protest, we were kissing, his lips exploring mine with a fervor I didn't know he possessed. After the initial shock wore off, I noticed I was responding in kind, my hands wrapped around his lower back.

Just as I wanted more, he pulled back and looked into my eyes. "I finally decided to take your advice." He pulled his hand around front to gingerly touch my face, and then sauntered off down the hall. I was still breathing heavily, my emotions so explosive in my head that every rose within fifty miles must have been changing color.

"I'll be in touch about our partnership," he called over his shoulder. I could still taste the sharp press of his tongue. At the door to the stairwell, he turned around in earnest and gave me a wicked smile. "I look forward to working together." He waved and went down the stairs.

What did I do to the White Knight I had met two weeks ago?

I was still a little unhinged as I stared out the paned window of the Count's office. He'd been going over a redrafting of my nondisclosure agreement for twenty minutes, and I just wanted to sign the damn thing, not listen to what limbs I'd lose if I was found to be in breach.

"…and the severed tongue shall be divided into at least four, but no more than eight pieces, and fed to any and all nearby dogs," he finished as my attention came back from a sense memory of Antoine's cologne. "Do you agree to the terms?" The Count sat back in his chair and stared at me over his half-moon reading spectacles.

"Sure. Yes. Sounds peachy," I quipped. I had to get out of there.

"Excellent," he said. "Then, in four to six weeks, after my legal team has finished hashing all of this out, you'll receive your payment."

The screams of anguish were so loud in my head, I was sure he could hear them. "That's great," I said, starting to get out of my chair. "Then, if there's nothing else, Your Grace—"

"Actually," the Count interrupted, "there is one more matter in which you could be of use to me."

Only sheer power of will kept me from sticking my fingers in my ears and running from the room. "Yes?" I prompted.

"As Mr. DuCarr may have told you, we are planning to go public with the story of Rick Pearson's kidnapping, while obscuring my daughter's involvement and blaming the entire incident on Elias Clewd."

I nodded. My first impulse had been to tell the whole world what had happened, but I finally agreed to take the Count's hush money after Tarris begged me. An investigation of his sister would just lead to more problems for him and Rick.

"But I was hoping to hire you on retainer in order to…manage my daughter during this difficult process and ease her state of mind. Make sure she doesn't do anything else confusing, that the media could misinterpret." The Count's voice was easy and diplomatic, as if he were suggesting which restaurant we should go to for lunch.

In a moment, I decoded the words. "You want me to enchant your daughter?"

"A little daily intervention from you would help her so much," he continued. "Just to remind her of the value of loyalty, and family."

I felt my stomach clench up in knots. I'd done similar jobs before, but after everything that happened on the rooftop…

"I'm sorry, Your Grace," I said, standing firmly. "I won't drug your daughter into obedience."

"Drug?" the Count scoffed. "Why, young lady, I would just like to help her achieve a healthier outlook—"

"Maybe," I began, knowing the words were unwise, even as I said them, "what she needs is someone in the Multiarchy who actually listens to her. Who values her for the ardent, intelligent person she is. Then she wouldn't be so determined to bring you all down."

The Count crossed his arms, clearly displeased with being overruled. "I am disappointed that you feel that way."

I wanted to run out the door right then, but I had to ask. "If Elias is taking the fall, what will happen to Miranda?" I remembered the outspoken, vivacious girl who had helped me get dressed for the ball and felt a strange pang of pity. The two of us weren't that different.

"We were hoping to have your assistance in the matter," the Count retorted icily, "but Braselyn and I have been looking into boarding schools that fit her special situation."

I knew people sent their rebellious teens to boarding school, but a boarding school for actual treasonous rebels? I didn't even want to know. "What about the Arsenic Queens? They were the ones who planned most of this and provided Elias and Miranda with a lot of the spells. Are you going to tell everyone there's a shadowy organization trying to take down the Multiarchy?"

"I believe you've given too much credit to the incoherent ramblings of my daughter. Whomever she was working for, I doubt they were as powerful as you imagine. And besides, without any sort of proof, there is no use frightening people with ghost stories."

"But they have powerful magic," I argued. "They were the ones who set up the geas that—"

"I have already made up my mind on the matter. Good day, Miss Pryce," the Count said dismissively, but he'd already turned his attention towards a scroll on his desk.

I left the office, part of me wondering if Antoine would be waiting for me outside. He wasn't, and the hallway was empty.

About halfway to the stairwell, the stones to my right suddenly shifted into an arch. My adrenaline spiked, and, before I could think, I drew Prick from my boot and shifted into a fighting stance.

Tarris stepped through the doorway and nearly dropped the box he was carrying when he saw me. "Briar! It's me!" he yelled.

I felt my face flush and put my dagger away. "Whoa. Sorry, Tarris. I just—I saw the stone move, and I must have had some sort of a PTSD episode."

"Not a problem," the prince said, a little paler than usual. "What are you doing here?"

"Just meeting with your father," I answered.

"I'm so sorry," he deadpanned. From behind him, Rick emerged carrying a duffel bag. It was unzipped and overstuffed with clothes.

"Hey, Briar!" Rick said cheerfully. The two weeks of rest had done wonders for the kid, and he grinned easily when he saw me.

"What are you guys doing?" I asked, looking at Tarris's box. It was full of picture frames, a mug or two, and a few other personal effects.

"Can I tell her?" Rick whispered to his boyfriend. Tarris nodded. "We're moving in together!" he gushed.

"Really? Congratulations! Are you moving into the tower, Rick?"

Tarris scoffed. "Perrault's panties, no. We've got a place of our own in Commontown."

"It's great," Rick said. I felt the lemony scent of his excitement reach all the way back in my nose, clearing my sinuses. "You'll have to come over and visit. It's in Havmercy! Not that far from your place."

I smiled. The giddiness they were both feeling was infectious, even without my powers. "Definitely. We'll have to throw you guys a housewarming party."

"That'd be fun," Tarris agreed, smiling. "Thank you." His voice rang with many meanings of the word.

I looked at the two of them and couldn't help but feel a little pride. "Any time."

"Well, we need to get going," Rick said. "We have a contractor coming in an hour. If we don't pull out those shitty 1960s shag carpets, I'm going to—"

"I'll mirror you about the party," Tarris interrupted, grinning with obvious good humor at Rick's antics. "Take care."

As they passed me, a small piece of paper fell from Rick's open duffle. I bent down to pick it up. "Hey, you forgot this."

Rick turned around and inspected it. "Oh, that? It's just that note the kidnappers sent me. Not exactly a keepsake I want lying around. Oh, that reminds me…"

He said something else, but my brain was totally focused on the note. It looked strangely familiar. Before I opened it, I had an idea of what I'd find. The paper, the size, everything was the same.

Inside, the note was filled with a circle full of swirling designs, all done in acid green ink. The geas that had sent Rick into the Harlem alleyway still smelled of spent magic, but it wasn't the design that made my heart stop.

The paper, the ink, even the handwriting of the symbols were all identical to the note I'd found on the cursed muffin basket. There was no doubt in my mind that whoever sent Rick to that alley was the same one who cursed Jacqui.

"Briar?" Rick asked. "Did you hear me? I said I Wikipedia-ed that crossword clue you asked me about. The answer is synchronicity."

THE END